Praise for *Such a Bad Influence*

"Mix one part juicy social media scandal, one part bitter family drama, and one part scintillating missing woman case—shaken up with urgent ruminations on what we lose by turning our identities into products for sale—and you have the heady cocktail that is *Such a Bad Influence*. Olivia Muenter's timely, riveting debut plunges readers into the dark underbelly of the influencer world, examining the unhealthy side of our parasocial relationships with the 'internet-famous.' This story is as addictive as scrolling Instagram, and marks the launch of a talented new writer. Highly recommend."

—Ashley Winstead, author of *Midnight Is the Darkest Hour*

"An addictive psychological thriller that will totally immerse you in the terrifying, overexposed world of child social media stars. Muenter's debut will have you rethinking everything about your Instagram scroll as you inhale this book in a single sitting."

—Jo Piazza, author of *The Sicilian Inheritance* and host of the *Under the Influence* podcast

"*Such a Bad Influence* is as addictive as Instagram. Woven into its twisty, propulsive story of a missing influencer are complicated questions about the cost of mining one's life for content. I was riveted the whole way through."

—Ana Reyes, author of *The House in the Pines*

"A fascinating exploration of the dangers of social media told through a propulsive mystery surrounding the sudden disappearance of a beloved mega influencer. In her smart and timely debut, Muenter probes the following questions: What do influencers owe their followers? What ownership do parents have over their children? And, perhaps most hauntingly, how do we reconcile the psychological perils of living in such an intensely online world?"

—Carola Lovering, author of *Tell Me Lies* and *Bye, Baby*

SUCH
A BAD
INFLUENCE

SUCH A BAD INFLUENCE

OLIVIA MUENTER

QUIRK BOOKS
PHILADELPHIA

Library of Congress Cataloging-in-Publication Data
Names: Muenter, Olivia, author.
Title: Such a bad influence / Olivia Muenter.
Description: Philadelphia : Quirk Books, 2024. | Summary: "Infamous social media
    influencer Evie Davis has spent her whole life online, since her mother shared a viral
    video of her at age five. When she suddenly disappears in the middle of a live stream,
    her older sister, Hazel, becomes determined to find Evie and the truth behind her
    disappearance"—Provided by publisher.
Identifiers: LCCN 2023050511 (print) | LCCN 2023050512 (ebook) | ISBN 9781683694014
    (hardcover) | ISBN 9781683694021 (ebook)
Subjects: LCGFT: Thrillers (Fiction) | Novels.
Classification: LCC PS3613.U3758 S83 2024 (print) | LCC PS3613.U3758 (ebook) | DDC
    813/.6—dc23/eng/20231106
LC record available at https://lccn.loc.gov/2023050511
LC ebook record available at https://lccn.loc.gov/2023050512

ISBN: 978-1-68369-401-4

Printed in China

Typeset in Georgia and Roboto

Designed by Elissa Flanigan
Production management by John J. McGurk
Interior photo by Vincent Burkhead on Unsplash

Quirk Books
215 Church Street
Philadelphia, PA 19106
quirkbooks.com

10 9 8 7 6 5 4 3 2 1

FOR MY PARENTS

Evelyn Davis has argued with every person she's never met.

In her mind, she has gone to battle with each stranger who has posted a negative comment on an Instagram post, every person who has somehow found her personal email address. The ones who have found her physical address, too. She has stood in front of them and laid it all out. She's made every point, every argument. She's memorized each counterpoint. Every caveat. She has looked into their eyes and convinced them that she gets it. She's willed into them the same belief that she's had to convince herself of for years: that she's as human as they are, soft and vulnerable in the very same spots.

Today, Evie drives and plays the game again, imagining all the usernames she sees on her phone as real people, giving them that benefit, even though they never gave it back to her. She turns up the volume and pictures the person who sent a handwritten letter to her house last week. The woman who had asked why she wasn't a better role model for people her age. Why she's not more grateful for her four million followers, for her success, her face, her body. "Don't you understand the power you have?" the stranger had written in neat, curving letters. "Don't you get it?"

The stranger's name was Susan, and it turned out that she, like Evie herself, was all over the internet. Single and in her late fifties, Susan lived outside of Columbus, Ohio, with a black lab named Muppet. Her passions, based on her digital footprint, included giving local restaurants highly detailed, lukewarm-to-scathing reviews and spoiling her two redheaded grandchildren whom she frequently referred to as "my life" or "my joy" or "my everything." Muppet, it seemed, didn't quite make the cut. Susan frequented Twitter less often, which made it easy enough for Evie to see her thoughts from any given time in the last ten years. It only took a few seconds of browsing, for example, for her to find a post from 2018 in which Susan wrote that she felt "truly devastated" when Matt Lauer lost his job on *The Today Show*. Her Instagram bio featured ten emojis and a Bible verse. And, of course, she had a lesson to teach Evie.

Evie imagines how they'd sit down together for coffee. "It's all a huge privilege, Susan," she'd say, ticking the box she knows Susan is so clearly waiting for her to skate right by. "An unbelievable, immense privilege. It really is."

Susan would cross her arms and lift her chin. A challenge.

"And?" she'd probably ask, pursing her lips. The unspoken second question suspended between them: "What do you plan to do with that, exactly?"

Evie smiles in real life, imagining the careful expression she'd strike in response to the question, knowing that whatever answer she gave next wouldn't really matter. Maybe she'd explain that she actively avoids promoting all the things that people her age are taught to avoid—drugs, alcohol, diet pills, bullying. She would reference the half dozen videos where she's made a point to mention that these things just aren't for her, that they've never been her thing. That they aren't cool. Maybe she would be honest and level with Susan. Tell the truth, that her vices have always been things that are entirely unique to her. That the things she can't quit are much more humiliating.

Even before people like Susan went out of their way to tell Evie what they thought of her, Evie has been addicted to seeking out the worst things people would say about her, to carefully cataloging the ways she is hated.

In the beginning, her mom half-heartedly tried to hide the snark sites from her, to block the Reddit forums that discussed influencers, to make sure Evie didn't learn about the darker, more hateful online message boards and chat rooms, too. To filter the worst comments. By the time Evie was eleven, though, she could find her way around most website child protection programs. A few years after that, Evie had nearly half a million followers, and the whole thing was too big to control, anyway. Her mom couldn't have hidden her from most of it if she'd tried. Besides, she had seen her mom browsing these same sites herself. She had gone through her mom's phone and found the screenshots of particularly hateful threads about her clothes, her body, her personality. Evie had wondered then if her mom was keeping them all to refer to later, to remind herself to not let Evie wear a certain outfit that the internet hated, or to nudge Evie to stop smiling in a way that seemed fake, forced. A million tiny road signs that illuminated the path to bulletproof adoration.

But Evie felt a pull to look at the sites, too. When most of her friends were desperate for first kisses and clear skin, she was fighting the same insatiable hunger to read more about herself. To know what everyone was really thinking about her, underneath it all. Most people might assume she'd mark the milestones of her life by career highlights (going viral at five, hitting 500,000 followers on Instagram by the time she was fifteen, becoming the most-followed teenager on TikTok shortly after), but instead she remembers ages by notable usernames.

At twelve, there was ShortCake23, who wrote that Evie was changing her voice in videos to sound more like an adult. That it was creepy the way she was trying to appeal to an older audience. Disturbing.

At thirteen, there was RioGranddd, who said she looked like "if JonBenét Ramsey was a hipster," adding an important disclaimer that they only said that because they were just "like, *really* concerned with her well-being."

At fifteen, it was NotMyTwin1993, who mocked her for wearing too much makeup. "God, if she needs this much cosmetic assistance *now*, just imagine what it'll be like in 20 years . . ."

You'd assume, maybe, that she'd fall back into this habit on her worst days, in her weakest moments, but it was in the happiest moments that she felt the urge to search more than anything else. She felt lucky, even, that she could cross-check her joy against the opinion of the rest of the world. That she had a built-in gauge for weighing her success, her pride. For knowing if she really deserved any of it.

There were thousands of comments that she had filed away in her mind, each one attached to a brief, unspoiled moment of joy. An achievement. A birthday. A crush. Each time she'd remind herself that she shouldn't look, but she'd do it anyway. It was like picking a scab, satisfying and shameful, always worse after than before. And in the end, she knew that the truth was the same thing that Susan would tell her, probably. That she had no one to blame but herself. That if she looked for room to complain there would always be none. She knew this, too.

"We didn't ask for this, but it doesn't mean we can't be grateful for it," her mom would often say when Evie mentioned a negative response to something she'd done online. An outfit. A life choice. A brand partnership. "This is just what happens when you share your life with the world."

It had been more than a decade since the Davises first became internet famous, all thanks to a viral video of Evie and her dad doing a coordinated dance. It was sweet, the kind of thing that makes people say, "Girl dads are just the best, aren't they?" Paired with the right music, the right exposure, the video might have been enough on its own, to go viral in a small way. But it was what happened after that made it explode. That led to daytime talk show appearances and enough social media followers to fund a new car, a new house, a new life.

"I'm grateful for all of it. I could never have imagined this in my wildest dreams," Evie would explain to Susan, to every follower she's imagined talking to, referencing the success she had found (or built, or had handed to her, depending on who you asked) on the internet.

She sighs as she pulls into the parking lot, shifts into park, and adjusts the sun visor. The Los Angeles sun feels like it's boring a hole into the side of her face, burning straight through to her teeth. She places her elbows on the steering wheel, pushing her hair out of her eyes. Evie is used to people not agreeing with her life decisions. She is used to the Susans of the world and their friends and their daughters going out of their way to tell her that reading paperback books is killing the planet or how her boyfriend doesn't really love her or how she would probably never get into college, not that she would even try. And yes, she is used to a million messages supporting her every move, too, but the one thing she has learned from both groups is that neither has helped her at all. Neither sees her or knows her. Believing the good stuff has sucked the soul out of her as much as believing the bad stuff has.

Evie checks her makeup in the mirror and grabs her phone, fluffing her hair and taking a deep breath before opening TikTok. She scrolls through some of the most recent comments, wondering what all those usernames would say if she decided to actually respond to them. To push back. To argue. To go through the points and counterpoints over coffee. She wonders if anything she said, even face-to-face, would change anything. As if answering the question, her brain automatically populates with the things she's read about herself recently.

How long do you think it'll be until Evie Davis gets a real job?

How much do you want to bet a ghostwriter writes Evie Davis's captions?

She doesn't even have shame about the ads anymore.

Evie exhales deeply, then hits the LIVE button, waiting for other users to populate the TikTok Live.

Evie Davis never posts about anything good anymore.

One hundred people are viewing the TikTok Live.

Evie Davis tries too hard.

One thousand people are viewing the TikTok Live.

I honestly wish Evie Davis would just disappear.

Evie watches the LIVE symbol in the top right corner blink red, and she nods and smiles, giving a half-hearted wave to no one and everyone as she watches heart emojis appear and float past her face to the top of the screen, popping and dissolving into nothing as fast as they appear.

"Just thought I'd hop on here . . ." she begins, but her mind is elsewhere. That thought is floating up again, bubbling to the surface of her brain and sticking there. And then there's something else rising in her chest, a feeling. Something bright and new. Sharp. She's still trying to place it when she sees the man approach her car from the corner of her eye.

I honestly wish Evie Davis would just disappear.

I honestly wish Evie Davis would just disappear.

I honestly wish Evie Davis would just disappear.

CHAPTER 1

I am the one degree. I am the familiar link. I am the tiny line that separates everyone I know from someone else, the connection that makes a fun fact slightly more interesting than all the others shared during a forced get-to-know-you group activity, the thing that makes someone finally tune in, perk up, say, "No. What? Really?" I am the second someone. Not the first mentioned when an acquaintance says, "Well, actually, I do kind of know someone famous—well, someone who *knows* someone famous." I am what comes after the part that matters.

I'm more than just that, of course. I know that. I can still name the qualities I know to be true about myself in the way that a former therapist suggested: I am a good friend. A truly top-notch giver of gifts. A person who asks "How are you?" and means it, who can physically feel when there's an undercurrent of shame or sadness moving through someone I love. I am a hard worker. A problem solver. More likely to get shit done than to complain about it. I am a seeker of beauty. I can see loveliness and humor in almost anything or anyone that isn't me. I do it automatically, unconsciously. I am always pointing and laughing. Isn't it funny? Isn't it gorgeous? But then there's everything else, the things I know to be just as true, that would make my former therapist slowly nod and close her eyes, as if she's heard all of this before (she has) and say, "Remember how we talked about being nicer to ourselves, Hazel?" I always imagined her eyes were rolling under her lids. I'd try to track their movement, but I'd never know for sure.

It didn't really matter, though, because niceness doesn't have anything to do with the truth. And the truth is that I am suspicious of most everyone I meet, distrusting and awkward. And I am stubborn. Not headstrong, or willful, or brave. I am the kind of stubborn that means I've held on to every slight, every hurt, every worst quality that I should have grown out of and let fall away from me years ago. I'm all of that, too.

But I am my sister's sister first. And mostly, I've learned to be okay with that. Mostly, I know the alternative is not much better.

There were years when it bothered me, of course. Huge swaths of my early twenties when the last thing I wanted to hear from a new friend was that they feel like they know my younger sister, that they've been following her since they first downloaded Instagram in college, or that she was the reason they started doing that one eyeliner trick that makes you look more awake, like you've gotten a full night of sleep. I always wanted to say, "Don't you mean more like *her*?" but I never did. Because it didn't really matter. Once they knew, once they confirmed that Evie Davis was my sister, I was something else to them already.

My sister would be the first to tell you that she isn't for everyone, though. It's what she's been saying for years in response to nasty messages, or particularly cruel comments. "No one's for everyone," she'll say, and shrug, seeming wise beyond her years, as if that explains a stranger leaving a vomiting emoji in response to her posting a selfie, or a direct message that just contains the copied-and-pasted Merriam-Webster definition of the word *slut*. I know she's right, of course. That it would be impossible for everyone to approve of her. I've remembered it a thousand times when I've zoomed out and tried to see her internet presence, her brand, in the same way that any stranger would on any given day. An ad for an antiaging moisturizer that features a close-up of her poreless eighteen-year-old skin. A photo where the tiniest ripple of fat inches over the top of her low-rise leggings. A caption about how you're beautiful just as you are. I've seen the daily story slides of Amazon finds, or cute dresses under $50, or "must-have" designer dupes. A lot of times, I'm tempted to hit BUY instantly, too. Sometimes I do. Other times, I do the rough math. I consider the single item she's shared and all the tens of thousands of people who will then buy it because of her, the subsection of those people who

olivia muenter

will share that item again, bolstered by the reassurance that they're endorsing something that Evie Davis loves, too. I've pictured hundreds of Evie Davis–specific landfills populating the earth. But then I circle back around. No one forced any of them to buy those things, right? No one forced any of them to follow her either. To stick around. No one's for everyone, after all.

And if I'm being honest, the fact that Evie Davis is my sister has been everyone else's fun fact almost as often as it's been mine. I sometimes love the extra surge of attention that people pay me when I explain that yes, she is ten years younger than me with a different face and a different body and a vastly different life, but we're sisters all the same. I liked knowing that everyone I met thought they knew her, but it was only me who actually did. It's why I have to bite my tongue when someone says something like, "So how much does an eighteen-year-old lifestyle content creator make, anyway?" They'll laugh, say something about how their most aspirational lifestyle content as a teenager would be the time they snuck out for a party or smoked weed in the school bathroom. I'll laugh along with them, say something like, "Yeah, same. She and I really couldn't be more different." They'll smile and nod, raise their eyebrows as they look me up and down as if to say, *yeah, you're sure right about that*. It always stings, but at least I know. "But she's incredible at what she does," I'll add, careful to sound both proud and protective. How big sisters should be. But that's not why I watch out for her, not really. Mostly, I protect her because I know how she got here. I've seen exactly what it takes to grow up under a microscope that you never asked for, to put a camera on that microscope, to monetize it into oblivion.

"A microscope isn't so bad if it's only pointing out the good stuff, Hazel," our mom used to say to me in high school when I'd explain why, exactly, I didn't want to be on camera in the same way Evie seemed so happy to be. I could practically hear my mom's eyes roll through my bedroom wall as I sat there, knees drawn toward my chest, back flat against the door to keep it shut. To keep everyone else out. "Suit yourself, honey. Just don't say I never asked you. These brands might only want your sister, but I'm out there fighting for you, okay? For all of us. We aren't excluding you. The option is always there for you, too. I make sure the option is always,

always there, no matter what. I'd make it happen."

Even before the viral video happened, before everything, my parents were always filming, snapping photos, reminding me again and again that this was for *all* of us. They were obsessed with documenting our life as a family of three via posts on a basic WordPress blog, then Facebook, then YouTube, and I rarely wanted anything to do with any of it. "People want to see your face, Haze," my mom would explain when I'd grumble about her filming again, hiding myself behind a pillow. She always said this, that people wanted to see my face. I always got the feeling that she assumed I was insecure about how I looked, that that was the reason I was so camera shy. I knew I had acne. Hair that always seemed to be too frizzy or too greasy or, somehow, both. But that wasn't the reason I was camera shy. In fact, it was her constant reassurance that first made me think that maybe I wasn't physically cut out for the spotlight.

But she'd give other reasons, too. "People want to see our house! Our life! Our beautiful family. You should be flattered, baby. It's simple, really: people watch us because we have something they don't. Isn't that so special?" I never *felt* particularly special, not really, but I knew what she was saying had an edge of truth to it. I had heard from enough friends at school that our life was indeed cool—that our house, a converted school bus, was *amazing*. And I agreed with them. I loved the bus, and the cross-country road trips it brought us on every summer and winter break, with stops from Disneyland to Acadia National Park and most landmarks in between. I loved the reading nook my dad built me in the back, the tiny cubby that was just big enough for me, the way it was surrounded by shelves, complete with tiny built-in straps for keeping the books secure while we were on the road. I loved the bus's strange and comforting groans and creaks. Its mint-green exterior. The way that our home was always with us, no matter where we were. People like to say now that my parents were the first real family vloggers, the first to feature a child growing up on camera in real time. But in a way, they were early to it all. The school bus. The filming. The money.

But as much as my mom liked to remind me that people were invested in the three of us and, eventually, my baby sister, too, the first few years of posting brought few followers, and even fewer who weren't curious friends or family. *The Davis Family Scrapbook*, as the blog (then the YouTube channel) was named, looked more like a family photo album than some sort of money-making machine. You can still scroll back through their blog and YouTube archives and find those early posts. Photos of my twelfth birthday party on the bus and our tiny Christmas tree, a miniature replica of our green bus in place of a star. Even my mom's pregnancy announcement with Evie is still there, complete with one thousand words about just how long she and my dad had been trying for another baby, how hard it'd been, how sad, how after five years of accepting that another child just wasn't in the cards it was finally happening. Everything was changing. It was a miracle. A complete family. Finally.

People have asked me sometimes why I didn't push back then, take a stand. Set a hard limit. But I wasn't thinking about boundaries then. About agency. About the fact that I had told them no to filming, to photos, to posting them, again and again, and they had brushed me off. I wasn't concerned about my identity one day being stolen or a far-off stranger on the internet seeing a photo of me as a naked toddler in a bathtub. I was more concerned with the more realistic, more present fear that haunted me daily: that even one person I knew in real life would see them. So I fought smaller battles, begging my mom to delete the picture and corresponding blog post about the day I finally got my braces off. I hated that photo. Me standing next to a six-foot-tall papier-mâché tooth, beaming like it's the best day of my life, and the caption reading, "Hazel's big day!" I couldn't imagine anything worse than that. Not yet.

Five years after Evie was born, there was the video. Evie and my dad, rehearsing for Evie's first big recital on the tiny patch of grass that made up our front yard. My dad coaching her through every single step, reminding her of the transitions, the movements. My mom laughing from behind the camera and saying, "Chris, did you memorize, like, this whole thing?" Then him joining Evie, taking it from the top, the two of them dancing in sync, alternating between looking gravely serious and then giggling their way through it all.

"I told her she could just look at me during the recital if she forgot something," my dad says with a shrug at the end of the performance. "It was fun." I was fifteen then, and grateful (as I always was) to let Evie take center stage while I hung back, careful to stay out of the camera's frame. I smiled at my sister's tiny buns perched on either side of her head, ever so slightly crooked. I rolled my eyes at most things then, but this? This was adorable. All of it. Part of me wonders if the video would have gone viral anyway, even if it hadn't turned into some kind of sick trauma porn, something that people talk about over lunch and say, "God, have you ever seen anything so sad? That poor girl."

Realistically, there were probably a million different factors that made the video explode in the particular kind of way that things did then, little bits of it landing everywhere, coloring our lives. In those days, it wasn't a question of if someone had seen that video that everyone was talking about, but an expectation. It was the era of the internet when a viral video, no matter how mundane, garnered you a daytime television interview almost immediately. Even without the cameras, the video, everything that happened as a result, that year would have been the hardest of my life. I knew I should have been grieving. I knew I should have been trying to process that I was fifteen and my dad was suddenly gone. That he was there one minute, spinning in front of me, alive and whole, and then he was somewhere else.

I sometimes wonder if strangers would be as protective of Evie as I am if they took a minute to remember. To trace backward from where she is now, to remember that she is that little girl from the video, that little girl who lost her dad when she was only five. I wonder if this would make people understand or empathize with her more. Not pity her, but rather consider each horrible stepping stone like I do, chart the ways that that kind of loss might change someone.

But aside from the most die-hard Evie fans, the ones who are as dedicated as they are unsettling, most people don't want to do this. To them, Evie is whatever they see on their phones on any given day. Her story holds so much less power than what she is today, than her privilege and her platform. They're more likely to ask me about who she's dating. "Is she really with that Gavin kid? The one who used to date that girl on the Netflix show? Or was it the singer?" they'll ask. I'll shrug and say yes, that's true (and he dated both). Yes, he sucks, but, you know . . . hasn't everyone dated someone horrible? I mean, does anyone remember that guy I dated during junior year? We've all been there. I try to find the common thread that reminds them that she's real.

Still, I wait for people to bring it up. To ask me about the one thing that Evie and I do have in common, that they could google and know about immediately. What's it like to lose your dad? To have him there one minute and gone the next? To see his death become the starting point of a big, important life instead of the end of everything you knew? Those questions rarely come, though. Instead, people always seem to work up the courage to ask about money, if the rumors are true about exactly how much Evie makes from an Instagram post or a sponsored TikTok. I can pivot easily by now, change the subject. Nothing good ever comes from knowing those exact numbers, not even within our family.

Part of protecting my sister has always meant staying under the radar myself—being the one person who can love her without trying to auction off a piece of her, too. It was the same when I was sixteen and she was six, and it's the same now, twelve years later, when our lives couldn't be more different. In so many ways, I'm in the exact same place I've always been. Stuck. And she's, well, she's—

· • • ● • • ·

"Ma'am." A voice cuts through the thought, shaking me. "Can you repeat your name for the record? And state your relationship to Evelyn Davis? A little louder this time, please."

"I'm her sister," I say again, my voice sounding flatter than I intended, the important part coming out first. "Hazel Davis."

"And can you tell us the last time you spoke to your sister?" the man says.

I open my mouth, imagining the answer will fall out easily, but the words don't come.

When *was* the last time we spoke?

"And where were you," the voice presses, "on the day she disappeared?"

CHAPTER 2

"Half sisters?" the male detective named Buxton asks, his thin, nearly translucent eyebrows pushed together like he doesn't trust what I'm saying, that it's not quite adding up.

"I'm ten years older," I say. "And we don't look alike."

"Big age gap, huh?" he says. His partner, Detective Williams, crosses her legs as she leans back in the lounge chair that sits in my mother's sprawling living room. I wonder when my mom bought the chair, if she bought it. Most items in this house arrived with a catch instead of a price tag. Payment in the form of promotion. It's what she does, and I can hardly blame her for that. But I wouldn't know where, exactly, the chair came from because I haven't been in this room, in this house, for a year now.

"Surprise!" I hear my mother from the kitchen, her voice moving closer to where the three of us are sitting. My skin prickles. "Evie was a surprise."

She stops in the doorway at the edge of the living room and leans on the frame, drying her hands with a towel, like she was just baking bread or chopping fresh herbs from her garden. She throws the towel over her shoulder, letting it rest there as she starts to roll up the sleeves of her linen button-down, which manages to strike the perfect balance of lived-in without seeming wrinkled or sloppy. All of it, right down to that damn dish towel, makes her seem cozy and laid-back, but thoughtful. Warm. Straight out of a Nancy Meyers set. But I can't be the only one here who realizes that most things in this house are like this. They can all double as props.

"Best surprise ever," she says softly, her face breaking into a pained smile before it falls apart, and suddenly she's pursing her lips to keep herself from crying.

Jesus Christ.

The ten years between Evelyn and me sometimes felt like they might as well have been a hundred. To grow up not side by side but staggered, not in the same world but in two vastly different ones, was exhausting. It made closeness something that required work, effort, energy that only I, as the older one, could give. It always seemed to feel so easy for Evie, but that was only because I made sure I was there. Present. That I tried. But as hard as that closeness could be, it was also wonderful.

I was old enough when Evie was born that I can remember it all. The scent of her skin, the fluffy patch of hair that would lift up from her head, staticky and soft as silk. The tiny curve of her finger around mine. The solid feel of her in my arms. I was ten when she was born, too young to mother her in any significant way, or to resent her for the chores she added to my only-child life. I was also old enough to appreciate the wonder of a newborn, then a baby, then a toddler. Unlike other sisters I knew, there was never competition between us when I was at home, never a battle over friends or being left out. We were in two separate worlds, and in a lot of ways, that made loving her that much easier. People sometimes assume that my fractured relationship with my mom has something to do with the way Evie was born and changed everything I had known. That I was used to a level of attention and then I suddenly had to share it. That I was jealous. But it was never that.

The thing that blew up all of that is not how old I was when Evie was born but how old I was when my mother hit POST on that first video, when that suddenly became the new foundation of our lives. Being old enough to have a choice and realizing that my sister wasn't—that's what changed it all.

"But it's also what makes us so close now," I explain to people who ask about what it's like to be Evie's older sister. "It's what helps me protect her. And I think she needs that, you know?"

People usually nod then, somberly, like they understand the logistics of what it means to be eighteen and have the kind of influence that Evie has, the kind of connections, the kind of money. The kind of mother. Like they understand what it means to think you chose a life when you never could have. Like they really want to talk about the fact that no one has agency when they're so young that they haven't yet learned to read.

"All right, ma'am, thank you. But we're just wanting to talk to your daughter right now," Buxton says before cringing and realizing his word choice. "Your other daughter, I mean. Hazel." He clears his throat and nods to where I'm sitting.

Well, someone had to remind her.

I give something like a half wave that says, *Yup, here I am*, and despite this being the worst day in the worst year I've had in my adult life, I almost laugh out loud at the absurdity of the interaction.

And then, right on cue, there are sobs.

My mother covers her mouth with her palm to stifle the noise. I steel myself to avoid rolling my eyes. I'm just as upset as she is, of course—or as she appears to be, anyway—but this is obscene. Utterly unhelpful. I don't know why I thought she would have turned it off now, though. Of all times.

"I understand this is a difficult situation," Williams says, softly. "But it will make everything more organized if we really take our time with the interviews, make sure we talk to people one-on-one. My colleague spoke to you at length yesterday, correct?"

"Yes." She shakes her head in a way that says *stupid, stupid me*, like we're all supposed to pity her. She inhales deeply, eyes closed. "Of course. I understand. I'm so sorry. I'll just be in here."

She heads back into the kitchen and the detectives watch her leave the room before they focus on me again.

"So," Williams asks me, pausing in a way that resets the conversation. "Would you say that you and Evelyn are close?"

I meet her gaze and take a beat as I decide how to answer. All the years of being the one degree that separates everyone else from my internet-famous sister, and it finally matters. Finally, someone else is realizing the thing that I've always known: That it doesn't matter how many people think my sister is their virtual best friend or little sister or big sister. It doesn't matter that she's beautiful enough to be aspirational and down-to-earth enough that it makes her impossible to despise. My sister makes everyone who follows her think that she's talking to them personally, that they're two people hanging out while she puts on her makeup or chooses an outfit, but it's never, ever been as much of a two-way conversation as people think. That's why the detectives are here talking to me and not them. It finally matters.

I'm sure the detectives have to ask these questions, all of them, even the obvious ones. But our relationship isn't really the point. Like everything else about Evie Davis, what they're looking for lives somewhere deeper, wedged between who she is and who she is to the world. That thing, the tiniest sliver of truth, is what it will take to figure out how, exactly, we got here. It's also what will determine why, if I'm as close to my sister as I think I am, that I'm left with the same question everyone else in this room is asking: where is Evie Davis?

r/InfluencerSnark

EvieDavisThread | June 12, 2023, 2:05 p.m. EDT

Mytoxictraitisthis34

Umm . . . did anyone just catch Evie Davis on TikTok Live? That was BIZARRE.

⬆ 67 ⬇   💬 44

> **LoneStarrrr**
>
> Explain????
>
> > **Mytoxictraitisthis34**
> >
> > OK, so. She was talking about . . . nothing, really (shocking), drinking out of that massive reusable cup she always has (side note: does she know liking Diet Coke is not a personality trait?) and then it just randomly cuts off. She hasn't posted since then and it's been like . . . hours, which, as we all know, is practically centuries for Eternally Online Evie. Eons, really.
> >
> > > **ImNotHere200**
> > >
> > > Maybe she's doing that ~social media cleanse~ that all the wellness influencers talk about now, like posting about it doesn't defeat the whole point. Just put down the phone, girlie, it's not that hard!!
> > >
> > > > **SwipeUpForBS**
> > > >
> > > > LOL I can't. It's like her former pal Ashlyn who is always talking about how little she needs to be truly satisfied. Like "you don't need anything but your own soul to be happy but also please buy this gluten-free moisturizer I'm shilling." I unfollowed her months ago, but I can't give up Evie for some reason. Too fun to hate.
> >
> > **PhoebeAllTheWay**
> >
> > You forgot to mention the weirdest thing of all . . . that she TOTALLY saw someone before the Live cut off. She looked to her left and *clearly* made eye contact with someone before it abruptly cut off.
> >
> > > **SwipeUpForBS**
> > >
> > > Psh, come on. That seems a little dramatic. Also I just checked and Gavin literally JUST posted a photo of them—it's old (from that stupid matching Christmas pajamas shoot they did), but why would you post a photo of you and your girlfriend if something serious is going on? If you know you're the very first person people will have questions for?

KarenButNot1983

You *clearly* don't spend much time in r/UnresolvedMysteries, my
friend.

> **P0is0nandWine**
>
> Both of you are giving that man way too much credit. I'm pretty
> sure the most forethought he's put into anything is that time he
> tried to set up a pay-per-view fight with the cow from Chick-fil-A.
>
> > **WinnietheBish**
> >
> > Our ally king.

LostOnline2001

I can't believe y'all are honestly complaining about having LESS Evelyn Davis
in your feeds. Personally, I've never been happier. Shoutout to mysterious,
nameless, faceless stranger entering stage left for taking care of that for us.
We salute you.

> **ImNotHere200**
>
> Lmao. DARK yet . . . relatable?
>
> > **LastGreatAmericanDynasty**
> >
> > And sooo fucked up if something is actually wrong.
> >
> > **HaroldsHouse**
> >
> > Please. She was just on that big beauty brand trip with literally every
> > other influencer. They were all posting their swag bags and whatnot.
> > She'll be on stories in full glam and apologizing for how she looks
> > "like, SO rough" in no time. Don't you worry.
> >
> > > **ImNotHere200**
> > >
> > > Tbh you're probably right. But how else am I going to find the 135
> > > Amazon basics that I *need* to transition my wardrobe from
> > > summer to fall in the meantime????
> > >
> > > **GatorChompCO2020**
> > >
> > > I guess we're all going to have to suffer together lmao
> > >
> > > > **OneHeadlightNight**
> > > >
> > > > Has anyone checked SABI??? Maybe she knows something.
> > > >
> > > > **RainDanceRecital4**
> > > >
> > > > SABI has been MIA for weeks now (months???). I've
> > > > never craved pointless influencer gossip more in my life.

BluexandGoldx

Well, if anything is going to bring them (we don't
know it's a HER, people!) out of hibernation, it's this.

CHAPTER 3

I've always thought it was lazy to build a personality around what you dislike. Never "I love this book" but "I can't stand that best seller everyone's raving about." Never "I adored this TV show, this movie, this restaurant" but "You know what I think is overrated?" It's not that I don't have opinions that seem to contradict what the general public seems to love. Everyone does. I just hate the idea that I would share my distaste for the beloved thing that everyone else seems to love and would unknowingly make someone else question something that had brought them joy, laughter. That I would make them feel wrong or out of place. This is how I walked through my twenties, ten steps ahead of myself and everyone else, accounting for each emotion in the room, the tiniest ripple of embarrassment or discomfort. It made me quieter than some, maybe, but when you grow up without anyone doing the same for you, you learn.

But flowers are different. I hate them. I hate them enough that I go against every impulse that tells me to be agreeable and flat-out say it, actively, openly dislike the thing that is universally beloved. I don't want flowers, I'd tell boyfriends. Not ever. "Oh, because they just rot and die and smell and all of that?" they'd ask, or "None of them? Really? I mean I know some people hate carnations, but . . . what about roses? Peonies? Tulips?" None of them, I'd say. None of them ever. I've turned away florists at the door, avoided the aisle in the grocery store. Taken a different path at the farmers market. All of them reminded me of being fifteen, the way my dad had turned to me midrecital and said, "Shit. I forgot to get her flowers. For after. Your mom said it's a thing that the dads do. Think I should go now? I can sneak out during the older kids' parts."

"Yeah." I had smiled, eyes glued to the stage, imagining my sister beaming at a bright bouquet, feeling special. "She won't even notice. Go."

Go. I had actually said the word. Pushed him out the door. He would be dead fifteen minutes later, convenience store flowers miraculously unruffled in the passenger seat. Barely even bruised. I've imagined they were roses, maybe. Or carnations. Lilies. A medley. I didn't remember the specifics now, just that they had been the more fragile thing, the stuff that was supposed to die and decompose first. Not him.

The police said it was instant. He sped through a yellow light turning red, likely trying to make sure he didn't miss the end of the recital. The other driver feels terrible, they had said. But really, it's no one's fault. Isn't it, though? I had wanted to say. Doesn't it have to be? Someone had told him to go, after all.

I didn't say anything for weeks after that. Didn't cry, either. Instead, I watched my mother weep for hours on end, sobs wracking her body so intensely that I knew she had to be physically sore, using all those muscles for so long. Bodies aren't supposed to work like this, I thought at the time, watching my mother wail that first week, her face constantly pinched, contorted. Evie was different. Not so much sad as lost, like she wasn't fully processing what had happened. She was always wandering aimlessly around the bus looking for a toy those first few weeks. It always felt like she was looking for him, though, as if he had simply been misplaced. The two of them seemed to have grief that fit neatly into the other's. My mom would weep and she'd pull my sister into a hug. I'd watch Evie rest her cheek on her shoulder, stroke my mother's hair.

"It's okay, Mommy," she'd whisper. "It's all going to be okay."

I recognized the sadness in all of it—in myself, too—but I couldn't access a physical response. I wanted to comfort them, my sister especially, but my lack of outward emotion felt like a mockery of their grief, their ceaseless crying. So I stayed away, silently moving through rooms, leaving them to their shared sadness, painfully aware that there wasn't quite enough room for me, for whatever was going on in my head.

And then, after exactly two weeks of this, I walked in the kitchen to find my mom sitting at our small, fold-down table, silent. For the first time since it happened, there were no damp tissues spread around her, no snot running down her face. Instead there was just the laptop, our family camera, and a USB converter. Silently, she turned the laptop toward me. It was a YouTube video, a headline that I didn't read at the time but now know said simply DADDY'S LAST DANCE WITH HIS LITTLE GIRL—AND NEITHER OF THEM KNOW IT.

All I could see then were their faces. They were right there, dancing, happy, giggling. It seemed impossible that this was taken only hours before everything was so hopelessly wrecked, before I said "Go" so easily, a smile on my face. I said nothing, stunned by the vibrance of them, the lightness. The sudden recognition of a before, an after. I felt like I was suffocating, like I needed to watch the video a thousand more times, and also like I wanted to destroy it forever. To erase it from the face of the earth, from my brain, my soul. It felt like something was tearing inside my chest, but I couldn't look away. Unconsciously, my hand went to my mouth, then my heart, like it was trying to keep everything from spilling out of me.

"I know," my mother said, shaking her head like she couldn't believe he was gone either. *At least she understands*, I thought. And then she kept talking.

"Already two hundred thousand views just in the last few hours," she went on. "And it just keeps going. Can you believe it, Haze? This is really happening."

No, I thought, I can't believe it. I can't believe any of this.

But my mother was right about this too. This was really happening.

And there was nothing, and never would be anything, I could to do stop it.

· • • ● • • ·

Even now, a few questions into our interview, I know that the detectives won't ask about my dad, at least not right away. Maybe the information is in a folder somewhere, a result of a preliminary Google search some junior detective did as background research before they started their interviews. Maybe they'll get to it eventually. But this guy, Buxton, he's exactly the person who would turn up his nose at the mere idea of Evie long before considering what kind of circumstances needed to exist for her to build her career. I knew who he was the second I heard him say the word *influencer*, the way it came out of his mouth with the slightest hiss, the same way it has with most guys I've dated, the ones who questioned what Evie and I had to talk about, anyway. "What's that supposed to mean?" I'd ask, and they'd back down, say something about her age. But I knew that it was because of the thing all of them were thinking, but always too afraid to say: that she must be dumber, must be shallower. Guys like Buxton talk about Evie as if she's a hologram, or a soulless, AI-generated robot instead of the person I love most in the world, someone I would die for.

"So this was her job?" Buxton asks, as if he wants to emphasize just how absurd he thinks the concept is. "Social media? That's it?"

I study him for a second, wonder where he's going after this. If he'll get in his car and turn on some right-wing vlogger's podcast, nod along as they whine about how it's hard to be a white man today, if he'll skip through ads about protein bars that taste like banana pudding or remind himself to order some soon. If he'll get home and spend an hour on the toilet, scrolling through his own Instagram feed. If he'll then sit in some faded gray recliner and play video games, or just watch people play video games on a streaming app.

"She has an audience," I say. Am I really explaining this? "Just like any other type of celebrity, brands see the value in that. She's a walking billboard, and her followers trust her recommendations. So, yes, that is her whole job. Always has been."

Williams's eyes narrow just slightly in my direction, but she just listens.

"And these fans of hers—all those millions of them . . ." Buxton goes on. "They love her? No bad apples in there?"

I stare at Williams as if to ask *Is this guy for real?* but she stays silent except for a small, almost undetectable sigh. I take this as confirmation that we, at least, are on the same page.

"Well, I mean, sure," I start. "Some people love her. Adore her. Would cry when they meet her, send her their deepest confessions. And then there are people who hate her. The ones who send her death threats, or creepy dolls they've made that look just like her or items of their clothing, or photos of their dicks."

Buxton visibly bristles at the last word, as if I'm supposed to believe he's somehow shocked by the word, the act. I almost laugh.

"She has, what, more than four million followers across all platforms by now?" I guess. "Something like that. Double that if you count TikTok, which is where everyone her age is right now, anyway. If you were to do a breakdown of all those millions of people, there's the ones who love her, sure. And absolutely the ones who hate her. But it's the people who sit in the middle of that Venn diagram who can be the scariest ones."

"What do you mean?" Williams says, breaking her silence.

"Her following . . . it's this amalgamation of love and obsession and admiration and envy and hatred and . . . ownership," I explain. "It's utterly fucked-up. In every way."

Buxton and Williams are silent for a beat, taking in what I'm saying.

I wonder for a moment if maybe this isn't the right setting for cursing. I hate that even now, I'm considering my audience, just like my mom would. Just like Evie would, too. "People see the numbers and think it means she's beloved by everyone and, yes, it's true, she has a lot of fans. But it's more complicated than that, too. Even the adoration is mixed up with all the other shit, too."

Buxton has leaned forward from where he's sitting, positioning his elbows on his knees, his hand stroking nonexistent facial hair. His eyebrows are pushed together again, like he's trying to get a better view of me or he's skeptical about something I said. Or skeptical of me.

"It's all darker than people realize. And way darker than you can grasp when you're eighteen," I say. "This is why I'm—"

I catch myself. I know better than to pile irrelevant family drama onto this situation. Not right now. I can count the ways it would make everything so much worse. I know my mom and I need to be a united front here, even if it kills me.

"This is why we're so worried about her," I go on. "Having the level of fame that Evie has isn't like being an actor or singer. Her thing isn't music or movies or writing or art. It's her. Her entire life. That's what people think she owes them. That's what *she* thinks she owes them."

"Well, I mean, if it's her job . . ." Buxton says.

In unison, Williams's and my heads both snap in his direction, as if we know what's coming but hope he doesn't say it.

"Then, doesn't she? Doesn't she owe them that? Or . . . like, something at least," he finishes.

I stare at him, heat rising in my temples, but Williams speaks before I can.

"I think we've gotten a little off track here. The point is to find your sister, Hazel. That's all we're here for. None of what she does or why matters unless it's something that helps us find her and clear all of this up," Williams says.

I nod, suddenly too tired to push back. I know she's right. That maybe Evie's social media presence shouldn't matter when it comes to finding her. But it's all I can think about. It's a neon sign flashing in my brain since last night, when her boyfriend called me and I learned that my sister had been missing for six days.

"Absolutely not," I said out loud in my empty apartment, Gavin's name scrolling across the center of the screen.

No way I would help this kid win back my sister after the fight I'm sure they've just had, probably so much like the other dozen fights I had heard about during their first year of dating. Nope. I wouldn't participate in some over-the-top display of flowers or I'M SORRY spelled out in pepperoni on a delivery pizza, holding his iPhone for him while he fell to his knees in a faux-dramatic pose.

But then, despite my first instinct, I answered anyway. Maybe Evie needed a ride from somewhere, or her phone died, or she was going through something with my mom.

"Hazel?" he said before I could even say *hello*.

"Gavin."

I already wanted to roll my eyes. Gavin Ramirez just had that effect on people.

"Hey." He cleared his throat, and it occurred to me that his voice sounded higher than usual. Younger. "So . . . have you talked to the police yet?"

I paused what I was doing, removing my hands from the keyboard in front of me and closing my laptop, where I had been filling out job applications for three hours. It turned out that trying to find a job was a job, too. Benefits include no benefits at all and a rapidly decreasing sense of self-worth.

"What?" I asked, my blood pressure rising. "What are you talking about?"

A beat passed, the silence hanging between us.

Police. *What does he mean,* police? I thought, my mind racing full speed toward the worst possible scenario. At first, of course, it was a car accident that I considered. Speeding through a yellow light. Taking a turn too fast. No one's fault. But then, the other fears started to creep in, the ones that are just as realistic when it comes to my sister. I imagined that someone finally did it. Finally made good on their worst threat. Finally got too angry, too jealous, too entitled. For a long time, I had seen my sister's career as something held up by a thousand impossibly taut threads. There was no telling which one had finally snapped.

And then I remembered who I was talking to. Who I was *really* talking to. Not just Gavin, Evie's on-again, off-again boyfriend of the last year. No. This was also Gavin Ramirez, the self-proclaimed king of pranks. Gavin Ramirez, who had recently entered some sort of new, dark tier of internet fame, thanks to the viral TikToks of him approaching women and asking them to rate themselves on a scale of one to ten. "Interesting," he would finally say in response to their self-rating before walking away. Men loved to reply to the videos, of course, with ratings of their own, though I suspected they liked the look of the women's eyes at the end more—the confusion, the way so many of them seemed slightly unsettled by the interaction, disarmed.

The first time I saw one of the videos, I had texted the link to Evie.

"Really, Ev?" I had written.

"He's not actually rating them himself, Hazel," she had texted back with the eye-roll emoji. "It's a social experiment."

I hadn't replied, distracted by something else at work, a job I still had then, but she texted again after a few minutes.

"A dumb social experiment, yes, I will admit," she wrote. "But an experiment nonetheless."

I wanted to laugh. I wanted to say, "Oh, is that what he told you it is?" but I had to remind myself, as I had so many times throughout my sister's teenage years, that this wasn't some twentysomething colleague I was talking to at a wine bar. This was an eighteen-year-old living a very particular kind of life, still living in a house with the nightmare that was Erin Davis. I needed to give her the room to fuck up on her own terms, to date questionable people. I needed to give her the benefit of doubt, the space to make a mistake that she so firmly believes isn't one, at least right now. That's the thing about being eighteen—you're always going to do the thing you want to do anyway. And she deserved that kind of normalcy.

And it's not like I could gesture toward my life, my romantic choices, and say that I was doing much better. Not when I was still being regularly ghosted by guys named Carter and Cade who said things like "The vibes are there, but they're also not, you know?" directly after having sex with me. The thing about the Gavins of the world is that when you want one, no amount of common sense or advice can sway you. It was true for me at eighteen and it still is, if I'm being honest. We all have to learn the hard way.

But it was a relief yesterday, when I remembered this conversation with Evie. I could breathe again. Of course that's what this is, I thought. A social experiment. A harmless prank that is only actually harmless to him. That's what it has to be.

I pulled the phone away from my ear for a moment and tilted my head toward the ceiling, pinching my nose with my free hand.

"Are you fucking kidding me, Gavin?" I finally said. "You're unbelievable."

"Hazel, I—" he said, his voice still sounding so very young, so small. Had he always sounded this way? Did he change his voice for videos? I wouldn't be surprised.

"This is fucked-up, even for you. You don't just joke about serious shit like this. You can't," I said. "It's not funny."

I waited to hear it—the eventual laughter that had to come. I could picture it, even: Him in some dark room, hunched over the phone in an absurdly priced gaming chair, sugar-free Red Bull cans scattered around the room. His YouTube friends spread around him in bean bags like giant,

olivia muenter

teenage-boy-sized lice, manspreading into infinity. All of them holding their breath, waiting for the prank to work. Not wanting to interrupt the footage, the audio recording of my fear. But it never came.

"Hazel," he said again, a little louder this time. "This is not a prank. I wish it was, but it's not. I swear to God. I thought Erin had talked to you . . . I thought you knew."

Erin. My mom. She knew this before me? That something was wrong with my sister?

My skin prickled.

"Told me what? What is going on, Gavin?" I said. "You're scaring me."

He exhaled into the speaker. "Fuck," he said. "Why am I the one telling you this? The person you hate with the passion of a million blazing suns?"

Those were Evie's words. I could practically hear her say them. Evie.

"I don't care about any of that. Please just tell me what is going on. Is she okay? Is anything okay? What the fuck is happening?"

"No," he said, his voice quiet again. Soft. "Nothing is okay. No one has seen Evie since Monday."

I quickly did the math, digging through my brain for the day. Sunday. It was Sunday. Almost a week. But . . . that wasn't possible, right? That couldn't be. She was in Los Angeles. It was a work thing. A brand trip. Right?

"No. Wait. What do you mean? She's . . . she's with Soleil, isn't she? That . . . sustainable razor company? That's what it is, right? Isn't she with, like, a hundred other people who all have a million more followers watching their every move? All of them are there with her, right? Posing photos of the same flower arrangements or whatever," I ramble on, rattling off the reasons why my sister is very much not missing. All the reasons why it's impossible.

"She was," he said. "But that ended days ago. And she hasn't been online . . . no texts, no calls, no posts, nothing. Erin thought she was meeting with the brand for longer. I thought she was just pissed off at me for some stupid shit I said."

My brain feels like it's about to split in half.

"I figured your mom would have called you . . . I know you guys are, like, no contact or whatever." He trailed off, suddenly sounding embarrassed to be talking about a situation that was so intimate, so personal. But he wasn't wrong.

My mom and I weren't entirely no contact. We were cordial enough to one another—if something involved Evie. It was less like I was her older daughter and more like I was a long-lost biological mother and she had adopted Evie. My mom couldn't deny our connection, couldn't deprive Evie of it, either. But she could only allow so much, lest she be replaced. And she certainly wasn't going to try to build a relationship with me that went beyond that, not anymore. She'd given up on that long ago, and so had I. Still, I thought she'd have the common sense to loop me in for an emergency.

But Erin Davis was still Erin Davis. I should have known.

"That's why I was calling you," he explained. "They said not to talk to anyone until everyone's been interviewed . . . the brand trip people, Erin, her friends. They wanted to make sure everyone was on the same page, I guess," he said. "With the detectives. Or the police? I don't know what the right terminology is, who's who . . . I just thought . . . I thought maybe she had talked to you. Maybe you knew something. Maybe you could tell me if I had done something wrong?"

This was probably when the anger should have started to settle in, arranging itself side by side with my fear. It should have made me curse my mother for the millionth time, because how dare she. How dare she not tell me that my sister was missing, possibly in danger. But of all the things Gavin had told me in the last five minutes, this part of things was the least surprising. This part of things made the most sense of all. My mother would want this all for herself, would be greedy to claim this type of panic as her own.

But Evie disappearing? Not responding to texts and calls, dropping off of social media without a single word? Without telling me? No. Nothing about that checked out. But maybe I had missed something . . . something vital. I had been a little preoccupied.

"No, I haven't . . ." I shook my head. "I haven't talked to her in a couple weeks, honestly. Things have just been . . . busy, and I haven't had the cash to drive all the way—"

I stopped myself then. I didn't need to share any of this with a kid, someone who once made a video about how much he spends on protein powder in a month (spoiler: too much). My sister's dipshit boyfriend. No, it didn't matter why Evie and I hadn't been talking much lately. All the reasons for that went far beyond the logistics of me being miserable, of losing my job while Evie made millions. We didn't have time for any of that, anyway. I didn't need to follow that rabbit hole any further down right now. I needed to know Evie was okay.

"What do I need to do?" I said instead. "How can I help? Who do I need to talk to?"

"I'll connect you with the detectives," Gavin offered. "They left me their contact information when they came by this morning."

"Thank you," I said, and now it was my voice sounding small, young.

I thought back to what he had asked, if he'd done anything wrong, and something about it kept repeating in my head.

"She—she probably is just taking some time away. Mad at you. Pissed off at my mom. Sick of working all the time," I suggested, grasping at explanations that could exist, ignoring all of the reasons it could be something darker—all the worst-case scenarios I've tried to brush off over the years as impossible, or unrealistic, but never could. The fears I know well from being a woman in the world, even one without millions of people tracking my every interest, my order at Shake Shack, my favorite time of day to take photos in that Target parking lot with great light.

"So," Gavin said, "I guess that means you haven't seen the video. Have you?"

I hadn't. I knew I hadn't because I hadn't seen much of anything that Evie had posted since I lost my job last month. I had hidden her content shortly after, muted her stories. I wasn't proud of it, but the juxtaposition of her happy, light posts with my current situation ate at me, and I hated that. I would watch an Instagram story that I knew had made her at least five figures, and it made my stomach churn with envy. I didn't want it to, but I couldn't stop it. I didn't want to have to hide any of it, but I didn't want to hate it more. And if I never saw it, there was nothing to hate, nothing to compare myself to. Besides, I knew the truth: @evelyn isn't Evie. So what did it really matter if I muted her? If I missed a smoky eye tutorial, a Trader Joe's haul?

I still checked in every now and then, and that was enough. I could see she was going on dates and applying face masks and going on trips with brands. Evie didn't need one more person watching it all anyway, one more flame-emoji reaction she'd never see in her DMs buried underneath thousands of other messages. She needed someone who was above all of that. Above the admiration, the jealousy, the greed. And not looking at any of it is what allowed me to be that person, at least in this particular phase of my life.

But it also meant that I missed things. I missed that it had been nearly a week since my sister had posted on social media. A week since she had texted me. I missed the ominous TikTok Live that Gavin texted me a link to after our call, a screen recording that was circulating everywhere now. The one where a man comes into view in the very last minute, right before everything goes dark. I missed the last thing she sent out into the world. I missed that she hadn't FaceTimed me, hadn't called. I missed that, actually, my sister was nowhere to be found at all.

CHAPTER 4

By the time my mom picked up my calls, it had been more than 144 hours since Evie was last seen. It took me almost five hours to drive through the long stretch of desert between Vegas and Phoenix, a distance that felt just far enough to me when I was first offered the digital editor job for a local newspaper a few years ago. It took twenty-five minutes to work up the nerve to get out of the car, even though I knew my mother had to know I was there since she had talked to the neighborhood security guard and buzzed me through the front gate. Even after I came inside, it took another twenty for her to look me in the eye.

It's less than twenty-four hours later, and I have spoken to two different detectives twice. I have watched the screen-recorded clip of Evie's TikTok Live no fewer than twenty-five times. I have scrolled through the 943 comments on the now-viral screen recording four times, my thumb carefully hovering over each username. Each time, I expect to find an answer that will make all of this seem explainable, laughable even, that will prove we're all just overreacting. And each time, all I find is strangers who don't know my sister at all. The video has three million views now.

I've never been particularly good with numbers, but I've always liked them. Ever since I was little, they felt comforting to me, predictable and cool. Numbers are all clean lines and solutions, things that feel manageable in a way that other descriptors don't. Hours seem like things you can hold in your hands. Minutes seem like tiny building blocks, something solid. But I've learned that even numbers can get out of control eventually, too. Days, weeks—those soon grow too large, looming over you in a way that makes them lose their shape, their scale. Eventually, they all start to mean too much. But for now, right now, sitting in my mother's house that has never really been my home, Evie has been missing for one week, six hours, twenty minutes, and thirty-five seconds or so, and I can still grip onto those figures, even as I feel them start to slip.

The detectives have told us repeatedly to stay put, stay quiet. Stick together. Ignore the media. No press. They know it's coming by now, that it's already started, really, but from our conversation earlier I've gathered enough to bet that they aren't even a little bit prepared for the shitshow that will ensue when the internet realizes Evelyn Davis is really, truly missing.

"No offense, miss, but I've never even heard of your sister," Buxton tells me when I try to explain the extent of Evie's notoriety, like he needs to make me understand that I am somehow too close to the situation, that I don't really realize how not-so-famous she is. Because if *he* doesn't know who she is, then how many fans could she *really* have? How big a deal could this *really* be? "I don't think we need to blow up the situation unnecessarily when we have our best people following every single lead. It will only turn this into a spectacle, and trust me, when the media gets a hold of this, because of what your sister looks like, it's a whole other ball game. You might think you want more attention on this, but it's going to get messy."

He chuckles, like something he thought had made him laugh but he can't quite share it with the group—not the way he wants to, anyway.

"Listen, when this goes public in a real way, half the stories will immediately be about the fact that your sister is a very beautiful, *very* white girl, and why don't we focus on other cases like we're focusing on this one, and then suddenly it's about how we're all a bunch of racist assholes and not about how we find your sister." He shakes his head, like I wouldn't believe the shit he has to deal with.

We both sit there for a beat, and I wonder if he wants me to—what? Feel bad for him and commiserate over his not-so-subtle racism? Not a chance, buddy.

"That happens whether she's famous or not," he goes on. "The only thing that changes, if she's really as well-known as you're saying, is that people are even less sympathetic. That's the cold hard truth, I'm sorry to say."

I'm angry now—that this is the guy who's in charge of finding my sister, sure, but also that I feel like I don't have much of a choice. For the first time it crosses my mind that maybe pushing back and making myself unlikable even here, even now, might backfire. That there's a possibility that the more disagreeable I am, the less this guy will want to do his job.

But before I can say anything, Williams cuts in.

"What we're saying is that right now, it's in our best interest to keep *our* eyes on this only," Williams says, leaning toward me with her elbows on her knees. "People knowing. That will happen. A statement from your family. That will happen, too, likely soon if nothing changes. But in this exact moment, if there is foul play at work here—and please understand, we have no reason to believe that that's not the case right now—then it only benefits us to make sure the perpetrator is in the dark."

The perpetrator? It strikes me as such a big, ugly loaded word to use for a situation, for something that I'm trying desperately to convince myself is simply a mistake, a misunderstanding. I suddenly feel helpless, struck with the realization that neither of these people are helping me in the ways I want to be helped. That I know nothing to do in this situation other than answer their questions, give them what they want, not get in the way.

I hear a sound from the kitchen then that I instantly recognize as my mother's sobs, fading as though they were muffled by something. Her own hand, or that fucking dish towel.

Williams exhales deeply and leans in closer.

"There will be a time and a place for a statement and for social media outreach, but it should only happen at our discretion," Williams says, her eyes darting behind me in the direction of the kitchen then back toward me again, a message. "Is that clear?"

"Crystal," I reply. It shouldn't surprise me that even now, I am charged with minimizing the wake of my parent's damage. A buffer until the very end.

The rest of our extensive interview is like everything I'd seen in hours of true crime docuseries, or British procedurals, right down to the detail that none of it felt even remotely real. None of it felt urgent, though of course it was. I had imagined emergencies all my life, especially those related to my sister. What if a crazed fan hid in her room? What if a stalker came to the door holding a gun? What if she sped through a light when driving, took a turn too fast, was in a hurry when she shouldn't have been? In all of those scenarios, there had been running, screaming, rushing. Nonstop frantic movement. There had been clear choices to make, an obvious path forward. A way to be useful or brave. In reality, there was nothing to do but wait, and answer these questions that all seem so pointless, and talk and talk and talk. I am at the mercy of these two people, and all I can do is follow their lead. They are the only ones in the room with a guide for how this works. Who else is going to tell me how to act, what to do, who to call, what to say? So I sit here in my mother's comfortable home, everything soft and beige, and I answer their questions calmly, one by one, hating myself for not running through the streets screaming my sister's name. For being safe and still and so very helpless.

Did Evie seem happy, they ask. Sure, I say. She just got back last month from an all-expenses-paid trip to the south of France where her only requirement was to wear a certain foundation once or twice. If she wanted. Who wouldn't be happy with a life like that?

What do I think of Gavin? How long do they have, I almost say, but I soften when I remember his call, the fear in his voice, the way he had helped me, and I think better of it. He's a twenty-year-old kid, I say. It won't last.

And how about Ashlyn Price, her former best friend? What about other friends, other people she talked to, other admirers?

She has more than four million followers across all social platforms, I emphasize again, only half trying to hide the other question in my tone: Do I have to do your job for you?

That quiets them for a minute, but we're soon back to the specifics of her relationships, her habits, her schedule.

"And she's never done anything like this before?" Williams asks. "It's completely out of character for her to disappear like this? To go off the grid for a bit, or to do something unexpected? To be deceptive, even?"

olivia muenter

This question makes me pause for a beat, something in the last few words snagging on a memory, but I know there is only one answer I can give them.

"No," I tell them. "She's never done anything like this. This is not normal. It's not her."

I make a point to make eye contact with them then, to show them how much I mean what I'm saying. How the answer I'm giving them is the only one that matters. By the time we're done, I feel like they believe it.

"We have a lot to go over," Williams says, standing to shake my hand. Her eyes are somewhere behind me, though, and I turn my head to see my mom leaning against the doorway. "We'll be in touch regularly. Please know that this case is our number-one priority right now. We'll be in touch later tonight, then tomorrow morning again. And, of course, as anything relevant comes in between. Call us if anything comes up before sharing information anywhere else. That's very, very important."

Williams looks at me then, her gaze steady and measured, full of implications. I nod as if to say: I'll try my best, same as always. Part of me is relieved that she seems to get the balance of things here. That it's not me she has to worry about. Another part of me resents that I'm back here, once again managing the selfishness of my mother and the damage it could do.

My mom walks toward us, shaking the detectives' hands herself before we both walk them to the door. As soon as the door shuts, my mother moves away from it as if even the forced proximity with me is too much for her, like it makes her skin crawl, too. I've been in the house for almost a whole day now, but we haven't managed to have a full conversation yet. The detectives and commotion have made it easy enough to ignore each other, to talk through other people instead of directly to each other. It's cleaner that way, anyway.

"I need some time," my mom says, pacing on the opposite side of the room for a minute, frantically detangling the three delicate gold necklaces she's wearing that have woven themselves together throughout the day. "To just . . . to figure this out. To be alone."

I nod, partially relieved that I'll soon be alone again, even though I still can't feel comfortable here. Mostly, it's been easy to distract myself, to avoid my mother during the odd times she wasn't with detectives, or on the phone. In the meantime, I've tried to be useful to pass the time. I called Evie multiple times, listening to her voicemail each time, letting it get all the way to the beep before I hang up. Now, I go through our text messages for a third time, desperate to find something. It's a two-week-old chain of live stream commentary about the newest season of *Lost in Love,* a survival-meets-dating show where singles are stranded on an island together.

No way Shaina makes it more than two days, Evie had written.

Honestly generous, I wrote back. *I give it two hours. And there will be crying.*

She responded with a skull emoji, and that was it. That was the last thing we talked about. The last stupid, stupid thing. My brain instantly imagines being interviewed one day, someone asking me what the last thing my sister said to me was, and the emoji popping up in my head. It's so mundane that it makes me almost embarrassed for her, for us. It makes me want to text every friend, every person I've ever dated, and say something meaningful, interesting. Anything so the last message I sent them wasn't something silly, so ridiculous that it almost distracted from the fact that it might be ominous, too.

But then I catch myself: What is wrong with me? Evie is coming back. People disappear sometimes, right? They come back more often than they don't. They show up. They're fine. I close my eyes and shake my head at the way I spiraled. My brain had been imagining this was the end without even wanting to. I hate that even now, I am outside myself, just like I was at work. A former boss once told me that I was so focused on the worst-case scenario that I prepared for that instead of doing my actual job, instead of considering what was actually in my control. "I swear you invite it into the room," she told me on her last day before transferring to another department. "Whatever the bad thing is you're thinking—how you're going to fail, how a story will fall apart, if someone hates you—I think you think about it so much that eventually it just appears." At the time I thought she was being dramatic, overanalyzing. In the end, though, she had been right.

I can't do that now, though. I can't get to that place again. I won't.

I hear the hum of the shower turning on upstairs and it reminds me of routine. Showering. Sleeping. Feeding myself. I need to focus on the basics if I'm going to keep my head above water. That's the only way I'll stay clearheaded now, in this place. I walk to the kitchen, where I decide I'll eat something. Something healthy, balanced. Fiber and nutrients and all that. The kitchen looks the same as it did the last time I was here, honed marble countertops, the type that are painfully beautiful but that design experts on TV always warn will stain easily. I search for a single mark, a ring from a coffee mug, the faint remnant of a spatter of tomato sauce, but they look as new as the day we moved into the house. I grab some sort of granola bar from the counter that looks trendy and vaguely healthy, opening the wrapper with my teeth. It smells like a Whole Foods, sterile and woody. It tastes the same. I choke it down anyway—I haven't eaten since lunch—and roam the rest of the downstairs, reacquainting myself with the space. I stop in front of the large gallery wall and I'm surprised to see some of the photos still feature me. I imagined Mom would remove them at some point after I stopped coming by. What's the point in pretending?

My eyes land on one of the four of us outside the bus turned tiny home, the familiar shade of green comforting me even now. My eyes are half closed in the image, and Evie's smile is bright and wide. Next to it is a shot of my sister, my mom, and me standing backstage before Evie's first appearance on a daytime talk show, the one where we were presented with a giant, human-sized check for "inspiring people."

"So . . . what? We're here because we made people cry?" I said to my mom backstage as Evie had her makeup touched up. "Because they feel bad for us?"

"Don't be ridiculous, Hazel," my mom said, eyes fixed on Evie's face in the mirror. "We're here because we touched people's hearts. Do you know how rare that is these days?"

Not that rare, I thought, imagining the slate of other sob stories the show would feature for the rest of the week.

"Perfect," my mom said, standing in front of Evie, adjusting her two tiny buns. I could have sworn she moved one just slightly down, so that they looked almost identical to how they were in the video.

We had walked into the hallway to meet with a production assistant, whom my mom promptly asked to take a photo of us. I had agreed to the appearance on the show—I had been excited to be on a television set. But I made my mom promise no photos. I didn't want to be on stage, or be interviewed. The spotlight of the viral video had made me feel hyperaware of my emotions, my body, my reactions to social cues. My mom and Evie had seemed to instinctively know what to do with it all, but I was never able to. I laughed when things were sad. I hunched when I should have stood up straight. I stared blankly when I should have smiled. It all made me feel scratchy, anxious, like I was tripping over my own body, my thoughts. If I disliked the photos before, the blog posts, now I hated it all.

I tried to push back when she thrust a digital camera into the hand of the intern, who didn't look much older than me at the time, but my mom wedged her arm between mine and my body, hooking us together there. Finally, I managed to squirm away, and they got a few more photos of just Evie and Mom. She could have used those for the gallery wall; I knew they existed somewhere, that they both looked great in them. But this was the one that Evie liked the most. Or that my mom liked the most. I couldn't remember now which. Either way, this was the one that they had framed and hung.

I could still hear what she had said to me afterward, when I groaned about the photos, our agreement.

"You promised," I said.

"We make people feel better about life, baby," she said, simultaneously pointing to the spot on Evie's cheekbone where she wanted the makeup artist to add a little bit more highlighter before they went onstage. Then she looked at me, hands on her hips. "If that's not worth celebrating, I don't know what is."

I didn't respond, but I remember thinking that she was right. I'm sure people loved knowing that at least they weren't us. That no matter what else was going on in their own lives, at least that had somehow dodged all of this. At least they hadn't lost what we had. At least they weren't parading around the worst thing that had happened to them like a badge of honor, or an opportunity. If nothing else, at least they had that.

olivia muenter

Re: Just thought I'd hop on here.

From: **Such a Bad Influence**

July 1, 2022

Good morning, friends. Just thought I'd hop on here and share what's on my heart this morning. Just something I've been thinking about during this season of life. Because I told y'all I'd always be honest about the highs and lows. And it's not all fake eyelashes and spray tans over here. Not all matcha and manifestations. Not all workouts and wine nights. Not all sunsets and slow dancing in the kitchen with my best-friend-who-happens-to-be-my-hubby. Not all highlights and highlighter. It's more than that. Yes, it might look glamorous, but that's only because it usually is.

That's how it feels, right? To sign on to your phone these days? To get on Instagram and expect to be entertained, only to find yourself annoyed? Yeah, yeah, we all know you *could* unfollow the Serena Bakers of the world, wave goodbye to the opportunity to find out what breed of pygmy goat the next Baker kid will get for their birthday (and actually, goats are great for clearing weeds— so it's an investment, really, an environmental fucking wonder). But will you? Will I? Probably not.

Look, I'm not saying it's noble to follow someone for the sole purpose of occasionally (or frequently) rolling your eyes at their ridiculous antics, acting like they're surviving on nothing but God's abundance and twenty jars of home-canned tomatoes when they have an inheritance to rival the GDP of a small nation. But I am here to say for all of us: It's not that hard, is it? To do the right thing? To have even an iota of self-awareness? To see the line between real and real fucking annoying? Wanting transparency from the people we follow is nothing new, but is it really too much for us to ask for a little self-awareness, too? For them to make note that several hundred thousand strangers follow them and think: *Huh, they'll probably have an opinion about all of this bullshit, too. I wonder if I should consider this from the other way around.*

I mean, of course, *they* don't think it's bullshit. It's their life. It doesn't have to look like anyone else's. That's why we follow them, right? To escape into a world that isn't ours? Or, wait, is it because their life *does* look like ours in some way? Is it the faux relatability we like, even if most of us have learned that this quickly slips away with time and followers and money, anyway? Is that why we stick around? Or is it because there's a weird type of satisfaction in knowing that we're doing this—existence—the harder way, the way that doesn't include validation from thousands of people immediately after we post a photo of ourselves, our kids, our homes, our homemade spelt fucking pie crusts, our lives?

I started this newsletter because I'm trying to figure this out myself. To make sense of the ever-shifting Venn diagram that is my own feed. The influencers I used to love to follow but now mostly hate-follow (don't judge me, I know you do it, too). The people I keep track of from afar (How are people still buying this bullshit? This pair of leggings? This aesthetically pleasing water bottle?). The people I enjoy following but, if I'm being honest, am always waiting to see mess up, or change. Because they always change, don't they? They give us one thing, we give them a platform, and then they make money off of it. And when the money changes them (because that's what money does) and we call them out on it, they're offended. Wounded. As if they don't need our approval anymore, anyway. As if we aren't giving them what they need to be relatable again: perspective.

So that's why I'm here. To put actual words to the passive-aggressive messages that make our favorite and not-so-favorite influencers cry on their stories. To bring some much-needed context to the mix. And to have a little fun, maybe. I could use some of that, too.

Won't you join me?

(Sign up at the link in my bio.)

(I'm kidding.)

(Or am I?)

Before I go, let's get to a quick roundup of the hottest tidbits around the industry this week, from Instagram-famous pet deaths to shapewear controversies:

olivia muenter

- Evie Davis's Insta-famous cat, Mochi, died suddenly this past week. With nearly 600K followers, Mochi was beloved by Davis family lovers and haters alike—and a testament to Erin Davis's ability to squeeze every single dollar out of any living creature in their home. Though Mochi's battle with cancer was sudden and shocking, we're pretty sure they were able to milk it for all it was worth, content-wise. RIP, Mochi, you were cute and fluffy, and we hope you enjoyed that four-story pet palace sponsored by Whole Foods half as much as we did.

- Laurie Arthur posted a single link to a voter registration website, prompting waves of praise and admiration from her millions of Gen Z followers. It seems that Arthur, who spent the majority of the last election cycle claiming that she "loves everyone" in response to questions about her political leanings (though, really, do we have to speculate?), is more compelled to speak up this year. If there's anything we can all count on, it's that doing the bare minimum is considered going above and beyond when the expectations are so, so low.

- Kelsey Steedmeyer has been skewered by your favorite online snark site for taking a paid trip to a Mexican resort only to lock herself in her ocean-view room because she "feared for her life." Steedmeyer, who lives in rural Idaho with one dead-eyed husband, three adorable children, and two doodle-adjacent dogs who I am personally considering saving from the chaos of it all, says that she wasn't expecting Mexico to be so "different" and that she has "had the worst diarrhea of her life for four days straight."

That's all for this week's newsletter. Check your inbox next week for the latest on the influencers, the influenced, and the in-between.

Until next time,

SABI

CHAPTER 5

I wake up to light streaming in through a window, stinging my eyes. My phone is on my chest. I scroll through the notifications with one eye open, slowly waking up as I read through the messages. Four notifications from LinkedIn about New York–based jobs that sound horrible but I should apply to anyway. One email from a recruiter that starts with "Unfortunately" and ends with "We'll keep you in mind for opportunities!" A 2:32 a.m., one-word text from a guy I had been hooking up with every seven weeks like clockwork for the last year.

Hazel, it said. That's it. Just my name, plus the single smiley face he sent fifteen minutes later.

I roll my eyes. I know this move. The name thing. It's not quite as direct as "You up?" Not so impersonal. But, of course, the meaning is largely the same. I think the goal is to be sexy and intimate, the way it is when someone says your name in bed. All a game to make you think that they know you, that they see you, they want you in a way that's somehow more interesting than the ways every other guy wants you. Please. I delete the text with a single swipe, thankful that I had fallen asleep before it came in.

There's one other text, from a name I don't recognize at first. I read the contact out loud, "Sierra Spanish," wracking my brain for who it could be. Then it clicks. We went to college together, were paired up for a group project in a Spanish class. We hadn't spoken since. And now she was texting me?

I know it's been forever, but I have to ask . . . Is this TikTok stuff for real? Is Evie okay?

And then I remember, a wave of nausea working its way through me when I realize I had forgotten. I stare at the ceiling, blinking the rest of the room into reality, remembering where I am and why. My mom's house. The couch. Evie, Evie, Evie.

The shame lights me up, makes me sit up straight, grab my glasses from the coffee table. I swing my feet to the ground and my toe lands on something that pokes me, then crunches beneath my weight when I stand up. I look down to inspect the area and realize it's my contact lens. Last night I pulled them out of my eyes and then was too lazy to go to the bathroom and throw them out. Erin will hate this.

"Look who's up," a voice chirps, as if on cue, from across the house, in the adjoining kitchen. My mom.

She's sitting at the kitchen table, hands wrapped around an earthenware mug, the kind that looks like she bought it from a third-generation artisan in Maine. I imagine her sharing it on Instagram: "My inbox is blowing up right now and I'm so, so very sorry I can't share a link for this *exact* piece. However, if you click through you can shop through 16 similar options—and all under $30, too!"

I roll my eyes without thinking and hope she can't see me, that the giant expanse of the open floor plan means she's too far away to catch it.

"Is there any news? Have you heard from her?" I ask, though I think I already know the answer.

I'm startled when a voice other than my mother's responds.

"I'm afraid not," the male voice booms from the just-out-of-sight kitchen. I already know it's Buxton. He walks to the kitchen table to sit across from my mother and sets his freshly poured cup of coffee down in front of him, translucent tendrils of steam rising from the mug.

How long has he been here? Have I slept through the whole thing?

"Morning," he says, the word loaded with judgment.

What kind of person sleeps in when their sister has been missing for more than a week? What kind of person isn't up all night, hysterical with worry?

I consider explaining myself, but everything sounds wrong in my head. It's been a long two days. A long month. A long year. I could sleep for a hundred more hours. A year. Sleep is the only time I'm not inside my own head.

I study my mother and I swear there's part of her that looks pleased. I can easily imagine a scenario in which she wants to make it clear to the detectives that she's the one who has her shit together here. She's the one to trust. To talk to. To focus on. That I'm the mess, and don't they have enough of that to deal with right now?

I walk over to the kitchen table, running my hands over my face, smoothing my hair, straightening my shirt. For the first time in my life, I'm thankful I fell asleep in my bra. I take a seat at the table across from the two of them, forgoing brushing my teeth or coffee, to make it clear that this is the priority. That it was an accident that I slept in this late. I look at my phone again, this time checking the time. It's almost eleven.

I wonder what my mom said to him, how that conversation went.

"She's always been a heavy sleeper."

"She said not to wake her."

"This is probably just her schedule now, being unemployed and all . . . back to being a nocturnal teenager, I guess. Kind of depressing."

Buxton raises an eyebrow the tiniest bit in my direction, like he's amused by my appearance, like I'm the one who owes everyone an explanation. I stare at the wall, determined not to let it bother me, straightening my posture against the feeling that I'm now even more on the outside of all of this than I was two days ago.

"Tell us what we should do," I say, my tone somber. "How we can help. We can't just sit here and wait forever."

"I was just going through all of that with your mother, actually," he says, glancing at my mom, a slight grin stretching across his face until he realizes I'm staring at it. My mom sees first, though.

"Detective Buxton is *very* helpful." My mom nods, adjusting the sleeves of her Lululemon zip-up jacket, the one that cinches at the waist, smooths out her already perfectly taut stomach. She sits up straighter, and her nipples show through the Lycra. "We're in good hands here."

My eyes dart toward Buxton, whose face has turned the color of strawberry-flavored Laffy Taffy.

He's actually blushing now, here, while talking about *this*.

I've always known my mom is attractive. I spent most of my childhood envying her dark hair, the smooth waves of it that cascaded down her back, the way it shined. Her eyes the lightest shade of green. She's petite, but curvy—she was even before the boob job, paid for by her first full year of Instagram partnerships. My mom could have done nothing at all to alter her appearance and she would have been stunning, the type of person who people walk by in a grocery aisle and remember later, wondering if she knows just how gorgeous she is, if people stop and tell her. But since Evie was born, since all of it, my mom has been obsessed with looking younger. Convinced the cameras would pick up wrinkles, frown lines. She was hyperfixated with people knowing she was forty, then fifty, like the further in age she seemed from Evie, the less people would care. She was the first in line to try the latest skin treatments and injections, the chemical peels that left her face looking like scabbed leather for days. She'd google "Erin Elliot Davis age" every few months and turn the phone toward me when she found a result she liked: "This one says I'm still in my *thirties*. Can you believe that?" It all seemed to confirm for her that she should keep going, even now (especially now, maybe), at fifty-three.

And yet, somehow, even with almost two decades of cosmetic treatments under her belt, she's always managed to avoid falling into the clichéd category of women her age, a specific brand of middle-aged mom that the world still thinks is hot enough to be fucked but just barely. You'd think it all would have made her look like everyone else, that it would have whittled away her beauty, but it never did. I waited for a botched procedure, an ill-advised extra syringe of filler—hoped for it some years, really—but it never came. In the end, her face was just like Evie's, so beautiful it was untouchable. She couldn't poke or prod or fill the shape of it away, no matter how hard she tried.

I had become used to her blushing and flirting long ago, the way male waiters would forget to take my order in my mom's presence, giggling to their coworkers as they left our table. The stares. And any of it, even this with Buxton, the sheer inappropriateness of it, was more bearable than what I endured in high school.

"Absolutely *loved* those yoga pants Erin was advertising last week, Haze," my male classmates would tease. "Has she been practicing her downward dog, because it's *really* showing . . ."

"Does your mom like younger men?"

"Want a new daddy, Hazel?"

There's a chance I would have been teased regardless, probably, that the MILF thing was inevitable. But there was something about the ads, the social media, the promotion of it all that made her, or me, an even easier target. Everyone knew that it all existed, at least partially, because of how she looked. Every post said "Look at me!" and they were all more than happy to do it.

Buxton clears his throat.

"Well, we are making progress, which is good. We have located the spot where she last posted from, which is her last known location at this point," he says, sounding proud. "It seems to be in the same spot where she filmed that TikTok Live."

"Right. The one with the man," I say, confused as to why this detail hasn't been explored more. Why Buxton seems so proud of himself for doing the bare minimum. "The one who appears in the left side of the frame. We haven't just . . . forgotten about that . . . right?"

I play the clip back in my head, the clear figure of a man walking toward the driver's side window. The hat, the beard. Those details could have been a shadow, maybe. A trick of light. But there's no doubt that was a person.

Buxton shifts in his seat, his eyes darting sideways to watch my mom as if he's wondering if this bothers her, too, if he's let her down.

"I just think it's important to remember that there are a lot of people out there determined to sensationalize situations like these . . . capitalize on the commotion, the buzz, create something to plug into their newest video. It can . . . confuse the investigation. If we took the internet's word for it every time, we would never solve a single case. Trust me."

I blink at him, trying to control my frustration, to smooth it down.

"I mean, have you ever wondered why all those true crime podcasts start with somewhat plausible sounding theories from amateur online sleuths and end with . . . no resolution? It's because that stuff doesn't solve cases. It's entertainment."

I flex my jaw.

"None of this is entertaining to me, I can assure you," I say, meeting his eyes.

"I never said it was, miss," he says, his jaw tilting slightly upward on the *miss*, like he's trying to remind me of the power dynamics here.

"As I was telling your mother while you were asleep, the most important thing that we've established since we last spoke is her last known location," he goes on. "The good news is that there is no evidence of foul play at the scene."

I try to swallow the lump in my throat. "And the bad news?"

"The bad news is that her car is not there, and we haven't located it yet."

A chemical taste fills my mouth, dry and scratchy. My mind races.

"But what does that . . ."

I trail off, and Buxton fills in the blanks.

"Best-case scenario is the simplest one. She drove there with her car and then she drove away with her car. We have a BOLO out for the plates, obviously, but nothing yet. The worst is that someone else moved her car. But it's not the more likely option of the two."

I stare at my mother, who is worrying at the sleeves of her jacket, pulling them so far over her palms that they almost reach her knuckles.

"My partner is working to obtain the security footage from the parking lot," Buxton continues. "It's stored remotely, and we had to obtain a warrant, which was a process. Turns out the parking lot is owned separately from the department store it's attached to . . . anyway, I'll be joining her when I leave here to go through all of that. Hopefully this will help us determine what exactly happened to both the car and your sister," he says. "I should probably be headed out to meet her at the office and work through all of that. But I wanted to stop by in person first. It's important that you all know you are in my top two priorities. My first, of course, being to find Evie."

He shifts his body toward my mom when he says this part, making eye contact in a way that makes me feel like they have some sort of understanding. His tone is so different from yesterday that I know immediately that something has changed, and I have a hunch as to what. I've seen it before, the shift that happens in men when they think Erin Davis is interested in them, too. That she's staring back. Maybe it was something else, or I'm reading too much into everything, but I would put money on the fact that my mother has done what she always does. That they had some conversation before I woke up that made him feel important, valued. Special. That she touched his shoulder or broke down in front of him. Left him believing that she needed him.

Fine, then, I think. If this is what helps him take my sister seriously, then so be it.

He talks for a few more minutes, emphasizing just how important it is that when we go public with this—*if* we need to go public with it at all—that it needs to be done as a collective unit.

"The worst thing that happens in situations like this is a splintering between the family and law enforcement," he says just before he walks out the door, where my mom is leaning on the frame, the slope of her hip curving outward, her crossed arms wrapped tightly around her tiny waist. "Things get messy real quick then."

"I bet. Of course, we'll wait for your direction," my mom says. "And you'll be in touch soon?"

"Absolutely, Erin. You have my number," he says. "That's my personal cell, by the way. Just so you know."

I nearly laugh from the kitchen as I pour myself a cup of coffee. We know it's your personal cell, buddy. We know.

I'm leaning against the kitchen island when my mom comes back in, looking deflated. The helpless, wide-eyed look that had been on her face all morning is gone now, replaced with something like exhaustion.

I raise my eyebrows at her, waiting for her to explain what, exactly, all of that was about. To say something like "All men are motivated by the same things, baby. It's biology, really." But she doesn't even look at me. She barely has since I've been here, not when it's been the two of us, anyway. It's like she doesn't know what to do with me.

"I'm going to take a nap," she says. "It's been a long morning. I can't . . . I can't think about this anymore. I need to do something else."

She turns and heads upstairs before I can say anything, and I listen to her steps as she pads up the stairs and walks down the long corridor of bedrooms on the second floor. I expect her footsteps to move away from me, opposite where I'm standing, but instead I hear her walking on the floor right above my head, in the room that was a home gym the last time I was here.

Maybe she changed her mind about the nap?

Or maybe she turned the room into a bedroom since I've been here last, switched it with the other guest room. It could be anything else now.

I spend the rest of the day in a loop on my phone: checking social media, refreshing Evie's pages, ignoring messages from friends, rereading Evie's and my texts, noting the tiny changes in her mood, overanalyzing meaningless updates about friends and relationships, screenshotting things that might mean something only to convince myself they're nothing five minutes later. I google her name again and again, anxious to see chatter about why she hasn't been on social media in more than a week appear anywhere other than the most niche influencer gossip forums.

My mom doesn't come downstairs for the rest of the afternoon, then the evening, not even when I text her.

Have you spoken to the detectives?

She leaves the message on read for two hours before she eventually replies:

No. Brendan said they'd call in the morning.

I only wonder who Brendan is for a second before I realize she means Detective Buxton.

I close my eyes for a moment then, exhaling as I wonder if this is the part that is somehow missed on all those true crime docuseries, all the procedurals. There's no episode for the waiting. For the desperation. The clawing reminder that you should do something but there's nothing to do. It's been a bad year, the kind when I spend most of my time holding myself up against past versions of myself. Thinner then. Better then. More successful then. But through it all, even in my lowest moments, I've never doubted that my relationship with my sister has always been the one thing I was good at. That I know her. See her. Understand her. That I would drop anything, in any lifetime, to help her. And yet, here I am. Completely unable to do anything but the same useless shit I've always done: scroll into infinity until my brain becomes nothing.

I rub my eyes as I feel tears coming on, the deep, biting kind that come from exhaustion that you feel in your bones. No. I don't deserve to be upset. Not when I will probably wake up tomorrow and all of this will be fine. It has to be fine. I sit up, shaking the emotion away. I want to curl into a warm bed, slide my hand under a cool pillow, and forget I exist.

First, I need to find a bed. A place where I can close the door, set my alarm, be alone. It's not even eight yet, but it doesn't matter. Maybe my mom had the same idea hours ago. Pretend not to exist until Evie comes home. Pretend it's not real. I stand at the top of the stairs and remind myself of the layout: Evie's room, my former room, and the former home gym to the left, Mom's room and another guest room to the right. It isn't until I'm opening the door of Evie's room that I realize I need to see it, be in it. Feel close to her. I take a step inside and it's only then that I consider that maybe I shouldn't be here. I imagine the swirl of my fingerprints illuminated on the doorframe. But then I remember what the detectives had told me, that they'd already searched her room.

I soon ignore all of this, though, because these are the questions you ask when someone isn't coming back. When something truly horrible has happened. When a person isn't going to show up tomorrow and say it's all a big misunderstanding. I won't ask those questions.

The stillness of the room chills me instantly. Everything is perfectly, neatly in its place. The bed made. The drawers closed. Her small antique vanity perfectly organized, products closed and clean. A stack of books on her bedside table with the spines all lined up evenly. Every surface gleaming. I wonder if my mom just had the housekeeper tidy up as I drag my fingers across the top of her dresser and note the utter lack of dust. But my mom is smart enough to know how that would look. Isn't she?

I open the door to Evie's walk-in closet, the familiarity comforting me before it quickly dissipates when I realize that this is the first time I've actually seen it in person since she's had it redone. It feels familiar to me not because I've been here, stood next to her while she tried to choose an outfit for a date or a photo shoot. It's familiar because I've seen it on Instagram, the same as her other followers. I open a drawer and there's her jewelry collection, the one that she did a tour of on TikTok six months ago. I can hear her voice in my head: "Number one rule: never get rid of jewelry. It's small enough to keep forever. I get a new piece every place I

olivia muenter

go, for every major life event—even if it's just costume jewelry. One day I'll be able to point to a piece and see my first kiss or my most memorable brand event or my first time in Fiji." I laugh out loud, remembering how much people had hated the Fiji line. It's not like I blamed them.

"Ev . . . your first time in Fiji," I had texted her, teasing. "How many more times will there BE?"

"I know, I know," she wrote back. "Not my finest work."

And then: "But you know what I meant."

I run my fingers over the heavy charm bracelet that she found at an estate sale last year. Her video about it went viral when the original owner's granddaughter recognized it. As it turned out, she was a fan of Evie's and insisted she keep it, even though it was a family heirloom.

I walk out of the giant closet, closing the doors behind me, taking in the rest of the room, remembering the first time I was in this place, this exact spot. It was just after my mom had bought the house, but before we had officially moved in. This house was her first major purchase after the viral video, the followers. When the brand partnerships initially started pouring in—the five-figure deals with mommy-and-me clothing brands, and detergent brands, and dance class companies, all of them desperate to have this adorable little girl, her mom, and their story attached to their image—we had moved from the bus to an apartment fairly quickly. ("Easier for deliveries," my mom said, gesturing toward the tower of fan mail and free products that took up half of our miniature living room.) Evie was too young to be fazed by the change in scenery, but leaving the bus broke my heart, because it meant leaving my dad, too. My mom seemed so desperate to be done with any version of life that reminded her of him that I didn't dare ask if part of her was sad, too. I was too afraid the truth was what it looked like on the surface: that she was happier now than she had ever been then. That a bigger, brighter life outweighed the sadness. I didn't want to know what it meant about me that my sadness outweighed everything, that it felt like it always would. I was drowning in it, and Evie and my mom were floating up, up, up.

I was seventeen when we moved into this house, and I can recall knowing, even then, that I would never feel attached to it the way I was to the bus, or the apartment even. Things were already too different by that point. But Evie was thrilled, which made it bearable. It was the same for me then as it was for all the followers, the fans: her joy made everything better.

"We can have, like, two million sleepovers," Evie said, spinning around the center of the giant space, the second-biggest bedroom in the house. My mom had said it was only fair that way. I would be moving out in a year for college, and after all, Evie was the reason we could afford this house at all. I registered that it was unfair, maybe, but I hardly cared. My life there was already on a countdown. It was more important to me that Evie was happy, that she'd be happy when I went to college. She was seven then, and obsessed with the idea of sleepovers, but our mom wouldn't allow them—too much risk, she'd say, as she posted Evie's latest sponsored content to her 700,000 followers, each post featuring a disclaimer that read, "Account run by mom <3 <3 <3." So instead, Evie and I had sleepovers, just us. At least once a month, we would pile in her room, the ground covered with every blanket and pillow we could find in the house, the floor turning into a giant cloud, and we'd watch movies, tell stories, do crafts. She'd tell me about what was happening at school, the latest drama of the second grade.

"All I said to her was that no one needs a full sandwich," she said one night, casually describing why, exactly, a friend wasn't speaking to her right now, as she drew on a piece of printer paper with a marker. I watched her trace a semicircle in the upper right-hand corner, connecting it with a million outward spikes. I remembered drawing a sun the same way as a kid and loved that even ten years apart, it turned out that all seven-year-olds' artistic interpretations of the sun were the same.

"What are you talking about, Ev?" I'd asked, more confused than concerned. "You told her she shouldn't be eating the sandwich?"

She shrugged as she continued drawing, moving on to sketching the outline of a house, a triangle roof sitting on top of a square, her knees curled up toward her chest.

"It's just, like, soooo much bread," she said. "I didn't say it in a mean way. I just said that one slice of bread is better. You know, like, healthier."

I felt my face go hot as I realized her meaning, exactly what was behind her story, dread gripping me.

olivia muenter

"Where did you learn that?" I asked, trying to make my tone seem neutral, though I knew what she'd say.

"Mommy," she said. "She said one piece is better."

"She told you that?"

Evie nodded, her brow knit together as she concentrated on the drawing. She had moved on to stick figures. The owners of the house, I guessed. I stayed quiet, though, unsure how to navigate this.

"I think it's working, too," she added, drawing a dress onto one of the stick figures, another triangle for a skirt. She nodded toward her stomach. "Less tummy."

I felt nauseous.

"Did Mom say that too?"

Evie stopped drawing then for a minute and stared at me, as if she suddenly sensed something unsafe about the conversation, like she had made a mistake. Revealed something she shouldn't have. But then she shrugged again, returning to what she was doing. Drawing another stick figure.

"You know it doesn't matter how many slices of bread you have," I said. "Right?"

"Then why don't you eat it?" she asked, her eyes still on the paper.

So she's noticed, I thought. She wasn't the only one who'd gotten the bread lecture from Erin and acted accordingly. I was just the one who had listened to it for longer, for so long in fact that I had cut back on bread long ago, gradually restricting it more and more throughout my teenage years until it wasn't part of my diet at all. Until there was nothing left for my mom to raise her eyebrows at. I wanted to be angry at my mom, to blame her for how Evie was feeling, but that wouldn't be entirely fair, I thought. Evie had been watching me, too.

"I eat it all the time," I lied, trying to seem casual, fun, and knowing I was failing. "It's the best."

Evie nodded, concentrating instead on the final touches of the drawing, placing a rectangle chimney on the triangle roof and adding flowers to the ground, the scale of them so that they were the same height as the house. I felt guilty, sick that my sister felt this way and that I felt this way and that I had let history repeat itself. What was going to happen when she was ten, or twelve, or fifteen? How much worse would it be then? What would happen when I wasn't here?

"So what's your drawing?" I asked, even though it seemed fairly straightforward. I was desperate to shake the feeling, to move on to a different subject.

"Dream house," she said. "Our art teacher said we could make it anything we wanted. Like, it could be magical or have a lake full of dolphins or whatever."

"It's really cool, Ev," I said, my eyes landing on the two people next to the house, one much shorter than the other. I pointed toward them. "You and Mom?"

She shook her head. "You and me."

· · • ● • · ·

The memory floods back to me now, here in this room, while I'm staring at the floor. I imagine it covered with layers of blankets and pillows and quilts and blankets once again. Suddenly, I want so badly to be seventeen again, for Evie to be seven. To be here together, safe and surrounded by soft things. I crave the chance to do things differently so intensely that the want of it makes me brace myself on the edge of the bed and sit there for a minute. I practice my breathing. Hold for seven. Release for eight. Or was it six? Five? What was it again? Mouth, nose? I'm nearly hyperventilating when I catch something out of the corner of my eye, a sliver of light poking through the door from the hallway. And in the crack, staring back at me, is my mother.

Episode 15: "An Interview with THE Evie Davis" |

The Contentious Podcast

May 22, 2022

Luna Thompson: *Welcome back to* Contentious, *y'all, the podcast where we talk about all things content creation. Today we have someone who has been on the internet since they were born, I'm pretty sure. Like, it's possible their follower count was larger than yours as they were actively coming out of the womb. I mean, am I wrong, Evie?*

Evie Davis: *I don't think that's exactly* how *things went, but* [laughs] *. . . thank you? I think?*

Luna: *It's a compliment, babe. Trust me. We all wish we had the audience you have. The sheer longevity of it is insane. The engagement you have? Unreal.*

Evie: *Well, thank you. It's definitely a crazy thing. I'm so grateful so many people have stuck around. And you're killing it, too, obviously.*

Luna: *I mean, look—I'm no Evie Davis, but who is? Except you, obviously. That's why we're so excited to finally have you on the pod. And you just hit a big milestone, right?*

Evie: *Yeah, yeah. A million on Instagram. It's so nuts.*

Luna: *And even more than that on TikTok, right?*

Evie: *I think so, yeah.*

Luna: *Holy shit. And you're, what? Seventeen?*

Evie: *Yeah, my birthday was this month.*

Luna: *Un. Real. I mean, you know how people talk about you, right? The OG influencer, the queen of content? The creator who has somehow managed to be all things . . . I mean . . . fashion, lifestyle, beauty . . . mental health! How did you* do this? Tell us everything. We want to know it all, girl. There are like a thousand baby influencers out there listening to this taking step-by-step notes.

Evie: [laughs] I mean, I don't know. I just post what I like. It's all I've ever done. I can't believe people are interested, to be honest. Or still interested. I mean, I'm thankful. So thankful, of course. But it's surreal. I try not to think about the numbers too much.

Luna: But, come on, you have to sometimes, right? How can you not?

Evie: Honestly, my mom handles a lot of that. The logistics of stuff. The insights. I mean, I know what's going on, but I'm not tracking things all the time. It gives me anxiety, really. So I'm glad my mom is there.

Luna: Right. Of course. I mean, it makes sense, I guess. Because—in case anyone out there is truly living under a rock—your mom is Erin Elliot Davis. I mean, she's kind of a badass. Right?

Evie: [laughs] Yeah, she's pretty great. I don't know what I'd do without her.

Luna: And she's a huge influencer in her own right, really—with that age group, anyway. If this podcast wasn't for our generation of creators, I would have totally had her on, too.

Evie: She would have loved that.

Luna: Maybe we'll make an exception for her sometime. I'm sure some of our millennial listeners would recognize her. She does more Instagram stuff, right?

Evie: She does it all, really, but . . . yeah. I guess so. She's killing it.

Luna: Totally, totally. But let's talk about you more. And before I get into the influencer biz of it all, the people have some questions. My DMs literally imploded when I mentioned you were coming on. I'm sure you can guess what people are wondering.

Evie: I'm scared to guess, to be honest. [laughs]

Luna: All right. You and Gavin Ramirez. What's the deal?

Evie: [laughs] *Oh, God, Are people really still talking about that?*

Luna: The king of YouTube and the queen of . . . like, every other social platform? Um. Yes, of course they're still talking.

Evie: I mean . . . I don't know, I don't want to start anything here.

Luna: It's not like it's a secret, is it? You two?

Evie: No, I mean . . . it's not that. I don't really have secrets. I just don't want to speak for someone else.

Luna: He'll survive.

Evie: Well . . . I guess I can say we're . . . having fun?

Luna: [squeals] I love this for you. A true power couple.

Evie: I don't know about that . . .

Luna: Oh, stop, you know it's true. But enough about your love life. Let's get into the real reason you're here: your career. Second to the Gavin thing, the most common question was what advice you had for up-and-coming influencers. Kids who look at you and want what you have. The brand deals, the money, the platform. All of it.

[long pause]

Luna: Evie?

Evie: Yeah, I'm sorry. Just thinking about the question . . . about the advice I'd give. I guess the truth is I don't . . . I don't really feel qualified to answer that.

such a bad influence

Luna: *Oh, please! I mean, if you aren't qualified, then who is? Don't sell yourself short here. You know this business better than anyone.*

Evie: [laughs] *Not anyone.*

Luna: *What do you mean?*

Evie: *I've never been as good at any of this as my mom is.*

CHAPTER 6

My mom watches me in silence for what feels like a full minute before she speaks. I wonder how long she's been standing there. What she's thinking. When she finally does say something, she doesn't crack the door any wider, like she's more comfortable when there's something solid between us.

"Dinner is downstairs," she finally says, turning away before I have a chance to reply.

Food. Right. Yes.

My stomach gurgles at the thought of it, and I'm reminded of last night, the way I told myself that I needed to keep my shit together right now. I can't slide into old habits, the things that are natural to me when everything is falling apart. Skipping meals. Staying in bed all day. Avoiding friends. Wearing the same T-shirt for three days. Letting my hair get so greasy it makes my scalp ache. I couldn't allow myself any of that right now. Evie needs my full attention. For me to be at my best, my sharpest.

I take one more minute to look at the room, the perfection of it, my eyes traveling from surface to surface as if I'm checking them off a list.

"Thank you," I say as I grab a salad from the stack of take-out boxes arranged on the kitchen island. "I can pay you back. Just let me know how much I owe you. You still have Venmo, right?"

"Hazel, please," my mom says with a sigh, shaking her head as she stabs a pile of spinach with her fork. "Not now."

I'm confused at first by her reply, but then I realize what she means.

Even now, she thinks I'm trying to make a point, even when I'm trying to be polite, to acknowledge the fact that it wasn't so long ago that I said I'd never come here again, never expect an ounce of her help. I want her to know that I don't want to be here, either, eating her food, sleeping in her home. Instead, she thinks it's a show, an act, a way to seem above it all.

We eat in silence, her scrolling on her phone, me doing the same, and then her phone rings.

"It's them," she says before picking up, taking the phone into the other room.

"Mhm.

"Of course.

"Where?

"Oh, God."

I stand, arms crossed as I watch her pace in the living room.

"Thank you.

"Yes.

"I understand.

"Okay. Bye."

She hangs up and walks right past me back to her salad, slipping her phone into the side pocket of her leggings and sitting back down at the table. I wait for her to speak to me, to relay whatever she just heard on the phone, but instead she starts eating again.

"So?" I finally say, embarrassed that I have to beg for information.

"Yes?" she asks, eyes fixed on her phone again, her fork suspended in between.

"What did they say?"

She sighs, like she resents being interrupted, like this isn't the time.

"They found her car."

I stare at her, but she still doesn't look up. How could she be this calm? Why wouldn't this warrant a meltdown? A discussion? A new level of fear? Is the car, somehow, a good thing? An indication that Evie's okay?

"Where?"

She finally looks up at me, setting down her fork with a clang.

"Near Palm Springs," she says. "In a parking lot."

Palm Springs? My mind reels. That's almost two hours east of Los Angeles. I close my eyes and try to picture it on a map, where it sits between here and LA. The route between the cities.

"Was she driving home, maybe?" I ask, considering that it would have been an easy stop on the way back to Phoenix.

"I don't know, Hazel." She sighs, standing to toss her salad, most of which is untouched, into the trash. "I don't fucking know anything."

I don't understand why she's being so difficult, so cagey, why she isn't more eager to let me in. In any other circumstance, yes, this would be expected, especially after last year. But this . . . this should be different. She's always known just how close Evie and I are, that my sister confides in me, that she needs me. There were lines my mother would never cross with me simply because she knew that it would push Evie away. Growing apart from Evie was unfathomable to her. Me being the reason for it? That wasn't even on the table.

I push for more answers, anyway.

"Well, did they get the security footage from the parking lot? Maybe that will explain it?"

"Tomorrow morning, they said," she replies. "They're focused on the car now. So far, they said no ID or wallet left behind. No purse sitting in the passenger seat. No . . . signs of a struggle."

She cringes on the last part, like it hurts her to say, to imagine what kind of evidence would be required to know someone had been hurt. Hair ripped from the roots. Blood pooled from a wound. Cracked fingernails from trying desperately to hold on to something.

I quickly shake the images away and remind myself that there was none of that. That my sister is somewhere unharmed. Safe.

"They said if it wasn't for the phone, it would be totally unremarkable," she says, opening the dishwasher as she loads items from the sink.

"The phone?" I ask.

"Her phone," she corrects me. "It was in the front passenger seat."

I wonder immediately why this isn't the first thing she said, why this doesn't seem to worry her more, why she isn't crying or yelling or beside herself.

"So can they . . . can they get into it? Track her GPS info, her recent searches . . ."

"That was what they were planning on doing, yes," she says, drying her hands with a kitchen towel. "That was before they realized it was wiped. Factory setting reset."

Fuck.

"So . . ." I start. "What does . . . what does that mean? That someone planned this? Why wouldn't they just dump it . . . I don't understand."

"I don't know what it means," she says, her voice softer now, her eyes clearer. She sits down across from me at the table again, folding her hands in front of her like she's about to pray. "But what I do know is that we have to be on the same page here, Hazel."

I don't understand. *Now* she wants to work together? To communicate?

"What do you mean?"

"I mean that we need to make sure the world knows that the three of us are solid. You and I especially. They need to know that we love Evie. That we'd never hurt her or take advantage of her," she explains.

I shake my head like I'm not following her. Why would anyone think that we had something to do with this?

"I know you're seeing the same stuff online I am. This is about to get very ugly, very quickly. And if we turn on each other . . . if everything comes out . . ." she says. "None of this will be about finding Evie anymore. It will be about last year . . . about all of it."

Last year.

"Are you . . . what? Threatening me?"

She laughs then, the sound eventually dissolving into a sigh, like I'm a child asking about something obvious.

"No, baby," she says. "I'm not threatening you. I'm reminding you of the same thing I've always told your sister . . . all this, the internet . . . what we do . . . it's work. It's not just being ourselves and hoping for the best. It's ugly, nasty, dirty work. So what I'm saying is, if you want to protect your sister, we both need to make sure no one is talking about last year. About all of that. We limit the distractions. We make sure this is never about us as much as it's about your sister, about how much we love her and want her back. How we'll do anything to make that happen."

I focus my eyes on her hands, which are still folded in front of her, each perfectly round nail painted the same almost-pink shade of nude, gleaming. I wonder when she got the manicure. On the third day Evie had been missing? The fourth? The one-week mark?

But she's right. I don't want to think about what happens if the world is suddenly talking about what happened last year. If Evie eventually comes home and that's what she's met with. It's the only thing I can think of that's almost as bad as the worst-case scenario, that she's not actually safe at all.

"Fine," I say. "Whatever brings Evie home."

"Good," she says, laying her hands flat on the table as she stands up, like she's exiting a board meeting. "It's like I've always said . . . you don't want to admit that you get it, but you do. You're like me in that way. Practical."

I ignore her, the thought making my stomach twist even though I've heard this all before, even though I shouldn't be surprised. She always did want an image of a family who sticks together in the hardest of times instead of what she had in reality: a thing that was splintered enough to draw blood.

· • ● ● ● • ·

I announce that I'm going to bed and walk straight upstairs, eager to put the entire day behind me, feeling more lost and uneasy than I did when I woke up this morning. I remember the last thing Williams had said to me after our interview. "The experience of someone you love being missing . . . the fear of it. It's the only thing in life that time makes worse. It grows instead of fades." In the moment, I had been uncomfortable with what she was saying. It had felt too ominous, too loaded. *I don't need someone to coach me through this emotionally*, I thought. *I need someone to find my sister*. But now I get it. She was preparing me for this part of things. The slow unraveling with each second of not knowing. The weight of it. She was saying: *You're going to feel like you're about to lose control, but you can't*.

I close the door of what was briefly, technically, my childhood bedroom, leaning against it before I slide to the ground. I was once a teenager in this exact same room, but it always felt more like what it is now—an impeccably designed space for a very temporary guest—than it ever felt like mine. I look around, noting the familiar layout, the changes.

It's cleaner now than it used to be, of course. This was the one room that my mom had instructed the housekeeper not to touch because it was never featured in content, so my clothing was always strewn across the floor. Now it's spotless. Instead of a stack of books gathering dust in the corner, there's a mini fridge stocked full of snacks and cold drinks with aesthetically pleasing labels. A small wicker basket of tiny skincare items rests on top of the dresser, right next to a stack of the fluffiest towels I've ever seen. It all is designed just so, down to the perfectly angled USB outlet beside the bed, to make the entire room feel comfortable, effortless. And yet here I am, crawling out of my skin.

I lie on the ground, stretching my limbs in all directions just to release the tension of the day, the stiffness I feel being in this place. Even the stretching seems to exhaust me, though. And now I'm just lying here, staring at a hole in the wall just above the baseboard. Almost hidden behind the dresser, but not quite. I stretch my hand to the spot, a flaw so small that it's hard to believe it's survived the many iterations this room has seen since I was seventeen, that it wasn't covered up by the paint or the plaster or the looming shadow of the professional-grade Pilates reformer my mom had insisted on buying five years ago, before she built the gym room. Evie had texted me about it when it arrived, describing it as "if Gwyneth Paltrow had designed a medieval torture device." I laugh at the memory now, the way we had referred to it in our conversations simply as "The Beast," right up until the day Mom sold it on Facebook Marketplace.

Through all of that, this little hole in the wall remained. I move my fingers over the spot, feel its grooves and remind myself that it's real, that I'm real, that my sister is real. And real people don't just vanish into nothing.

"Hazel. Truth or dare," Evie had once asked me, looking over at me from where she lay on my living room floor, a borrowed air mattress beneath us. It was the first time she had been allowed to stay at my place after I had moved back west and accepted the job in Vegas. I missed my friends from college, Brooklyn. Seasons. Feeling like I was doing something hard but noble, letting myself and everyone else believe I was doing

olivia muenter

it all on my own.

But after seven years of roommates and cockroach-infested apartments, I was proud to have my own space, somewhere with central air conditioning and an in-unit laundry machine. It wasn't exactly glamorous—the faucet constantly dripped and the walls were tissue-thin, but it was mine, and that thought made any other complaint seem manageable. That, and the fact that I was finally able to be there for the small stuff in Evie's life—the friends and school dances and first kisses—made it bearable that I was giving up the dream of living somewhere else, of making it in a big city. Besides, Las Vegas was a big city. The job was an opportunity to catch my breath. I told myself I'd work hard, make some great connections, and save enough money that wherever I lived next would be somewhere that didn't make me feel like I was drowning. In the beginning, it all seemed temporary. And when I did panic, sure I had made a mistake, I thought about my sister. That this meant I could be there for her high school years, for her.

I was finally close enough for Evie to come visit. It was almost a five-hour drive, but after a month of begging, my mom let me meet her halfway in my own car, picking up Evie for the weekend. I loved those drives, the long stretches of desert, the songs she'd play for me. The conversations we'd have. Sometimes, I was embarrassed that I didn't have glamorous, exciting stories from New York to share with her anymore. I knew on some level that she must have thought it, too, that it was so clear I had given up on my dream. But other times it felt like I was teaching her about how life really worked. That it was okay to try something different, to press pause, to reassess what works for you and what doesn't. It's what I told myself to feel better, anyway.

"Truth or dare," she pressed again, peeking out from the edge of a blanket, her eyes blinking behind the sharp beam of a flashlight. Before I could reply, she went on, anyway. "Great. Truth it is."

"Oh, that's how it is? What if I wanted dare, huh?" I teased. We both knew I would go along with it. These sleepovers were more about her than me, no matter how old she was.

Evie was propped up on her elbow now, her face resting on her hand. It was summer and her freckles had darkened and spread farther up her cheeks, while her auburn hair had lightened. Both features were from my dad, my mom's green eyes sandwiched between them. "You got his face," I'd tell her sometimes, and she'd sigh and say, "And you got to remember him more." I never told her that that only made things harder.

"A true tragedy," she responds to my complaint about the game. She had started talking like this recently, everything tinged with a hint of sarcasm and drama. I couldn't tell if it was because she was trying to be funny or just trying to seem older. "There's time for dares later. First, let's hear the truth: Have you ever broken anything? At home?"

I didn't follow. "What do you mean?"

"Like, something nice. Important. You knocked over a vase, or you spilled a soda on the couch and then flipped the cushion before Mom got home. When you were my age, maybe. Did you ever have secrets that were just yours?"

It was a weird question, maybe, but Evie was barely fifteen. Who wasn't a little odd at that age? I could remember me then, could still practically feel the discomfort I felt in my own body, the way I felt paralyzed with fear around adults, all of it only emphasized by five-year-old Evie—always perfect and adorable and charming in all the ways I was gangly and awkward and nervous. Plus, Evie had always asked questions like this when it was just us. Strange hypotheticals. Silly stuff. The questions she was too scared to ask everyone else. I thought for a minute, remembering.

"I smashed all of Mom's lipsticks once," I offered. "In high school. I forgot to put the lipstick part down before I put the lids back on. Every single one was wrecked. I never told her, though."

Evie blinked hard through the beam of the flashlight instead of laughing, like I expected.

"And what happened?"

"What do you mean, what happened?"

"I mean, did you get in trouble?" she asked. "Did she mention it to you?"

"No, never," I said. "I just figured she never noticed they were broken, or she just bought a thousand new ones. Had some brand send her some. I don't know. Maybe they just got lost in the mountain of makeup she had then. But no, it never came up. I never got in trouble."

What I didn't say was: She always suspected it was Evie who did it. A five-year-old messing around with her mom's makeup. A five-year-old who she couldn't risk reprimanding lest she look sad on television or refuse to take photos together.

Evie smiled and rested her head on the pillow again. I could just make out the outline of her head beside me, slowly nodding in the dark.

"That's the question you use when I say truth?" I laughed. "Aren't you supposed to ask me if I ever hooked up with Blake Sokolowski or, like, if I pee in pools or something?

She laughed a bit at that, and then I saw a small sliver of white flash. A quick eye roll.

"Boring," she said. "Plus, I think we both know that Blake Sokolowski was far, far out of your league."

Blake was a boy who had lived next door to us when we moved into the big house. I was seventeen and he was eighteen, and beautiful. My mom teased me relentlessly about being in love with him, even though she knew that he looked at her more than he ever did at me.

"Oh, shut up." I laughed, lightly punching her on the shoulder. "What about you then? If you think it's such a good question."

"I think we both know I only pee in the pool in emergencies."

"I mean about breaking things." I rolled my eyes. "What things have you broken, then? I find it hard to believe that Mom would fail to notice, like, virtually anything you do."

She hesitated for a moment, eyes fixed at the ceiling.

"Lots of things," she said finally.

This surprised me.

"What do you mean, lots of things?"

"Big things. Small things. Silly things." She sighed. "All the time."

"Like what, exactly?" I asked, having trouble picturing my little sister silently moving around my mom's house, destroying things.

"Like things no one notices," she said. "Things they don't care about, anyway."

I forced myself to stay silent then, to encourage her to keep talking instead of cutting her off, something I had learned from a journalism professor in college.

"At first, it was by accident," she started. "I was in the laundry room looking for a safety pin and accidentally spilled bleach on one of Mom's sweaters, so I hid it in my room, balled it up under my mattress. I figured it was easier than explaining it and getting in trouble. She never even asked about it. It was like it never existed, so I tried it again. I drew on the walls of the closets in the rooms that no one ever goes in. Wrote my name in Sharpie on the bottom of shoes that she hasn't worn in years. Scratched smiley faces in walls that no one ever looks at. Whatever I wanted. Not that I really wanted it. I just did it. I barely thought about it sometimes. I put all these tiny holes into the walls of the guest rooms, all along the baseboards. They've been there for years, and no one has ever noticed."

My pulse had raced faster with each admission. None of this felt like the Evie I knew. It was all harmless, damage that no one would notice, but oddly that made it feel worse. Less understandable.

"She never noticed?" I said. "Not once?"

"Not once." Evie laughed as she bent her arms at the elbow, cradling her head as she stared up at the ceiling, despite the darkness. I wondered if she could see the outline of the slow-growing water stain above, the one that had been there since I moved in months ago. "You haven't noticed either, you know. You never did."

I tried to make out her expression in the dark. Had she really been doing it that long, since she was seven or eight and I was still at home? Or was she saying something else, I wondered, like she had been changing things now, too?

"Here?" I asked, expecting her to laugh off my suggestion.

"Sure, here," she said. "It doesn't matter where. It's not, like, personal. Or angry. It's not like your landlord will notice. It's not like you have."

"Okay, well, obviously you have to tell me where it is now, tiny Banksy . . ."

I joked, but I was unsettled. I wracked my mind to think back to the day before, the morning and the afternoon, trying to figure out when she could have possibly damaged something.

"Oh, chill." She sighed. "It's not, like, graffiti, Hazel."

She pointed the flashlight to a tiny spot next to the TV, just barely visible underneath a picture frame. I got up and moved closer to where the light was shining. There it was, the tiniest, faintest hint of a stick figure, its face serious, a jagged line where the upturned smile should be.

"Not very good graffiti, maybe," I said, forcing my voice to sound lighter despite the chill I felt. "Here I was expecting your name written in bright red marker or something. This is nothing. It could have been from anyone, any of the previous tenants."

"Sure, it could have been," Evie said, turning the flashlight around so the room was dark again except for her face, the beam making her green eyes look paler than usual. "But it was me."

"But it was you." I heard myself laugh, but it didn't sound funny, or light. None of this should have been serious, really. It's not like she was hurting anyone, or herself. Like she said, it was harmless, small. So why didn't it feel that way? "Mom is always so worried about you going to parties without telling her or dating without telling her or having some footage of you drinking out of a Solo cup go viral. Whatever. Little does she know . . . this is what she has to worry about. Stick figures and barely visible pin holes. Miniature moments of destruction."

I expected her to laugh. I wanted her to laugh. If she laughed, then it would be proof that none of this was as strange as it felt to me. That it was all in my head, something that seemed scarier at night in the dark than it would in the light of day. We'd laugh about this tomorrow, for real, I reminded myself.

"It's hard to worry about things you don't really see at all," she finally said.

I wasn't sure what to do with that.

"Okay, well, no more drawing on my walls, please?" I said, still trying to keep things light. Trying to be the cool sister. "You can go to town at home, though. Be my guest."

"Gladly," she said before clicking the flashlight off.

I fell asleep then, and now, thinking of all the other hidden places in my room, the well-shadowed corners of the world that we were missing.

LoneStarrrrr

Holy shit. I think Evie Davis is actually missing. Like, for real.

⬆ 363 ⬇   💬 97

> **Incoherentbabble**
>
> I was JUST coming here to talk about this . . . did you see Pour Toi's post???
> It's basically confirmed.
>
> **HowYallDoin**
>
> Maybe it's time for *some* people to feel bad about joking about this now
>
> > **PrincessLeona**
> >
> > Oh please. You clearly don't know anything about the Davises. Erin
> > basically molded her out of silly putty while still in the womb and then
> > catapulted her into the world as some perfectly designed child robot to
> > sell us all diet pills and loungewear and make herself unholy amounts of
> > money. It wouldn't surprise me if she's in on this whole thing, too.
> >
> > > **CartwheelHart**
> > >
> > > Evie has never advertised diet pills . . . or tummy tea. None of that.
> > > She's VERY against that stuff. She's told us.
> > >
> > > > **Tattletale**
> > > >
> > > > Honey, you do know that she isn't talking to *you* right? Just
> > > > because you've watched her grow up like she's your little sister and
> > > > now all-grown-up bestie doesn't mean that she—brace yourself for
> > > > this—actually cares.
>
> **P0is0nandWine**
>
> Wait, wait, wait . . . how do you know this? For sure? Has Erin released a
> statement or something?? Did she delete it? I've been searching her feed and
> nothing . . . just vague posts from her of, like, mugs of tea and captions that
> say "really needed this today" I mean, slightly less deranged than usual, sure
> . . . but would you be posting photos of TEA when your kid is missing?
>
> > **PrincessLeona**
> >
> > Hmmm, I don't know, would you exploit your kid for your own financial
> > gain, giving every creep across the world hundreds of photos of her face
> > to jerk off to in their basement? Maybe not!! But Erin Davis sure would.

olivia muenter

CartwheelHart

That's disgusting. Evie herself has said she loves what she does . . . and the pedo thing is just a rumor. It doesn't actually work that way.

> **PrincessLeona**
>
> I'm a private investigator. And I can tell you that it does. These monsters take photos of famous kids and superimpose them on the darkest, sickest images you've ever seen. Just because they like their particular face. Erin has been told this, I'm sure. She must have been told a hundred times by now. I wouldn't be surprised if there's a whole FBI file of the dark web sites Evie Davis's face has ended up on, starting from when she was 5. She kept putting her fucking kid on the internet, though. And now here we are. Gee, I wonder what could have happened . . .
>
> > **ForEvieandEver**
> >
> > Oh, wonderful. Another private investigator on Reddit. Just what the world needs. Truly, thank God. /s Anyone who has followed Evie for a while knows that that whole narrative is bullshit. Evie loves what she does. She helps people. She's the reason why I started going to therapy.
> >
> > > **PrincessLeona**
> > >
> > > Yeah. And all I'm saying is that her parents are the reason *she* started going.

SwipeUpForBS

Has anyone heard that Darker is covering the Davises on their episode next week? Apparently they hinted at it in their latest episode and teased some sort of exclusive guest to finally address the rumors about "the internet's favorite influencer." The pod subreddit is absolutely losing it.

> **LoneStarrrrr**
>
> You're shitting me.
>
> **Incoherentbabble**
>
> I fucking knew it.
>
> **PrincessLeona**
>
> Oh. Oh my god. This is going to be so, so good.

such a bad influence

CHAPTER 7

When I got to my mom's house three days ago, all I wanted to do was answer questions. Ask me everything. Anything. I would have told them everything there is to know about my sister. How she takes her coffee. The word she misspells constantly. Her most embarrassing stories. I would have answered it all if it would have been helpful. But now, I'm learning that more talking means there's nothing else to do. Today, for example, it means that Buxton and Williams and their team haven't been able to access the security footage yet. The system resets weekly, apparently, and they now have to access a separate hard drive for the archival footage. I want to say: *You have one job. Figure it out.* But instead I just keep answering questions, doing as I'm told, spinning my wheels, pushing myself into the most agreeable mold I can imagine.

"What is her relationship with your mom like?" Williams asks. "What can you tell us about that?"

"She's eighteen," I say. "It's complicated, I guess."

We're sitting outside, and it's so hot that I can feel my makeup slowly sloughing off my face, giving up.

"Define complicated," Buxton says, rolling up the sleeves of his shirt, the armpits soaked in sweat.

I glance toward the house, my eyes roaming over the small window by my mom's bathroom, the one that sits right above the clawfoot bathtub that she had imported from a castle in France.

"She is literally bathing in the dead skin cells of, like, ancient, long-dead royalty," Evie told me when it arrived two years ago. "It is vile."

The truth was that Evie and my mom's relationship had all the hallmarks of a normal mother-teenage daughter dynamic. It could be explosive, emotional, frustrating, impossible. But it also wasn't as simple as Evie knowing she'd be off to college in a year, that soon she'd be an adult and the space would make it all easier. Evie's entire career was built through and around my mother.

"They grew up together, in a way, I guess," I explain, looking up toward the window again, the sliding glass door. Making sure my mom was away. "My dad died . . . the video happened . . . all of it happened. And suddenly they were doing this thing together, becoming internet famous together, getting brand deals together . . . even when Evie started to get way more popular than my mom ever was, my mom still managed her brand deals. Negotiated. Handled the money stuff. I mean, yeah. It was all complicated. It is complicated."

"Did Evie resent that?" Williams asks. "Not having control of her finances?"

I adjust in my seat, try to get comfortable. I feel a bead of sweat creep down my lower back. My mind says: *Careful, careful, careful.*

"Again, she's eighteen," I say. "She resents a lot of things."

"Like what, then?" Buxton says, his tone a little stiffer, like he's frustrated. "Being vague won't help us."

My eyes drift upward again toward the bathroom window, and I wonder what my mom had already told them.

"Lack of privacy, for one. From the world, but from our mom, too," I say, trying to walk the line between careful and honest. "My mom thinks most of Evie's personal decisions are business decisions, too. And I mean, she has a point. If Evie dyes her hair right before a hair campaign . . . yeah, it makes a difference. If Evie posts about how bad a day she's having right before a mood-boosting supplement ad, yeah, it doesn't play well. If Evie makes some political statement, sure, there are implications to everything."

"Sounds like a good manager to me," Buxton offers.

I roll my eyes.

"Maybe if that manager is not also your mother," I mutter. "And your friend."

"And your competition?" Williams suggests, but it doesn't sound like a question.

I don't reply.

"I understand how that could be . . . tense," Williams says. "I can see how it would lead to arguments. Disagreements. Work conflict."

"Sometimes." I shrug. "But their relationship was not one specific thing, and it never really has been."

"I mean, correct me if I'm wrong, but for the most part . . . all they had was each other," Buxton says. "That kind of closeness can be intense. Doesn't mean it's bad, right?"

My eyes slice in his direction. It feels like a jab. I don't like remembering that Evie was only eight when I moved to Manhattan for college. That my dad was gone and then I was, too. Buxton doesn't say it directly, but he might as well have: At least my mom stayed. At least someone showed up for Evie.

"I never said it was bad," I reply. "I said it was *complicated*."

I want so badly to get into all of it, the levels of betrayal and mistrust, but I know I can't. Not without ruining everything. Not without hurting Evie.

"Let's talk about something else complicated, then," Williams says, sitting up a bit straighter. "Money."

"Money?" I ask, though I'm not sure why, because I knew the question was coming.

"How exactly does that work?"

I inhale, then quickly exhale while I consider where to begin. How to explain that part of things. How much they may already know. Because they have to know something, right? Even if my mom didn't tell them anything. There has to be a reason they're interviewing me out here, on my own, instead of in the cool, comfortable beige cocoon that is my mother's living room.

I tuck a curl behind my ear, smoothing it down with my own sweat.

"It's . . ." I start, but then stop when my eyes land on my mom's bathroom window.

This time, it's wide open.

Episode 349: "The Mysterious Appearance and Disappearance of Evelyn Davis" | *Darker: A True Crime Podcast*

Kira James: Hi, everyone. Welcome back to Darker: A True Crime Podcast. *Today we are doing something that makes August's skin crawl. Who's excited?*

August Cho: It really does. She's not lying.

Kira: We are talking about a case that . . . is . . . controversial.

August: Tell the people why it's controversial, Kira.

Kira: It's controversial because it's not, per se, an official case yet. Nothing is confirmed. Yet.

August: Enter: my intense, all-consuming fear of being sued.

Kira: Okay, okay, yes. August has a point. They do. But they've agreed to do this episode with me on one very specific condition.

August: Indeed.

Kira: So this episode is going to be more of a . . . let's say, more of a cultural deep dive than some of our episodes in the past. With some crime-ish aspects, depending on who you ask. But the most important part—and why August said yes to this—is that it will feature an exclusive source. Someone close to the Davises.

August: The second part is the only reason I've agreed to do this one. It felt too important. Like too much of an opportunity.

Kira: [laughs] But please let the record show that it still took days for me to convince August. Days of me telling them what I've researched and how important I think this could be. Usually when we do an episode, we surprise each other and do a case that the other one has never, ever heard about or researched, but this time it felt important to make sure August was fully on board and understood, you know, the stakes of everything beforehand.

August: *Yes. Thank you for that, friend. I think people are going to want to buckle up for this one. So. Kira. Tell the good people what you've learned. Tell us everything you know about the wild world of Evie Davis and how, exactly, we got here.*

Kira: *Gladly. So, Evelyn Elliot Davis was born on May 15, 2005, to Chris Davis and Erin Elliot Davis. It's not talked about much, but Evie has an older sister named Hazel. They're ten years apart. You can see Hazel on some of their oldest vlogs and stuff, but by the time Evie is really sort of, like, center stage, Hazel basically fades away. And I don't want to invade her privacy here by, like, diving too deep into her life, which she has clearly chosen—unlike the rest of her family—not to publicize and monetize.*

August: *What a concept.*

Kira: *I know. It's wild. Almost as if not everyone is into having every moment of their life filmed.*

August: *Especially when you're an anxiety-ridden teenager.*

Kira: *I'm pretty sure I would have rather run into moving traffic than had my parents filming me for their YouTube channel when I was that age.*

August: *One hundred percent. But wait—they weren't always making money from this stuff, were they? What about before?*

Kira: *When it comes to what her parents did other than their blog and then some YouTube stuff, or what they did before Evie was born, it's hard to get any definitive facts. I think her mom said in one vlog she used to be an artist? Maybe a painter or something? And her dad was sort of a jack-of-all-trades . . . computer software salesman, personal trainer, motivational speaker—ha, I know—listeners, August is giving me the "Okay, now I'm skeptical" look but . . . yeah, well. Just wait. Juuuuust wait.*

August: *My spidey senses are automatically set off anytime the phrase* motivational speaker *is uttered. I can't help it. That and* essential oils.

Kira: *That's fair enough. But trust me, this is only the tip of the iceberg.*

August: *I'm ready. I mean, I'm not. But I am.*

Kira: *So, look, pretty early on—before Evie was even born, Chris and Erin started this blog called* The Davis Family Scrapbook. *Then when YouTube rolls around in 2005, they start filming pretty much everything. It's basically just a catalog of their life, with the first couple years spent traveling around in a school bus-turned-tiny home. Evie is freaking adorable. She's smart, she's charismatic, she's . . . all over their videos. She's the star of the show and it's pretty clear from the beginning.*

August: *Woof.*

Kira: *I know. Same. But, it is fair to mention that back then, in the early aughts . . . I don't know. People didn't think about how they put kids online the same way they do now. I mean, people don't even think about it that much today, so you can imagine what it was like almost twenty years ago. So, you know, we can maybe cut them a little slack? Maybe? It's tough. But look, what I can say for sure is that most of the videos—if you take the glaring issue of a child possibly being exploited or used for entertainment—are pretty wholesome. It's a hard task to separate the two ideas, I know, but for the sake of giving them the benefit of the doubt here, it's fair to mention that the videos seem, to many people, harmless. She's the cutest kid I've ever seen. I get why her parents were like, "The world needs to see this child!" And she seemed to like the spotlight, people seemed to like the family content, so there it was.*

August: *Sure, sure. Let's go with that for now.*

Kira: *So as the years go on, the Davises build up a tiny bit of a following. I think they had, like, maybe ten thousand subscribers by the time Evie was about five. Not terrible, but not mind-blowing, either. They might have been making some money from it, but serious cash? Not a chance. It's not until 2010 that that*

such a bad influence

such a bad influence

happens, thanks to this super-viral video—or, well, just a clip, really—of Evie and Chris. It's of the two of them dancing together before one of her recitals. He's memorized the entire routine, kind of half performing it himself, half coaching her through it. It feels very natural, very off the cuff. They do this little coordinated pirouette thing. Evie is wearing this adorable tutu.

August: *That's . . . sweet . . . I guess.*

Kira: *It honestly is. Here, I'll send it to you now so you can watch.*

August: *Fuck. It is cute. I wanted to despise it so much, Kira!! So much! I still disagree with putting it on the World Wide Web, but it's really cute!!*

Kira: *I know. But . . . well, the story gets much darker at this point.*

August: *Oh, no.*

Kira: *So, right after this video was taken . . . just a couple hours after it, I guess, Chris was killed in a car accident.*

August: *What! No. Oh my God. That's horrible.*

Kira: *It's very sad. He was only thirty-seven. And so, when Erin uploads the video—*

August: *I don't like where this is going at all. I do not like it one single bit.*

Kira: *—she basically positions it as a . . . "you will cry when you learn the whole story behind it" kind of thing. And it explodes.*

August: *Jesus Christ, this is dark.*

Kira: *I know. It becomes this weird combination of "aw, look, how cute" and trauma porn. Ellen DeGeneres ends up having them on the show, like, a month later, talking about their experience, the video, how great Chris was . . .*

olivia muenter

August: Just so I'm understanding . . . so . . . a five-year-old is forced to relive her trauma on national television? Like, what, mere weeks after she's lost her dad?

Kira: Yeah. But . . . even in that first TV interview, the audience loves her pretty much immediately. She's like this little comedian slash talk show host in a tiny person's body. You can probably guess what happens next.

August: When was this, 2010?

Kira: Yup. For those who were just kids then—God, this makes me feel old—it's important to know that this was such a weird era of the internet. And such a weird time in the country . . . the world. It was the middle of a recession. Viral videos were newish and fun and exciting, and I feel like cute videos were the only thing getting us all through. I mean, when you're faced with deciding between thinking about the collapse of the housing market or watching a video of a cat playing the piano on YouTube . . . the choice is very clear.

August: That makes a lot of sense. I'm twenty-five, so not that much older than Evie, but ohhhh, I can still remember this time. Watching YouTube videos after school. The concept of viral videos. It was a thing.

Kira: Totally. And I was watching the same shit but while stoned in my college dorm room with all my friends crowded around one laptop.

August: Same difference, really.

Kira: Anyway, because of all of that, unsurprisingly, the Davises' channel explodes. Within a year, they have a million subscribers—one of the first few channels to hit the number, actually. And from there things get . . . intense. Erin goes from posting one vlog a week or so to three or five a week.

August: Whoa. That is . . . so much filming. And this is just, like, them going to the dentist or whatever? Or more cutesy shit? Or . . . God, don't say it's more stuff about her dead dad? That's so fucked-up . . .

such a bad influence

Kira: *It's honestly a little bit of everything. I think the newly single mom aspect of it, the uniqueness of their lifestyle . . . it all kind of works together to make people want to root for them. And, I mean, they had just lost Chris—Erin's husband, Evie's dad. I don't think anyone really wanted to be the person who questioned if all the exposure was good for Evie or not. Who criticized the widowed mom who was making the best of a horrible situation. And then, I mean, it was the fact that their daily life was just . . . different from most people's. That first year, they become super well-known for their US travel content, traveling around in their school-bus house with Evie every summer—Hazel is there, too, but it's more of the Evie and Erin show, really. They were really some of the first people doing the tiny home thing, and people loved it. The way they decorated the house. The renovation stuff they'd highlight. The trip itineraries. They made everything look, well . . . fun. Easy. Beautiful.*

August: *So they were truly the OG van lifers, then?*

Kira: *Exactly. And overall, even as the money was clearly pouring in—the ads and sponsored videos and eventual paid Instagram content, I think people were just happy to see the adorable little girl from the sad video . . . well, happy. I think people liked this so much that even when things started to really change—when they moved into an apartment, then a giant McMansion in Phoenix, or when Evie got older and the filming only got more and more intense, they already had a soft spot for her, you know?*

August: *And then . . .*

Kira: *And then, well, I mean, it all just continued to grow. At first, Erin was kind of the main event, at least when it came to followers. That mom who seems to have it all together, who makes you think that you can, too. But then, after Evie got her own Instagram account—*

August: *Do I even want to know how old she was then?*

Kira: *Seven.*

August: Nooooo . . .

Kira: I know. Erin claims that she monitored or ran the account herself until Evie turned twelve, but . . . it's hard to say.

August: I mean, still! Why! That is so young. So, so, so young. Like, imagine you at twelve just having FULL access to the internet?? And a whole-ass personal brand?

Kira: I know. It's terrifying. But also, like, imagine having access to a whole business . . . a career that is . . . you. She was basically an influencer by the time she was thirteen. One of the first, really, if you really go back far enough. By the time she was a teenager she had a built-in audience of hundreds of thousands of people on Instagram . . . and then TikTok. You get the idea.

August: The ultimate early adopter of new social platforms.

Kira: Basically, yeah. Thanks to her mom.

August: Thanks *is an interesting word . . .*

Kira: Right, well, that's the thing. There's been a significant amount of pushback to the sort of Kris Jenner–esque, stage-mommy feel to this whole thing. The issue isn't really that Evie seems to hate the spotlight—she continues to find new ways to monetize it and grow her platform—but rather that she never really had a choice. I mean, a lot of people argue that this was inevitable. That she was so clearly born for fame of some kind.

August: Like she was bound to become an actor or a singer anyway, right? A performer? So what difference does it make? Especially if this just makes any other performance-focused jobs that much easier for her now?

Kira: Yeah, that's the argument. The counterpoint being that . . .

August: She never had the chance to tell them, or decide, otherwise. Right?

Kira: That's what a lot of people think, yes.

August: I mean, it makes sense. From what you're saying, she was basically conditioned from a young age to only know this life. Of course she wants the attention and fame to keep coming. How could she not? And that doesn't even begin to cover the other stuff . . . the constant stream of outside validation that she had become completely used to. I'm sure she couldn't even think about tying her shoes without wondering how the world would perceive it, let alone, I don't know . . . puberty, relationships, core values . . . anything! All those eyes on you all the time . . . It makes my skin crawl.

Kira: Same. I know. Actually, this is kind of a good way to lead into the . . . I don't want to say crime, because it's unclear if a crime has even taken place here . . . but the . . . mystery that's currently surrounding the Davises.

August: This is where I usually start to get nervous, Kira. This is where I have to start every sentence with allegedly.

Kira: Well, this time you don't have to be nervous, because we have a source.

August: And before everyone starts screaming at us in the comments, no, Reddit is not a source! We have a real source.

Kira: Yes. A real person. A guest. An exclusive interview.

August: Dun, dun, duuuun . . .

Kira: Yes, in the second part of this episode, we will have someone who is close to the Davises on the pod to confirm what, exactly, has been going on. What's true and what's not. A Darker exclusive.

August: Cue the entire world freaking out.

Kira: Cue me freaking out.

olivia muenter

August: *Personally, I'm ready.*

Kira: *Well, that makes one of us. But first, let's take an ad break.*

CHAPTER 8

I don't know why I expected Gavin to stop posting videos. To suddenly stop performing for all his followers. Maybe it was the way he had sounded on the phone that day—unsure of himself, scared. I couldn't connect that voice with the twenty-year-old I had known before, all bravado and charisma. It didn't take long to realize it was all still there, though. That maybe he was built for exactly this, a shining spotlight. A framework for drama.

The title of the first video was just two words: "Dear Evie." It was simple, really. Him talking to the camera as if it was my sister, spilling his most romantic thoughts, trying to bring her back, or to win her back, depending on which comments you read. It was equal parts intimate and uncomfortable, like we were all watching something that we weren't supposed to. I watched it with my finger hovering over the pause button, waiting for the disgust to hit me, but I couldn't look away. It was a more casual video than his usual content. Just him in his bedroom, wearing a threadbare blue hoodie that matched his eyes. It was obvious he had been crying or barely sleeping or both, his lash line red and swollen. Even so, he looked good. I'm sure he knew it. His skin was rich and golden, browned by the sun, the color of a terra-cotta pot. His lashes were jet-black, the same color as his hair, though he kept it buzzed.

"It's because he knows he doesn't need it, right?" I teased Evie once. "That he's so good-looking that he can just willingly, happily shave off a head of hair that most guys would kill for and still look that good? Men

olivia muenter

have literally gone to war for less."

Evie had laughed, rolling her eyes. I could tell she was satisfied, though. Or proud. Happy to know that I thought he was handsome.

"It's because he gets too hot," she said. "It's too thick."

I had put my hand across my chest in faux sympathy. "His cross to bear."

Since that first vlog, I've avoided all the ones that have come after, reading the Reddit recaps instead. Every day, there's another video. One more letter to Evie. After the first went semiviral, I'm sure his plan was to capitalize on the curiosity and rumors and keep the content coming—and based on the comments and views, no one could stop watching them, or wondering if they were the surest sign that Evie Davis was really, truly missing.

But then something seemed to shift, the way public opinion does on the internet: slowly, then all at once. The more people watched and speculated on the videos, the more Gavin posted, and the more people started to believe it was all part of an elaborate prank. His biggest prank yet, because he'd finally convinced Evelyn Davis to join the trickery, too. The detectives told us to ignore him, to not entertain any of it. To not respond or set the record straight. And then Gavin posted today's vlog.

"Today's video changes things," Buxton says, his voice booming from the speaker of my mom's iPhone where it sits between us on the couch. "He's involved himself in the investigation now. He's implied he knows things he shouldn't. It's not as simple as some sad boyfriend crying online anymore."

This vlog *was* different. I had watched it earlier, after the detectives had flagged it to us in an email. It wasn't just a letter to Evie but an announcement that Gavin had decided to organize a search party for the following day. It was an effort to search Evie's last known location with any friends and family who were willing to participate, Gavin had said, "with or without law enforcement's cooperation."

I was sure that it was the wording that had made Buxton and Williams panic, concerned it would make them look like they were the ones who should be organizing a search party, but instead were dragging their feet.

But it was a fair question: why *hadn't* they suggested that already?

"I think this could actually be an opportunity, though," Williams adds as if she could sense my question and wanted to deflect, her voice cutting through the speaker. "If he's so determined to center himself in all of this . . . maybe there's a reason why."

I glance at my mom, whose expression is completely neutral. Why isn't she as confused as I am? Haven't the detectives interviewed Gavin by now? Isn't that what he had said to me on the phone when he first called? Haven't they cleared him already?

"Is he a suspect?" I ask.

There's silence for a beat.

"He has a strong alibi," Williams says.

"Rock-solid," Buxton adds. "Doctor's appointment. Scottsdale, not in LA. Security footage showing him going into the appointment. Nurses and doctors confirming he was there. Time stamps. Records for everything."

"So, technically, no," Williams says, getting to the point, "he's not a suspect right now. But that doesn't mean he might not know more than he says."

What are they saying? That Gavin didn't do anything to Evie *himself*, but he . . . what? Arranged for her to be taken? Is hiding her somewhere? Worse?

I play through the vlog in my head and another thought occurs to me.

"How does he know her last location? I mean, *does* he even know?" I ask, realizing he didn't mention a location in the video. I'm relieved at the thought, knowing that without a place to gather, the search can't attract the hundreds of curious fans that would be there otherwise. "Did someone tell him about Palm Springs? The car?"

"We're not sure," Williams says, and her tone is apologetic, or embarrassed maybe. "Based on this video . . . we don't even know where he's planning to go. If he's going to go to Palm Springs or somewhere totally different. Maybe he's just making things up. Trying to keep the content coming while he knows there's no one to cross-check what he's saying."

"Can't you just . . . ask him?" my mom says, and it somehow manages to sound naive instead of patronizing. Nonthreatening.

"Of course we could, Erin," Buxton says, and my mother's name might as well be *babe*. Gross. "But we think it's more beneficial if we let him believe that we're ignoring him. That we've cleared him and it's as simple as that. Especially if there's a way to see what he may know without making him second-guess anything he's doing."

"So . . ." I say, my brain already calculating what I think they're going to suggest.

"We want you to join him," Williams says. "To tell us what he knows, where he goes. What he's trying to do, exactly."

This is their best plan? After all these days and no progress? This is how they think we're going to find my sister? Us spying on her dumb boyfriend? Following him around? Doing their job? It feels like a massive waste of our time, like the very last thing we should be paying attention to. Isn't that what they had said just a few days ago? Ignore him. Don't play into the drama, the theatrics.

"He's trying to go viral," I say, frustrated. "As many times as he can. This is how his brain works. It's literally the only thing that's there. His brain is the equivalent of one of those bulk containers of whey protein, but there's nothing in there except his desire to get more views, more followers. I promise you. He's not some mastermind sociopath inserting himself in the investigation, offering to help because he gets off on it. He's a narcissist, I'm sure, but not that brand of narcissist."

I sound like I'm trying to convince myself of this as much as I am them.

"Maybe so," Williams says. "But that would be a pretty good reason to orchestrate all of this, don't you think?"

I had thought about it, of course, that all of this was a detailed, layered, supremely fucked-up—and potentially illegal, given the involvement of law enforcement—prank. But I know enough about my sister to know she wouldn't agree to this. She wouldn't let us worry like this. She wouldn't stay out of touch this long. Not for a joke. And certainly not for Gavin. There's no way.

And the other option? That she said no and Gavin made it happen anyway? Forced it to happen? That feels equally unbelievable. Almost.

"When is this thing happening?" my mom says, her face going the faintest shade of red. It's the first time she's looked uncomfortable for the entire call. "If it's tomorrow, I . . . I had a previously scheduled thing . . .

it's . . ."

I stare at her, blinking wildly. A work thing? A hair appointment? Now?

"Therapy," she says. "I really can't miss it . . . not now."

I lower my chin in her direction, my eyebrows raised. Since when does my mother go to therapy? And since when does therapy take the entire day?

But my brain sees an opening, an opportunity to be by myself, to get some space from my mother and to actually do something. To be useful.

"I'll go," I say. "I can go by myself. And . . . report back or whatever."

"Great," Williams says. "That would be great."

"I'll text him right now."

I tap out the question quickly.

Can I come help tomorrow?

He reacts to the text with a thumbs-up almost immediately, and then ten seconds later, there's an address in my inbox.

Museum Way and Belardo Road, Palm Springs, California

· • • • • • ·

The meeting point turns out to be a newly renovated downtown park by the art museum. I had googled it beforehand, trying to get a lay of the land. To know what to expect. I arrived to find it looking the same as it had online, save for some minor construction in certain areas. The grounds are dotted with scraggly palm trees and an expansive water feature, a dozen fountains shooting straight up from the ground, cutting through the heavy curtain of heat.

I had been afraid that I'd arrive to find that Gavin had shared the address online anyway, that there would be hundreds of obsessed fans gathered to drool over him and the intrigue of it all. But in the end, there's just a handful of us. Me, Gavin, plus a couple of girls I remember from Evie's high school swim team, though I couldn't recall them ever being particularly close to her otherwise. I wrack my brain for their names—for one of their names, even. Haley, maybe? Or Hallie? Kaleigh? I have no idea. Add it to the list of things I missed about my sister's life, I guess.

I don't know what I thought we would do once we got here—make small talk, or something more serious. Cry. Go over what we all know about the

olivia muenter

investigation, what we think. I half thought Gavin would instantly grill me for more information for his vlogs. Instead, he seems to keep his distance aside from greeting me with a quick hug, our bodies barely touching.

"We're just waiting for one more person," Gavin announces. "And then we'll get started."

I look around at the park, the fountains, a toddler running through the spouts of water half naked, squealing every time the water surprises them yet again. It is the epitome of innocence and joy. Delight. And then there's this.

Gavin glances at his phone. "All right, she's just about here."

I instinctively look behind me, checking for who the mystery guest could be, wracking my brain for names of Evie's friends. Old boyfriends. Distant family. Trying to figure out who would have watched Gavin's videos, who he would have asked to join him, if not me or my mom. Who would have believed him enough to be here, or who would have been curious enough to come anyway.

"I must have had five hundred messages from strangers wanting to join us, wanting to help . . . but I wanted to keep this small," Gavin starts, and I'm relieved to hear someone cutting through the awkward silence. "Just family and friends. This isn't some spectacle. It's real life."

I resist the urge to roll my eyes. Everything is a spectacle with Gavin. And that reminds me.

"I don't want to be on camera," I say.

"Don't worry." Gavin shakes his head, pushing his Wayfarers to the top of his brow, like he wants to make eye contact with me for this next part. It's well over a hundred degrees now, and he hasn't even broken a sweat yet. Of course. "I'm not filming today. The full focus is on looking for Evie today. For clues. On trying to figure out what happened. That's all that matters to me."

I'm about to push back, to make sure he really means what he's saying, but then there's a hand on my shoulder.

"Hi, guys," a small, high voice says.

Ashlyn.

Ashlyn Price is *here*? For this? Now?

I spin around and she's standing next to me, looking the same as she always has on my phone: smooth, golden, hydrated within an inch of her life. I instinctively stand up straighter, instantly self-conscious.

I see her hair first, all of it gathered to one side, woven together in a braid as elaborate as a sailor's knot. It's the color of honey and impossibly thick, so shiny and healthy-looking that it reminds me of an illustration of a Disney princess. If my brown curls are a biological inevitability, her hair is something else: a marvel, a thing to be thrown through a window and climbed.

My mind flashes to the time I was staring at photo of her wearing a ponytail and I showed it to Evie in awe. It was so thick and full that it made me wonder if I had been putting my hair in a ponytail the wrong way for my entire life. It cascaded from her crown perfectly, a bouncy, full shock of hair curving outward from her head, a section of it wrapped around the elastic holding it up, disguising the effort. These are the things that Ashlyn Price taught me to think about.

"Can you please explain to me why I look like a Revolutionary foot soldier when I attempt to do my hair like this?" I asked Evie, both of us lounging in her room one Saturday afternoon a few years ago. She and Ashlyn had been friends for about a year at that point, and though I had never met Ashlyn, I followed her even before she and Evie were close. It was one of those parasocial relationships that I couldn't trace the beginning of anymore. It felt like as long as I had been on Instagram, Ashlyn Price had been in my feed, too, like that one U2 album that came preloaded on everyone's iPods. Once she was there, she stuck.

"Because you, much like a Revolutionary War foot soldier, are not wearing seven hundred dollars of the best fake hair money can buy," Evie replied casually.

I laughed, but she stopped staring at her own phone then, eyes narrowed in my direction.

"Wait, you don't think my hair is real too, do you?" she asked as she took out a section of hair and threw it at me. "What? Do you think we're all out here just consuming collagen powder by the fistful or something?"

I caught the section of hair in midair and attached it loosely on the top of my head. My own hair was much darker and frizzier than Evie's, so I knew I must have looked ridiculous, and would have even if I had any idea how to insert it in a way that looked normal. I twirled it around my finger and placed one hand under my chin, modeling it dramatically.

"Of course I know it isn't real," I said, but the truth was that I had never once thought about it. "And honestly, based on about twenty 'my daily routine' TikToks I've seen in the past week, yes, the collagen powder things seems possible."

She threw her head back and laughed.

I'm surprised to find the fake hair doesn't even matter, though. Not in person. It doesn't stand out even now, with the full power of the sun looming above us, illuminating everything. It looks real. Plus, I know Ashlyn is open about wearing extensions now. She's beautiful, and she's honest. What else matters?

I had played out this situation in my head before. What it'd be like to meet Ashlyn Price in real life. Even if she was my sister's friend, she still felt distant to me. I pictured meeting her in person and knowing immediately that she and I weren't that different, after all. She'd have pores. Acne. Extensions that I could spot from a mile away. I'd remember that no one is what they look like online. I thought I'd see all that effort that went into being beautiful and it would make me stand up straighter, but looking at her now, all I can find is the same beauty I'd been staring at on my phone for years. Not effortless, maybe, but real and undeniable.

She takes her hand off my shoulder, and I notice that each finger is dotted with an almond-shaped nail, each nail painted with tiny rainbow hearts. Instinctively, I look for the giant, oval-shaped engagement ring she had been wearing on Instagram for the past year but I'm surprised to find it's gone. Instead, I'm searching her hands to try to spot the hallmark evidence of a spray tan, some tiny bit of orangey-brown residue left behind, to prove she's just a person who's trying, too, but there's nothing but an even glow. She looks like goddamn human sunshine. I suddenly feel very small, hyperaware of my body, my outfit, the way I'm sweating. I haven't prepared for any of this.

Before I can say anything, Gavin continues talking.

"Well, I want to start by saying thank you to everyone who made time to be here today. I know we've all known and loved Evie. And I know we all want to find her. And that most of us drove a hell of a long way to get here. So let's not waste any more time."

He splits us up into groups—he and Ashlyn take one area of the city, the swim team girls take another area, and I take a third on my own. I'm relieved, really, that I'm not stuck with Ashlyn, that I don't have to pretend like it makes sense that she's here right now, after what happened between her and Evie. I make a mental note that he and Ashlyn are searching the area where the car was found, though I don't say anything, in case it's a coincidence. It's not until everyone has started to walk away that I speak up.

"What . . ." I say, clearing my throat. "What do you want us to look for . . . just, anything?"

Gavin hesitates for a minute, and I wonder how much he's willing to reveal here—how much, exactly, he knows.

"The easiest thing to spot is her car. It's a black 2021 Range Rover. Tan interior. A beauty, really," he says. "I doubt you'd be able to miss it if it was just sitting untouched."

I look at him, eyes narrowed, waiting for him to say more. So he does know her car was here.

He stares at me for a minute, and I watch the first beads of sweat form on his forehead.

"Anything," he says calmly, though the question seems to fluster him, like he hasn't really gotten that far. Maybe this is why he's not filming right now. "Just . . . anything, I guess. Anything that could help find our Evie."

· • • ● • • ·

I drive around my allotted twenty-mile radius without knowing what I'm looking for, feeling equally comforted and unsettled by the fact that my sister was here at some point, probably driving the same roads. Was she scared? Was she alone? Was she already bruised or bleeding? Begging? Desperate? I can't imagine my sister pleading for anything, but I try to make myself see it now. Feel it. I'm getting worse at pushing back against the worst questions and images that pop up: In her most vulnerable moment, would she ask for Mom? Or me? Who would she need more as the world went to black? Why does it feel like there's a right and wrong answer?

olivia muenter

Three hours later, I've covered nearly every square inch of my part of the city and then some. I can't look at the same buildings anymore, can't imagine that the reason I'm not finding anything is because Evie is in one of the places I can't see. Deep below the earth. Covered by bags of days-old trash. Locked in a room we'd never see from the outside. I can't do that anymore.

We'd agreed to meet back at the park, but I arrive to find no one there. I consider going to wait in my car, conscious of how it will look to be the person who stopped looking for clues first, but before I can, I hear someone say my name. I look over to see Ashlyn getting up from a bench that was obscured by a palm tree.

"Hey," she says quietly, her voice humming with a vocal fry that I have to remind myself not to judge. I cringe at my internalized misogyny, the way it lingers. Even my instinct to criticize her feels like a win in her column. The fact that I'm clearly the only one comparing the two of us another. "I've been wanting to talk to you."

I'm suddenly exhausted from the day, from everything. The temperature must be at least 110 degrees by now, tame compared to what I've gotten used to in Las Vegas these last few years but still overwhelming. I feel like an egg that's been cooked on a driveway. I'm also nervous. I don't have time to assess whether it's because it's Ashlyn Price, someone I've admired from afar for years, or because it's my sister's former best friend, or because between the two of us, she's the one who knows why she and Evie don't talk anymore. I'm the one who was shut out.

"I can't imagine what you've been going through," she starts, and I can't ignore that her voice is all empathy, all warmth. I instantly understand, more than ever, why so many people online look up to her and take comfort in her posts. She's only twenty-two, but it's obvious to me already that she's the mom of every friend group, the nurturer in every situation. And though I don't want to admit it, it feels good. For someone to think of me now, too. "It must be so hard."

"Thanks," I say, fidgeting with the edge of my T-shirt. "Did . . . did Gavin ask you to come help?"

Part of me doesn't want to know the answer. Why would Gavin have asked her, but not me? Is it because of her followers? Her platform?

"Yeah, I . . . well, I was in Arizona already," she says sheepishly, and I remember that, of course: Ashlyn lives in Utah. Not here, and not Phoenix, either. "I was visiting my aunt and uncle for my cousin's graduation party. I was supposed to go home a few days ago, but after all the rumors started popping up online, I don't know . . . I just felt like it was important to stay for a bit. To make sure she was okay."

I now remember Evie saying something about Ashlyn's massive family, how she was close to her cousins, the dozen or so aunts and uncles she had spread out all across the west. Still, it's convenient, isn't it? That she was in town? I wait for her to go on, to talk more.

She clears her throat, continuing in my silence. "And Gavin said he could use the help.

"Look," she says. "I don't know how much Hazel told you about what happened with us last year. I know you were going through your own thing with Erin at the time . . . and it was all so stupid, really. So fucking dumb."

My eyes go wide at the sound of her cursing, despite myself. Ashlyn's brand of conservatism had evolved over the years, but there were still certain things that allowed her to be categorized as wholesome, or pure, or all the things that the conservative Christian corners of the internet need to feel safe. One of those things is language. But here we are, in our first-ever conversation, and she's talking just like I would. I'm as unfazed by curse words as anyone, so why do I feel . . . annoyed? Like I've been fooled, too.

"I just . . . even if we hadn't been talking . . . I still know my friend," she says, her eyes fixed on where she's tearing the edge of the cardboard sleeve of a watery iced coffee instead of on me, for the first time since she approached me. It's the first time I've felt older than her, somehow. I wait for her to go on. "So when I started reading the rumors . . . after last year, after everything, I just knew that something was really wrong."

My mind whirs at what she's saying, what she's implying. Does she know something about why Evie would have disappeared? About someone who could have hurt her? Or taken her?

"And then Gavin called you?"

She looks down at the disintegrating cardboard sleeve again.

"Yeah," she says. "He told me. That it was real. But it was like . . . it was like I already knew. Gut feeling."

Also convenient, I think.

"I have no idea what Evie told you about us. About what happened. And if she did, I'm sure you must think the worst of me, especially since I know you two have gotten closer in the last couple years and—"

"What does that mean?" I cut her off, my defensiveness a knee-jerk reaction. In the last couple years? What does she think—that I was just absent from Evie's life before? Is that what Evie told her?

"No, no," Ashlyn starts, her voice cracking with nervousness, the smallest hint of blush poking through her tan. "I just meant . . . I meant that, you know, she wasn't the same with everyone. She's not the same as she was online."

"I know that," I say, my jaw tightening.

What Ashlyn is telling me isn't just obvious, it's insulting.

"I've known her for her entire life," I add, but what I really want to say is: I knew her before you did. Before anyone did. Before she was online at all.

"Right, of course," Ashlyn says. "I know how much she meant to you . . . and vice versa. I do. But I guess I just mean . . . there was your version of Evie, and my version, and Gavin's version, and . . . I don't know which parts of her you got, I guess. And which I did. What overlapped."

I picture a dozen different versions of Evie, strung together like paper dolls, each one wearing a different outfit that's been drawn on with crayons.

"And you just assume that you knew the real version?" I ask. "That somehow you, the person she chose to stop talking to altogether, saw the real her?"

She looks wounded, and for a second I feel bad. Embarrassed. I know I sound overly defensive. Too sensitive. But my reaction doesn't surprise me, either. This is how I've always operated. If Ashlyn was all warm and soft, I would be ice-cold, spiky. I would make us so different that no one could ever compare us in the first place.

"Right," Ashlyn says, eyes turned downward, then shooting up again to meet mine. "So you know, then."

I blink back at her, a challenge.

"About everything?" she adds, but I'm unsure if it's a question. "Of course you know."

She's staring at me, her gaze earnest, and I'm suspicious of it, if all of this is just her calling my bluff. Before I can say anything, I spot the swim team girls walking toward us, whispering to each other, their eyes fixed on Ashlyn, who turns and looks toward them expectantly.

"Any luck?" she says, hopeful. "Hazel and I were just talking about what we found . . . a whole lot of nothing, really. I don't even know what I was looking for. I feel so useless."

It's a definitive change of subject. She's even angled her body away from me now, making it clear that our conversation is done. That she doesn't want to talk about any of this around them, that she doesn't trust them, and it confirms what I already thought: that they somehow snuck their way into this, inserted themselves into the drama in the same way the detectives think Gavin is doing. He isn't far behind the other girls now, walking toward us. His shirt is so soaked in sweat now that it looks like he's been walking since we left him hours earlier. It's molded to his chest, all the knotted muscle more apparent than it is usually.

"He wanted to keep looking," Ashlyn says quietly, explaining why they split up at some point, though I hadn't thought of it until now. "He's driving himself insane with all of this, I swear."

I study him as he talks to the swim girls, shaking his head, a familiar version of defeat on his face, too. Unconsciously, my eyes drift down toward his midsection as he peels the shirt away from his torso to wipe sweat from his brow, all those abs. He looks healthy, vital, lush. I look away, suddenly aware that I'm staring, and blot the sweat from my upper lip.

He turns to Ashlyn and me and debriefs us on his search, his version of the afternoon sounding a lot like ours: aimless, pointless, fruitless. We're all in the same spot we were when we started.

Was this his plan, exactly? To waste time like this? Or did he genuinely think we'd find something, see something? After all, Evie's car was found here. Evie was here. And somehow, he knew that. I wait for someone to ask why *here*, why this spot, but no one does. I consider for a second if

Ashlyn knows everything, too, and it makes me trust her less.

"Thank you all, anyway," Gavin says, hands on his hips. "I know we've all got a long drive head of us . . . you know how to reach me if you think of anything. If anything clicks . . ." he trails off, shaking his head, like he isn't even sure what he's saying anymore, like it isn't making sense to him either. "I don't know. Just . . . thank you."

It occurs to me that maybe I should be thanking everyone, as Evie's only family member present, but I don't have that in me. I am already looking forward to the four-hour drive back to my mom's, to sitting in silence.

The swim team girls leave, hugging me before I can avoid it, their sweat pressing into my shoulders. I wait for Gavin to walk away too, to leave Ashlyn and me alone again. I wonder if she'll ask me to go get a drink or a bite to eat. If we'll talk like we're friends and I'll finally get answers to some of the questions I've been asking myself for the past five days, or the new ones I'm asking myself now. But that doesn't happen.

"He's my ride," Ashlyn says quietly, tilting her head toward Gavin.

They carpooled here? Together? Or . . . did someone drop her off and she decided it'd just be better to go back with Gavin? I try to remember if they were ever friends when Ashlyn and Evie were close. Did they get along? Did Ashlyn hate him too? I hate that both options seem equally plausible. How have I forgotten something like that so quickly?

"We'll . . . we'll talk. I'll send you my number," Ashlyn says, her body lurching ever so slightly forward, like she's about to hug me, before she steps a little farther away, toward Gavin, who is waving goodbye.

"I'm here if y'all need anything, Hazel," he says, kindly. "Just like I told your mom. Anything you need. We'll find her. I promise."

I say thank you and turn in the opposite direction toward where I'm parked, but all I can think is: what did he tell my mom?

And then: what did she tell him?

I was at the Evie Davis search party | June 23, 2023, 11:43 p.m. EDT

Butt3rflyButt3rcup

Long time lurker, first time poster. Trust me when I say this is *not* my usual thing . . . but here's the thing: I know Evie Davis. Or did, I guess. I don't want to dox myself, but let's just say we had hobbies in common.

I never really gave a shit about @evelyn ~The Influencer~ in the same way everyone else did, but mean . . . I'm only human. It's been basically impossible to ignore the rumors and the crazy ass shit Gavin has been posting on YouTube since she disappeared.

At first, I was skeptical of the whole thing tbh, but when he mentioned this friends and family search party thing . . . I thought . . . well, we were friends. Ish. I bet I could join. I could help. I DM'd Gavin and asked to go. And long story short, after sending him some photos I had of Evie and me to prove I wasn't some random psycho, he gave me an address. I expected there to be more people, tbh, but it was a super small group. It made me wonder how tf I got in, but whatever. It ended up just being me and a friend of mine—another person who knew Evie—Gavin, and Evie's older sister, Hazel. And get this: Ashlyn fucking Price showed up. Ashlyn. Isn't that weird? I could have *sworn* they weren't a thing anymore. Evie doesn't even follow her anymore. I checked. But let me back up.

So, I got there early. Like an hour before the thing was supposed to start. Killed time and went to grab a coffee a few blocks away, but before I walked in . . . I noticed Gavin's car across the street. I'm not some fan girl, but like . . . it's a lifted vintage Bronco that he posts all over his Instagram. Not exactly subtle. At first I thought, whatever. He's here early, too. And then I saw Ashlyn in the front seat, too. At first I was like: WTF is Ashlyn Price doing here? But then I thought . . . idk, maybe she and Evie reconciled. And I mean, did it really make any less sense that she was there than that I was there? So, whatever. But then I noticed . . . she looked upset. Not, "oh my god my best friend is missing" upset, not sad or worried, but like . . . *pissed*. I couldn't make out what she was saying, but she was sort of shouting at Gavin, and he mostly just looked annoyed. The search itself ended up being a bust (found nothing, by the way, no idea why we even dragged our asses all the way to Palm Springs), but I just keep thinking about the way the two of them had looked at first. What it could mean. Like, that must mean something, right? That they were so angry at each other?

⬆ 298 ⬇   💬 43

> **Don'tTrustGarthBrooks**
>
> Just so I'm clear here . . . your shocking, boots-on-the-ground theory that you're bringing to us today is that . . . maybe the boyfriend had something to do with it?
>
> > **IBlameTheOwl**
> >
> > I honestly think you're giving OP too much credit here. This mostly just reads as gossip. Who knows if they were even really there . . .
> >
> > > **NotAConspiracyIfTru3**
> > >
> > > Wait, what about the Palm Springs detail though . . . why were they in Palm Springs??? Is everyone just ignoring that!!
>
> **StayxxWeirdxStayxAlive**
>
> You know who's probably absolutely loving this post right now, and the way its conveniently directing all attention away from them riiiiight when shit is about to really hit the fan? Erin fucking Davis.

CHAPTER 9

My mother has never looked better.

It's been six days since I arrived at her house. Twelve days since Evie was last seen. I've spent the majority of my time here talking in circles with the detectives, scrolling on my phone, and waiting for news that hasn't come. I've distracted myself with hours-long walks in the blistering heat, repeated listens to Evie's favorite playlists. I can see what days she added certain songs, and I listen to them and picture the Tuesday or Thursday or Saturday in my head, imagine she was happy or sad or heartbroken. Seeking out more of her feels natural to me, like it's the only thing to do. It's taking care of myself that feels harder. It is taking everything in me to do the bare minimum—brush my teeth, shower, feed myself.

Meanwhile, my mother has the energy of someone who's been on vacation for a week. Not happy, necessarily. Not unbothered. But there's something about the situation that makes her seem like she's in her element, the balanced eye of the storm while everything is in chaos around her. Terrifying, but unshakable. All the adrenaline has left her with something that I can only describe as a glow. I'm studying her face now, as we both sit at the giant antique farmhouse table in the kitchen. The table is ten feet long, and she's all the way at the other end, staring at her phone, scrolling.

This is what we do now for dinners. We avoid each other most of the day, if the detectives aren't here, but dinners we eat at the table. It's our only time to really look at each other, to occupy the same space. We've

olivia muenter

learned to coexist in the house again, the same way we did when I was seventeen and eighteen, silently keeping an eye on each other, neither of us willing to back down.

"Hungry?" she says suddenly, looking up from her phone. "I made a kale salad. Lemon dressing."

My mother eats salad like it's been medically prescribed to her. She's had one every single evening I've been here, even after the worst days— the one when the detectives finally told us they weren't able to recover the parking lot security footage after all, for example, or when they explained that they found a set of prints on Evie's phone and male DNA on the steering wheel, both unidentified.

On the nights that I'm able to feel my hunger, it hits me all at once, and I dream of escaping into my favorite foods—a heaping bowl of spaghetti pomodoro made with basil so fresh that the smell of it lingers on your hands the next morning. Thick, crispy hunks of sourdough toast topped with burrata and tomato jam. Stove-top popcorn, still warm, with pieces of dark chocolate thrown in, melting into the salt and butter. I fantasize about all of it, right here at this table, just like I did when I was seventeen. But I refuse to give her the satisfaction of knowing that I need more than a nightly salad. That I'm weak enough to crave something richer, heavier. That I need more. All of this is the same as it was at seventeen, too.

"Sure," I say lightly. "Thank you."

She moves to the kitchen to prepare it as I go back to my phone. In a different house, a different family maybe, this is when I would offer to help. To set the table. Grab two glasses of water. But that's not how things work with us. We may be in this house together, but we aren't working together on anything. We're not cooking together. Not spiraling together. And we're certainly not grieving together. No one wants to be the first person to do that. No one wants to be the first person to admit there might be something to grieve, not yet. There are tears, always from my mother, but only when the detectives are here. Like she's saving the emotion for the people who can actually do something with it. And I can't say I blame her. What am I going to do with her tears? What would she do with mine? This has never been a place for comfort.

A few minutes pass and my mom puts a wide, low-rimmed bowl in front of me, and it's beautiful. The bowl, the salad, its tiny, gem-colored pomegranate seeds popping against the lush green of the kale. She brings her own bowl to the opposite end of the table and sits down. Her portion, I notice, is much smaller than mine.

"I just don't crave a big dinner like you always did," she says, noticing the way I'm eyeing the plates. "The lighter the meal, the better I sleep."

It's the kind of small talk that I've heard a million times before, a completely unnecessary tidbit of information that no one asked for. It might be a bit of a dig, but mostly it's a family habit. My mom does it. I'm sure her mom did it. I've taught myself not to do it out loud, but it still happens in my head. And now Evie does, too, despite my best efforts to make sure she was safer. Hunger has always required an explanation in this family.

The last time I saw Evie in person was more than a month ago. She had driven all the way to Vegas to visit me, her first major trip in a brand-new car. She had insisted we spend the afternoon driving around together, even though she had been driving all morning long. I chose the playlist, and we spent an hour or so blasting our favorite songs and driving down long, empty stretches of highway, clouds of dust everywhere. The sky was starting to fade to pink and orange when we had stopped for In-N-Out for dinner, a tradition on these road trips to nowhere, as we called them. We had just pulled into a parking spot to eat when I'd lifted my phone above our meals—double-double for me, protein style for Evie—to snap a photo without thinking. Evie groaned before I had even put down the phone.

"What?" I said, confused. "Is it because it's a millennial thing? Am I cringe? I am, aren't I? I get it. And you know what? I've accepted it. I'm owning it. I am cringe and I have a side part and I am *alive*."

"No," Evie said, though she didn't say it with a laugh like I was hoping. "It's not that. And I've already told you that the side part thing is a myth. It's the jeans that are the real problem."

I threw one of my fries at her. "How *dare* you. My ass looks phenomenal in these jeans."

She laughed that time, but she was still stuck on the photo. "Just don't post it, okay?"

The request surprised me, because I knew Evie had seen how carefully I had approached my own social media when it came to her. My account was private, though a few Evie superfans had managed to start following me over the years; I'd drunkenly pressed ACCEPT on random requests or misread a username. It didn't really matter, though, because there wasn't much for these fans to see. I had made a point for years not to share photos of my sister on social media. I was all too aware of just how much it looked like I was trying to use the photos to selfishly signal something to the world. To say: look who my sister is! So instead, I didn't really share photos of Evie. Or even myself, for that matter. At this point, my Instagram grid was mostly made of pictures of books, food, and nature. No Evie in sight. So where was this concern coming from?

"You're not even in it, Ev," I said gently. "But that's fine. I won't post."

"The car. They'll know it's mine from the color of the interior," she said, matter-of-factly, like it didn't sound insane at all. "And it's just—the burger. The lettuce instead of the bun. They'll assume I'm dieting."

I took a sip of my drink, studying her slightly anxious expression as I decide how to reply now. I've always treaded carefully around food with my sister.

"Well . . . aren't you?" I eventually asked, making a point to keep my tone light, casual, anything but accusatory or judgmental. Immediately, though, I saw how sad the question made her, how the anxious line across her brow seemed to deepen. Wrong question.

"Not really. It's not—it's not forever or anything. I just have this big campaign coming up and I really can't deal with the comments. If I'm dieting, I'm a bad influence on everyone who follows me. If I'm not dieting, I'm too big."

Evie? Too big? The idea was so utterly absurd that I wanted to laugh, but I kept quiet.

I forced myself not to say anything.

"I saw a comment the other day that said, 'Our midsized queen!'" Evie went on. "I'm a size four. Sometimes a six, I guess. But also sometimes a two. I couldn't tell if they were joking or not. Is four midsize now? Should I, like, lean into that?"

She can't be serious, I thought. Could she?

I looked over and she was pulling apart the piece of lettuce that was poorly substituting as a bun. She seemed nervous, worried. Embarrassed, even.

I knew the feeling, of course; I had been a teenager once, too. I had felt the same pressures, the same concerns about not fitting into whatever box of attractiveness was required that year. I still remembered the agonizing span of my early twenties when I realized that I was still doing the same thing I had at fifteen, staring in the mirror and waiting for a new body and face to arrive. I still hadn't accepted they might never come.

Part of me always thought that Evie's beauty—those eyes and that face and all the other things about her that made her so easy for the world to look at every day—would give her a different story. She'd never feel as bad as I did, I thought. She'd never be as hard on herself as Mom was, as quick to change her face. She'd check her messages, her comments, and realize that everyone wants to look like her. That *she's* the standard. And even if she didn't see it, I figured the mere existence of social media would remind her of the thing I never really believed in middle school or high school: that there are all kinds of ways to be beautiful. I thought a world with body positivity and plus-size models and a universal condemnation of "almond moms" would be easier to navigate. But the opposite had proved true.

Evie was like any other eighteen-year-old, oblivious to her own smooth skin and shiny hair, hyperfocused on becoming that impossible level of desirable in which you stand out and fit in in equal measure. Our mom certainly didn't help. But what made things particularly hard was that Evie couldn't talk about any of it. Couldn't acknowledge it even once. No one wants to hear a beautiful girl cry that she's not beautiful enough or see someone diet who is already thin by any standard. No one wants to hear how hard it is to be a teenage girl, even if everyone knows being a teenage girl is impossible. I knew this because I felt the same way sometimes. I couldn't stand to see her most human moments—the dieting, the obsession with angles, the Photoshop of a barely there stretch mark. If I was honest with myself, I was just like everyone else. I said if I looked like her, if I had what she had, then I wouldn't waste a single second trying to change any of it, and I hated it when she did.

"You look great. Always," I reassured her, trying again to keep things positive, uplifting. "And a four is only midsize if you consider that the largest size a human could be is, like, a size eight. And that is . . . a pretty disturbing concept."

She smiled, finally taking a bite of her food.

"Though," I added, "based on the truly horrific experience I had last weekend in a Zara dressing room, that may actually be the case for some brands."

A laugh then from Evie. A real one. It felt like winning.

I smiled and pushed back the memory behind the joke, ignoring the rest of the story—the fact that I had gone to the mall searching for a dress that I had seen Evie wear on Instagram. I made a point not to dress like my sister, for a lot of reasons. I was older, we had different body types, and the last thing I was searching for was more comparisons between the two of us. But I had my college roommate's wedding coming up and had bought and returned so many other options that I was starting to worry that I'd end up wearing an oversized sleep shirt and a pair of heels to the ceremony. Plus, this particular dress was *cute*. Really cute. It had looked so good on Evie, and on so many of the people who had bought it, who'd tagged her in their fitting room photos, who she'd reposted to her stories. Besides, who said I was immune to being influenced, too? In the end, I fell into the same state of mind that everyone who follows my sister does, thinking that maybe we're not that different. Plus, the dress came in multiple colors and patterns—it's not like I was going to wear the same exact one as Evie Davis, SuperInfluencer.

It was only halfway over my shoulders in the dressing room when I considered that I should turn back, not pass go. There was a very clear series of red flags telling me that if I forced this garment on my body it would not be coming off without a fight. But Evie wore this dress. So why couldn't I?

I pushed on. *I will make this work*, I told myself. It's a dress, not a wetsuit. It felt like a wetsuit, yes, but that was beside the point. After a few completely unnatural contortions and a good deal of sweat, I got the garment on my body. By that point, though, I was floating above myself somewhere near the large fluorescent lights overhead, watching me below, my body stuffed uncomfortably into the dress. I looked like a piece of fried chicken sitting under a heat lamp. Lumpy, greasy, overheated. I had gotten the dress on, sure, but at what cost? Blood flow was being cut off somewhere, I just knew it. I imagined that the only way I'd be getting out of this thing would be via the Jaws of Life, that a very hot (they're always hot) fireman would make his way through the fitting room curtain and be forced to cut the dress off my body.

Eventually, using this scenario as motivation, I managed to get myself out of the thing. I exhaled, letting my body expand to its normal size once again, and looked at the tag, but I already knew. It was the largest size they sold. And, I realized, the side seam of the dress had ripped.

Maybe I could have just left it there, pretended that it was already damaged before. Or simply explained the situation. But I didn't have it in me. The dress from hell was going home with me. I emerged from the fitting room drenched in my own sweat, my hair matted to my forehead, my face flushed. I balled the dress up in one of my hands, hiding the damaged seam, and went to the counter to buy it.

The associate at the cash register smiled and asked me if I found everything I was looking for today and what I really wanted to say was: *you have no idea what I've been through.* And: *why is it eighty-five degrees in there?* And: *curtains instead of doors in dressing rooms should be illegal.* But instead I smiled and nodded.

The associate carefully folded the garment, and then their eyes lit up. "Oh, my gosh," they said. "Do you follow Evie Davis? We've been selling out of this left and right ever since she shared it. I can't believe you got the last in this size."

"Me either!" I replied, forcing an extra-wide smile on my face as I handed over my credit card and walked out of the store, forty dollars less to my name and filled with the intense urge to cry.

I got to my car and threw the dress in the trunk, where it would likely stay for months. I didn't want to look at it. I knew it was just a dress. That I should brush it off, watch some body-neutral video content about how clothes are supposed to be made to fit our bodies and not the other way around, blah, blah, blah, but I can't. I can't get over how effortlessly beautiful the dress had looked on my little sister, how quickly I had forgotten just how good she was at this. How good she was at making one dress represent a whole other way of existing, an easier, lighter, more beautiful

olivia muenter

way of being you. That was the appeal of Evie, I remembered, she made it all look so easy. I tried not to hold it against her that it never really was for me.

· ● ● ● ● ● ·

I'm midbite, barely tasting the salad, when I feel a knot start to form in my throat. The same one that always comes now when I think of Evie, her face, her laugh. The ways I failed her, the tiny cracks in our relationship that I ignored. Every day she's gone feels one day closer to learning the worst. I desperately want to leave here, to deal with this somewhere else. Cry and eat and fall apart alone, like I always have. But leaving would mean there's nothing else to do. That she's a more permanent type of gone, the kind that means it's time to move on. And I'm not ready for that. As long as I'm here, it means there's still hope.

I set my fork down and take a drink of water, swallowing down the emotion. Not now. Like every other time this has happened since I've been here, I calm myself down by walking through the facts of the last few days. The things I know. I start at the beginning, replaying the first conversation with Gavin in my head. I remember the words he had used to describe my relationship with my mom. "No contact." It sounded like legalese, cold and official. I bet he hadn't pictured this, the two of us politely sharing a kale salad in silence, sleeping under the same roof. But none of this is new to us.

It would be easy to say it started with Evie. That she was born, and then my dad was gone, and then everything looked different. That that's what killed my mom's and my relationship. It might even be easy to say I was jealous of Evie's success. Resentful of my mother and sister's relationship, their intertwined careers. That I missed when things were simpler. But I think part of me had an inkling before all of that, before there was a platform to share any of it. I felt it as soon as I could say no to the endless photos or push away the digital camera that seemed to follow me to every event, every milestone. I saw the disappointment in my mother's face every time, the longing. I learned to count the ways that I wasn't anything like she expected.

"You know I grew you in here and everything," she'd say, pointing to her abdomen. "You'd think that would mean I could show you off to the world. Be proud of my little girl."

She'd look at my dad. "Can you believe it, Chris? Twenty-three hours of labor and everything, and now the child I pushed out of my vagina won't even let me take her photo. Unbelievable!"

My mom's tone always said she was joking, just teasing me for being so stubborn, but I knew that she meant it. That deep down, it really did bother her that her body had put so much time and energy into someone who didn't have the decency to like the same things she liked, to want the same things. It was the photos, sure, but it was everything else, too. I never thought about aesthetics the way she did—decorations for birthday parties and dress-up and dance recital tutus. I was an introvert from the start, more likely to be curled up with a book in my reading nook than I was to enter a room and announce, "Hey, Mom, look at this!"

"Ew, Mom," I'd say, and my dad would laugh and pull me in for a hug, tell me that we had plenty of photos already. That I was fine.

I couldn't have known for sure then that the blog and Facebook posts about me would go up anyway, even without the photos. It was her outlet, she said, her way of making sense of her life, motherhood. She was never trying to be famous, she'll say now. She just wrote about and shared what she knew. And what she knew, what she shared with that then tiny group of followers and readers, was often about me. Long, rambling posts about the talk she had with me about my changing body, or confessionals about how I still wet the bed occasionally during bad dreams, like it was her shame to carry instead of mine. I didn't see every post then; some of them didn't surface until years later, when fans were mining the archives of the blog for never-before-seen content. But even at age eight or nine, I had a feeling. A gut instinct that I needed to tiptoe around my life, conscious that it belonged to her before it ever belonged to me.

"Your mom's just *so* proud of you, Haze," my dad would assure me in these moments, freckles curving up his face with his grin, and I'd nod, telling myself he was probably right even though I didn't believe him.

Everyone assumes that Evie being born made me feel angry or jealous, but it was more like relief. The second I saw toddler Evie twirling in front of a camera, my mom beaming as she stared at her face on the screen, I knew that my mom finally had a daughter she could see herself in, and that I had an out. It's part of why I always felt like I had to protect Evie. I owed it to her.

CHAPTER 10

"So what did you tell them?" my mom says, breaking the silence sitting between us. Her fork is suspended in the air, a shiny piece of kale spiked on the end. It's the first time she's brought up the fact that I've talked to the detectives separately—that they made a point to get me alone.

"About what?"

"About Evie," she says, as if that should explain what she means entirely. "Obviously."

"I don't know," I reply. "I told them the truth. What I know about her. Her personality. The same things you told them, I'm sure."

"Did they ask you about me?" she says. "About how she feels about me?"

So maybe she was listening then. Or trying to.

I wait a beat, searching for desperation on her face. Fear. But all I see is that same damn inexplicable glow. Like even now, she's somehow still carrying something good inside her, something bright.

"I just told them the truth," I say again.

She blinks at me, waiting.

"I said she's eighteen and you're her mom. And that you work together, too," I explain. "That things can get messy."

"*Messy*, Hazel?" she says, setting the fork down. "Really?"

"All I said was that you manage her career like, well, a manager would, and that sometimes Evie doesn't exactly love that," I say. "Buxton seems to think you're doing a *great* job at it, for what it's worth."

She shakes her head, pausing to twist her hair into a gold claw clip, only to let it fall and repeat the motion immediately, a nervous tic she's had for as long as I can remember. "Oh, I'm sure you were very quick to correct him there. Did you share a theory about how Erin Davis forced her daughter into some horrible situation she couldn't come back from, didn't protect her? Did you bring up the push-up bra story then and there, or are you saving it to leak to the press?"

I roll my eyes. The push-up bra story. Really?

It had happened a couple years ago. Evie was sixteen, and I had been back from New York for almost a year. I was lying in bed scrolling when I saw the photo on Instagram, two images posted back-to-back. Evie and my mom standing in a giant walk-in closet, both wearing the same type of bra. My mom in a half-open robe, reaching for a hanger, Evie in sweatpants. Both of them laughing, their matching cleavage angled toward the camera. The caption said something about how getting ready together is one of their favorite things to do, how having the right foundation to any outfit makes everything easier, "no matter what your body type is!" I knew what they were trying to do. It was the peak of the "one item on two different body types" trend, though I didn't quite understand how they thought that angle made sense when one person was a 34DDD and the other person was a 36D. That wasn't the thing about it that bothered me, though, or that made me call my mom for the first time in weeks and ask her what the fuck she was thinking.

"It's like catnip for perverts, Mom," I said. "What could you have possibly been thinking letting her do this? Is this even legal?"

"It's a *bra*, Hazel." My mom sighed. "Not a negligee. Sixteen-year-olds wear bras. Not everyone is as small chested as you were at that age."

"She's *sixteen*," I said, ignoring the barb. "You literally did a half-naked Mommy and me photo shoot with your underage daughter . . . and then posted it for millions of people to see. Do you know the kinds of fucked-up internet forums these pictures will end up on?"

"You know I can't control any of that, honey." She sighed. "People like that have existed since the beginning of time. If it wasn't these pictures, they'd find others."

"Well, actually, you can control some things," I said. "You can say no to shit like this pretty easily, actually. Do it yourself and leave Evie out of it."

She sighed again. "You're making this into a much bigger thing than it is."

The phone was on speaker, and I scrolled back to read the comments. "'Wowza. Someone's all grown up!'" I read aloud. "'Not sure which one I'm into more now, tbh.'" Bile was rising in my throat as I tried to keep my tone measured, serious. "This isn't fair to her. There have to be boundaries."

She laughed then. "I swear, your generation is always talking about hypersexualizing women just for existing . . . and then you lose your mind over stuff like this. It's basically the equivalent of a bikini."

She was right. There *was* arguably more fabric on the bra than some bathing suits Evie had worn in photos she'd posted. So why did this feel so different?

"Besides, your sister wanted this campaign. She insisted on it, really," my mom went on.

I hesitated. Evie had wanted this? Who would want to be photographed shirtless at sixteen? While wearing matching outfits with their mom? What amount of money could possibly make that worth it, especially if she was splitting it with my mom? That was how I thought money worked for them then, at least.

When I didn't respond, my mom kept talking.

"Here," she said. "Ask her yourself."

There's a pause, and then my sister's voice comes through the speaker.

"Hey, Haze," she said. "What's up?"

"This Instagram post . . . the bras?" I started, suddenly conscious that I felt awkward talking about this with my sister. *Do I really need to get into the details?* I thought. To explain how fucking *weird* this was? Did I need to put all of that on her if she wasn't already thinking about all of that in the first place? "It feels . . . off."

I heard the familiar sound of the back door closing, birdsong floating in the background. She had gone outside. Away from Mom?

"Yeah, I had a feeling you wouldn't be a fan," she said quietly.

"Mom said you insisted on doing it?" I pushed. "It doesn't even really seem like your aesthetic or anything? Am I missing something?"

She inhaled deeply, then lowered her voice. "Yeah, I can't say it was my favorite thing in the world. I'm honestly afraid to even read the comments. And for the shit I'm about to get from my friends at school."

"So then why?" I asked. "Did she pressure you? Is that what this is? You need to tell me if that's what's happening here, Ev. It's not okay."

"No," she said quickly. "It's not that."

"So? Then what?"

"They pitched it to both of us," she began. "Mom was all in immediately, obviously—you know that the brand deals really haven't been the same for her in the past few years. That things have dropped off. It's a huge name brand. They had a huge budget. This was going to be the first five-figure post Mom had gotten in a while—maybe all year. She was thrilled. I passed on it, said I was too busy with other projects, which was true . . . but when the brand found out I wasn't willing to do the campaign *with* her, they started to back out altogether."

This was the first time that Evie had confirmed what I had assumed for a while—that the money wasn't the same for my mom as it had been, or at least that it didn't compare anymore to what Evie was making. I had watched my mom's spending from afar, the aspirational lifestyle remaining mostly the same, but I knew that didn't mean much. So much of that, right down to the Botox, was from the endless stream of free products she could wield. A post for a new couch. A post for a new fridge. A post for a new face.

But I had also seen the way Evie had blown up on TikTok. How natural it had been, and how my mom never managed to find her footing there. Her videos felt forced, awkward. Her longtime followers on Instagram and YouTube followed her because of her and Evie's story—the way they had been attached at the hip for all those years. These followers loved to see them together now, to check in and see what they looked like now, if they were successful, happy. But Evie's audience was different. Many of them didn't even know about our mom, or the viral video that started it all. About our dad. They just knew that everyone else followed Evie Davis, so they did, too. Mom may have had nostalgia going for her, but Evie had everything.

"So, what?" I pressed. "You backtracked? Said you'd do it, anyway?"

Evie sighed. "I saw how upset Mom was . . . how embarrassed. It was like she was disappointed that I wasn't doing the campaign, yeah, but even more disappointed that she needed me for it. That she wasn't a big enough get on her own anymore."

I hated that Evie felt this way. It reminded me so much of my own childhood that it made me feel dizzy. I knew exactly how heavy it was to believe that your parent's happiness was your job.

"So I changed my mind and told her it made sense to do it. A huge name brand. The potential for a long-term partnership. Made up some shit about maybe how it would go viral, get picked up by *People* or something. I don't know. It was just a few photos. I could handle it," she said. "Mom asked if I was sure a few times, but I did insist, yeah. She seemed genuinely relieved. It was fine. It is fine."

"Is it?" I asked.

"Come on, Hazel," she said. "I don't want to do this right now."

I had tried to pick my battles with Evie over the years, to push back on content and career decisions as rarely as possible. I was determined not to be the out-of-touch, judgmental older sister, not to assume she didn't have agency in her career, even though I knew that she never really had a choice. If *she* thought she did, then what did my opinion matter? Why burst that bubble for her? But this was different.

"You have to set boundaries with her, Evie," I insisted. "This is something that should never have been on the table for *either* of you. You're too young. It's too weird. I hate it."

"Shocking." She laughed.

"You should have called me. If I was there, I would have made sure this didn't happen," I said.

"But you weren't." Evie laughed again. "You haven't been for, like, basically forever. It's Mom and me, on our own, figuring it out. Same as it's been since I was eight."

I swallowed, stung by her honesty.

"Look, I love you, Haze," she said, her voice softer. "I do. I know you want the best for me. But you can't bring your and Mom's shit into everything I do. And you can't look down at me from a million miles away and say you know better, like you somehow see it all more clearly than I do."

olivia muenter

Yes, I can, I wanted to say. *I see it all, everything you can't.* But I stayed quiet.

"When it comes to Mom, to this kind of stuff . . . the bottom line is that I wouldn't have any of this without her," she added.

"Yeah," I said. "I know. That's my whole point."

I should have left it at that, but when she didn't reply for a beat, I kept going.

"I know you, Ev," I said quietly. "You're better than all of this."

"Thanks for that," she replied. "Look, I've gotta go."

And then she hung up.

We didn't talk for weeks after that, the longest we had gone in years. Eventually, I apologized, said I didn't know what I was talking about. That I couldn't speak on an industry I'm not part of. That she was free to do whatever she wants. We moved on. My mother still brought it up, though, whenever she thought I was criticizing her parenting skills. I wondered if on a certain level, it was because she still felt guilty. Because maybe she knew why Evie had changed her mind and agreed to do the photos all along. Because she felt so pathetic about that that she had to deflect somehow. But she'd never tell me any of that, of course.

"I didn't bring up anything specific," I say now, staring at the far end of the table, where my mother is still sitting, her salad bowl pushed forward, signaling that she's done. "I told them you were close. *Are* close," I correct myself, embarrassed.

This had been happening more and more in the past two days, my body slipping into past tense when talking about Evie. It's like something in my brain has registered the span of her absence, the way it's stretching, before I can.

Like my brain is trying to prepare me for the truth that with each passing minute, the possibility that she is gone for good is more realistic than the possibility that she's still out there somewhere, living in the present tense.

My mother's expression doesn't change.

"And that you and I are not?" she asks.

The doorbell rings then, and I look down at my phone. It's after eight now, and neither of us had been expecting the detectives to stop by today.

"Did you order something?" I ask my mom, who shakes her head no, though I notice that she doesn't look entirely surprised, or even worried really. Was she expecting something else?

She makes her way to the door and I trail a few feet behind her. When my mother opens the door, both Buxton and Williams are standing there, and I feel my whole body tighten. They both look somewhat flustered, but serious, and I know in my gut that this is bad. This has to be bad.

"Hi?" I say.

"Is everything okay?" My mother cuts right to the chase.

Neither of the detectives answer right away, and I feel panic start to rise in my chest, hot and swirling.

Is this it? Have they found her? Are they about to tell us to sit down before they deliver the news? Am I standing smack-dab in the worst moment of my life?

"Well, frankly ma'am, no," Buxton says, stepping into the entryway.

His tone is colder than it's been in the past. No hint of flirtation. No "Mrs. Davis," no "Erin."

My brain whirs, running through a Rolodex of a million horrible headlines about young women dying horrible deaths. All the different possibilities for violence and terror and pain. I want to kick myself, hit myself. One hard punch in the gut. How could I have been so stupid? So naive to have let my guard down? Every part of being a woman in this world has taught me that there are things to fear. It's suddenly so clear to me that I forgot. That I had let myself be gaslit into thinking that it was all paranoia, exaggeration, the result of a million hours of consuming true crime in podcasts, television. If only I had trusted myself, then maybe this wouldn't be happening. Then maybe I wouldn't be about to learn that my sister is—

"We don't have any news about Evie," Williams cuts in, in a way that feels like she's correcting her partner, like she's the only one who realizes the conclusion that we must have jumped to, or the only one who cares that we might have, anyway. "Nothing has changed there. We came back because we received . . ."

I take a deep breath.

"We received a link to a podcast." Buxton finishes his partner's sentence.

This . . . this is not what I expect them to say.

"What?" I snap.

I look at my mom, and her expression is completely neutral. Why isn't she confused, too?

"What are you talking about? What kind of podcast?" I ask again.

Neither of the detectives are looking at me, though. Their eyes, instead, are fixed in front of me, staring knowingly at my mother.

Why isn't she saying anything? Why do they keep looking at her like that?

She stands up straighter, crossing her arms in front of her, and it feels defiant.

"Maybe you should ask your mother that," Buxton says to me, but he's still staring at her, too. I can't shake the feeling that he feels personally slighted here, that he felt like the two of them had some sort of rock-solid understanding and she's betrayed it. It makes me pity him, almost.

"Well, Hazel, it seems we're about to get a *very* stern talking to, from the looks of it," she says, turning back toward the kitchen.

We?

I shoot a look at the detectives to let them know I have no idea what she's talking about. What they're talking about.

"Sit, please. Sit down," she says to the detectives, waving them to walk across the living room to the kitchen table. She grabs a pitcher of water from the fridge and nods toward the remains of the salad on the counter. "Water, anyone? Salad?"

Williams and Buxton exchange a glance, and they look uneasy. They don't understand why she's acting like this, and neither do I. They both shake their heads.

She shrugs. "Suit yourself."

I don't understand anything about what's happening here.

"So," Williams starts, her fingers forming a steeple in front of her. "The podcast."

"What about it?" my mother says.

"I thought we discussed the importance of keeping the investigation insular, just for right now—" Williams starts.

"You honestly expected me to, what?" my mom cuts her off. "Protect you all forever? Not use the platform I spent my entire life building? Not do everything in my power personally to find Evie? Please."

What has she done?

"I had no possible way of knowing it would go like that," she adds.

I suddenly feel claustrophobic, nauseous. I swear I can feel the kale disintegrating into acid inside my stomach. I need air.

I walk outside and pull my phone out of my pocket, quickly googling a series of words that bring me to what I'm looking for almost immediately.

For the rest of the time the detectives are there, I sit outside, listening to the podcast from start to finish. Twice. In the end, the only thing that is clear to me is that if the world wasn't already suspicious of my mother, of her involvement in Evie's disappearance, of her character—they definitely are now.

Episode 349: "The Mysterious Appearance and Disappearance of Evelyn Davis" | *Darker: A True Crime Podcast*

August: Trust us, the SquatPot is going to change your life. You will never go to the bathroom the same way again. And that's a good thing. Use the code DARKER10 for 10 percent off your first order from SquatPot. That's D-A-R-K-E-R-1-0. Now back to our episode.

Kira: So, look, we've been building up the anticipation behind this reveal for a long time now . . . so let's just do it. We want to go ahead and welcome Erin Davis, Evie Davis's mother, to Darker today. She's going to be telling us what exactly has been going on in her world, confirming for the first time, exclusively, which rumors about her daughter's absence from social media are true and which aren't.

Kira: Mrs. Davis, welcome to Darker. Thank you so much for talking to us today. Though of course we wish it were under different circumstances.

August: Yes, welcome.

Erin: Hi. Yes. Me too. And you can call me Erin. Please. I'm not that old . . . [laughs]

Kira: Erin. Sure, yes.

Erin: I'm a huge fan of the podcast, and I just . . . I honestly feel a little starstruck right now talking to you girls.

Kira: Well . . . um, thank you. That's very kind. But actually, August is nonbinary, so . . .

August: My pronouns are they/them.

Erin: Of course they are.

August: Excuse me?

such a bad influence

Erin: Oh. I just meant that of course they are, that I should know that. I should have remembered that. I apologize.

Kira: [clears throat] *Well. Erin. Let's get right to the reason why you're here today, which are the rumors surrounding your daughter Evie's recent disappearance from social media. I understand you have an official statement you'd like to read.*

Erin: Yes, I do. [sniffles] *Just give me a minute. This is the first time I've said all of this out loud. It's just . . . it's a lot.*

Kira: I'm sure it is. Take your time.

Erin: Thank you. [takes a deep breath] *My daughter Evelyn Davis, or Evie as she's known to most people who love her, has not been seen or heard from in eleven days. Her last known location was a parking lot in Los Angeles, where she broadcasted on TikTok Live from her phone on the afternoon of June 12. Since then, Evie has not posted on any of her social accounts or attempted to make contact with her friends and family, which is completely out of character. We've been working with law enforcement to determine her whereabouts and bring her home safely, and while we thank the detectives for their work and have made some progress in locating her car and cell phone, the leads seem to be diminishing quickly. This is where we need all of your help. We are asking the public to share any and all information on where she could be by visiting FindEvieDavis.com or calling 1-800-FIND-EVIE. There's also a hashtag you can use to share anything you might know, or any tips: #FINDEVIE. We are beside ourselves with worry and desperate to have our friend, daughter, and sister home again. Thank you.*

Kira: We really appreciate you choosing Darker to spread the word about what you're going through right now. I think it will help our audience to have as much information as possible about the case thus far. I know they'll want to help as much as they possibly can. But . . . before we get into that—and I'm sure this is a sensitive subject, so forgive me for being so blunt, but I have to ask . . . is it true that detectives have instructed you not to speak to the media at this time?

olivia muenter

Erin: Yes.

August: So you're actively disobeying law enforcement's advice because . . . ?

Erin: Because the more people who know that Evie is missing, the faster we can find her. Because I'm not going to protect people who don't want a spotlight on their mediocre work, or lack thereof, just because they ask me to. Not anymore, at least.

August: Are you saying that law enforcement isn't doing their job?

Erin: I don't know what they're doing, to be quite honest. We are almost as in the dark as you are. That's why I'm here. To shine a light on all of it. To get answers.

Kira: Let's back up a bit, maybe. Can you walk us through this entire situation, from your point of view? Everything that's happened so far? What's been done to find Evie up to now?

Erin: Gosh, I don't even know where to begin, August.

August: She's Kira. I'm August.

Erin: Right, of course, I'm sorry. I'm just a little flustered. It's been . . . a journey. It's been overwhelming. That's why Evie's sister couldn't be here today to speak, actually. It's just too much for her. It's been too much for both of us.

August: Hazel, right?

Erin: Yes. Hazel's very private, but she wanted to be here too, very badly—to speak out and demand answers for her sister. In the end, she just couldn't bring herself to do it. So . . . I'm here, even though it is quite overwhelming.

Kira: Just start wherever is comfortable, Erin.

August: Or at the beginning. Like, waaaay back.

such a bad influence

Erin: What do you mean?

August: As in, the beginning of Evie's career. How she ended up on the internet in the first place.

Erin: Oh, well. Sure. If you think that's helpful . . .

Kira: I think what August means is that it would be beneficial for our audience to understand as much of Evie's life as possible up until this point, from your perspective.

Erin: Well, it does always make me smile to tell the story.

August: Smile? Even given how it all started?

Kira: We're very sorry for your loss, by the way. It's a lot of trauma for one person to endure.

Erin: Thank you. It is. But that's exactly why the entire journey still makes me smile, I think. Being on social media, all of the opportunities we've been blessed with . . . it all came from the worst moment of our lives. It made it bearable. Almost as if . . . I don't know . . .

August: It happened for a reason?

Erin: Exactly.

August: Wow.

Kira: [clears throat] Well. I guess, can you tell us a little bit about Evie, Erin? What she was like then, what she's like now . . .

August: If she had a choice in any of it, et cetera, et cetera.

Kira: August . . .

olivia muenter

Erin: I don't understand what you're implying by that. If she had a choice?

August: I mean, it's pretty simple. Don't you think that that's part of her story, too? Even now? Especially now? Don't you think that in order to talk about how you're protecting her today, we have to talk about how you've done—or some would say not done—that her entire life?

Erin: If you think that there's literally anything I could force that child to do, you clearly don't know my daughter. [laughs] From the second she was born, she had a mind of her own. She wanted to be in front of the camera. She wanted to perform. To share her personality, her likes, her dislikes, everything, with anyone and everyone who would listen. I couldn't have forced any of it on her if I wanted to—which I never did, for the record. I wanted her to love it all, yes, but she did. She wanted every bit of it.

August: That doesn't mean she could understand what any of it meant at five or six. The implications, the ripple effect of it all. Wanting to be on camera and understanding that footage will be seen by millions of people, by gross old men sitting in their basements . . . those are different things.

Erin: Look. I don't see how any of this will help find my daughter—that's what I'm here to discuss, nothing else. That is what we agreed to discuss. That's what we talked about.

August: Well, sure, that and how much money you would make from this, right?

Erin: I . . .

August: I was cc'd on those emails, too. What was the agreement you wanted, again, before you gave us an exclusive? Half of ad revenue? Or was it personal intros to advertisers we landed on instead because, you know, interview ethics?

Erin: This is not appropriate—

Kira: Erin, I apologize. This wasn't what August and I discussed either, was it,

such a bad influence

August . . .

August: *I mean, someone here has to be honest.*

Erin: [laughs]

August: *Is something funny?*

Erin: *Honest. It's an interesting word choice.*

Kira: *Listen, maybe we should just cut the interview here—*

August: *No, let her finish. What's funny about it? Tell us. Here's your chance. Your spotlight.*

Erin: *You really, honestly think you're better than me? Different? Because, what? You're younger? You're woke? Because you know exactly the right charities to donate to in order to distract your audience from the fact that you are capitalizing on the horrors of the world? People's deepest, darkest, most vile miseries? And you want to judge me? How I supported my child's success and fostered her career? You really want to do that while you're advertising fucking bidets as you discuss murder and rape like it's entertainment? Be my guest.*

Kira: *Erin, this is really not the place to—*

Erin: *You want to call out my request for revenue sharing? For making the introduction to advertisers? Fine. Then at least be honest about how you both knew what you got with me giving you this exclusive, too. You both know the kind of traffic it would bring. Wasn't it you, Kira, who asked for my statistics and engagement numbers, right after I explained that my daughter had vanished? That she could be in danger. You wanted to know the numbers because you knew you could use it to negotiate a higher ad rate. Or did you conveniently forget that part, too? You people, I swear to God . . .*

August: *You people?*

olivia muenter

Erin: Sorry, was that not the right pronouns, either?

Kira: Well, I think this has gotten a bit out of hand, you two. Let's just stop—

August: No, please. By all means, let's take it from Erin Davis, the expert on parenting. The person who monetized her daughter's most vulnerable years. Do you know that you posted 150 vlogs featuring Evie the year she turned eleven? That in half of those, she's at gymnastics competitions and swim meets and dance recitals? Barely dressed? As someone who seems very aware of statistics, I'm sure you noticed the same correlations I did when I started doing some research. That those are the videos with the most views. The most comments, many of them from men. I'm sure you saw it in real time, sifted through the much uglier feedback from perverts and hid it from what the public could see. And yet . . . you kept filming. Kept posting. The next year there was even more swim team content, even more gymnastics competitions. You had to fucking know. And yet you kept doing it. So, forgive me if I can't sit here and feel totally bad for you, or ignore the part that you had in exploiting your daughter, the very clear ways it could have something to do with why you're here today. But, you know, sure. Be my guest. Any other advice you'd like to pass along, Erin? To share?

Kira: No, really. I think we should just stop—

Erin: You know, I do have something. My advice would be for the two of you, and anyone else listening and nodding along, to get off the fucking high horse that lets you think you're doing anything other than the same exact thing I am: working with what you have and monetizing it. Oh, and fuck you, too.

Kira: Well, I don't think that's quite the—

August: She's gone, Kira. She left the Zoom.

Kira: Jesus Christ, August.

August: Personally, I think that went great.

CHAPTER 11

I don't go back inside to listen to what the detectives have to say. I already know. I can imagine, anyway. I've read through all the comments online, against my better judgment. I know it looks almost as bad for the people running the investigation as it does for my mom—for me, even, thanks to her implying that I knew about the podcast beforehand. But I imagine they'll survive the aftermath better than we will.

We. I hate that I'm thinking as a we again, that she's pulled me deeper into this mess, made it even uglier. That I'm lumped in with a person who would choose to do an interview like that, who makes it so clear that the worst things that happen to this family are just as much about attention and spotlight and money as they've ever been.

Darker had apparently released the episode outside of its usual schedule. This led people to conclude that the hosts thought it was important that people heard it right away—and that people heard all of it. It had been posted four hours ago, accompanied by a short bit of text that read: "The only thing that matters is finding Evie," paired with the same website, hashtag, and phone number my mom had mentioned for sharing tips. And from what everyone could gather, it hadn't been edited at all. Even the things that would have likely been easier for them to cut—the discussion of ad revenue, the criticism of the true crime genre, the clear lack of cohesion between the two hosts—were all left in.

There were some people expressing sympathy for my mom online, for our family. Who suggested that any normal person would be a wreck if their child had gone missing. Any normal person could snap at a stranger or make a poor decision. Any normal person would make choices to find their child, to get more information, that would seem desperate to someone else. But Erin Davis, others said, is not a normal person. Isn't that much obvious by now? Still others said, wait—was everyone letting *Darker* off the hook, too? Was what Erin said really that wrong? The stuff about selling bidets while selling stories about murder and rape? It might have been crass or aggressive, but was she really wrong? Maybe it's time we talked about that, too, people wrote in online discussion threads and through Instagram comments.

Most of all, the episode had seemed to set off an internet-wide panic that no one was really prepared for, even with all the rumors that had been swirling about my sister's absence from social media. Evie Davis was really, truly gone. Her lack of posts wasn't a social media fast or the prelude to a big rebrand, but a sign that she could be in serious danger. That the worst really could be possible. Everything is different now, and though part of me is relieved that more people know—that this doesn't just exist in our own miserable heads—another part of me hates it. It makes it real.

I've finally managed to put my phone down and take a deep breath of fresh air when I hear the back door close, and I look over to see my mom walk over where I'm sitting.

I'm not in the mood to talk about this. Not now.

She's drinking a glass of wine, and she hands me one, too, when she reaches where I'm sitting. I take it. We don't toast, which I'm grateful for. What is there to toast to now? Even surviving feels like failure at this point.

"Did they leave?" I ask, even though I heard the detectives' car pull out of the driveway twenty minutes ago.

"Yeah," she says. "They seemed more concerned with the podcast than the fact that they can't seem to figure anything out. Can't get the security footage. Can't get into the phone. 'We're doing everything we can with the resources we have access to, ma'am,' they say. Well, you know, so am I. That's what that was."

The last four words all blend together, and I know then that this isn't her first glass. I wonder if she had poured herself one before they even left. I'm sure the detectives would have loved that.

I snort. "That's all that was? Come on, Mom."

She sips, sinking into the seat next to me.

"It was a train wreck," I say. "You sounded . . . unhinged."

"Yeah, well," she starts. "What makes more sense to you in our situation? Someone staying cool, calm, and collected . . . or someone losing their shit? Having a meltdown?"

What she's saying is so reminiscent of some of the comments I read, almost word for word, that I'm somewhat impressed.

She blinks into the string lights that hang above our patio chairs. "It was a human moment."

"But you lied," I explain. "I didn't know about the podcast, like you said. I didn't want to be there."

"And you weren't."

"But you told them that I wanted to be . . . you know how many of my friends listen to that podcast? It makes me look . . ."

"Desperate?" she says. "Like that isn't what we are? Look at us. We have nothing to do but sit here and wait. I couldn't wait anymore, Hazel. I couldn't just do nothing."

"So what about the money stuff, then? How could you even think of leveraging the podcast for cash, or connections?"

She shakes her head as if she doesn't understand how I'm not putting this together.

"Eventually, if your sister doesn't come home, if she isn't found, do you know what we're going to have to do? Hire private investigators. With our own money. And I'm just going to go out on a limb here and say that isn't really feasible for you right now, given your situation . . ."

My mind flashes to the balance of my bank account, barely enough cash in my checking account to cover rent for the next month. I take a sip of my wine, and we both sit there staring at the night sky for a moment, silent.

"It wasn't always like this," she says, her eyes still fixed upward. "Or I wasn't, anyway, I guess."

It's such an out-of-character comment that goosebumps rise on my arm. I wait for her to keep talking, wondering if she will.

"Before your dad and I left New Hampshire, all I could think about was art. Pottery, to be specific. And I was good. I made these beautiful things out of nothing, built these shapeless pieces of clay into forms and textures that were surprising. Bold and soft, warm and cool. It wasn't like painting, people didn't know how to talk about it. What adjectives to use. But I'd always watch people look at my work . . . see how their eyes lingered on a piece. This feeling of creating beauty for the sake of it . . . I knew that it was all I ever wanted to do, or at least that nothing I did would ever feel as good as that."

For the first time in my life, I try to imagine my mom as a teenager. A teenager who's in love with art. It seems impossible. I must look as confused as I feel, as awkward, because my mom catches my expression and laughs.

"I know," she says. "It's hard to believe."

It is, but as the thought sinks in, it starts to make sense. If there's one thing a successful career on social media requires, it's an appreciation for how things look. For making people stop and stare. A talent for sculpting an aesthetic that people want more of.

"I saved up for the first two years of high school for my own potter's wheel, so I wouldn't have to use the one at school. Eventually, I had enough to get one secondhand from a local community college, and then it was all I thought about," she goes on. "Your dad would sneak out at night and tap on my window only to realize that I was in the garage making things, one lightbulb hanging above the wheel. I never got tired there. I always told him that I couldn't talk, I was busy, and he'd wait. Just sit there and watch me quietly."

There's a sadness in her voice that I haven't heard in years, not since my dad's funeral maybe. I hadn't thought in years about the fact that my parents had been high-school sweethearts. In the beginning, though, it had been part of the whole narrative, the sob story. High-school sweethearts. Beloved father. Gone.

"I think I fell in love with him then, just seeing him sitting there, watching me be happy," she says, and for the first time in more than a decade, I remember them together again. The way he rooted for her.

"By the time I was set to graduate, I had a whole portfolio of pieces. Dozens of them. Maybe more than a hundred. It's all I ever did and where every cent of the money I earned from babysitting jobs went. But my parents were . . . I don't know. Practical, I guess. They reminded me so often that they had worked their way up from nothing, that they had to fight for every single dollar. And they didn't do that just so I could choose a career that wasn't a career at all. They had come from so little, and in their mind it was only natural that I move a step beyond what they had done. A doctor. A lawyer. Anything but an artist."

I try to conjure memories of my maternal grandparents, and all I can think of is stilted Christmas dinners, gray hair, scratchy sweaters. They lived far away and both died before Evie was born. I've had so few conversations with my mom about her childhood that this feels totally foreign. Uncomfortable. Like she's supposed to be saying it all to someone else, but I'm the only one here. The thought crosses my mind that maybe who she really wants to say all of this to is Evie, but I push it down with another gulp of wine.

"I had applied to this prestigious ceramic course in Italy and kept it secret, but my dad found some pamphlet in my room and freaked out. They both just . . . lost it. I told them that I'd handle it, but they just dug their heels in. They said it didn't matter if I would pay for it, because what would happen after? They said they *certainly* couldn't afford to support me when I was unable to get a job after I finished 'arts and crafts.' It was a different time, I guess, with different expectations about what a career should look like, but . . . I don't know. It broke my heart, I guess."

I look down at my wineglass, now almost empty, and I am struck by a feeling of panic. Of knowing that if we were other people, this is the point when I would hug her, place my hand on her shoulder, offer comfort. But I can't get myself to do it, so I just sit and stare.

"I didn't know that," I manage.

"Why would you? I haven't talked about it in years," she says, throwing back the last drops of her wine. She gets up and walks toward the wine fridge attached to the outdoor kitchen, pulling out another bottle of sauvignon blanc. It's not the worst idea she's ever had.

"So . . . that's it, then? You decided not to go, just because they were against it?" I ask.

"Well, no, actually," she answers, pouring more wine in my glass. "I made a plan instead."

And suddenly I see a teenage version of my mother that I recognize.

"I had all these pieces I had spent the last two years making. So I sold my wheel for gas money and convinced Dad that we could take his van on the road that summer. We would travel the country, camp when we could, sleep in the car other times, and I'd sell my pieces at flea markets, craft fairs, boutiques. Then, when it was all sold, I'd figure out what to do next. Maybe it was the Italy course. Maybe it was opening a studio. It was a good plan, really. It made sense. Your dad didn't want to work at your grandpa's furniture warehouse anyway. Neither of us thought college was for us. The plan fit. I think I was proud of us, even then, for taking the time to figure out what we wanted. I honestly believed that it would all work out, even if it didn't."

I almost say "that does sound like you," but instead I just nod, waiting for what I know must be coming. She closes her eyes, like she's remembering the moment.

"My dad found out the week before we were supposed to leave. He was angry. Furious, really, but I thought . . . you know, he'll get over it. He has to. And by that point, I was eighteen. It didn't matter what he wanted. I was leaving either way. He was still drinking then, though, and when we got into an argument the night before your dad and I were supposed to leave, it just all exploded. He said it was a slap in the face after all the time and energy they had spent on raising me, educating me. I still thought he'd cool off, though. That I would prove to him one day that it all made sense. That I was right. I would make him see."

"Did he?" I press.

She peels the label off the side of the sweating wine bottle, shaking her head.

"No," she says. "But I was so convinced he'd eventually understand that I walked out that night. Went to your dad's. I figured things would cool off by the morning. But when I got back, he had broken every single piece I had packed for the trip. Everything I had ever made, really. It was all destroyed. All of it . . . just gone. I'm still surprised he didn't trash the van, too."

I feel my soul deflate, all those broken pieces jabbing into my insides.

"And then . . . we left anyway. Drove away that same day," she says. "I never sat at a potter's wheel again, but I still left. And honestly, thank God."

She still hasn't really looked at me, but she raises her glass anyway as a dramatic final flourish to the story, a "good riddance," maybe.

"I don't even know what made me tell you that . . . I guess I just . . . I know you look at me and you see every mistake I've ever made. Every worst quality. And I know there have been plenty. There are plenty. I do. But none of us—not even me—are one thing. It's all more complicated than our worst decisions or the slow-motion trainwrecks that make up our lives. I know you've . . ."

She lets out a small hiccup, and it breaks the seriousness of the moment for a second, but she carries on.

"I know you've always thought that I've loved your sister more—"

I start to protest, to push back on the idea that I'm jealous, or needy, but she holds up a hand to stop me.

"Let me finish. I know you've always thought I've loved your sister more, but it's never been that. Not once. It was more like . . . Evie needed me, period, no matter what, and you . . . well, you mostly just needed me to be better. And I just . . . I couldn't handle that."

My head is swimming, the back-to-back glasses of wine not helping. I repeat in my mind what my mother has just said. It's the kind of honesty that I feel before I understand it.

Before I can say anything, though, she stands up, tucking the two empty wine bottles under one armpit.

"I need to sleep," she says. "Tomorrow is going to be . . ."

I think of what tomorrow will be like. The media frenzy. The endless calls.

"It will be a lot," I say. "But maybe you're right . . ."

She raises an eyebrow at me, like she can't believe what she's hearing.

"I just mean that despite the mess . . . maybe it will drum up some leads . . . maybe it'll help us find her," I say. "And then the rest won't matter."

"I hope so, baby," my mom says, turning to walk back to the house.

Baby. She's always called me this. Or honey. Or sweetie. Or doll. It's intimate sounding, personal. But even now, after everything she just told

olivia muenter

me, the word lands like it always has, the same way it does when a stranger says it at a restaurant or a gas station. A thing that comes from habit more than sentiment. It feels nice, even if it's not real.

She's almost inside when I call out, surprising myself. "Hey, Mom?"

She turns, her gaze expectant, illuminated by the warm glow of the kitchen.

"Did you know?" I ask. "About the videos, the statistics? What they said in the podcast. The fact that whenever she was dressed a certain way, the views went up . . ."

She waits for a beat, her gaze fixed on her reflection in the glass door.

"The only thing I've ever really known for sure is that I want what's best for our family," she says, her voice flat. She opens the door and walks inside before I can say anything else.

"So do I," I say into the darkness, to no one.

But that's not really true.

I just want what's best for my sister.

Where in the World Is Evie Davis?

By Loren Fasuco

It's officially been two weeks since mega lifestyle influencer Evelyn Davis has posted online. Fourteen days of no Instagram stories or vlogs from the internet's little sister or best friend or dream girl, depending on who you're talking to. Fourteen days with no branded content from someone who is rumored to be the youngest person to ever garner seven figures from a sponsored TikTok. Fourteen days of silence.

The rumors, though, have been quite loud for almost as long as she's been gone. A quick Google search will land you in forums where people discuss where, exactly, Evie has gone. Is it a stunt? A way to drum up even more attention? A political statement? An allotted period of recovery from plastic surgery? Rehab?

Last week, Evie's mother and fellow social media star, Erin Davis, was interviewed about her daughter's disappearance on the beloved true crime podcast *Darker*, confirming what the internet had been speculating: Evie Davis is officially missing. It's been twenty-four hours since law enforcement was forced to issue a statement of their own, one in which they confirmed Evie's disappearance, and that they are continuing to search for Evie around the clock.

The internet is not giving up, either. Evie fans and critics alike seem dedicated to finding answers, sharing theories, and pointing fingers—anything to get to the bottom of where Evie has gone and why. As of publication, there are more than 5,000 posts under the #FindEvie hashtag, and that's only one iteration. It's concerning when any person goes missing, of course, but some might say this level of public attention and concern feels different. More intense. And it's not just because this person is beautiful, or young, or white (though, of course, that is always part of it), but because she feels so *close* to so many people. Evie isn't some distant, blurry stranger to all those people, but a face they see every day. A voice they recognize. Someone who's part of their day. For many, Evie Davis has been on their screens for as long as they've been looking at one. And it's not so easy to just let go of something that you've had access to for more than a decade. But this isn't the first time an influencer has disappeared from our screens.

Take @HeyMadisonLee (2.1 million followers) for example, the mommy blogger-turned-momfluencer who spent years posting the elaborate birthday cakes she made for her six children and many throwback photos of her bespectacled husband—only to stop altogether at the beginning of last year after criticism about a political post, though apolitical is really the better word for it. Madison posted an apology saying that she now understands "*everything* is political when you have a platform," but she's since turned off all comments and stopped posting, much to the horror of her dedicated followers. It has been more than a year since she was last online publicly. Still, you'll see her name pop up on message boards if you frequent the places that talk about influencers the most. There are reports she now lives with her family in the Midwest on a sprawling 1960s ranch. You'll still hear chatter from the dedicated people who follow her husband's private account, too. But for most of us, Madison remains gone.

There are darker shades of disappearing, too, of course. Take the mysterious case of Cheryl Danielsen, a twenty-eight-year-old Louisiana wife, mother, and momfluencer who made headlines in late 2019 after disappearing for nearly two months. After seven weeks of searches and nonstop media coverage, Danielsen wandered back into her home bloody and bruised on a Wednesday morning, explaining that she had been abducted from a jogging trail. It took a few more weeks for police and then, of course, the public, to discover that the entire event was staged by Danielsen, for reasons that are still mostly unclear to investigators. The evidence may be murky, but theories have been out there to scroll through since she disappeared. Some guess it was an affair turned botched attempt to escape her own life and the online persona she built. Others believe the opposite: it was all a stunt for more followers.

Again, there is no publicly available evidence to support any of these theories. But if we were to consider that the latter was true—that it was all a dark stunt for attention—then you could say it was a successful endeavor for Danielsen, who gained more than 750,000 followers in the time she was missing. She hit one million three days before she was arrested and charged with making a false report. Currently, she is serving month twelve of an eighteen-month sentence. Her account is silent, but it's still there. And one day she may be back on our screens, and we'll all find out together how long the internet's collective memory is.

And then there are stories that are less flashy, easier to forget. Take Dani Tan, a clean beauty influencer who built her brand and following by outlining the ways our deodorant and other personal care products were "poisoning" us, according to her. One day she was posting five ways to use apple cider vinegar, and the next she was gone. Tan simply stopped signing on one day in 2021, leaving her followers—"Tanatics," as they called themselves—to wonder where she had gone. Was she going through a breakup, or having health issues? Did she hate them? Hate Instagram? If you know where to look online, there's still chatter about Dani. People have reported spotting her on a little-known trail in Joshua Tree, but others are skeptical. And either way, Dani continues to stay silent on social media. Believe it or not, Dani Tan doesn't think she owes anyone an explanation.

So what *do* influencers owe the fans that built their platforms, their wealth? The answer is a matter of opinion, or maybe of values. What are the boundaries of a job like this? What qualifies as entertainment, or as a relationship? Wherever you land on these questions, it does make you wonder if the Cheryls and Danis and Evies and Madisons of the world are getting sick of us the way so many of us seem to get sick of them. Even the mysterious SABI, the go-to source for all things influencer

olivia muenter

gossip and rumors (plus surprisingly thoughtful, witty commentary about it all), has seemed to quietly fade into the background lately, leaving its 25,000+ subscribers hungry for more, waiting, asking similar questions to the ones we all have about Evie Davis: What happened? Why did it happen? What do we do now?

For now, if you ask the police and her family, Evelyn Davis is missing. If you ask the internet, however, Evelyn Davis is everywhere. One look under the #FindEvie hashtag and you will be met with dozens of blurry photos of women around the world who look, from one angle or another, like Evie. She's on a yacht in St. Barts. She's on a ferry in Croatia. She's in a museum in London. She's on a hike in Asheville. And though law enforcement has found her car and her phone, details that media outlets have run wild with, they insist that evidence has stopped cold after that. The rest of us know the feeling. There's no evidence that she just went shopping at the mall. No evidence of her go-to order from Sweetgreen. No evidence of what she thinks of the newest season of *Love Is Blind*. No evidence of her morning smoothie, her evening lemon water, her latest workout set. Her opinion on abortion bans. Her thoughts about Botox. There's none of that for us to sift through anymore.

Maybe she had a mental health episode, the internet says. Maybe her boyfriend killed her, the internet suggests with a shrug. Maybe she's exactly where she wants to be or maybe she's in the darkest, scariest corner of the earth, the kind of place where women disappear to when they wear the wrong thing or give someone the wrong idea or are too nice or not nice enough. All the speculation can sound like concern on its face, or maybe just curiosity if you're a bit more cynical. But if you look a bit closer what you'll find is what has always been there. A raw, shameless need. A hunger to know everything there is to be known about a person. You'll see exactly what it looks like when people are suddenly denied access to something they've consumed for years.

The Cut has reached out to Erin Davis and law enforcement for comment but has not received a response at the time of publication.

CHAPTER 12

Twenty-two felt like it would last forever. I had finally graduated from college with a journalism degree (plus a mountain of student debt that I ignored) and found a studio apartment, a roommate who was willing to split the rent with me, and a food service job that paid just enough to get me from week to week. I was old enough to be totally independent and young enough that it didn't matter that I was striking out on job after job, barely making ends meet.

Sasha, my roommate, had moved to New York City from Florida, determined to make it as a photographer. It felt like it fit perfectly with my goal of becoming a reporter, a real journalist, someone who wrote stories that made people feel as much as think. I dreamt of crafting human-interest stories, deep dives into strange, specific pockets of culture and society. I pictured sitting down with someone and watching them settle into the conversation and realize that I wasn't going anywhere. That they had my full attention. It was what I had dreamt of having as a kid. A person to listen, to ask me the right questions.

Beyond our career goals and the fact that we had left painfully hot climates, Sasha and I had little in common, but that didn't matter much at twenty-two. We were both flailing spectacularly, but determined, and the first time it snowed that winter, we both stood outside with our arms outstretched, tongues stuck out, waiting, still amazed by something as mundane as true, changing seasons.

We both worked odd hours and spent the rest of them chasing various

olivia muenter

highs—booze, sex, love—and debriefing about our adventures at a diner one block from our apartment, a jumbo-sized plate of greasy fries always placed between us. At the time, it felt like we were in it together. Even after a year of restaurant jobs and bartending and interviews that went nowhere, we weren't as discouraged or as worried as we should have been. I would have said then that it was because we were on our way, that I knew I'd make it at *some* point, but I know now that I was just distracted. I spent so much time obsessing over the latest bearded guy I had met at a bar, or the cook at work I hooked up with (often enough to convince myself he actually liked me) that I didn't have time to assess anything else. I didn't worry about credit card bills stacking up into infinity, piling neatly on top of my already overwhelming student debt. I didn't consider that I couldn't share a one-room apartment for the rest of my twenties. I didn't ask myself what it would mean if I didn't get hired by a newspaper or a magazine or a website for another year, or another year after that. If I had spent less time with Sasha debating what a text meant or recapping the highlights of a particularly wild weekend, then maybe I would have had more time to *make it*. Maybe I could have avoided it all. The move back home. The new job. The way I lost the new job. The decision I made with my mom. Everything.

We'd spend entire afternoons nursing fountain Diet Cokes with unlimited refills, the bubbles easing our turbulent, alcohol-soaked guts. Every time, it'd be the same. I cared too much. I wanted too much. I drank too much. And always, for both of us, we were on our phones too much. It became a game between us, eventually.

"I want to put my phone in a suitcase," I'd say, my thighs sticking to the vinyl seat of the booth, straw swirling in the caramel-colored liquid.

"With a lock and a 243-digit combination," Sasha would offer in response, playing along.

"But this lock is also magic, so in order to open it I'd also have to provide the secret musical code," I'd add.

"Ah, yes, of course." She'd nod along seriously. "And that secret code would be the exact lyrics and choreography to Rihanna's 'Pon de Replay.'"

"Too easy," I'd quip.

"Hmm," Sasha said. "The exact lyrics and choreography to Rihanna's

'Pon de Replay,' but . . . *backwards*."

"Better, but honestly, do you know me at all?" I'd use a french fry to point toward myself. "That's simply too easy."

We'd go back and forth like this for half an hour, joking about the lengths we'd both go to in order to make sure that we didn't once again call a person who treated us like shit. That we didn't respond to the late-night texts, that we didn't send them ourselves. That we stopped ordering delivery ramen at three a.m. just because we could, and stopped trying to figure out the subtext of a crush's tweet for hours instead of applying to jobs.

"These things are the root of all of our problems, I swear," she'd say, eyes fixed on her Instagram feed as she talked.

It was just a game, of course, but really, it was the perfect way to expertly skirt the fact that if either of us really wanted to, we could stop looking at our phones right now. We could turn them off, put them in a drawer, take a break. We could do it for a day, or a weekend, and we'd be just fine. But we both knew we wouldn't. The other part of the game was knowing that we wouldn't, that we were as chained to our phones as every other person our age—that neither of us wanted to be the one to say, "If you do it, I'll do it."

Neither of us wanted to get rid of the instant ability to numb out, either. It was too easy, too present, more socially acceptable than any other vice we had, though I would venture to guess it wasn't much healthier than any of those things, at least not emotionally. Our phones were a steady stream of distraction from anything that really mattered, a welcome source of dopamine. And the inevitable emotional crash that they brought? Well, I guess we decided, like everyone else in the world, that it was all worth it. Right?

In my most clearheaded moments, I'd scroll through my phone and see the damage of a weekend spread out like an intervention: The messages I shouldn't have replied to. The Instagram posts I shouldn't have liked. The credit card statement that made my throat tighten. I'd see it all and consider, for a minute, that I should buckle down. Get serious. Fix my life. *But am I really that weak?* I thought. Did I really have that little willpower? Why should I be the one that has to give up the dopamine, the fun, the excitement? It was the first time in my life that I wondered if maybe Evie and I were feeling the same way—that maybe she had always felt this way.

I'd often think to call her during moments like these and remember that she was in school, that by the time she'd be home I would be working at the restaurant. I'd check her Instagram instead, making a note of the ads, the organic posts, the small details. Evie was twelve then, not quite a teenager yet, but I could see the ways her content was shifting, maturing. Each month, there were fewer partnerships that seemed to be handpicked by our mom and more of her own content. Silly stuff. Off-the-cuff, in-the-moment photos and videos. I could still spot the photos that had been Facetuned, but the edits were a little more obvious. It made me think that she was doing it herself now, rather than Mom. I didn't know if that made it better or worse.

I texted her once that year, thinking of Sasha's and my game.

Do you ever wish you could just throw your phone to the bottom of the ocean? I wrote.

It was a few hours before she replied, my phone buzzing in my back pocket as I walked home from a waitressing shift.

Boy troubles? her text read.

I almost snorted in surprise, and then I felt my face go hot. I still liked to think that Evie thought of me as her older, cooler, important sister living in New York. Her sister with a journalism degree from a prestigious college. An apartment in Brooklyn. Is this the image she had of me now, from Mom, or maybe just my own Instagram?

First of all: How dare you, I texted back.

Second of all: No. I just don't think I've ever asked you if you ever felt as overwhelmed with it as I do. I mean, you must. Times like a thousand. Right?

This time, she replied instantly.

Idk, not really? Is that weird?

Yes, I thought. It is kind of weird.

Before I could say anything, though, she texted again.

Mom says when you love something, nothing is ever *that* hard. It's kind of like that, I guess? idk

It should have comforted me, maybe, this idea that social media was my little sister's passion. If other kids had soccer and piano and poetry and she had . . . Instagram, that was fine, right? But it unsettled me.

I typed out three different responses before I deleted them, conscious of sounding judgmental, or harsh.

So you never think about what it would be like if you woke up tomorrow and it was all just gone? I wrote.

I'd feel like I was living on a different planet lol

· ·● ● ●· ·

If there ever was a time to destroy my phone, or at least put it away for a few hours to protect my mental health, it's now. Four days after the podcast went live, the updates from the detectives have become few and far between and the media attention is constant. Suffocating in a way that is anything but helpful. I scroll through Twitter, Instagram, Facebook, TikTok like a zombie and all I can think about is the game I used to play with Sasha. Locked suitcase. A 243-digit combination. I want to get this thing far, far away from me.

Even the most promising tips that have emerged since the interview— the few that have stuck out among the heaps of utter bullshit and attention-grabbing fake headlines—have proved unhelpful. Still, it's only too easy to keep refreshing the feeds, keep staring at the photos, type out a message to some online amateur sleuth posting an obscure theory and then delete it, even if I knew she wasn't in any of the beautiful places people wanted her to be. A yacht. A beachside bar. A tiny mountain town. I felt it.

What's worse is that it's all become a steady stream of entertainment for the world; there are even TikTok accounts dedicated to posting updates on the case, so they can be the first to share the latest news. The "news" is almost always an unsubstantiated rumor.

I hate the phrase *the case*. I hate that even now, there's a new way for the world to dehumanize my sister, to boil her down to a single word. A case. An influencer. A girl. But I can't stop looking at any of it, either. I'm afraid if I do, I'll miss something. An update. A call. A sign. Every time I scroll, it feels like the very next thing I see will lead me to something useful. Or maybe it's the thing after that. Or the thing after that.

Until finally, it does.

I'm refreshing my Instagram feed for the tenth time in an hour when I see the post. Shiny and new, no likes yet. It takes me a minute to realize it's real. That it's not from a fan account or spam or an imposter. No, it's Evie's account, the thumbnail of her profile image the same as it's been since she was twelve, a close-up of her eye partially obscured by a swoop of auburn hair. It's hers. A grid post with some text. I force my brain to slow down, to stop jumping to the end or reading every other word, searching for something important instead of starting at the beginning.

Hi everyone! I know there's been a lot of speculation about where I've been. But I wanted to let everyone know that I'm doing absolutely fine. Better than ever, really. Thank you for your messages. I'll see you in the real world.

I read it again.

And then a third time, then a fourth.

By the fifth time I read it, I hear my mom scream upstairs.

CHAPTER 13

It feels off. From the minute I see the post and read the text I know something is wrong. The image, though, is familiar. Evie had showed it to me a couple years ago during one of our long drives between Vegas and Phoenix after a weekend spent together. I'd meet Mom halfway sometimes, but usually I'd drive the whole way, enjoying the distraction-free time with Evie. We'd turn the whole thing into an event, a road trip movie montage complete with curated snacks and playlists.

She thrust her phone into my line of vision, the photo frozen on her screen.

"It's fine, I mostly just use intuition to drive anyway," I'd joked, pushing her hand down. "Vision is merely a secondary benefit."

"Isn't it great?" she said. "The photo?"

My eyes darted quickly toward the image, only for a second, studying the photo. It was a cactus, not dissimilar to the thousands we passed on that drive, or on most drives we've ever been on together. On top of the cactus, though, there was a balloon, its red string tangled in the spikes.

"What's it say?" I directed my eyes back to the road. "The balloon?"

"Congratulations." Evie laughed. "Great, right?"

I roll through the memory in my head, willing it to go on, but it won't.

And then what? Did I ask her why she liked it? What it meant to her? If she was the one who took it, or if it was something she found online? It couldn't have been more than two or three years ago that she showed me, but when I search, the memory fades to black.

I glance again at the Instagram post, the balloon's cheery message sprawled across my screen, and I feel it in my gut. Something about this is wrong. I know it *should* settle me; this is proof of life, right? Something we've been desperate for. No one should have this photo but Evie. She's telling us herself that she's okay. But all I feel is dread.

"Holy shit, holy shit, holy shit, holy shit," my mother says, bounding down the stairs. "She's . . . she's alive? She's okay?"

I silently nod from where I'm seated, phone in my hand, the post still pulled up, frozen. I have to remind myself that this assuages my worst fear, the one that had been slowly sinking into me with each passing day. The longer it's been since Evie disappeared, the more often I fall asleep each night imagining the worst-case scenarios. The specifics of her fear. Of what it would be like to know it's all ending. I imagine things I don't want to: Dirty hands crushing her windpipe, the world fading around her. A sharp blade pressing into soft skin. Rock cracking through a skull. Desert sand pouring into open wounds. I wondered if there's feeling then, or knowing, or if there's just pain. Would she have thought about how she was going to get out of this and survive? Or is it simpler, more primal? Maybe the only thought that would occupy her brain is: air, relief, the end.

I tried to calculate the exact tipping point so many times, the point of suffering that would make you wish for the end more than for life. I didn't want to think about any of it, but I had spent so many nights trying not to go there that eventually I just let the thoughts flood in. I was too exhausted to fight it.

So I know I should be relieved now. Elated. But all I feel is the same familiar sense that something is very, very wrong. I can't access the joy my mom seems to be feeling. I glance over at her, and then I see it. A cloud passes over her face. Anger.

"How could she do this?" she whispers, so quietly that I almost don't hear it. "To leave . . . to leave is one thing. But then to do this without even calling me first. Without even explaining *why* she left. People know us *together*," she goes on. "A unit. Evie and Erin. I mean, do you know what people are going to think now, Hazel? That I'm a monster. That I pushed her to do this. That she ran away from me like she's a battered child or something."

I cringe at the comparison.

"Before? Maybe some people thought she hated me. But now . . . God. What am I supposed to say to everyone? That I heard from her the same time the rest of the world did?"

I study her face, the anger mixed with panic. For a moment I had gauged that her reaction was something closer to mine, that she had an inkling that this post shouldn't be taken at face value. But *this* is what is bothering her?

"No brand is going to want to touch me now," she says. "Not after this."

I am tempted to say: Is that really the only reason? And: Haven't you known that was the case for a long time? But I don't. It's the same as it's always been, even now; Evie is as responsible for my mom's career as she is for her own. It's the first time I consider that maybe all the attention in the past two weeks had been welcome, somehow. The podcast. The rumors. Gavin's vlogs. The endless online mentions of Erin Davis, links to her old videos going around. View counts and engagement levels that had been stagnant for years finally going up. Maybe she's been enjoying being back in the spotlight, alone, more than I realized.

"This is a nightmare," she says.

On that, at least, we agree.

"Are you sure it's her?" I finally say. "Could she have been hacked?"

My mom's head snaps in my direction and she blinks, as if she hasn't considered this.

"The real world . . ." I say, quoting the post as I study it. "It doesn't even sound like her."

I watch the comments populate on the post. It now has 12,000 likes.

By the time the detectives call us to tell us they're investigating the legitimacy of the post, that they'll be in touch soon, it has 50,000.

And when they arrive at our house that evening, hours later, it's approaching half a million.

As soon as I see the detectives' faces, I know that something is wrong. Not because they look sad, or worried, but because, for the first time since I met them, they look relaxed. Buxton looks more at ease than he has since I met him more than a week ago. Williams looks so well-rested that it occurs to me that she's been exhausted during every previous conversation we've had. And as the four of us sit around my mother's kitchen table, I know. I know that they're going to tell me that the message was real. That they've confirmed it was her, somehow. And that she isn't coming home, not because she's hurt or lost or in danger but because she simply doesn't want to.

I also know that I think they're wrong.

"Evie is an adult," Williams says after she shares what they've learned, that the Instagram message led them to an unnamed source who was able to corroborate that the message was real, and ultimately confirm that Evie is alive and well. "And that means that, technically, she's not a runaway—even if it feels like that to you, Erin."

My mom bristles.

"So, what? You're just not going to tell us what this source is?" my mom pushes. "Who they are? This is absurd."

"What if . . . what if she was forced to post that? Blackmailed or . . . threatened?" I ask.

I flash back to one theory I had read on an internet sleuths forum yesterday. It proposed that the man who had approached her car during the TikTok Live was an obsessed, lifelong Evie fan, a man named Charlie who had commented obsessively on all of Evie's content, especially the younger stuff. He had left hearts in the comments of every dance recital video, every swim competition montage, and people online had noticed. On all her videos, all of my mom's vlogs, he was the person who showed up in the comments the most often, they said. By far. I went back and checked myself after I read the theory, feeling guilty that I had never noticed. His wasn't the only username that popped up repeatedly, not by a long shot, but they were right. His comments were always there. He had been watching Evie's content for years. More than a decade.

"What if it was him in the Live?" someone had theorized. "What if he took her and brought her back to somewhere in the middle of nowhere, insisted that he wants her to stay little forever? I could see it."

After scrolling to the end of the comments in the forum, I could see it, too.

Obsessed fans aren't exactly a novelty in Evie's world, though. Or my mom's either. I think of two years ago when Evie and I had been lounging by the pool and Mom emerged from the house, waving her phone in the air.

"Done," she says. "They're officially banned."

I had no idea what she was talking about, but when I glanced over at Evie for an explanation, she looked relieved. She leaned back in the chair, and I could see every muscle in her body relax. "Thank God," she said.

My mom did a little fist bump into the air, and Evie smiled, doing the same motion in return, like a victory dance. I felt like a third wheel. My mom started to walk toward us, but then her phone rang. She held up a finger signaling that she'd be right back.

"Some lunatic on Instagram," Evie said. Her eyes were closed, lids translucent in the light. Every vein was illuminated, tiny blue rivers cutting through sunlight. "They wouldn't stop bombarding every sponsored post and story with comments, lies, insults . . . disgusting, next-level stuff. I mean, not just one or two comments a month, but I'm talking every single day, multiple times a day. For months now. To the point that brands have been bringing it up in meetings, like, 'Uh, who's this weirdo? Should we be worried? Should you?'"

I didn't know if I felt worse that I hadn't noticed this person in her comments already, or that this was the first time anyone had told me about it.

"That's horrible. I wish you told me sooner."

She turned her head toward me so that her chin was touching her shoulder when she smiled, eyebrows raised half an inch. "Hazel," she said. "Come on."

"What?"

"You would have freaked out," she said, laughing. "You would have been guarding my door with a steak knife or something. Day and night."

"And that would be a bad thing how, exactly . . ."

"Oh, it would have been great." She laughed. "Not creepy at all."

She reached for the sunscreen stick on the side table between us and applied some to her nose where freckles had started to bloom.

"If there's anything I've learned in this fucked-up world of social, it's that taking care of shit like this . . . it honestly just comes down to what

olivia muenter

everything else does: knowing the right people." She shrugged. "When you know the right people you can take away someone's ability to hide behind a screen faster than you might think. And, as you know, Mom knows everyone."

"She does," I said, my voice straining to keep my tone neutral, measured.

"I mean, don't get me wrong, she's terrifying, too," she said. "Just in a different way than you."

"Ah, yes, an 'I will ruin your entire life, both online and otherwise' kind of way rather than an 'I can maybe use my car keys as a weapon if cornered' kind of way," I mused.

"See?" She smiled, turning to face the sun again. "You get it."

· · · • · · ·

I tell all of this to the detectives. The banned accounts. The theories circulating online. Williams gives me a look that is all pity, that seems to say she's disappointed that she can't tell me more, or maybe that I haven't guessed more myself. I hate it.

"Based on our source, we are confident that she wasn't coerced by anyone," Buxton adds.

Their source.

Who could that possibly be? What aren't they telling us, and why?

"Unfortunately, disappearing is not a crime when it's your choice. Not when you're over eighteen," Williams adds. "I know it may feel like we're being deliberately obtuse here . . . that we're leaving you in the dark now. But please understand that we gave more care and attention to this case than we would to a lot of others that are very similar. You'd be surprised how many young adults simply choose another life one day. But because of her notoriety, because of the implications of that TikTok Live, because you all claimed it was so extremely out of character for her, we went above and beyond here, despite what you may think. But again . . . she is an adult."

"An adult . . ." my mom sneers, her forehead resting on her hands. "She lived here. She worked here. With me. Her mother. She didn't even clean her room. Do her own laundry. File her own taxes. How, exactly, is that adulthood? Please. Tell me."

"It's what the law says, ma'am," Buxton says, and I wonder if I'm the only one who notices a small trace of a satisfaction in his expression, like part of him is glad to see her feel bad after she made him look bad on the podcast.

"I'm sure this is difficult after the . . . trauma of this experience," Williams offers. "But as hard as it might be to understand, this is the best outcome we could have hoped for."

"Oh, is it?" My mom laughs. "Is it really?"

"Mom . . ." I start, already exhausted by this conversation. Embarrassed that she's giving them even more reason to believe that Evie would want to leave her. Us.

"I have lost *everything*, Hazel. And they're sitting here saying that there's nothing I can do about it. That it's all fine. Best-case scenario," she says, her voice breaking. "No daughter. No business. No credibility."

Both detectives look at me for a moment, like they wonder if I realize what she's just said, how she's erased me in real time as I'm sitting right next to her and, somehow, invoked money now. The business of it all. I feel my face go hot at their expressions, embarrassed that they think this would surprise me. Haven't they been paying attention? Don't they know that I know my place here?

I know when my time is up, too. When it's time to go.

I spend the rest of the meeting trying to name the strange feeling that's seemed to burrow its way into my chest and stay there. I know I should feel lighter, free of the anxiety that's organized the contents of my brain since my sister went missing, the worries that have robbed me of sleep, of focus, of comfort, but I don't. I can't stop going over the Instagram post in my mind, all the ways it doesn't sound like my sister.

But maybe this is what my sister sounds like now. Maybe this is how she talks. Maybe it would seem exactly like her if I had been paying attention for the past six months, if I had taken the calls that I had started to ignore because I was too depressed to talk, too guilty, too insecure to admit all the ways I had failed.

My friends had looked so disappointed when I said I was moving back west, taking the only thing that resembled a reporting job that I could find. I couldn't do it anymore, I said. Weird hours. Clothes always smelling of grease. Never enough energy to hustle to get the job I had gone to college for, or to pay off my student loans.

It was so clear that they thought I was giving up, especially Sasha, but to me it was what had to be done. I would get my shit together. I would be closer to my sister. I would spend her last few years of childhood showing her that success didn't have to look like one thing. And then, by the time she was eighteen, I'd have enough money saved to go back to the East Coast. I'd have clips and bylines and a resume that I could build into an actual career. My own apartment. A life that would make Evie want something different than the only world she had known. Maybe she'd come with me. Decide a career in social media wasn't really for her. Do something different, just like I was doing.

I knew that Sasha wasn't wrong. That leaving New York was a little like failing. That I had had this big dream and I had let it die for something more practical. But I had a plan. I was like my mother that way, I guess.

But I wasn't Erin Davis—not in the ways that mattered. And when everything fell apart in Vegas, and I somehow ended up in a shittier, darker place that I had ever been in New York, I became a version of myself I didn't like. I ignored Sasha's texts until they didn't come anymore, too embarrassed to admit I had somehow failed at this, too.

It was all a perfect example of why Evie couldn't have possibly looked up to me, or considered a different type of career for herself. I had nothing in me anymore that felt admirable, like something she would envy, or want, or dream about. I know now it's why I made the choices I did last year. Why when my mother offered me an out, I took it. Why I didn't stop to think that I could lie for only so long. That eventually it would be hard for me to even look at my sister, let alone feel close to her.

I know this is why I missed something. Because I had to have missed something, something big, for what they are telling me about my sister to be possible.

By the time the detectives get up to leave, my mother's rage has morphed into messy, heaving sobs. Williams and Buxton share a look that says this is their cue and announce that they'll call us with any new information as they wrap up the investigation. It's so casual that I wonder if they're going to add, "And if you want to leave us a review on Yelp, that'd be much appreciated," but they just shake my hand and walk out the front door.

It's not until I've closed it that I realize I need to ask one more time. In a split second, I open the door again and follow them to their car, closing the door behind me.

"You're sure?" I ask, and they both spin around, though Buxton looks more surprised to see me than Williams, who seems to relax when she realizes it's just me and not my mom. For the first time since we met, her face is all empathy.

"We are fairly certain, Hazel, yes," she says. "I know it's hard. But these things happen."

"I just, I know her, and it feels like . . ." I start. But no. I will not be like my mother. I will not assume ownership of my sister. I will not be so desperate to have a person in my life that I will ignore what they want, what they say, what they do. Not when I don't deserve their trust at all. I will not. I will not. I will not. And yet . . .

Williams walks toward me, leaving the driver's side door halfway open.

"Hazel," she says, putting her hand on my shoulder. "I don't know why. Sometimes this is how it goes. It's not really our job to know the exact 'why' when it comes to adults. But . . . I mean . . ."

She pauses, glancing at the house looming over us, and I understand. What she wants to say is: *Look at who she lived with. Look where she lived. Do you blame her?*

"From what I can tell, your sister has been working and moving through this world like an adult for a long time now. In a lot of ways," she says quietly. "The money, the choices, the pressure . . . those are all adult things. Now imagine handling all of that while you're living with your boss . . . your mom? Your best friend? I don't know. I don't claim to understand all the dynamics here. You know more than I do. But I think we can both agree that your sister was more mature than most people probably give her credit for."

Again, she glances toward the house. I know what she means. That my mother underestimated her. But I'm not my mother. Even if I've made some bad choices, I'm still not her. It's different.

olivia muenter

"I just . . . she and I were close . . ." I say. "She would have told me . . ."

"Maybe she did, I don't know," she offers, and it feels like pity. "In her own way. Maybe you just missed it. Sometimes in cases like this, everything only becomes clear later. It takes time. Distance."

I nod, a reaction more than an agreement.

"Can I give you some advice?" she says, and I nod again. "Go back to your own life. Get out of here. Evie made a choice, you know? A hard one, probably. We have to respect that. You owe it to yourself to make some choices of your own now, don't you think?"

I resent the implication that I don't know how to do that. I want to tell her that I've been making choices for a long time now. A choice not to want the same things my mom and Evie wanted. A choice to leave home. To make my own way, my own career. All things that have only left me more alone.

But I just nod again, and she squeezes my shoulder gently before getting into the car.

"It'll get easier," she says before ducking into the driver's seat and rolling her window down. "You'll be okay, Hazel." But I believe that part less.

CHAPTER 14

I walk back into the house and immediately start packing up my overnight bag, the one I had thrown a few pieces of clothing into back when Gavin first called me, when everything somehow felt both more horrible and more bearable than it does now. My mom doesn't say anything as I walk down the stairs with my bag over my shoulder. We both know that there's no need for me to be here now, not really.

"Headed back to my place," I say. I expect her to stay seated, to ignore me as I walk out the door, same as she did last year, but she stands to see me go.

"You know I'm here if you need me," she says slowly, like it feels as awkward for her to say as it does for me to hear. "Right?"

"Yeah . . ." I say, my body tensing. "I just . . . need some space right now. After everything."

"I get it," she says, and her face says that she really does.

She gives me a half hug that I don't lean into, but as I start to pull away, she whispers something in my ear.

"Baby . . ." she says, her arm gripping me closer to her. And though I know I shouldn't, maybe it's the exhaustion that makes it so easy for me to settle into the affection for a split second. To let myself be comforted and admit that I need it. Or I need her, maybe.

"If you know where she is, you need to tell me," she finishes, stroking my hair. "You have to."

I pull away, feeling somehow even lonelier than I did ten seconds ago.

olivia muenter

Before I can see her reaction, I'm in my car, my bag flung in the passenger seat. I drive the whole four hours and forty-five minutes to my apartment in silence. No music. No podcasts. No thoughts, if I can help it. The silence feels like safety.

The view out the window is unchanged from the last time I was here, the same familiar shades of brown and green sandwiching the highway. The sky stark blue above. Eventually I let it all blur together until it's nothing but color, until I can feel it more than I can see it. I pick at a patch of dry skin on my face with one hand as I drive with the other. I can't remember the last time I drank water. Put on moisturizer. I feel as brittle as the scruff of desert plants out the window, the few things that have managed to adapt and survive here over time. Miracles, really. Any other living thing would die out here in time. As I approach Vegas, I feel that, too. Like there's not a single good thing that could survive in me either.

I feel guilty that part of me wants them to be wrong. That part of me wants to believe she didn't just choose this, to leave us. Leave me. The feeling that there is something I'm missing, that everyone is missing, sinks through me and sits at the bottom of my stomach like a rock. It piles up against every rumor I'd read on the internet, every conspiracy theory that has crossed my mind, everything I know about my mother, myself. Everything I thought I knew about my sister. It's sitting beside everything else I've pushed down over the last two weeks, a tiny monument to my panic.

But I walk myself through it again: if it were true that she didn't leave of her own free will, other things would have to be true, too. It would mean she is hurt. Or scared. Or dead. The detectives were right. If this was her choice, then it's better than the alternatives. And I have to live with that.

When I pull into the parking lot of my apartment building, it finally hits me. The grief. The loss I'm now left with. The feeling that I'm supposed to be thankful for because it's not death or violence. Because my sister is apparently still in the world, even if she's not the sister I knew.

Without thinking, I open my phone, the surest way to stop feeling. To focus on something else. I check my DMs on Instagram, and there are five new messages since I've last been on my phone. Two of them are a version of "Hey, girl! Saw the news. Can't believe you're going through all of that" that were sent by people I had known years ago, in past jobs, college. Not even friends, I realize as I click through, but acquaintances. It shouldn't surprise me; acquaintances are all I've had for a while now. I can imagine the series of events that led to them messaging me, the BOGO margaritas, the friends they looked at and told "Actually, omg, I totally forgot—I, like, know Evie Davis. Well, I know her sister. See, we're friends on Instagram and everything" before sending the message.

I delete both of them without reading them all the way through. There's a third message from Ashlyn, Evie's former best friend, sent right after the search, with her number included in the body of the message. I had thought to call her but was waiting for the right moment, maybe. For the right words to admit I didn't know about anything she had implied.

The fourth is from a distant relative, a cousin of a cousin of a cousin who always seemed to come out of the woodwork whenever my mom or Evie were on the news.

She's just brought so much joy to my life, you know? I can't believe this.

I roll my eyes.

People have talked about my sister this way for years; I'd once gone to get my hair colored and the stylist couldn't stop saying it once she realized who I was.

I've just loved watching her grow up.

I can't believe how old she looks now! How mature!

I remember when she won her first gymnastics competition!

They said this like she was some distant niece they were keeping up with through Facebook instead of someone they'd never met and probably never would. But it was always the same, this sense of amazement and gratitude. People seemed to regard watching my sister get older as some sort of gift, even when they had their own children at home. It was like they were somehow too close to those kids to notice the changes. Too tired to view any of it as a gift or privilege when it wasn't packaged as carefully as my sister's life was, all the pain and strife edited away.

"These are the same people who get mad when I do change," Evie told me once, not long before I lost the job at the Vegas newspaper. "Who message me things like 'So disappointed to see you no longer embrace your natural beauty' when I get highlights or post about antiaging skin care." She rolled her eyes.

I knew she was joking, that maybe she was just trying to deflect the attention to remind me of the darker side of admiration, that being beloved isn't all that great. But I was distracted. Just as she had started talking, an email had popped up on my phone from my boss, telling me about a correction I needed to make online as soon as possible. I had written about a new company for a digital story and had spelled the CEO's last name incorrectly. I scrolled through our correspondence, and sure enough, I had made a mistake, even though I could have sworn I had double-checked the name before. Triple-checked.

"Be better than this," my boss had written in the body of the forwarded email, and I knew I should have been. I quickly corrected the issue from my phone, scrambling to do it in as little time as possible, to show it was important to me, too. I could feel my face get warm, embarrassment coursing through my body as I reread the words again and again. Be better. Be better. Be better.

But I didn't want Evie to see me react to any of this. Didn't want to her to ask if everything was okay. I was determined to make her believe that my work was somehow meaningful. That real work could be rewarding. That she should want to do something with her life other than post ads on social media. I didn't want to admit that this job that was supposed to be an easy, breezy stepping stone to a big, important career wasn't actually easy or breezy at all. That I hated the work. I hated the hours. I hated that I left New York for this. And all of it meant that I made mistakes constantly. I was a poorly paid cog in a machine that ultimately made money for some man somewhere. Even if it required a degree and came with a 401(k).

Evie had a million people telling her every month that her life, her outfits, her face, her thoughts were all so very cool. What she needed was someone showing her that there was a different way to be valuable in the world. A more boring way, sure, but a different way. I wasn't about to let her know that I was beginning to suspect that way was bullshit, too.

"Well . . ." I said, tuning back into the conversation, about what she had said about the people who complain when she changes. "They still stick around anyway, don't they?"

"What do you mean?"

"They are still there, right? In your comments? Your DMs? Still giving you the likes, the views, the follows? The numbers for big brand partnerships?" I said, still typing away on my phone, sending off the final email saying that the issue had been fixed. "That's pretty convenient."

I could hear the edge in my voice, the way it was so obvious that I was dismissing her perspective because of my own shit, my own work frustrations. I hoped she didn't catch it, but at the same time, I didn't understand how she could be complaining at all. How could she not see what a privilege it was to be her? How even the people who were the most committed to seeing her fail were still there watching, still feeding into all the statistics that directly corresponded with her ever-increasing paychecks? Even the people who hated her the most were helping her be more successful. Even they couldn't help themselves.

"I guess." She shrugged, like it didn't really matter, like she didn't really need those people.

And wasn't that a privilege, too? That they needed her more than she would ever need them? I considered pushing it, but in the end I changed the subject.

"The interview I worked on is finally live," I told her, turning my phone to show her the story, complete with the spelling correction. "I'm super proud of it."

· • • • • • ·

I glance down at my phone again, mindlessly refreshing my feed, pushing away the memory. I'm about to close Instagram and make myself go inside when I think to check my message requests folder. There's one message from a username made up mostly of numbers. Spam, probably. But I click on it and read anyway.

It's truly been the honor and thrill of my life to watch your sister grow up into the beautiful and talented young woman she's become. I would love to connect with you to discuss what I've learned about her over the years.

I only make it through the first line before goosebumps prick my forearms, shoulders, and legs, a chill spreading through me. The sentiment, of course, isn't entirely foreign to me, but it's the intensity of the words that sticks with me, the way they seem to have real weight behind them. A knowing. I feel a fizz of adrenaline in my chest and I try to follow it down to the root. To decide whether I should believe it or not. Trust it. "My little worrier," Mom would always say when I was little, too scared to jump off a diving board or get on a skateboard. As I got older, it only got harder, a constant seesaw of: Am I scared of this because I'm scared of everything? Or because I should be? But this doesn't feel like blind anxiety. It feels like a sign. A lead maybe, or perhaps just a reminder from the universe that there are plenty of reasons to follow this gut feeling I have, the one that says very clearly that I should keep going, keep pushing. That Evie might not be safe at all.

I think of all the theories online, the Evie fans speculating about what really happened, discussing how they just have a really bad gut feeling about it all. My skin prickles with fear again, but this time it's because I'm realizing that I'm the same as them now, desperately clawing for a way to get closer to Evie, to get more of her. That after years of having access to her all the time, of taking it for granted, it's suddenly gone, and none of us have the faintest idea what to do with that now.

Admit it: It sounds nice. Delicious, even. You log off social media, you shut off your phone, put your laptop in a drawer, and you feel yourself start to dissolve. Suddenly, your world is smaller, quieter, more still. Softer. You see people in person more often than on a screen. You don't worry about perfectly packaging and displaying every new outfit, every vacation, every milestone for the world to see just so. You don't worry about editing those moments, either. You don't worry about inventing them altogether. It feels like going back to something and like starting over, too. But is it even possible?

We all know that person. A friend, or a friend of a friend, who has somehow found a way to give up their smartphone or sign off of Instagram for good. They say they're happier, lighter, free. But it's never as simple as that. Think of the last time you dated someone new and immediately searched for their name only to find a slate wiped clean, no digital footprint whatsoever. Did it make you feel safer? Or did it make you suspicious? Did it make you wonder what they were hiding? When they told you "I just don't like social media" or "I don't like putting everything out there for the world to see" or "Instagram isn't my thing anymore," did you feel intrigued? Or did it make you want to ask where, exactly, they were on January 6?

We've all toyed with the idea of leaving it all behind, right? Considered who, exactly, we would be without it all. I have too, as I've watched the Dani Tans and Madison Lees of the world disappear from my feed and wondered if they'll stay away for good. Lately, though, I'm wondering if a freer, happier, internet-free version of any of us (or of Dani and Madison and all the rest) is just fantasy.

Being alive today means being online, leveraging that version of you to benefit the real-life, less optimized you. Maybe you're in high school and you've wiped your entire feed and started from scratch, offering up only one photo a month or so—striking the perfect balance between visibly popular and somewhat mysterious, too. Or maybe you're older and you don't think any of this applies to you, even though you've curated your LinkedIn profile just so for a job search.

Have you used your face, your body, your interests, your humor to convey who you are, what you like, what you want? Have you posted an affiliate link or clicked on one? Have you simply realized that people feel safer with the doctors, designers, writers, accountants that they can find online and know immediately? A dentist who you know nothing about: sketchy. A dentist with a golden retriever named Stanley: charming, trustworthy. Appointment booked.

But besides the obvious benefits of being on the internet, it's still easy to romanticize the opposite choice. To wonder if leaving it all would make you better. But there's another thing that happens when you attempt to leave the internet, the thing that no one really considers. It's your absence from it that defines you. You are a curious exception to an accepted rule of our modern world. And no matter how long you spend away from it all, nothing changes the fact that the internet? Well, the internet is forever.

- Evie Davis has been accused of Facetuning her body in Instagram posts again—pinching and pulling the dimensions of her waist, her hips, her butt until she manages to convey the exact type of body that is just real enough to be attainable but just fake enough to be inspirational, too. The darker version of this piece of gossip: her mom is still the one editing her photos, her body. I mean, would *you* put it past Erin Davis?
- Rachel Song has officially created the latest, greatest TikTok parenting trend: cracking an egg on your unsuspecting toddler's head. I mean, what could be more adorable? What could be more charming than a prank on a small human who still relies on you for validation, security, love, and comfort? What could be better than using their surprise and disgust for views?
- Self-proclaimed animal lover and "low-key" vegan Ashlyn Price is in hot water after a Bernedoodle breeder tagged her in a post, which announced that a puppy from their latest litter found a home with Ashlyn and her fiancé. The post disappeared quickly, but not before Ashlyn's followers (and haters) noticed. The problem? Ashlyn had previously shared that her puppy was adopted from a shelter—saved from a puppy mill, in fact. Oops!

That's it for this week, friends. Check in next week for more about the influencers we love to hate and hate to love.

SABI

olivia muenter

CHAPTER 15

The only thing that distracts me from the eeriness of the message is the state of my apartment. As soon as I open the door, stale air hits me. I tiptoe around piles of clothes, no idea which are clean and which aren't. I navigate what seems like a dozen empty, discarded shipping packages, reminders of online shopping I certainly shouldn't have done and definitely can't afford. I kick two cardboard boxes to the side as I make my way to the couch, taking inventory of the chaos. The trash can is overflowing with moldy take-out containers. At least three sticky-looking bottles of wine are poking out of the recycling bin, the contents gone long ago. And if I close my eyes and concentrate, I can hear the faint sound of a fly or mosquito buzzing somewhere. They're probably wondering how the hell they got here, too.

Every bit of it, from the trash to the clothes to the bug, is worse because of where I've just spent the last ten days. Every bit of my mother's house had reminded me of the ease of new things, of comfort. Of when I moved back home four years ago.

When I first came to Vegas, I moved into an apartment that looked like it could have been located anywhere in the country. Everything in it was gray and sparkling new, right down to the fake wood floors that were approximately the same shade as a sidewalk. There was no prewar molding or exposed brick or one-hundred-year-old character, but I was okay with that. I had had enough of character and the catches it comes with in Brooklyn, the tiny, nocturnal creatures that I'd wake to find on the pillow next to me or hear scurrying around the basin of our tub in the dead of night. I told myself that for this phase of my life—this very brief phase—I simply wanted to be comfortable. I could have spent even less on rent, but the apartment was still so affordable compared to what I could afford in Brooklyn, it was impossible to resist. It had central air, a dishwasher, an in-unit washer and dryer, a shower with actual water pressure. Nothing about it was glamorous or charming—the location wasn't even particularly convenient—but it felt adult. Like, for the first time, I was doing the things you have to do to succeed. I was getting somewhere.

My first night in the apartment, I sat on the living room floor and fantasized about a savings account balance that wasn't laughable, a number that I could watch grow. I thought about carrying groceries through my front door and cooking dinner in the ice-cold air-conditioning, the smells of food being sucked out the vent above the stove instead of sinking into my comforter and couch cushions and pores. I pictured myself hand in hand with a version of me a few years from now who would be so grateful I did this. Who was back in New York with a reporting job to be proud of, with a life that was so much bigger than this, and comfortable too. Where having dreams and goals didn't mean everything else was so hard.

And then that plan fell apart, too. Within two years, I lost my job, moved to a shittier, cheaper apartment, and found another waitressing job to make ends meet—one that I'm likely now in risk of losing after so many days of taking time off while my sister's been missing. Except this time, I'm not in a city I love, commiserating about it all with someone who gets it. I'm stuck in a studio again, another place with a tiny bathroom and minimal natural light. No roommate this time, but somehow that's only made it more depressing. The only time I ever feel compelled to keep this place clean is when Evie is coming over. Though I guess that's over now, too.

I drop my bag on the floor and assess the mess, trying to gauge where to start. If I want to start. I look around at the clutter, vintage furniture covered in old picture frames, vintage glassware half-wrapped in yellowing newspaper. So many beautiful things without homes. Evie and I loved thrifting together. We'd visit estate sales of fabulous women in gigantic mansions on the outskirts of Vegas. She would comb through their costume jewelry, and I would find the most unique furniture and home décor that I could—bergère chairs upholstered with loud floral fabric, velvet love seats, threadbare Persian rugs. I'd buy it all and imagine how I'd style it, even here, in this tiny studio, and then I'd freeze. Nothing ever seemed to come together how I'd imagined, how I saw it on the interiors accounts I followed on Instagram. The pieces sat strewn around my room, piled with other secondhand finds. A guy had slept over once and told me my apartment felt like a fabulous, "carefully curated yet chaotic" thrift store, and I had laughed, told him he didn't have to try that hard. He was already in my bed. I knew what the space actually was: proof of someone whose grand ideas always outweighed their follow-through.

I look at a pile of dirty clothes teetering on a mid-century modern lounge chair. I had loved its lines when I bought it, the smooth curve of the seat, its faded leather. Now it feels like a waste in here, a reminder of all my mistakes. I'm glad it's hidden.

My mind flashes to the paranoid place I'm trying to avoid, the one where something feels wrong, and I recall the Instagram message again before I push it away and tell myself that it can wait. I can be paranoid later. I can trust what Detective Williams told me. I can respect Evie's decision for her life while I try to grab hold of my own again. I need that, for my own sanity. For my mental health. There's something in the back of my mind that tells me I need to get my shit together. That whatever comes next will require my focus. A clear mind. And for that, I need to clean my apartment for the first time in months.

I twist my hair into a bun on top of my head and put my hands on my hips, pacing around the room, picking up things as I go and throwing trash away. I spot a mildewy towel on the floor, still in the exact same place I had left it on the day Gavin had called me. I wince at the memory now, the way I had chosen to get ready, to shower and polish myself before I got in the car and drove to my mom's house. I should have been in the car before I'd even hung up the phone, already on my way to find out what was going on. To help. But I couldn't fight the urge to arm myself before I got there, like I had to be better than I was as is, even then.

I pick up the towel with my pointer finger and thumb and toss it to the mountain of dirty clothes that I've told myself I'm accumulating for one massive load of laundry. I'm about to take the trash out when my phone buzzes in my pocket.

I dig it out and see a Salt Lake City number on the caller ID. I've answered every random phone call since Evie went missing, on the off chance that it will be her on the other end of the line.

"Hello?"

"Hazel?" a voice squeaks. "It's Ashlyn."

My stomach drops. "Hi," I say. "I . . ."

"I got your number from Gavin. I . . . I know I sent you my number and I'm sure you've seen it by now . . . and maybe you don't really want to talk to me at all, but . . . I just . . . I had to get in touch."

I take a deep breath, my heart racing. What does she know?

"I was wondering if we could talk," Ashlyn says, and it's the first thing she's said that hasn't sounded like a question. "For real."

"Now?"

"Yeah," she says. "I . . . I think that's best."

I hear the sound of muffled laughter and conversation in the background, like a TV is blaring in the next room.

"Are you back in Utah?"

A beat of silence.

"I mean, now that it's all . . . over, I guess . . ." I add, my mind begging me to bring the conversation closer to where I know it needs to be: Evie.

She clears her throat, and I can hear the sound of air whooshing past the speaker now, like she's moving to a different section of the house. Or going outside.

"Do you really believe that?" Ashlyn asks.

My heart races.

"That it's over? That she posted that?" she presses.

I want to scream: *No, I don't, not even a little bit*, but I steady myself. Instead, I decide to offer a tiny bit of truth, of vulnerability. One admission for another.

"She didn't talk to me," I say, and it startles me as it comes out. "About whatever happened between you two. She wouldn't talk about any of it."

It feels like a confession.

"That makes sense," she says, like she isn't surprised at all. "She never did want to burden you with any of it."

It's meant to be kind, maybe, but it's the worst thing she could have said. The last thing I wanted was to be another adult Evie had to tiptoe around, whose happiness she had learned to manage.

Ashlyn inhales deeply for a second or two and there's a faint cracking sound, a popping. I imagine her pressing her hands flat on a table as she exhales the breath, using the leverage to twist side to side, cracking her back. The sound makes my skin crawl, but something about it is so raw, so plainly human, that it feels satisfying, like a win. A window into Ashlyn that no one could see but me.

"It started with these emails," she begins. "About a year ago, this newsletter started popping up everywhere. It was about the industry, influencers. Who was making what mistake. Who was getting canceled. Who should be canceled. Everything wrong with influencer culture. It would call out specific creators who were making too much money or taking shady brand deals or lying to their followers . . . it was pretty brutal. I mean, it was good. Don't get me wrong. There's a reason it got so popular. I actually read it every week, despite the fact that I was terrified of seeing my name there. Of doing something wrong and being called on it . . ." She laughs a little. "I guess that was part of the point—to force us to do better. I don't know. Either way, like I said . . . it was brutal."

Evie had never mentioned anything about this to me. I would have remembered.

"And then, one day, there I was. They were writing about me."

"Who's *they*?" I ask.

"That's the thing. No one knew. It was totally anonymous. People had theories, of course, but no one knew for sure. And at first, I didn't really care. I mean, people hate on influencers all the time, for a million different reasons or no reason at all. I was used to it—to people messaging me to say that I was evil or selfish or stupid. The first time I saw my name in SABI—that's the name of the newsletter—I was horrified, but almost relieved. It had happened. I could stop waiting. But then, week after week, more was written about me. It was relentless. And all of it was stuff that no one should have known. Not my manager. Not my parents. Not my fiancé, even."

As she talks I feel like I'm walking into a familiar room, but every detail is different from how it should be, everything ever so slightly out of place. And I think I know what's coming next.

"I should have unsubscribed. Blocked the email. Pushed it out of my brain. But I couldn't stop thinking about it. Obsessing over who would have this information . . . how. And then I started to notice who else was in these newsletters all the time . . . what they had in common."

It sounds like she's gearing up for something. I steady my breath.

"And like, look . . . it's not that it was *just* me, or just Gavin. You know Serena Baker? That homesteading mom with, like, nine children who lives in the middle of South Dakota with a $40,000 stove? She was in there constantly, too, but the stuff they wrote about her was . . . I don't know, knowable. Like if someone wanted to google that she was the heir to a fertilizer fortune, they could have. The stuff about me, about Gavin, too . . . it just seemed different. More private."

I only recognize what she's saying as sounding paranoid because I'm familiar with paranoia from constantly measuring it in myself, making sure too much of it doesn't slip out.

"Evie was in there too, obviously. I mean, of course. She's too popular not to be. But her stuff was . . . I don't know, it was either common knowledge, like Serena's stuff, or it was . . . tame. Boring. It wasn't the same, once you started to pay attention. And look, I'll admit I got a bit crazy about it. Obsessive. But after a few months . . . I just couldn't ignore this gut feeling. I just felt like I knew. I felt like it had to be her."

"Evie?" I ask. "You thought Evie was writing about all of you?"

"Yes."

"About . . . herself?" I add.

"I know," she says. "I know how it sounds. And honestly, when I brought it up to her last year, I was relieved because she denied it immediately. She laughed. She said, 'Ash, do you really think I have time for that shit? Come on,' and I wanted to believe her, so I did."

"But . . . ?"

"But I also wanted to be sure. I felt like I couldn't be honest with her otherwise, like I was holding things back, trying to make sure that they didn't show up in the stupid newsletter. I was paranoid and secretive and worried all the time. It was ruining our friendship. Eventually I just thought . . . well, I'll do a test. I'll truly eliminate the possibility from my brain once and for all. So I started creating stories . . . to see if they'd end up there. Stuff I wouldn't tell anyone else. Stuff that was completely false," she says.

I try to keep my voice neutral, but it's hard to hide my skepticism. "Isn't that kind of . . . risky?"

"Yeah," she says. "But she had told me it wasn't her, so I thought I was just . . . I don't know, easing my own anxiety. One last thing and then I'd know for sure. Finally relax. Go back to the way things were."

I stare at my apartment as I wait for her to go on, the in-progress cleaning that had gone nowhere. The hazy-with-age, gold-rimmed mirror where Evie had done her makeup once. The dresser where she had picked my clothes up one by one and tried to date them, always aging them ten or fifteen years on purpose, just to tease me. The antique dish she bought me when I moved to Vegas, as a place to put my keys every day.

"And then?" I press.

Ashlyn exhales. "And then I realized that I had been right the whole time. The first thing that I had told her—some made-up story about buying my dog Arlo from a pet store instead of adopting him at a shelter—ended up in the newsletter the next week," Ashlyn says. "But even then, when I confronted her, gave her the chance to be honest, she denied it. Said I was spiraling. That I could have told that to anyone. That she would never do that to me."

I can imagine how much the accusation would hurt my sister. Can feel it even now.

"She tried to convince me for a while, but eventually she just got angry," Ashlyn says. "Said I should find bigger things to worry about, that I should go focus on making $50,000 for a teeth-whitening ad, or I should maybe consider what it means that my fiancé thinks early-onset male pattern baldness is the worst thing that can happen to a person. That maybe I should worry about myself before I spiral over some email."

Ashlyn stops suddenly, like she realizes that maybe she didn't need to tell me all of that, to expose all her most vulnerable spots so plainly. But it does sound like Evie. I don't doubt that she's telling the truth.

When I don't reply right away, Ashlyn lowers her voice. "That was the last time we talked," she says. "Until . . ."

My body tenses. I had been almost disappointed when Ashlyn told me about the emails, not because Evie hadn't told me about what Evie had accused her of, but because it seemed so meaningless. What could any of it possibly have to do with where Evie was now? I didn't expect there to be more.

"Until the texts," she finishes.

"What are you talking about?"

She sighs. "You have to understand . . . I hadn't heard from her in weeks, Hazel," she says. "No apology. No truce. Nothing. And then, all of a sudden . . . there she was, texting me, asking for help. And suddenly it was her sounding like the paranoid one, the obsessive one, the spiraling one, the one who was reading too much into something. I thought . . . no, no way. I'm not just going to go back to being friends without at least an apology."

I want her to get to the point, and I suspect that the fact that she seems to be avoiding it isn't a good sign.

"What did she say, Ashlyn?" I ask, trying to make myself sound assertive, if not a little annoyed. "What was she so paranoid about?"

"She thought she was being watched."

Image description: Evie's last Instagram post before her disappearance, a candid photo of her laughing with Gavin's hand wrapped around her waist. His body is mostly out of shot. She's wearing low-rise cargo pants and a cropped tube top. Her hair is slicked back into a braided ponytail.

Comments:

lucyinthesky 4 weeks ago
I can't get over this look omg

seanhunt29 4 weeks ago
the things I would do . . .

bodyloveclub 4 weeks ago
mother is mothering

richarddawsonuk 3 weeks ago
feet pics?

soleilskin ⬤ 3 weeks ago
um, GLOWING! we love working with a self-confident QUEEN!

clementinedenner 2 weeks ago
LIKE THIS IF YOU'RE OK EVIE

amyamyamyyy 2 weeks ago
How's it feel to be ghosted in the most embarrassing way of all time
@gavinramirez? You deserve it. Evie could always do so much better.

> **girlgamerreally** 2 weeks ago
> he's seriously so cringe

tomasrojas 2 weeks ago
$$$ SIX FIGURES FOR EVIE DAVIS NUDES $$$

such a bad influence

eviedavispicsss 1 week ago

omg what if this is the last evie davis fit we ever get

>**xcxmarie** 1 week ago
>
>really?

>**anonpanda** 1 week ago
>
>lucky for you every other influencer looks exactly like her, so you've got outfit inspo for daysss girlie 😵

whereiseviedavis 20m ago

Tell us where she is, Gavin.

View all 2,385 comments . . .

olivia muenter

CHAPTER 16

I stop breathing for a second.

"Hazel?" Ashlyn says, as if she can sense the way I'm spiraling.

When I don't reply, she keeps going.

"I just thought," she says, "how convenient that after *years* of being followed by the creepiest men on the internet, now is when you have a stalker. She thought her phone was bugged. Her house. It just all seemed like an elaborate excuse to imply that there was another reason someone would have been writing all that stuff about me. That they had hacked our conversations or had recordings of us somewhere. I'm sorry. I just . . . I didn't buy it."

I want to say that this isn't my sister, that there's no way she would do something so extreme just to make amends, to protect herself. No way she would lie like that, but then I remember what happened four years ago.

It was her last year at a Montessori school before she moved to the public high school. By that point I was planning to move back west but was still in New York, mostly keeping up with Evie's life through weekly FaceTimes and daily texts. We talked about everything, but when I asked her about dating, she always brushed me off. I remembered that age, the hunger to be loved, touched. So overwhelming and thorough that it colored everything. I wasn't so naive to imagine that my sister was immune to it, even if she had a never-ending cascade of attention on social media. When I was her age, I would have died to know that a single boy in my class thought I was pretty. Average, even. She merely had to open Instagram to have thousands of strangers telling her she was gorgeous. That she got prettier every day. Still, I knew there had to be someone.

"So, any crushes lately?" I'd ask, trying to seem casual, cool. "Anyone special? A boy? A girl?"

Almost every time, she'd laugh, say no. Not like she was embarrassed, but like it should be obvious that she didn't have time for crushes. And then one day, it was different.

"There was this one kid," she said, and I had to force myself to sound unfazed on the phone.

"Oh?"

"Yeah, well . . ." she started. "You have to promise not to tell Mom."

I tried to hide my excitement. A secret that was mine? And not my mom's? "Of course. Always."

"I was talking to this guy from a high school in Scottsdale," she said, and I already knew by her voice that there was a line of darkness running through the story that I wasn't expecting. She doesn't sound giddy, or shy, but guilty. Maybe a little defensive. "It was harmless, really. He sent me some pics. I sent him some. Whatever."

I gritted my teeth, trying to remind myself that my sister was a teenager. And this was what teenagers do.

"He wasn't even that much older," she said.

My stomach lurched. "Ev . . ."

"He literally *just* turned eighteen. Like, the day before we started talking."

Jesus Christ, I thought. This was worse than I thought. Maybe I didn't want to know this.

"It was whatever, really. We were just talking. Followed each other on Snapchat," she said. "Flirted. Not a big deal. But for him, it was different . . . he was, like, in *love* with me."

I can see it now: The too-old-for-her stalker showing up at the door. Our mom freaking out. The details that would leak. The headlines that would follow.

"I was over it, so I ended it, blocked him—I mean, we literally never even hung out in person." She sighed. "But he sent this letter last month. Left it in the mailbox. I got it before Mom found it, thank *God*."

I'm picturing: A teenage boy's messy scrawl. Threats written in nearly illegible handwriting. Reminders that she was his.

"I know what you're thinking, Haze," she said. "This isn't *Law & Order*. It was . . . sweet. I mean, a little pathetic, but sweet. He said he would love me forever. He wanted the best for me. He would never forget me. I would do big things in high school. Blah, blah, blah . . ."

A chill went up my arm.

"And then I forgot about it, really. Put it in my backpack and brought it to school. Stuffed it in my locker between some books. Whatever. And I guess Aiden got the picture—that was his name, by the way," she said, and I wondered why it mattered. "He never sent anything else. Never even texted me. I forgot the letter was there, honestly. I should have thrown it out, *obviously*. No idea why I didn't. Laziness, I guess. It was also probably laziness that led me to leave my locker unlocked one day, and . . ."

"Oh, Jesus, Evie . . ."

"Yeah, Regan found the letter. Fucking *Regan*. I swear she's still annoyed about me not including her in my 'best of summer' Instagram carousel. As if she would want any of the photos I had of her online anyway. Let me tell you: not good. But whatever. She snooped. She found the letter. Obsessed with me as always."

I cringed, hearing my sister talk that way, though in a way it was what I always wanted for her—to be an impossible, headstrong teenager concerned with petty school drama, boys, friends.

"And then she . . . ugh, I swear to God I'm still so mad at her, Haze." She groaned into the phone. "She gave the letter to the principal."

Good, I think, imagining the eighteen-year-old being disciplined accordingly. That's what you get for going for an underage girl. A fucking *middle schooler*.

"I have no idea why Principal Locklear saw the name Aiden and thought, 'well, I guess there's only one other Aiden in the world. And he happens to work here.' And is one of my teachers . . . and that I'm, I don't know, pervert bait or whatever it is people think because of social media . . . whatever, anyway . . . she was convinced it was my history teacher, Mr. Jernigan. *Aiden* Jernigan, I guess. Though it feels weird to, like, say his first name like that. Ew."

Something in her voice sounded so light and airy, so distant, that it made my pulse race. Why didn't this seem like a big deal to her?

"And you told her it wasn't him, right . . . ?"

"Well, that would mean I would have to tell her it was *my* Aiden . . . and then she would tell Mom that . . . so . . . yeah, no," Evie says.

I had been walking, pacing the apartment, and I stopped in my tracks. Who was this person I was talking to?

"No?" I repeated.

She sighed loudly, but I spoke before she could say anything. "I don't get this, Evie . . . I thought you were over him. Why would you want to protect him?"

"I mean, the photos, for one," she started. "He screenshotted a few . . . At the time, I was, I don't know, flattered that he thought I was hot enough. That I looked old enough. But then afterward, I realized that there was no telling where the photos would end up if he was pissed. Even if he got in trouble. You know how guys are. They feel betrayed and boom: scorched earth. Plus, the money he could make on them . . . I'm sure you get it."

"So you just . . . let your teacher take the fall . . . and . . . what? Get fired?" I pushed, trying to make sense of what she was saying, putting together what must have come next. "Get arrested?"

"Look, it's not like the letters were *sexual*, Hazel," she said, drawing out the word like she wants to make it clear that she's comfortable with this situation. That it doesn't faze her. That this is all no big deal. "I knew they weren't going to, like, immediately send him to jail. I mean, the letter seemed weird, sure. I knew he wouldn't be back next year, but neither would I. We could all move on. And once I explained to Principal Locklear how many people would care about something like this because I was in-volved, if it ended up on the news, what would happen to the school . . ."

She sounded calculated, both younger and older than I'd ever heard before. She sounded like my mom.

"Evie," I said quietly. "You could have figured out a different way. You could have . . . I don't know . . . talked to me. Something. That man didn't do anything wrong."

"Yeah, well," she said, and I could practically hear her shrug through the phone. "He's not in jail. And neither is the other Aiden. And Mom isn't

olivia muenter

losing her shit. So it's fine."

"It's really not."

"I mean, it's not like Mr. Jernigan was an angel, either, Haze. He was *very* open about the whole 'in this classroom, hugs are free' policy." She sighed. "A little sus if you ask me."

It was clear that Evie had thought the whole thing through. That it all made sense to her, even if it was scorched earth, even if it was destroying so much more than was necessary or even remotely fair.

"You *promised*, Hazel," she whined, sensing the depths of my disapproval through the phone. "You cannot tell Mom. She'll kill me. Or she'll, like, immediately go public. We'll be on *The Today Show* in four days talking about child predators. She'll put Mr. Jernigan's face everywhere. I can see the Instagram caption now: THIS IS THE FACE OF A MONSTER. MY BABY IS A VICTIM."

She wasn't wrong.

"Please don't make me do that. Don't make me lie on television."

Would that really be so hard for you? I wondered, but didn't say it out loud.

· • • ● • • ·

We never talked about it again. I tried not to think about it, either, other than the occasional times I googled Aiden Jernigan over the years. Last I checked he was running an SAT prep course out of his house in the Midwest. Now, on the phone with Ashlyn, I think of him for the first time in a while. About what Evie had done, what I had let her do.

Had Evie thought she was being watched? Stalked? And if she had, why didn't she tell me—the one person who would have taken it seriously right away? Or did she make it all up to win Ashlyn back?

"So, what?" I say, doing my best not to sound annoyed, panicked, angry. "You just didn't reply?"

"No," Ashlyn says, and she sounds genuinely ashamed.

"And you didn't tell the detectives either?"

"I was scared," she says. "I thought maybe I would be implicated somehow, or . . . I don't know . . . maybe I was just embarrassed. I told myself that if the police reached out to me for questioning, I'd tell them then. I'd explain that I had genuinely thought she was making it up. It's not that I didn't care about her enough to be worried, even though we weren't in a good place . . . I just thought there was nothing to actually worry about."

This part doesn't make me feel any better, but I do understand it. There are things I've waited to tell the detectives, too. Things that I've told myself must not be important if no one else is bringing them up. Even if that is the more convenient version of things for me.

"And then the Instagram post and detective statement happened . . ." Ashlyn says.

"So, what?" I sneer. "You just thought, 'well, I guess I'll just continue to keep my mouth shut.' What a relief, huh? That you never had to really involve yourself . . ."

I don't care if she knows I'm angry now, that I resent the fact that she protected herself instead of protecting my sister. That she didn't assume the worst-case scenario, too.

"It's just . . ." she starts. "That's what she said she wanted, right? In that post? If it's her that's saying it, then what else was there for me to do?"

"So then why are we having this conversation now?" I push. "Why call me at all?"

"I needed to tell someone," she says, her voice small, wavering. "I needed someone else to see the emails, the texts. I couldn't just . . . sit with it forever."

I think of why that someone couldn't be the detectives. "Someone who didn't have the power to hold you accountable? And when the world is already paying less attention than they were three days ago? Convenient."

There's a beat of silence, and when she talks again her voice is still small, but confident. Steady. "Ignoring a text isn't a crime," she says. "And neither is leaving your family."

I'm stunned by how matter-of-fact she seems. And angry that this whole conversation feels centered on Ashlyn unburdening herself instead of on Evie.

"You know, as fucked-up as the emails were, I thought that telling you about them might help. That you'd want to read them and then you'd see that Evie was more complex than you thought. That she was smart," Ashlyn says, somehow managing to sound warm despite the bite behind her words. "That maybe there is a lot you didn't understand about her. That you couldn't understand. I thought maybe we'd have that in common."

I don't reply, stung by what she's said. Is this how Evie talked about me? How she thought I felt about her?

"Look, I'm not asking you to look at the texts and emails and have some epiphany about me or her or anything. Just read them, okay?"

"Fine," I say, too deflated to push anymore.

"Thank you," she says, and something in her voice feels lighter, like she's been treading water and has now finally peeled off a layer of clothing, a pair of boots.

It's not that she sounds happy, really. But sunnier. Like she's going to hang up the phone and run or jump, take long strides into a lake. She reminds me of a golden retriever.

And suddenly it isn't just her or the memory of her tan or her perfect hair that makes me wish I was a little more like her, but instead it's the weightlessness, the ability to pass something along to someone else and know your job is complete. To wash your hands of it, shrug your shoulders, and be done. To tell the truth, and have that be enough.

CHAPTER 17

The PDF is color coded. I expected screenshots of texts, emails. But instead, it's all cataloged. Each section of the PDF corresponding with a shade of pink, orange, or lilac. It looks ridiculous. I can only imagine Detective Buxton's reaction to all of this. He's exactly the type of person who would never take this seriously, not even if what was written on the pages was helpful. He would never believe that something so beautiful could be truly useful, too.

I sit cross-legged on my apartment floor as I swipe through the pages of the PDF, the palette of colors reminding me of something Ashlyn had posted in response to an Instagram Q&A once. "What's your favorite color?" someone had asked. But Ashlyn hadn't responded by saying green or pink or purple or orange. Instead, she'd written: "The colors of a desert sunset." I can't help but smile at the memory, the PDF. The aesthetically pleasing absurdity of it. Even now, even with everything that's happened, this is perfectly, deliberately Ashlyn. Relentlessly on brand.

I know I should start at the beginning of what she sent over, that it's probably organized in a way that makes perfect sense, each piece connecting, but all I can think of are the texts from Evie to Ashlyn. I keep thumbing through the documents, waiting to land on those. I find it eventually—only one sheet, and only texts from Evie. No replies from Ashlyn, either because they never came or because she intentionally cropped them out.

I know that even what I'm seeing could have been edited. That it could have been generated with some computer program. But as soon as I start reading, I can hear them in my sister's voice. I can feel the fear, the panic. It was one thing to hear about it secondhand from Ashlyn, but reading the texts, sensing Evie's desperation, was different. It was a tone that was so different from the versions of Evie I'd heard before, even the darkest ones, the one I heard on the phone four years ago after the Aiden letter. And though they're not any different from what Ashlyn had prepared me for, it feels different to see them so plainly spelled out like this. There's a reason why she hadn't read the messages to me.

Evie, 12:07 a.m.

Hey. I know we haven't talked for a while, but I really need to talk. I wouldn't reach out if it wasn't serious. I just am really freaking the fuck out right now.

Evie, 12:25 a.m.

Please, Ash. I really, really need someone to tell me I'm not losing my mind right now.

Evie, 12:42 a.m.

You know me. Would I ever triple text if something weren't serious?

Evie, 12:49 a.m.

Look. It's going to sound insane written out like this . . . but I think I'm being followed. Or that my phone is bugged. Something is so off. Weird shit has been happening. My stuff has gone missing . . . personal things. Just gone. At first I thought I was just losing it but then I thought . . . maybe *this* is why the stupid newsletter thing happened. Maybe someone has been listening. I don't know, but I'm freaked out.

Evie, 12:50 a.m.

I'm scared.

I swear I could hear her say the words in my head, and none of it sounded rehearsed. It sounded like she was spiraling, falling deeper down into something she knew she wasn't prepared to face alone.

But maybe I'm wrong. They're just words, after all. All she had to do was type them.

But whether they were real or not, the fact remains: Ashlyn ignored her. If Evie had texted me this, I would have canceled any job interview, dropped everything, maxed out every credit card I could find just to get to her, protect her, know that I had done everything I could as her sister, her friend. Even if she was lying, at least I would have known that I did that.

Had she tried to tell me something was wrong and I missed it? I avoided her calls more than I should have. I became less available. It was easier that way, to convince myself that what I had done was some version of fair. The best thing. I knew I had missed things, but something this big?

A memory of us sitting on my tiny couch one weekend last fall pops into my head. I had looked over at her laptop and noticed a tiny cover on the spot where her camera was, just above the screen. I had bought one for her as a stocking stuffer years before, but she had never used it, even though I'd told her horror stories about computer hacking and security breaches.

"Oh, my God," I said. "Has hell frozen over? Do my eyes deceive me?"

"What?" Evie had said.

I pointed toward the camera cover. "Don't tell me that Gavin got it for you or something, and that's why you're using it," I said. "I can't take that."

"No, no, I just hadn't gotten around to putting it on until now," she said. "More important things to do."

"Ah, yes," I said, gesturing toward the TV screen in front of us. "More important things like . . . watching *Lost* in its entirety for the . . . let me check my notes . . . third time in two years?"

The show was one of the first things I had shown Evie from my own childhood. I had loved it then—the absurdity of it, the mystery—and I thought she would, too. I was right.

"It's the smoke monster, Hazel," she said matter-of-factly, pressing PLAY on the remote. "I still don't understand the smoke monster. I need to understand!!! I must!!"

Should that small moment have set off some sort of alarm bells in my mind? Should it have made me ask why she was concerned about privacy now, after all these years? But that was months ago. Who knows what else had happened since then?

I swipe on my phone, getting the texts off my screen, deciding to focus on something else. Something that feels more understandable. The SABI newsletters. I tell myself I'll try to see what Ashlyn saw. And sure enough, by the time I get to the third or fourth email that Ashlyn has included in the PDF, I can almost see it. I start to notice the tiny turns of phrase that do sound so much like my sister. The whisper of sarcasm throughout everything that echoes her sense of humor, the rhythm of her speech. But even after I read all of them, and then read them again, something still feels off. I don't know how Ashlyn and I could know the same person if she really thinks Evie was capable of this.

I close the PDF and open Instagram immediately, a mindless tic. I scroll through my feed for a few seconds before Ashlyn is there, a photo of her sitting by a pool, her feet curled up under her. She's wearing a crocheted cover-up with extra-long sleeves, her fingers barely visible even though they're holding a book, some feminist self-help best seller. I go to the comments.

"Where's her man???" one person had written. "Oh my god does this finally mean that bestie is free of the trad wife pipeline???"

I've never known too much about "B," as Ashlyn referred to him on Instagram, since the two of them had started dating after her and Evie's falling-out. Most of what I do know I'm ashamed to have gathered on Reddit, where people constantly speculated what "B" stood for.

"It's probably just, like, Ben," someone had written.

"Maybe it stands for . . . Biblically conservative, but also fiscally conservative, too," another person had joked.

The most recent drama surrounding A + B, as Reddit called them (or at least what I had read before Evie went missing), was why, exactly, they weren't married and popping out babies yet. They were both from traditional Mormon families and had followed the typical trajectory: three to five months of dating followed by an engagement. A temple wedding would be held no more than six months later, followed by a carefully crafted mansion in various shades of white with two laundry rooms, one basketball court, a walk-in closet the size of a basketball court, and, of course, a view of some snow-capped mountains. But the wedding that everyone was waiting for had never come. Ashlyn would reply to curious comments with things like "We're taking our time!" and "There's no rush!" It didn't fit with the rest of what the internet knew about Ashlyn Price. Last I checked, A + B had been engaged for more than a year. But not anymore, it seems. I see Ashlyn has liked one of the comments about her finally being "free." Maybe she *is* finally taking a cue from Evie.

I had promised to text her as soon as I read through the texts and newsletters, though I suspected what she wanted was something I couldn't give her: to hear me say that she didn't do anything wrong.

Hazel

> Hey. I looked over everything. Thanks for sending all of that.

She responds immediately.

Ashlyn

> I've been sitting here so worried that you hated me now . . . but you get it, right? You see why I was skeptical of the texts?

No, I think, *I don't really see it*. Not completely. I take a second before replying to scan through the newsletters. It's true that most of them weren't kind to Ashlyn. But it is also true that they weren't exactly cruel, either. Most of the stories were . . . survivable. And I mean, she is living proof that it's true, right? Like pretty much every other influencer mentioned in the emails, she hasn't been canceled. She hasn't been ruined. She has more business than ever, more followers. An entire new product line coming out in the fall. For every person who criticized her, I know there are people who said, "Oh my gosh, I'm so glad to hear Arlo is from a reputable breeder too. It's like, if no one buys those dogs, then won't the shelters just fill up even more?" Maybe the criticism had been uncomfortable for Ashlyn, or inconvenient. But none of it was as damning as she had made it seem. None of it would make a difference for someone like her in the end. And none of it was reason enough to ignore my sister's pleas for

olivia muenter

help, even if Evie had been the one writing the newsletters.

As I try to figure out what to say to her next, I realize for the first time that I'm angry. Furious, really. If only Ashlyn had replied to her texts, called her to check in, then maybe Evie would still be here, safe. And yet I find myself deleting every reply I type out. I'm finding it impossible to say any of it. To chastise Ashlyn Price, Person Who Lives on My Phone. I've consumed as much content and commentary about Ashlyn's shortcomings and missteps as I have images of her outfits, or recommendations of her favorite skin care products. So why do I still feel intimidated by her, even now?

In the end, I decide to tell the truth. Just an easier one.

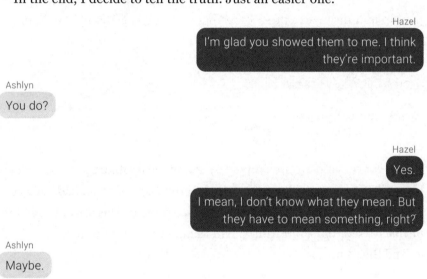

I almost laugh. Maybe? Your best friend tells you she thinks she's being stalked, then disappears from the face of the earth, and you think *maybe* those two things are connected? I had always brushed off all the criticism about Ashlyn being vapid or dull as inherently sexist. This is a woman who had built a whole business herself, an entire brand. Products that people loved. She is anything but stupid. But maybe I had been wrong to give her the benefit of the doubt all this time.

Ashlyn

Gavin said she could be like that sometimes, though.

> That she would make things up. Create chaos just for the sake of it.

I should be annoyed by the dig at Evie, even if I know firsthand that it's true. But something about Gavin being mentioned tickles my brain. Did Ashlyn already talk about all of this with Gavin at the search in Palm Springs? And if so, what did he tell her?

Hazel

> Did he ever tell you why Palm Springs? Why he thought that would be the best place to look?

She doesn't reply for a minute this time. I watch the "typing" bubble pop up and disappear three times before a message finally lands in my inbox.

Ashlyn

> You should really ask him that.

> You should probably ask him about a lot of things, actually.

Our conversation is interrupted by my phone lighting up: a notification from TikTok. A new video from the true crime account that had been covering Evie's case. The title scrolls across my screen: "Has anyone seen this *insane* leaked transcript from Gavin Ramirez??? Let's discuss!"

And then I press PLAY.

olivia muenter

Interview with Gavin Ramirez

June 17, 2023, 5:47 p.m.

Detective
Brendan Buxton: *So, Gavin, thank you for coming in to talk to us today. What you know about Evie will go a long way toward us understanding more about who she really is, and hopefully where she is. Can I get you some water before we get started? A soda? Coffee?*

Gavin Ramirez: *Nah, I'm good.*

BB: *All right, well, you just let us know if you need anything from us, okay? I want to start by asking you about your and Evie's relationship. What was it like?*

GR: *It was good. Fun.*

BB: *Oh, I bet. But I know how it is. That fun comes with some drama, too, right?*

GR: *I don't know what you mean.*

BB: *Look, man, I've been there. I was crazy in love with this girl, but she just couldn't figure out what she wanted. More of me, less of me. She hated me, she loved me. Hot and cold, all the time. It was a lot. Was that kind of what it was like for you two?*

GR: *[laughs]*

BB: *Is something funny?*

GR: *No. it's just . . . it wasn't like that.*

BB: *So what was it like, then?*

GR: Evie always knew exactly what she wanted, as far as I could tell.

BB: Tell me what you mean by that.

GR: She was focused.

BB: A man of few words, Mr. Ramirez, huh? You know—I had no clue you were even Hispanic before I saw your last name. Never would have guessed.

GR: I'm half Mexican.

BB: Exactly. Could have fooled me. I'm sure that helps with what you do, right? Get a leg up for brand deals or whatever? I imagine it helps that you can tick that box, but still have that all-American boy-next-door thing going on too? Pretty ideal.

GR: Uh . . .

BB: It must only add to the competition between you two, right?

GR: I don't know what you're talking about.

BB: You and Evie. I mean, seeing who could get the most deals, the most sponsorships, make the most money . . . I can't imagine the demand for basic white girls is really very high right now.

GR: Evie isn't basic. And last I checked, white girls are doing just fine on Instagram.

BB: Exactly. See, you get it.

GR: That's not what I . . . look, I don't know exactly what you're getting at, but Evie and I have totally different lanes. And we've always been supportive of each other . . . that was our whole thing.

BB: Right, right . . . so give me an example. Of how she was supportive.

GR: Okay, so I had been working on this . . . new thing. Something different. She supported me in that from the very beginning. She was right there in it with me. Never doubted me.

BB: Can you tell me more about that?

GR: Well . . .

BB: If you can't be honest with us, Gav, we can't help you, either.

GR: It was a docuseries. I wanted to take my video skills and put them toward something important. She was all in, excited about it. We both were. It's another reason why none of this makes sense.

BB: What was this docuseries about?

GR: We hadn't decided yet. There were a dozen different options. It was less about the subject and more about the vibes.

BB: The vibes?

GR: Yes.

BB: *Right. Of course. The vibes. So. Let me just get this straight real quick. You two were totally supportive, totally honest with each other . . . sounds pretty perfect. Perfect relationship . . . perfect girl . . . perfect life. No secrets. Doesn't seem like a reason for someone to just disappear.*

GR: *Yeah, so you can imagine why we're all worried . . . But . . .*

BB: *But?*

GR: *Just because she was happy doesn't mean things were perfect.*

BB: *Things with you two, you mean?*

GR: *No. We . . . we were fine. We've always been fine. It's not that. It's her family.*

BB: *Erin, you mean? Her mom?*

GR: *I mean her whole family.*

olivia muenter

CHAPTER 18

I thought it would feel like a decision. Or like flipping a switch. A hard right turn from accepting what the detectives had said, what the Instagram post had said, to pushing for more answers instead. In reality, it's more like holding on to something for dear life, afraid that it will all get worse when I let go. So even though it didn't feel like a decision, I woke up this morning knowing exactly what I was going to do next anyway. I was getting in my car and driving back to Arizona. I was going to see Gavin.

I could have called him, read him the mysterious texts from Ashlyn and grilled him about the interview. But I wanted to see his face, to watch what happens when there is no camera to perform in front of, no captive audience except one person who doesn't like you to begin with. I had given him so much of my patience. I had let the videos play out, the letters to Evie, the pointless search party. I had given him what he wanted: the unchecked time and space to manipulate his audience the way he wanted. And for what? To be the bigger person? To not fan the flame? To not make him mad? I think of how the transcript had ended. What he had implied. He can explain that to my face now.

I drive all morning, and I'm fifteen minutes away from Gavin's house when I realize my hair is matted. It was damp from the shower when I left, and I had had the brilliant idea of air-drying it by opening the window once I hit the highway. I imagined I'd arrive looking unbothered, a natural, didn't-even-think-about-styling-my-hair kind of casual. Instead, based on what I can see in the rearview mirror as I crawl through the innards of a sprawling Phoenix suburb, I look unhinged. The opposite of unbothered. I use one hand to comb my fingers through the mess, desperately trying to tame it.

It's thanks to my paranoia that I have Gavin's address. I had insisted that Evie send it to me when they first started dating, even though she said I was being dramatic. That she was safe with him.

I go as slowly as possible, but eventually, there it is. Gavin's house. I pull into the driveway, my car easing into its looming shadow. I had expected a boxy, ultramodern bachelor pad, all slate-gray lines and minimalism. In reality it's a beige, cookie-cutter McMansion, not unlike my mom's house. Or most houses in these kinds of neighborhoods—huge, grand. It looks more dated than I expected, a symbol of wealth from a different time. But then I see the backside of a white Tesla through the windows of the garage, and I'm sure I'm in the right spot.

I had rolled my eyes the first time I saw Gavin drop Evie off in the thing.

"Please don't tell me he's an Elon Musk guy," I said. "Please. I beg of you."

She rolled her eyes back at me. "It's not like he's endorsing him for public office, Hazel," she said. "It's a car. A very environmentally friendly one, I might add."

"Sure, you say that now," I said. "And the next thing you know he's packing his bags for a long weekend aboard a space shuttle and paying for a little blue checkmark. It's like a Jimmy Buffet song. One second, you're thinking, 'Hey, that's kind of catchy,' and the next you're tailgating at every East Coast show and using a specialty blender. It happens quickly. And none of us are above it."

"I'm pretty sure some of us are, indeed, above it, Hazel." Evie laughed.

"No one," I said, faux serious, as I watched him pull out of the driveway. "and I mean no one, is above loving 'Cheeseburger in Paradise.'"

I almost laugh at the memory now, thinking of how much Evie would have loved this, to see Gavin and me hanging out, one-on-one, bonding, but then I'm panicking again. I think of my sister and remember that I might be the only person looking for her, the only person who believes she's not okay, and I let the horror of that reality pull me forward instead of down, down, down.

I take a final deep breath and step out of the car, making my way across the expansive driveway and sidewalk to the front porch. By the time I get there, Gavin is outside, leaning against a giant Grecian-style pillar on the front steps.

"Hazel," he says casually. "This is a surprise."

I hadn't heard him walk out. Hadn't seen him there when I pulled in the driveway, either. And it would have been hard to miss him. He's shirtless, wearing only a pair of gray sweatpants that are slung low across his hips in a way that feels vaguely pornographic.

"Is it?" I say, forcing myself to seem casual, cool, relaxed. "A surprise?"

He shrugs. "Not really, I guess," he says, turning away from me and gesturing for me to follow him through the front door. "That fucking transcript brought all kinds of weird shit out of the woodwork."

"I bet," I say, letting the implications hang between us.

"Yeah, it didn't make me look that great, I guess."

"You and me both," I say, staring at him.

He stops in the kitchen and leans on the giant island. I perch myself on a barstool on the opposite side, adjusting my posture until it feels confident, but not stilted.

"About that . . ." he starts, his forearms resting on the cool marble, biceps flexing.

Does he just always . . . *look like this*?

"I'm sorry about that. I just . . . I honestly didn't even realize what I was saying. Not really. I just hated how Buxton seemed to be overanalyzing every single thing I was saying."

"So you gave him something else to overanalyze?" I say. "Someone else?"

"I mean, not intentionally, no," he says. "I was overwhelmed."

I look around the room. The cabinets and shelves are lined with the kind of vaguely Italian-looking items that you buy in the clearance section of an extremely American home décor store. There are tall glass bottles filled with bloated vegetables suspended in what I think is supposed to be olive oil, though I have my doubts about that. There are four metal roosters of various sizes. There is one small sign that says BON APPÉTIT! and a larger one that features no words but instead a wooden carving of a giant fork.

"Not what you expected?" Gavin looks up at me through dark lashes, his torso leaning farther over the marble now. He's smiling, like a part of him is loving this, that I'm surprised, or confused. A dimple peeks out from one side of his face. How had I not noticed this before? How had Evie never mentioned it? It's the kind of thing you mention.

I shiver from the air-conditioning, and I suddenly have absolutely no idea how he's not wearing more clothing in here. I cross my arms in front of myself, sitting up straighter again. His smile deepens, like he can read every thought that's going through my head.

"Not . . . exactly," I say. "I mean, it's nice. It's . . . huge."

The smile's still there, but he bites his lip and narrows his eyes in my direction now, like he knows exactly what I really mean but won't say. Like I'm a kid at dinner who turns down broccoli by saying, "I don't care for that," as if the manners make the meaning less obvious. He's amused by me.

He looks around and laughs. "It certainly is that."

I glance around the room for a third time, desperate to avoid eye contact, suddenly too uncomfortable and disarmed to ask the questions that really brought me here. It feels better to let the conversation happen naturally. Safer.

"You smoke?" he says, opening a drawer and pulling out a joint.

I shrug instinctively, in a way that says *sure*, though I instantly regret it. Because the answer, really, is no. Not for years. And even if it wasn't, the answer should be no, anyway. I came here to get answers, to tell him how angry I was. And now, what, five minutes and one shirt later, I'm saying *sure* to smoking a joint with my sister's boyfriend? Ex-boyfriend? I'm not sure which now. A smoother, rational part of my brain speaks up: Maybe this will help you relax. Maybe he'll be more likely to open up.

Gavin lights the joint and brings it to his lips as he walks around the island to where I'm sitting, taking the barstool next to me. I have to hop off of mine to move it farther away, so our foreheads aren't practically touching if I turn toward him to talk. It's undeniably awkward, the chair clanging across the tile floor as I drag it over, but he only smiles, like he's not bothered by any of it. When I'm seated again, he hands me the joint, and I take a drag, feeling him watch me the entire time. I blow the smoke out and away from him, aiming for one of the giant metal roosters, trying to distract myself from the odd intimacy of the moment.

"You know, you look like her," he says, and I choke. I cough wildly for a minute before the air finally settles in my lungs.

"Sorry, is that a weird thing to say?" he says. "It's not even really what I meant. I wouldn't know you were related if I had to pick you two out of a crowd or something, but . . . you both have this . . . this light about you, I guess."

What is he *talking* about? I ignore the part of me that deflates because he took back his slightly creepy, quasi-compliment and said something corny.

"Uh-huh," I say. "Right. I get that a lot on Hinge lately. 'Great light, but unfortunately I see us more as friends.'"

He laughs, and it seems genuine.

Then he's quiet for a minute, staring out one of the windows in the room behind us, like he's deep in thought.

"What I meant," he continues, "was something more like: There's attractiveness. Features. Body type, whatever. And then there's beauty, like actual beauty. The kind that makes us stare at nature or art or poetry, I don't know. That kind. Those are two different things, don't you think?"

Yes, I think, nodding.

"I think I just meant, before I managed to say it like two different equally weird ways," he says, smiling in a self-deprecating way, "is that whatever made her beautiful is what makes you beautiful too, even if it resulted in two people who don't really look alike on the surface."

Something he's saying peels a layer away from me, exposes something, but I don't let the feeling stay.

"Right," I say, handing the joint back to him. "In other words, Evie is beautiful, and I'm beautiful on the inside."

He shifts on the barstool so he's facing me now, one arm resting on the island. One of his knees brushes mine, and I stare at my own leg, willing it to move, but it stays.

"No, Hazel," he says, and his voice is deeper than it was a moment ago.

The smile is gone, but he doesn't look angry, either. "That's not at all what I'm saying."

We make eye contact for a second, and it takes me what feels like two minutes to look away first. The weed must be dulling my reaction time. How has this thing gone so wildly off the rails?

I'm about to get up and run to the bathroom, splash some water on my face or throw up or both, when Gavin starts talking again, like he knows we need to change the subject.

"It's not my place, by the way," he says. "It's my parents'."

I snort; the weed has dulled my social graces, too. "You still live with your parents?" I ask. He'd never struck me as the type to live at home for longer than he had to—especially not when he has as much money he does. Then again, neither did Evie.

"No, actually, I'm house-sitting. I sent my parents on an around-the-world cruise." He goes to the pantry and pulls out a bag of kettle chips, then sits down next to me.

My eyebrows shoot up. I just listened to a podcast about these types of cruises and know the tickets could be upwards of $50,000—sometimes much more.

He offers me the bag and I take a handful of chips. "Wow," I say. "That's . . . so nice of you."

I pop the chips into my mouth in what feels like slow motion, trying to ignore the new edge of paranoia that's cut into my thoughts. The one that says that it seems convenient, too, that his parents haven't been here during the investigation, the detective interviews, the nonstop social media frenzy.

"Well, anything for some good old-fashioned validation." He shrugs. "Daddy issues, you know?"

I smile, but I know it looks tense, forced.

"My dad has early-onset Alzheimer's disease. I wanted them to have the experience while he's still somewhat okay. The symptoms aren't debilitating yet. But time is not our friend, as I'm sure you know. It's pretty scary."

"I'm sure," I manage. I don't know what else to say, so I eat some chips with an embarrassingly loud crunch. I didn't expect this kind of depth or self-awareness from him.

"So now you know a little more about me, right?" he says, with a wry smile. "There's no reason to tiptoe around each other. And I guess, weirdly, we do have something in common."

"What do you mean?"

"Last time I checked," he says, standing up so I have to tilt my chin upward to see his face, "she left us both."

I swallow. He walks around me to the fridge, grabbing a protein shake from the fridge.

He offers me one and I shake my head no.

"It's taken me a while to accept it, though. To be rational about it. At first, I literally refused to believe it," he says. "It didn't make any sense. We had this entire project going on, we were on the same page about a lot of stuff. We were happy. But then . . . I don't know, the sightings, the Instagram post, what the detectives said . . . at a certain point I just started to feel . . ."

"Pathetic." I offer.

"Bingo," he says, spinning the bottle cap on the counter. "That's exactly it. Pathetic. I mean, who am I to doubt what she literally posted, what she said, what the detectives said, who do this for a living. At a certain point I just started to feel like the boyfriend who can't take a hint that he's been broken up with. Who can't let it go."

He feels real to me in this moment—authentic, refreshing. Maybe I was reading him wrong, through the lens of his YouTube channel. Maybe this is why Evie liked him so much.

"It still doesn't make sense to me," he says. "I doubt it ever will unless Ev suddenly comes back from wherever the fuck she is and explains it all. Even then, I'm sure I'd still have questions. But things happen all the time that don't make sense. That doesn't mean they're not reality."

He has a point, of course.

He shakes his head. "I miss her like hell, all the time. But what am I supposed to do? I don't even know what there is to do except just . . . move on."

I say the only thing that feels true. "I miss her too."

"Would you look at that," he says, and there's that hint of a dimple again. "Now we have two things in common."

I smile too, and to my horror, I realize I'm blushing.

"Would you look at that," I repeat back to him.

"I guess I get it now," he says, leaning back against the countertop now, feet crossed in front of him. His hip bones jut out slightly, creating the tiniest gap between his skin and waistband.

"Get what?" I ask, leaning forward. I feel myself licking my lips.

Jesus Christ, Hazel. Really?

"Why she thought we'd get along," he says. "She always said that we'd hit it off. That on paper it didn't make sense, but in person we'd click."

"Is that what this is?" I laugh, even though he seems serious now. "Clicking?"

He picks up a tangerine from the counter and starts to peel it. "Could be."

The smell of citrus hits my nose and it steadies me just enough to remember: Whatever this is . . . cannot happen. Will not happen. And yet I feel like I'm watching him eat this piece of fruit at half speed, eyes hovering at his mouth. My brain feels warm and liquid, like all I'd have to do is lean an inch right or left and it'd all shift. I'd be propelled toward him.

I can see it: The way he'd fuck me. The heat and need and particular kind of release that comes from doing The Bad Thing. The tiny sliver of time when you've already chosen it, it's already decided, there's no going backward. You're all in, consumed with only the knowledge that it's happening, so you might as well enjoy it. You might as well do it again and again and again, luxuriate in the obliteration. You might as well bleed the pleasure out of it until there's nothing left, before the guilt hits you and you have the clarity to remember that you're the type of person who does something like this. Who knew they should say no but didn't.

I stare at him, a challenge.

I tell myself that he'll make the choice, the move. And if it happens, it happens. It won't be my mistake, not really.

He walks toward me and my pulse races, my skin electric. But then he stops short of where I'm sitting, eyes narrowing at me, considering something.

And then like a candle that's run out of wax, whatever was happening is burned out and done. Whatever was there is gone.

"So what did you really come here to talk about, Hazel?" he says, but it might as well be, *You didn't actually think that was going to happen, did you?*

And I hate myself for a minute, not for entertaining a fantasy but for believing that giving up control is ever worth it. Ever truly satisfying.

"I want to talk about what you and Evie were working on before she disappeared."

CHAPTER 19

"The transcript thing was ridiculous," Gavin says. "I was in there for, like, four hours. None of that stuff was leaked to TikTok, of course. Not the parts where I was crying, where I was a mess. Just the parts where I came off like the unemotional, detached loser boyfriend. I mean, you have to know that they grilled me for forever even though they cleared me, right? I have an airtight alibi. A doctor's appointment in Scottsdale—cameras, time stamps, witnesses. All of it."

"Okay, but what about the docuseries?" I say. "I never heard about that from Evie. It felt . . . made-up."

We're sitting on his couch now and he's leaning all the way back into the cushions, arms stretched out on either side. I'm directly under the AC vent now, and I have the urge to drape a blanket over my lap, tuck my legs under myself, but it feels too intimate. Too comfortable.

"Well, it wasn't." He laughs. "We really were working on something. Something pretty cool."

"Right," I say, rereading the transcript in my head. "Vibes."

"Well, yeah." He laughs again. "But I lied when I said we didn't have a subject."

I shoot him a look that says: *Explain. Now.*

"Well, not a lie. It was mostly true," he backtracks. "We did have a lot of different ideas. We had just recently focused in on one. I mean, it wasn't even an official decision, we were just researching one subject more than the others. It was completely irrelevant to the interview, to what we were talking about . . . there was no point in going down that rabbit hole with him. It would have distracted us from actually finding Evie."

I stare at him again, my nails digging into the leather couch cushion beside me. "Why don't you tell me what it was, and I'll be the judge of whether it matters or not?"

"I'll tell you whatever you want, Hazel," he says, his voice dropping lower than it was a minute ago. "Under one condition. You tell me why you hate me so much."

It feels playful, like a challenge. For a moment I feel myself slipping back into whatever was happening in the kitchen, weighing how easy it would be to simply let it happen. But the blast of the air-conditioning has sobered me enough to know that I can't go there. Not now. Not if I'm ever going to figure out what happened to my sister.

"Fine," I say, eager to get answers from him, to escape the intensity of this charge between us again. "It was . . . I didn't want more of that world for Evie. More followers, more spotlight, more scrutiny . . . I wanted something normal for her. Boring. And you were . . ."

"Not boring?" His hands are folded in his lap now, and he's staring at them, but then he looks up and smiles.

"No," I admit. "Not boring. I wanted her to have something that looked a little. . . simpler. A life that was quieter for once. That was . . ."

"Like yours?" he says quickly, maintaining eye contact with me.

I'm taken aback. "I mean, in a way . . . I guess, yes. She needed that," I say, trying my best not to sound defensive.

"She knew that, you know," he says. "That you wanted that for her. That you thought that was best."

I hate that I can't tell from his tone if she resented me for it, and I hate even more that I'm afraid to ask.

"I think that was why I said that in the interview," he says. "I shouldn't have. I know she loved you, both you and your mom. Especially you. You know that. It was just complicated, to be on the outside watching it all. To see the pressure she put on herself to please everyone. It was impossible. At the time, I thought . . . her being gone had to do with that. It must. But I had never considered I might be part of it, too, so what do I know? Nothing, clearly."

I don't know what to say.

"So." He slaps the back of the couch with his hand, as if signaling the end of that part of the bargain, and the beginning of his part. "What do you want to know?"

"The docuseries," I say. "What was that?"

As soon as I saw the word *docuseries* in the transcript, I guessed the same thing everyone else on the internet seemed to, based on the comments: They were filming something about Evie. About how she had grown up on social media. I could picture it so clearly that I was almost mad that I hadn't thought of it first. An in-depth docuseries about what it's like to grow up in the public eye, online, what it's like to have your childhood mined for content regularly. A critical analysis of the failings of my mother, of her selfishness, her own success, maybe. I could see it all now. It would be genius.

"It wasn't about Evie, if that's what you think," he says. I make a mental note that the growing-up-online docuseries is still on the table, then. But what would the ending be?

"It was about this management company," he goes on. "It was all top-secret, like, a month ago . . . but I guess it doesn't really matter if I tell you now, now that the project is on hold or, I don't even know. I can't imagine touching it without Evie now. The whole thing was her idea in the first place. But, yeah, it was about an influencer management company that is . . . sketchy."

"Sketchy how?"

"They take advantage of people like Ev and me," he says. "They're called ReBrand. Like other agencies, they manage influencers, negotiate brand deals, take a cut. Whatever. Not a big deal. Evie told me about it first, that she had heard some rumor about it. And when they reached out to me to work together, I was skeptical at first, but the more I talked to them, the more interested I was."

I settle into my spot on the couch, comfortable for the first time since I got to Gavin's house.

"They reached out to me, right?" he says. "But before I knew it, it became like . . . I had to convince them that I was the right person for the agency. There were endless interviews. They'd call me out of nowhere, always from a blocked number, and just quiz me on everything. My life, my family, my goals, my dreams. It sounds nuts, I know, but the more intense it became, the longer it went on, the more I wanted to be part of it. I was invested, you know? It seemed like a real opportunity, something deeper than other agencies had offered, other partnerships."

His phone buzzes then, a phone call. He studies the caller ID and I can swear his face goes a shade paler for a second, but he sends it to voicemail.

"Anyway, after eight weeks or so of this, things started to get a little weird," he goes on. "Maybe I should have known it was weird all along, but I don't know . . . I get so many people in my inbox begging me to work with them, the fact that they were doing the opposite seemed somehow . . . meaningful. The final step to this thing was apparently this big, three-day-long meeting, a big pitch, where I'd finally find out if I made the cut. And I had agreed and everything. My flight to California was booked. And then they started asking me about my dad."

"About your dad?" I say. "What? About him being sick?"

"Yes," he says. "And the thing is, almost no one knew about the Alzheimer's other than the people closest to me. I know you probably think . . . the videos, the Dear Evie stuff . . . I know you think that I'd monetize anything. But this was different. There was a line for me. And at first, they asked around it . . . 'Are there any traumas you're processing at the moment?' and 'Is anyone in your life going through a particularly hard time right now?' but I guess they didn't like the answers I was giving because by the end of it, they were flat-out asking me. 'It must be hard, to know that someone you love won't even recognize you in a few years. Isn't life so fragile, Gavin?' Shit like that."

I suddenly feel cold again, like the weed has worn off out of nowhere.

"That's very weird," I say. "How would they know?"

"I have no idea. I still don't," he says, shaking his head. "But eventually it became clear what they were getting at. They wanted me to use it."

"What? What do you mean, use it?"

"They wanted me to share about it . . . to monetize it, really," he says. "I mean, they didn't say that *exactly*, but it was clear. They kept saying that the only way social media works is with humans behind it, and the only way you master your platform is if you continually remind people of that humanity. If you use that part of you to help the greater good. They had been saying some version of this from the beginning, that they're only looking for people who don't filter themselves, blah, blah, blah . . . but I thought they meant *literal* filters at first. Not . . . we want people who show the world everything. Every horrible thing."

He laughs, and it comes out bitter.

"From what Evie and I learned, ReBrand's whole thing was this idea of the Greater Good—capital G's—that they'd find people willing to share the darkest things that had happened to them, and when people inevitably engaged with that stuff, and more followers and bigger partnerships came . . . because, you know, they always do . . . part of the money we made would go back to people in need. Nonprofits. The Greater Good. It was included in their cut, they said—if they took 40 percent, then half of that would go to worthy causes, they said. They gave me some insane number, seven figures at least, and told me that *that's* what I could generate for Alzheimer's research if I signed up with them. I was freaked out and a little pissed, obviously, but I also thought, for a split second, that maybe this is how I make something good of all of this. Maybe this is my opportunity to really make a name for myself for something honestly, truly . . . well, good."

It sounds like a scam. Or an MLM. But I also see how the pitch would appeal to creators, especially those who are regularly categorized as shallow or dumb or problematic. A thing to point to and say, "Would I really do this if I was as vapid as you think I am?"

"By the time I realized what was going on, how fucked-up it all was . . . that they were using people's issues, their pain and sadness, to make themselves money . . . they were packaging it and selling it, I knew I wanted the world to know about it," he says. "People needed to know how wrong it was."

I wonder how people would react. I've been on the internet even longer than Gavin has, after all. I've seen the way people gain a following after tragedy—had experienced it firsthand. Once I saw it with my dad and my mom and Evie, I saw it everywhere. People sharing about their child dying or their spouse leaving or a terrible diagnosis and suddenly gaining a whole new audience, people who tuned in for trauma porn and then ended up sticking around. I know it says more, maybe, about the people following along—their inability to look away, to turn down the sick sort of relief that comes from a good cry, a sad movie, even if they know what they are consuming comes from someone else's very real pain.

But I understand the inclination to share, anyway. I know the desperation to feel less alone in your grief. On the fifth anniversary of my dad's death, I was twenty and having what felt like my best year of life yet. My classes were going well, and I had an internship lined up for the summer and a boyfriend who seemed promising at the time. For the first time in years, I felt like anything was possible. But I missed my dad in a way that felt bottomless, too painful to articulate even to myself most of the time. I found the words that year, though. I wrote paragraphs describing every horrible corner of grief and loss, to see if someone out there would recognize them. If anyone had been to those places, too. And though I rarely posted anything personal on Instagram, I shared it that day, pasted it all in a caption of a photo of my dad and me. I'm seven or eight in the shot, and we're sitting in front of the half-built reading nook on the bus, a book in my hands, a hammer in his. I hit POST and felt instantly lighter, as if the writing (and sharing it) had lifted something that had been sitting on my chest for years. It was one of the first moments that made me want to switch my major to journalism. Figuring out the truth and writing it all down. I could do that forever, I thought.

As it turned out, though, my mother had beat me to it—I knew she scheduled an anniversary post every year, with a still of the viral video of Evie and Dad and a caption about how life had never been the same since he died—and my stomach sank. It wasn't too dissimilar to my post, but it felt performative somehow. I wondered if people would think my post was performative, too. If our whole family was still trying to capitalize on our tragedy.

Based on how my family became famous, it shouldn't surprise me that some company out there had turned suffering into a business model.

"I had the skills. I had the cameras. I had the contacts. I had the perspective," Gavin continues, bringing me back. "I knew I could pitch it to Netflix for some serious money and honestly, I really wanted it. I thought it would be a great way to do something different, to prove that I could succeed doing something else . . . a different avenue within content creation. Something my dad could see before . . . before it all gets worse, and he would know I had tried to do something important."

I nod, thinking about what the docuseries would look like on my Netflix home screen. How quickly I would have hit PLAY. People would be skeptical at first if they heard Gavin had created it. But I also knew they would watch.

"And Evie knew about all of this?" I ask.

"One hundred percent." He nods. "She was all about it. Honestly, it was another reason why her leaving made sense to me. We were in this thing together. I was going to go meet up with them, she was going to produce it from here. We were going to pitch it to the streaming services as a joint thing. She was excited about it."

"So, what?" I say. "She was going to go with you to this big meeting? Join in and secretly film the whole thing?"

"No, that was the thing . . . she was never supposed to go," he says. "They actually didn't even want her. Evie even reached out to them. I thought surely they'll want Evie. Surely, they'll want this huge name. But Ev said they told her that unless she had something else to offer them, there was no more work for them to do. She'd already shared too much."

Something in me prickles with anger at the idea of some board room of people, somewhere deciding that my sister wasn't good enough for them. That her pain wasn't good enough.

"Or her mom had," I said. "Right?"

"Right. They said that Evie's trauma already seemed . . . hollowed out. Branded within an inch of its life. Those were their exact words, according to Evie. It made me want to expose them even more."

It was true that Evie always shared on social media about our dad, mental health, breakups . . . she was open about it all, the way people seemed to want her to be. The problem was that being open about so much also seemed to make people think that there wasn't still a line. That there weren't certain things that stayed tied down, even when you let everything else come to the surface.

"Anyway, I said no to the Alzheimer's pitch, and they ghosted me," he says. "Two weeks later, Evie went missing, so I haven't really thought about it since. I don't want to do the docuseries without her. At least not anytime soon. And by the time I get to it . . . well who knows what Re-Brand will be, or if someone else will expose them first. So, that project is dead and gone. And Evie is just gone. And here I am."

"Here we are," I say quietly, still processing everything.

"You know, it's part of why I did the search party," Gavin says. "I thought, maybe I could honor Evie by still doing a docuseries—just not the one we planned."

I think back to Palm Springs, the way he had insisted on no cameras.

"I thought you didn't film anything there . . ."

"Well, I wanted people to be natural." He shrugs. "And, you know, focused, of course. On finding Evie."

Right. His main priority.

"The dashcam stuff only featured Ashlyn and me . . . and the drone was more of a B-roll situation, to be honest," he goes on. "At that point, it was all about leads, but now . . . I don't know, I thought I could use my vlogs, the footage from the search . . . all of it to create something about her legacy. I think she'd love that."

I shake my head. How had I not noticed the drone? How could I not have assumed that he'd have some kind of plan to capitalize further on this? It makes perfect sense. I can imagine the sponsors. The views. People would eat it up. God knows everyone is still clamoring for more of Evie, that there's a certain portion of the internet that feels the same way I do. Like we all deserve more answers. Like they're out there.

And then I remember another unanswered question.

"How did you even know about the car? About Palm Springs?" I ask. "The detectives said they didn't tell you. You weren't supposed to know."

He laughs, then looks at me expectantly, like he's waiting for me to admit that I'm joking—like there's some unspoken thing between us that I should already know. He waits for a minute and then clears his throat, shrugging.

"Well, I mean, look at the transcript on TikTok," he offers. "It's not like the investigation was exactly airtight."

"So, what?" I say. "You just wanted to use the information for yourself?"

"I just wanted to see if I could find her. And to show all the people who thought the other videos were fake. That I wasn't really crying, or upset, or that I didn't really miss her . . . that it was all a prank," he says. "Like it would signal I was doing something instead of just talking about doing something. Instead of just making videos."

It sounds less creepy this way. Less creepy than it looked, anyway. But it's also more calculated.

"I had to try," he adds.

Did he?

"I did care, Hazel," he says, staring directly into my eyes now. "I do."

I meet his gaze, and I'm surprised to find that I want to believe him.

"Why do you think that I only let the five of us go?" he presses. "That I said no to the people who reached out to me two or three or four times about joining? The people who claimed to know her so well, but I had never heard of? There were hundreds of them."

I had to give him that; he kept the location from Evie fans, true crime aficionados, journalists who must have wanted their own angle on the investigation. But who else had wanted to join? I had been so focused on the way Gavin was inserting himself in the investigation that I hadn't even thought to ask who else had.

"Like who?" I ask.

"So many people," he says, seeming relieved to shift the conversation. "Teenage girls. Older women. Dudes. A ton of people."

"Did anyone push harder? Really try to make a case for themselves, beg you?" I press.

"I mean, they were all kind of nuts . . ." he says, shaking his head slowly like he's trying to dislodge a piece of information. But then something seems to occur to him, and his eyes light up.

"There was this one guy . . . an older guy, I guess," he says. "He insisted he and Evie were close. That he had the privilege of watching her grow up for years and knew everything about her. That she was like his *daughter*."

"Ew," I say.

"I know," he says. "That was a hard no. I blocked him pretty quick and that was that. But man, he sent a lot of weird messages before that."

"Do you remember his name?" I ask, my brain whirring. "Or username?"

"Something with a C . . ." Gavin muses. "I think?"

Then I remember the message in my inbox. The person who had said it was a privilege to know Evie, to watch her grow older. And then I remember the other popular Reddit theory. The one about Evie's most-frequent commenter.

"Charlie?" I ask. "Was it Charlie?"

Gavin's eyes light up with recognition.

"Yes."

CHAPTER 20

My brain is full of tiny red flags, all of them waving in unison, as I desperately try to remember the theory I had read online, the one that said this person took Evie just to keep her to himself. Wouldn't that be exactly the type of person who would insist on joining a search party? Who would get off on watching Gavin's videos, watching him cry about how he missed his girlfriend?

It was also exactly the type of person who my sister would ignore entirely, if she even noticed them at all. Dismiss as harmless if I had begged her to worry. I understood, of course, that a person like this was normal to her in the way that anything you grow up with becomes average, boring. Sometimes, when my anxiety subsided, I was grateful she could tune it all out. I knew that if she panicked at every creepy thing someone sent to her, she'd been panicked all the time. I didn't want that for her, either.

I think of when she was ten and some crazed fan sent her a doll that had been pieced together with mismatched parts, a face painted on to match Evie's. She had sent me a picture like it was nothing. Like it was funny.

"It's like, *really* weird looking, isn't it, Hazey?" she had said on the phone later, using a nickname that I only heard once in a blue moon. "Mom says it's because I'm an *inspiration.*"

I tried to give my mom the benefit of the doubt for a minute. Maybe this was her way of shielding Evie from the darker side. From having to explain to her how truly messed up it was. When I visited Evie a couple

olivia muenter

years later, just after I had graduated from college, she was twelve but the doll was still there, sitting on the top shelf of her closet, staring down at us between some old dance costumes.

"God, that's creepy," I had said, pulling it from the shelf and holding it away from myself as though it smelled bad. "Can we please get rid of this, Evie? Please. I swear it's haunted."

"Get rid of *Evianna*?" She gasped. "I could never."

"It has a nickname?" I said. "Good God. Please don't tell me that was Mom's idea."

"No." She laughed. "I came up with it. She's like my uglier, scarier twin. No one wants to take her picture or film her, but you know . . . I kind of like that about her. She lives a nice, quiet, relaxing life up there on the shelf. Weird and free."

I stared at the misshapen, fading facial features on the doll, the messy shock of auburn hair, the freckles that had been dotted on with Magic Marker, that made it look like someone was trying to cancel out her face. It was the ugliest thing I had ever seen. It made my skin crawl.

"This is definitely when my job as a big sister requires to inform you that there is like an *entire* genre of horror films about dolls that come to life and kill their owners," I said.

"Oh, don't be dramatic," she brushed me off, taking the doll from my hand and tossing it back on the shelf. "It's not like it's real."

Was this like that stupid doll, I wondered? Has it always been this way with Evie, not fearing the things she should? I think of her texts to Ashlyn. Could I even imagine an Evie who was ever genuinely that scared?

I am scrolling on my phone now, ignoring Gavin, desperate to spot Charlie's comments anywhere I can find them. To somehow string them together in a way that makes sense, that will lead me to answers.

"Hazel," he says, insistently, like maybe this isn't the first time he's said my name since I started scrolling. "What are you doing?"

"What if this guy has her? What if he held a gun to her head somewhere, made her post that she's okay?" I ask. "I need to find him. To figure out who he is. Where he is. I need to. It has to mean something."

"What about the other 250 people that messaged me asking to look for her, too, Hazel?" he says. "And the hundred other people I have in my inbox right now, sending me their theories of what really happened to her? You can't do this forever. You'll go insane."

I glare at him and finally feel sober. "So, what? It's back to business as usual for you, then? Back to ads and videos and just pretending that she didn't exist? This just isn't good enough content for *Dear Evie: The Feature Film*?"

He looks at me with something like pity for a second, and I hate it.

"What I'm making . . . it's about the investigation. What happened. Not what's happening. It's over, Hazel. Don't you get it? She told us to drop it."

Every retort I can think of pulses through me, but I say nothing. I feel like he's scolding me.

"Think for a second how it would look," he says. "How it would go. If I keep pushing this thing, keep asking questions, ignore what Evie literally said herself—"

"You don't know if that was really her," I interrupt, my voice quieter than I mean for it to be.

"—ignore what the detectives said . . ." he goes on, pressing his point. "I'll look obsessive. Controlling. The psycho ex."

I stand, ready to walk out the door, confident that there's nothing else here for me, but he speaks as I turn to go.

"I want answers, too. I do," he says. "But I can't beg someone to come back if they've already said they're not going to. Even if I want to. They would eat me alive for it."

I know he means the internet, but I wonder if that should really matter. If he really wanted to know where Evie was so badly, if he really cared, then how could he take any of the possible judgment or fallout into account? How could that be more important than finding my sister?

But I don't want to fight. To beg him to care. To convince him. I'll do this on my own, same as always. Same as everything. Maybe that's why I've been here so long—to feel like I'm not alone in it. Suddenly I can't stay a moment longer.

"I should go," I say, gesturing toward the door. "I didn't mean to take up so much of your day." Gavin stands and raises his arms as if to give me a hug, but I walk by him, through the house, out the door, and to my car.

olivia muenter

Even now, after everything, touching him feels too dangerous, a starting point instead of an end.

My car is scorching hot from baking in the Arizona sun for the last couple of hours, the steering wheel too hot to touch. I check my phone while the AC kicks in; no texts or calls. Part of me still believes, every time I pick up my phone, that this might be the moment I finally have a missed call from Evie.

I open Instagram. There's another message in my inbox from a username I don't recognize, and I tap through. I'm committed to following every lead now, no matter how unlikely, how dark.

It's a picture. The sender and I don't follow each other, so I have to tap the screen to reveal the image. I expect to see a screenshot of some story about my sister, a rumor, a #WhereInTheWorldIsEvieDavis shot in Amsterdam. But it's not.

The picture takes a minute to load, and my eyes drift from the screen to Gavin's house to the screen again as I wait. When I look back for the third time, the image is there staring back at me. It's a closeup of what anyone else would think is a scribble, a child's messy drawing. But I recognize it right away. It's a photo of a face I know well, though the last time I saw it was almost a decade ago. A chill crawls up my back.

It's Evianna. Evie's ugly, horrible doll. And it's staring right at me.

r/WhereIsEvieDavis

SwipeUpForBS

Look. I need to speak my truth. I never thought this day would come, never thought I'd be here, but I need to be honest. I miss Evie Davis. There! I said it! It's done. I miss her. I can't believe bitch just up and LEFT US HERE. High and dry! Where are my links! My OOTDs! My GRWM videos that make me feel like shit about my body, face, and life! Forget everything I said before. I want them back!! Nay, I need them back! I have a sickness.

⬆ 426 ⬇   💬 88

> **KendallICanFixU**
>
> Omg. Yes. Same. Ok, I've found my people. I am regularly struck with this feeling to go check her stories and then I remember. Did I enjoy hating her before? No. Do I miss hating her now? Yes. Yes I do. It's so depressing.
>
> **EmotionalMotionSickness**
>
> Sometimes I just watch Gavin's stories just to feel something now. Just to remember. Shit has gotten DARK.
>
> > **LostOnline2001**
> >
> > Speak for yourselves. I feel free. I haven't shopped on Amazon in weeks. My 9-year-old has finally stopped asking when she's going to post a new TikTok. It's wonderful.
> >
> > > **PrincessLeona**
> > >
> > > Lol who lets their 9-year-old on TikTok
> > >
> > > > **LostOnline2001**
> > > >
> > > > There are plenty of other places to parent-shame on this cursed website if you're looking for one . . . but this ain't it.
> > > >
> > > > > **PrincessLeona**
> > > > >
> > > > > I just think it's funny that someone can criticize Evie Davis and then let their elementary-school-aged child on an app that is actively rotting their brain
>
> **123LetsGoB1tch**
>
> Is anyone else still feeling weird about ALL of this? I'm still not buying that she's just living a new life somewhere. I can't. I simply won't. That *Darker* interview? The weird-ass way she sounded in that Instagram post or, like,

allegedly did, I guess? Nope, no way. Something is very sus here. It's gotta be.

LostOnline2001

Y'all honestly think that she didn't plan all of this? She's probably still actively making money off of all of us as we speak as she lounges in some sprawling beachside villa in Mexico, free of her crazy-ass mother and her toxic boyfriend and her boring friends. There's no conspiracy theory. She literally told us what was going on here!!!! Point blank! Let it go!!

User4815162342

What about her sister, though? Weren't they close?

EmotionalMotionSickness

EVIE DAVIS HAS A SISTER? WTF?

CHAPTER 21

I don't trust myself to drive the five hours home. I was hazy before from the weed, the heat, the hours trying to get a true read on Gavin, but the Instagram message is acting like a stimulant. My brain is scrambled, but one thing is clear: I need to see if the doll is still in Evie's room.

My mother opens the door wearing a cashmere robe. I have never known enough about fashion to be able to identify fabric on the spot, but immediately, I know. This is cashmere. This is buttery, expensive, the type of clothing the lead in a movie is wearing when someone unexpectedly shows up at their door. It's the thing they're supposed to cocoon into as they say "Who is it?" like they just feel so exposed in this state of undress, so embarrassed to be wearing an item of clothing that was handmade in Mongolia and cost $500.

This is how my mother looks when she sees me. Not shocked, exactly, but like this wasn't how she imagined her night going. Like I'm a friend from high school who's visiting town and said she might stop by. The understanding being, of course, that they won't. But here I am.

"I was in the neighborhood," I say. "Can I . . ."

I don't know whether to finish the question with "come in" or "ask you some questions" or "search upstairs" but eventually she puts me out of my misery, opening the door wider and stepping aside.

I expect her to ask why I'm here, if something happened, if I heard something about Evie, but instead she walks toward the couch. The TV is paused on some Netflix show that I don't recognize. There are pillows and blankets piled on the couch in a way that makes me think she's been here a while. Sleeping here, maybe.

She sits down in a corner of the couch and gestures toward the seat opposite her, a sweeping arm motion that says *join me*.

It's not even happy hour yet, but there's a near-empty bottle of wine on the coffee table, a glass perched on the side table next to her. I've spent more time around my mother in the past month than I have in the past four years, but this feels like the first time we have sat in silence, unsure what we're waiting for. No detectives at the door. No call we're anticipating. Is this what our family has boiled down to now? Is this how it will be?

I really look at her, concentrate. Beyond the cashmere, the veneers, the Botox, she looks tired. Her eyes are swollen and red, fixed on the TV, though she's yet to press PLAY. She reaches for her glass now and takes a big sip of wine.

"So . . . how are you?" I finally say.

Her eyes dart my way and stay there, like she's studying me, trying to gauge if I'm being serious or not. Eventually, she laughs.

"I'm doing spectacularly, Hazel," she says, gesturing around the room with her wineglass. Her sarcasm shouldn't wound me, not after all these years. After everything. But it does. Even when everything tilts off its axis, some things are exactly the same.

"Got it," I say, pushing myself up from the edge of the couch, remembering why I came here. The doll. A night of sleep. I was planning to ask my mom if she leaked the Palm Springs information to Gavin, but I don't even know if it matters anymore. If it should have been surprising to me at all.

"Wait," she says when I'm halfway to the stairs. "That was rude."

I pause, a bit surprised at the admission.

"I'm stressed, okay? Sad. Devastated. And work is, well . . . you can imagine. Worse than ever. Any brand deals I had in flux are gone. No one wants to touch this drama with a ten-foot pole, especially since it's all so . . . mysterious. Why did Evie leave? Why doesn't Erin know? What *horrors* occurred in her house to cause this? And it's not like I could just hop on Stories and sell some workout gear now, anyway, right? I'm just . . . done. It's all done."

I imagine the podcast didn't help things, I consider saying, but I bite my tongue.

"And let me tell you," she goes on, laughing darkly, "it certainly doesn't help anything when your own daughter doesn't seem to trust you, either."

"Evie's post could have meant all kinds of things, Mom . . ."

"I mean *you*, Hazel," she says. "*You* don't believe me. Though I guess you're right, in a way. Evie didn't trust me, either. I mean, clearly." She laughs again. She looks around the room, and I wonder if she's thinking the same thing I am, at the same time: *I've never felt this alone.* It crosses my mind that this is the one thing we agree on, that life without Evie is unbearable. It's more obvious than ever that we were never meant to be here without her.

"Look," she starts again, and I can tell she's trying to overenunciate, to disguise the way her words have started to blend, her consonants dulled by alcohol. "I know I fucked up with you. I know. There's no sugarcoating it. It's just the truth."

I open my mouth to respond, to tell her that she's wrong without thinking, to make myself agreeable, to make all of this easier. I want to say that we don't have to do this, not now, not ever, maybe. But she holds up her free hand, the one that isn't balancing her wineglass, to stop me.

"Let me just say this," she says softly. "Please."

I nod once. What else is there to do?

"I know you never wanted anything to do with any of it. Not from the very beginning. Even before your dad died. You hated it all, and you let me know again and again, every single time I tried to include you. And I thought—okay, fine. Let her hate it. Let her do her own thing," she says. "And so I did. I watched you distance yourself from all of it, from us, and I let it happen."

She's staring toward the wall of photos behind me, her eyes traveling over the memories, so many of which include only the smallest snippets of me.

"Before . . . what happened with your dad, before the video went viral . . . it was fine, right? You drove me insane with your stubbornness, but I also loved it. I thought: That's my girl. That's just like me. Maybe the only thing that was like me. And then it all changed. It got so much bigger, and you got so much more independent. I missed your dad so much every day and the only thing that seemed to make it even remotely bearable was to throw myself into this world. I told myself I would build this thing. For the three of us . . . even if you wanted nothing to do with it. Or me."

The unexpectedness of what she's saying hits me all at once, and I feel my throat pinch with tears. I dig my nails into my palm to keep from crying. I won't do that. Not now.

And what does she want from me? To tell her it's all okay? That I wasn't grieving and traumatized from losing Dad, too? That she was the adult I needed her to be, and I had been the child? No, I won't do that. Before I can reply, though, she keeps talking.

"I honestly thought I was nurturing the thing in you that seemed most important. In both of you. You hated the photos, the videos, the posts. My job. So I kept it all away from you. Evie couldn't get enough of it, so I gave her more of it. I thought I was doing the right thing. But I get it now. I pushed you so far away that it made it impossible for you to ever really come back, even when you needed me," she says, nodding as she talks. She takes another swig of wine and then she turns my way again. "I guess this is just who I am. What I do. I have to live with that."

What she's saying is so raw and honest that I don't know what to do with it, or with myself. I'm both relieved and surprised when she keeps going.

"I think there was part of me, for a little while at least, who was waiting for you to come around. I thought that'd you'd see everything I did for Evie and know that I'd do that for you, too. I'd champion whatever you wanted me to champion. I'd be there cheering for you, shoving a camera in your face and making you famous for whatever it is you wanted to be famous for."

"Not everyone wants to be famous, Mom," I say quietly.

"I don't mean famous, maybe. Just . . . successful. Happy. Whatever that meant to you. I wanted to help you make that happen. When I first got pregnant with you, I was so young. Your dad and I were surprised, and, frankly, scared shitless, but all I could think about was that fight with my dad. The way he had crushed my dreams. Doubted me so completely. I told myself I would never be that person. I would make my child know that I thought they should be shown off to the world. I would celebrate them on every mountaintop. We barely had any money, but I knew I could do that."

She laughs.

"And then you were born. And you grew up. And I realized that it was never going to be that simple. I was so proud of our life, of you, of the three of us," she says. "And then after years of not being able to have a baby . . . Evie."

She stops for a moment, like she's going to cry, but she clears her throat, sits up straighter, and keeps going.

"All the joy was just amplified. I couldn't keep it in. I had to share it," she says. "And when things got bad, when they were horrible, when we lost your dad . . . I didn't know what to do but to share that, too. The grief was spilling out of me just as much as any of the happiness was. I didn't know where to put it, Hazel. On you? On your sister? I couldn't do that to you. So into the world it went. And then it just . . . I don't know what happened. People suddenly were paying me for this thing that for years I had been doing for free, for fun. Was I supposed to stop when I had myself and two children to support? Maybe I should apologize for that, but I won't. Other things, though . . . the way you got lost in it all. Yes, I'm sorry for that, baby. I am."

It's maybe the first time I've heard my mother apologize to me about anything.

"I . . ." I start, completely unsure what to say. "Thanks. Thank you."

In response she thrusts her empty wineglass in my direction, like a toast, and then lifts herself off the couch, walking past me toward the kitchen. I can hear her open another bottle of wine and pour it as I walk back to the couch and sit down.

I'm used to my rock-hard thrift store loveseat, something with cushions so dense and solid that I could probably do a back handspring off of them. This thing, though? This thing is made for melting into. Everything about it is designed to keep you right where you are, to make sure you don't leave. It makes me feel uneasy, this level of comfort, like it dulls my senses slightly. It occurs to me that I need to be sharp for this, whatever this is.

I'm adjusting myself amid all the pillows when a wineglass pops into the corner of my vision. I look over my shoulder and my mom is standing there, a full glass in one hand and another held out for me. I take it, grateful that I'll at least have something to do instead of talk.

"Thanks," I say, taking a small sip.

"I figured it couldn't hurt." She smiles. "You know a brand sent this when everything first happened? When Evie first went missing? Some sort of PR thing with a note that was like, 'To make a hard time easier'—I mean, they're not wrong, but really?"

"God," I say. "That's dark."

We both laugh a little, if awkwardly. This is new for us. Hanging out on the couch. Talking about something real. Her apologizing. The fact that I've just shown up here, no explanation, and she hasn't asked why I'm here or when I'm leaving. This is what Evie and my mom do, not us.

"My therapist says this is the first step." She sighs, scooching herself back into the L-shaped corner of the couch, stretching her legs out in front of her.

"Your therapist," I say back to her. "The one you mentioned the other day with the detectives? That therapist?"

"Well, yes," she says.

"So you weren't recording the *Darker* interview that day then?"

She takes a sip of wine, slowly. "Well, two things can happen on one day."

I sigh.

"Plus, I mean, I didn't really need to be there. Gavin kept me posted," she adds casually. "It was part of the agreement. He could use the location, the cameras . . . and I could handle other avenues."

Of course she was the one who told Gavin about Palm Springs, the car. Of course it wouldn't have just been the podcast, a one-off thing. Erin Davis always had a bigger plan.

"I mean, no good media blitz involves one platform," she goes on, as if reading my mind "YouTube, podcasts, blog posts . . . if *Darker* hadn't blown up in my face so spectacularly, it all would have worked seamlessly together, serving the intended purpose: more eyes on what was happening."

I notice she doesn't say "finding your sister."

"But, I mean, the therapy part is true, too," she says. "Isn't this what people your age are always going on about? What Evie's always telling me to do? I thought you'd be proud of me," she says.

"No, no," I say. "It's good. It is."

It is, right?

"Anyway, she's been saying that I should talk to you for months now. Months. All year, really. Since . . ."

Don't say it. Come on.

"Since last year, you know . . . and now, with all of this . . ."

She takes another long sip of wine, nodding as she does, as if she's telling herself a story, or coaching herself, reminding herself of how this is supposed to go. "Honestly, I haven't been ready for any of it yet, but she said I'd know when I was, when it was the right time, that a door would open and we'd finally have a real conversation about all of it, and wouldn't you know . . . here you are. At the door," she says. "So why not?"

Something about her tone is making me uncomfortable, and it's not the slight slurring. It's like we've turned off the path I thought we were on and now we're headed toward something different.

"Oh, yeah," I hear myself saying anyway. "That makes sense."

"It's up to you and me to open the lane of communication, she said, and it's on me to let you know that I'm ready at any point to listen," she says, her posture straightening as she speaks, like she's proud of herself. "To hear you out."

I take another sip of my wine, my eyes narrowing in confusion. "To hear me out?"

She smiles at me sweetly.

"We're both adults here, Hazel," she says. "We can both admit when we've done something wrong. We can both apologize, right?"

So that's what this is.

She looks at me expectantly for a moment. Waiting for me to apologize, I guess. My expression must give me away, because she rolls her eyes.

"Oh, please," she says. "Don't act like you haven't made mistakes here too. You can't be the victim in every room, every time, Hazel. Haven't you learned that by now?"

I stare at her, imagining the face of Evie's doll floating in front of her features, something ugly amidst all the beauty of the room. The doll. I need to go look for the doll. What was I thinking sitting here, drinking wine, trying to have a conversation like we'd ever have a normal relationship?

"I should go to bed," I say, though what I really want to say is: *You're drunk, and a narcissist. And this—us—it's the same thing it's always been: pointless.*

But I'm eager to change the subject. To look for the hideous doll that I can't close my eyes without seeing, and then go to sleep and wake up and go somewhere far, far away from this. Somewhere where I can actually help Evie, maybe.

"Oh, you're staying, then?" She laughs. "By all means. Make yourself at home. Glad you feel so comfortable taking advantage of it all again. That didn't last very long, did it?"

She means last year, of course. Last year when we sat in this house and I told myself that this is the last time. The last time I ever took anything from her.

"I'll be gone first thing," I say, and for a moment I've never hated myself more. All those years I told Evie to stand up to our mother, and I can't even walk out the door.

I'm halfway up the stairs, making my way to Evie's room, my mind flashing to that shelf in her closet, when my mom yells up behind me.

"I couldn't have protected her anyway, you know," she says. "I never could have. So why should I have been the one to change? In a world of people plastering their kids and their ugly babies with faces like wrinkled elbows on the internet every single second of every goddamn day, why should it have been me who has to say no more, to make some sweeping, moral choice? To lose out on money, on a career, on a whole world of opportunity? Me, who's bringing joy to people? Who's supporting your sister's dream? Why should I have to be better than all of it? It's not my fault the world loved your sister as much as we did from the beginning. That's not on me. Everyone acts like it's my responsibility to set some standard for parenting, when really I'm just following the same impulse every other person sharing their small, stupid life on Facebook has. Pride. Excitement. The urge to shove your kid into the world and say, hey, that amazing thing is part of me, too. I did that. I built that. I created that. And one day, that kid may hate me or judge or resent me or push me away, but there's nothing that changes that fact that without me, they're nothing. Not even an idea of a person."

She's leaning halfway on the back of the couch now, steadying herself.

"You can judge me all you want, Hazel," she says. "But you'll never understand until you have kids. That is human fucking nature, baby. Sure, there were years when I could have pulled back. But guess what? I didn't want to. I wanted to be someone more than I didn't want to be a lesson. And now I have to live with that. Now I'm both instead of nothing at all."

This time I don't say anything, just turn and walk up the stairs to my sister's room, missing her so much it makes my teeth ache. I open her door and turn on the light, and everything looks exactly the same. Everything in its place. I walk to her enormous walk-in closet, shelves and hangers full of clothes from high-end designers and indie brands, tags still attached to so many of them.

I flick on the light and stand on my tiptoes. I've never wanted to see an ugly thing so badly. But when I find the spot where the doll lives in my memories, and all the shelves around it, it's nowhere. It's gone, just like Evie.

CHAPTER 22

I wake up with a jolt, and all of me feels wrong. My whole body feels pinched. My neck is drenched in sweat, my feet freezing cold. I feel sore, like I've been exercising, though I know that's not right. But it's something else that's bothering me, a feeling like I'm lost, like I have no idea where I am. I pull at the comforter on top of me, running my fingers over the fabric, trying to remember it. This isn't the guest room. And then I remember: this is Evie's room. I fell asleep in Evie's room.

I remember the horrible conversation with my mother, the closet, the missing doll. I was bone-tired, like all I wanted to do was lie down and be crushed by a ten-foot wave of sleep. I'd laid down on Evie's bed and imagined the wave flattening me before I could even take a single deep breath. I hadn't meant to sleep here, in her room. Or maybe I had. Maybe it's the only thing that made me feel settled.

I run my hand over the linen bedspread, the familiar shade of sage. And then the memory is floating into my consciousness, bringing me right back to that day last year.

Evie and I had spent the day in her room talking, watching TV, opening mailers from brands who wanted to send her free things in the hopes that she'd post it online. She'd been scrolling through Pinterest on her laptop, making a mood board of everything she wanted for her senior year.

"I want this to be the year where I just let myself go a bit," Evie had said, as if she was sixty instead of seventeen. "Do whatever I want. No more rules. No more worrying about what everyone will say."

"I love that for you," I said, and she had thrust the laptop toward me then, trying to show me the collage of images she had made, the aesthetic she was hoping to mold the next year of her life into. But my thumb moved the mouse when I grabbed the laptop, accidentally clicking on another browser tab. By the time I realized exactly what I was looking at—her bank account—it was all right there in front of me, my brain already making sense of the figures. There was a checking account with just over $4,000 in it, and a savings account with even less.

"Evie," I said, treading carefully, knowing that I had inadvertently invaded her privacy. "I accidentally clicked this tab but . . . is this your only bank account?"

"Snooping, are we?" she teased, in a way that said she didn't really care if I looked. That it wasn't that big of a deal to her.

But it was to me.

"Seriously, Evie," I pushed. "Is this it? There's nothing else?"

This wasn't right. She should have had hundreds of thousands of dollars in savings and investments, minimum. Seven figures would have made more sense to me. Enough money to put herself through college and then do whatever she wanted to do after that.

"I mean, there's other money, obviously," she said. "But I don't handle that."

My chest tightened.

"Mom does," she said.

"Mom does," I repeated back to her. "She controls all of it?"

"Not all of it, obviously. She pays me every month from what I make—a few thousand, usually, enough to cover basically anything I want." She shrugged, clicking back to Pinterest, to building her dream life. "And then if I want something bigger—the car, for example, I just ask. It's easier this way. What am I going to do with all that money right now? Buy the entire skin care section of Sephora on a whim? Maybe. I wouldn't put it past myself."

A few thousand dollars a month was a lot of money for a teenager, I knew that. But Evie was making so much more than that. She had to be. Still, she seemed so unfazed by my concern, so unbothered by it, that I wanted to believe her. That this setup really did make sense. That my

olivia muenter

mom really was saving and monitoring her money, safeguarding it for when Evie was ready to go to college, or buy her first home.

"So you get it all when you turn eighteen, then?" I asked. "Next year?"

"That's the plan," she said. "And in the meantime, I can just . . . chill. I mean, we have meetings, Hazel. She tells me the balances or whatever. I'm not worried about it."

"And then she's no longer your manager, right? You go to college, and you take over everything?"

"Well, maybe," she said.

She was lying face down on the bed, propped up on her elbows, her feet swinging behind her.

"What do you mean, *maybe*?"

"I mean, it's worked out this long," she said. "And do you know how many horrible influencer agencies are out there? The number of partnerships I would bring a new manager that they'd take a cut of automatically, despite the fact that they had nothing to do with them? Despite the fact that they had done zero work to negotiate them or create them at all? That doesn't exactly seem fair to me."

I considered her point, though I could easily imagine my mother feeding her all of these reasons. Was she right, though? Was my mother more trustworthy than some random manager who had never known my sister before? Could a stranger ever care as much as family? Maybe not.

"Besides, I don't know if college is for me," she mused, like it was the most casual thought in the world. "If it even makes sense, really."

"Of course it makes sense," I said, immediately regretting how tense I must have sounded, how panicked. "It's absolutely for you. You're the smartest person I know."

"Well, thanks," she said, shutting the laptop and sitting up on the bed to face me, her back against the headboard. "I know I *could* do it. It's not that. It's whether it would really be worth it. I mean, *is it* really worth doing if most of the reason I'd be doing it is to prove to the world that I'm not actually some hollow, idiotic robot? That I'm intelligent? Does that make sense to *you*? Because I don't know if it makes sense to me."

"That's not what college is for," I snapped.

"Not for *you*, maybe," she said. "For you it was what gave you the experience and platform to pursue the career you wanted—the one you're doing now. The one that's going to bring you back to New York, have you working for the *Atlantic* or something before we know it."

I looked away, studying the cuticle that I'd been tearing on my thumb since we'd started talking about this. I had told Evie the month prior that I had to move into a smaller place because I wanted an apartment that was simpler, more manageable, but I had avoided the part about how I had lost my job. She still had no idea I was back in the same cycle I had left New York to avoid, just as far away from my dream job as I'd always been. Farther, maybe.

"But I already *have* that platform. I could write a book. Go on a television show. Travel the world for a year. I could do anything. I don't need college to make it possible," she said. "I have the money."

"Well, Mom does," I said, reminding her of how this conversation had started.

"You know what I mean." She rolled her eyes, checking her phone, then typing out a quick message. "Gavin's almost here. We can continue this another time. Are you staying over?"

"Maybe," I managed, still distracted by the conversation. "I don't know."

"Cool, well, we'll talk more," she said, grabbing her wallet from the top of the dresser. "Don't worry about me, Haze. You always did that way more than was necessary. I made it this far, right?"

I had waited until I heard Evie's car pull out of the driveway to walk downstairs and confront my mom. She was sitting at the kitchen table with her laptop, a scene that reminded me so much of the mornings I'd leave my lofted bed in the bus and find her editing videos at our tiny dining table that it made me a little nostalgic. We weren't close, not by a long shot, but we were cordial, for Evie. We coexisted peacefully, if not happily. So when I sat down across from her, she looked up, surprised.

"Oh," she said. "I thought you left when Evie did. You're waiting for her to come back, I guess?"

"I wanted to talk to you."

She slowly closed the laptop, like she was curious, then strummed her long nails on the table.

"Okay . . ." she said.

"What's the deal with the money?" I asked. "Evie's money. I saw her bank account . . . her savings."

For a split second, I thought I saw fear on her face, but then it relaxed away.

"Well, it's really *our* money. Evie and I's," she said matter-of-factly. "That's how partnership works."

"Partnership?" I asked. "So, what? It's all fifty-fifty? Even the deals that have nothing to do with you?"

"Something like that."

"Something like that?" I asked. "How much of her money are you taking, exactly? How much *have* you taken?"

She sighed, standing up from the table and moving to the kitchen, where she filled a glass of water from the tap.

"Enough to make sure you had a roof over your head for years, for one," she said.

A chill ran through me. I knew, of course, that Evie's fame, and to a lesser extent my mother's, had funded our lives for the last few years I was at home before college. I knew this well enough that when my mom had offered to pay for my college tuition, had insisted on it, really, I refused. I told myself I would build a world that didn't include any of that. When I got drunk once and told Sasha that there could have been a scenario in which I wouldn't have had student loans to pay back, I'd expected her to praise me for being principled, for not taking money made from the years-long exploitation of my little sister. Instead, she looked at me like I was the single dumbest person in the world. "That's the most privileged shit I have ever heard in my life," she said. I never brought it up again.

"But you're going to give it all to her when she turns eighteen?" I said. "Right? Half of everything she earned? More than that, I hope? You owe her at least that."

"Well, according to the law, I don't really *owe* her anything, baby," she said. "There's no law for what we do. No requirement that I have to save money for her when she's older. The fact that I did put money away should tell you that I've gone above and beyond. And trust me, eventually I'm going to get every cent of it back for her."

"What do you mean?" I asked. "Get it back?"

"That's actually something I've been wanting to talk to you about. I could really . . . use your help with something," she said. "Something for Evie."

I blinked at her, waiting for what was next.

"The thing is, I made some bad investments," she said. "A few years ago. My brand deals had started to fade away. I couldn't seem to get the hang of short-form video to save my life. I panicked. When a brand came to me with the opportunity to create a product line, I thought, this . . . this is the next thing that will build our career."

I placed my hands flat on the table, as if to brace myself.

"It seemed legitimate, I swear," she added. "They pitched it to me as something like Ashlyn's skin care line . . . it seemed like a slam dunk."

"But . . ."

"But it wasn't," she said, her gaze focused out the window instead of on me. "I lost . . . I lost a lot."

"How much?" I pressed. "How much of it did you lose, Mom?"

"Two million," she said quietly.

My mouth went dry.

"Oh, my God," I said, trying to do the math. I had no idea how much money my sister earned in a year, specifically, but I knew it had to be seven figures at least, especially recently. "How much is even left after that . . . I mean, it still must be a lot, right?"

"There's some left," she said, still staring out the window.

"Define *some*," I said, standing up.

"Fifty thousand, give or take."

And then I was angry, livid, furious. How could this have happened? How could I have let it happen?

"Where did all go?" I asked. "It can't all be to the product line . . . what the hell did you spend it on, Mom?"

"I don't know, honey. It just . . . there was always more money for the longest time. This steady stream of it. I didn't even think about it half the time. There was always enough for your sister's allowance, for whatever she wanted to do. And when you were here, for whatever you wanted to do . . . it just felt like it wouldn't run out."

"And then it did."

"Yes," she said, crossing her arms in front of herself, defiant. "But we can fix this."

"We?" I asked.

"Yes. We can make it so that Evie never knows about it."

I waited for her to explain, a familiar-feeling mix of resentment and rage stewing somewhere in my gut.

"With the way Evie's partnerships are going right now . . . the way everything is exploding, I just need two more years. To get back to where I was before. Where we were. Just two more years of working together," she said. "And then she never has to feel like I failed her. Like her only remaining parent has let her down."

And suddenly it clicked for me.

"Is this why she doesn't want to go to college? Why she seems so intent on continuing to work with you?" I asked.

"Well, I don't know how she feels, but that's the goal . . . yes," she said. "And I think that's what will happen. If you don't keep pushing her."

"I don't know what you're talking about."

"Come on, Hazel," she said. "You're always pitching college, a real job, some boring nine-to-five that seems important and meaningful on paper. Let's just be honest here. You make her feel less than for even *considering* that she could keep doing what she's doing, like if she turns eighteen and still does it then she's officially choosing it, instead of it all being pushed on her. As it's always been in your mind, I'm sure."

Is that what Evie thinks? I wondered. *Do I make her feel less than?*

"I'm not going to lie to her," I said.

"I'm not telling you to lie to her. I'm telling you to let it happen. Let her make the decision. Don't go whining to her about all of this. The money. Just encourage her to do what feels right. I know my daughter," she said. "She wants this. Us, working together. It feels safe to her. Do you really want to take that away? Make her doubt it all? For her to suddenly be on her own when it comes to business, finances? Even if I gave her every dime left right now, she wouldn't know what to do with it. It would be gone in two months."

And you're so great with money, I thought, but another thought was taking up more of my brain: what version of life I'm willing to destroy for my sister, the one in which my sister can still trust her only living parent, or the one in which her sister always tells her the truth.

"Is it really so fun, Hazel?" she said. "To do things the hard way like you are? To battle for a life that you don't even like that much? That's what you want for her?"

"My life is fine," I hissed.

"Right," she said. "So you just moved into that horrible studio apartment in Vegas because you were bored?

"I don't know what you're talking about," I lied.

"She's seventeen, baby. Give her two more years of ignorant bliss. Please. Two years when she doesn't have to worry about any of this," she begged. "I'll make the money back for both of us. For all of us."

For all of us?

"The offer still stands, you know," she explained. "I could still pay for college, even now. Take those student loans off your plate. Give you enough breathing room to go back to New York, find a job that you love, an apartment you like. In a year, we'd have enough coming in for that. Easy. And all you have to do in the meantime is . . . nothing. Let her continue to enjoy life as it is. Don't push her for more."

Instantly, I remembered Sasha's reaction to what I had told her about paying for college, the way she had looked at me like I was out of my mind. I thought, would this really be so bad? Does leaving things as they are hurt my sister any more than it would if I told her everything when she comes home tonight, if I told her that she can't trust anyone anymore—not her mother, and certainly not herself? Do I really want to create a world where my sister is thinking more about money, about contracts, about the millions of dollars that should be sitting in her bank account but aren't? It might be naive of her not to be thinking about all that money, all its implications, but it's not worse than the alternative, is it? Plus, Evie had offered multiple times to buy me things, whatever I wanted, but I always brushed her off. I didn't need charity from my little sister. I didn't need her to think that I needed it. So was this any different?

I imagined how it would feel to have a massive chunk of debt off my plate, how easy it would be to finally move on, focus on work, create a life that made me feel proud. One that Evie could admire, or maybe even consider for herself. Two years. That's it. I could give her two more years of this world, and then she could move on. Not because she was backed into a corner, or angry at our mother, but because she saw another option. And in half that time, I could be back in the city, far away from all of this. But I knew there was a bigger catch to this, too.

"So, what?" I said. "You want me to just stop coming here, stop talking to her?"

"No," my mom said, looking offended. "Of course not. That would seem a little weird to Ev, don't you think? Do whatever it is that you two always do. Hang out. Chill. Just don't pressure her about college. Don't push her about money. About where it's going. Just let things exist as they have been."

I shook my head. "And then what? This whole cycle starts again? You make all the same money mistakes, and she keeps working her ass off?"

She sighed and moved her head from side to side, her spine cracking. "Obviously not. I've learned. This would be no more fifty-fifty. Everything that I don't need to survive goes to her."

I wondered what, exactly, my mother needed to survive. I imagined it's not a short list.

"Just let things be, Hazel."

"Because that's worked out so well for her . . ." I scoffed.

"I mean, has it really been so bad, Haze?" she said. "You talk to her all the time. You think she really seems so depressed? So unhappy? Tortured? Please. Let her be seventeen and naive. And next year, when she signs our partnership contract as an adult, and the deals are still pouring in, you can be twenty-eight and debt free in no time. One step closer to the big bad life you're trying to build."

She was staring at me, daring me to look her in the eye. My gaze rested on an enormous canvas on the wall behind her. A black-and-white photo of Evie at thirteen, taken at a shoot for a popular tween clothing brand. I remembered that partnership, the way Evie had described it to me on the phone: six figures for six posts. She told me later that she didn't even like the clothes, but the next year she signed another contract with the brand anyway—that time, for even more money, I was sure. I thought about how quickly that money had materialized, how easy it was for her. "I'll think about it," I heard myself say to my mom, hating the words as they fell out of my mouth, hating myself for not being more definitive.

It should have been the easiest *no* in the world, but I left the door open anyway. Even this ate at me afterward, when I told myself I had never agreed to anything, or I pretended the conversation had never happened, committing myself to finding other ways to pay off my debt—side hustles, freelancing on top of working full-time at the newspaper.

But I had left the option there, like a part of me knew I wouldn't be strong enough to resist it, not forever. And sure enough, when I lost my job earlier in the year, my mom's offer was the first thing I thought of. I wasn't even waitressing for a week when I called her and asked if it was still on the table. I tried to tell myself that I was giving Evie exactly what she had asked for that afternoon in her room: Fewer questions. Less pressure. I would just step back from this role I was trying to fill, and soon enough, I would have an easier life. I'd be farther away, back in a city I loved, debt free. Evie would want that for me anyway, I told myself. She would.

But in the weeks after, the guilt set in like an illness I couldn't quite shake, a tickle at the back of my throat, then a gnawing. I had only accepted the thing that Evie had always offered—to give me money, to help me out. To buy me whatever I wanted. But I knew it was a betrayal. I knew all the ways that I had protected my ego before I had protected her. In the end, I comforted myself with the same idea my mom had planted in my brain: knowing would only hurt her more.

· • • ● • • ·

I am telling myself this now, too, as I lie awake in my sister's bed. Of course, everything is different now. Evie's disappearance means no more seven-figure income for the Davis family, the student loans won't be paid off. A life and career back in New York are out of reach, and not just because I lost my job in Vegas. I was focused on all the wrong things.

I check my phone. Nearly four a.m. now. No point in going back to sleep. I stand up, pacing the room. Desperate for movement, to distract myself.

olivia muenter

I walk across the room to the en suite bathroom and flick on the light, my reflection startling me. I lean in close and cringe. Every part of me looks dry, tired. My hair is brittle at the ends and greasy at the roots. My skin is red and splotchy. My entire body seems thirsty. I need sleep, but I want to be out of this house more. I can't believe I ever thought it would be a good idea to stay here. I check my phone again mindlessly, a nervous tic. I feel like Evie is further away than ever, and I'm only falling apart more in the meantime. Becoming less sharp. More fragile. More paranoid. Like I won't be able to handle whatever answers I eventually find.

I open the medicine cabinet, searching for an unused toothbrush, some mouthwash. Instead I find perfectly organized rows of skin care products, brightly colored tubes and matte white bottles of all sizes, each of them mostly full. Unlike my bathroom at home, none of the products are stacked upon one another. They all have their space, their spot.

I take a cleanser out, study its label. Is this the one Evie used every day? I splash my face with water and massage some of it into my skin, scrubbing the grime of the past twenty-four hours from my face, then pat it dry with a soft towel. I grab a moisturizer next, the one that seems the emptiest. Was this Evie's favorite? I try a rich eye cream next, one that I can tell is more expensive than anything I've ever used on my face. I find foundation, a cream blush, eyeliner, and a mascara I know has a cult following on TikTok.

In a haze, I find myself staring at a fully made-up version of my reflection. The white eyeliner tightlining my eyes looks garish and neon. The foundation isn't the right shade; Evie was always just the right amount of sun-kissed. The final effect is undeniable: This is the face of someone trying to be something they aren't. This is the face of someone on the edge.

What are you doing, Hazel?

I wash it all off, scrubbing until my face feels raw and tight.

I'm pressing the towel to my face again when I see something blinking behind me. Or I think I do. A tiny white light—or is just exhaustion? A visual trick from opening and closing my eyes so many times, pressing the towel against my face and removing it again?

But I stare at the spot for a moment, and there it is again. Right inside the air-conditioning vent. I flick off the studio lights over the mirror for a clearer view, and there it is again. A faint light, blinking every sixty seconds or so, barely noticeable, really, but it's there.

I rush to pull in Evie's vanity chair from the bedroom, placing it close enough to the bathroom wall that I can stand on it and be eye to eye with the vent. As I test the sturdiness of the chair with one foot, it occurs to me that I have no idea what I'm going to do next. Remove the vent cover? With what? Stare into the darkness? Why? I climb onto the chair with both hands and turn on the flashlight on my phone, pointing it toward the grates of the vent, illuminating the dark space on the other side.

It takes a few seconds to focus my eyes in the dark, to understand what I'm seeing perched just beyond the air-conditioning vent. A sensor? A smoke alarm?

But the longer I look, the surer I become. It's a camera.

CHAPTER 23

There are cameras in my sister's bathroom.

My sister, who was worried in the weeks before she disappeared that someone was following her, recording her, bugging her phone.

She was right.

Every possibility crashes over me in seconds: An HVAC repairman who recognized Evie and quickly formulated a plan. A contractor who saw a beautiful eighteen-year-old girl who didn't seem very cautious and took it as an opportunity. A jealous ex-boyfriend or hookup I'd never met who knew exactly how much people would pay for scandalous photos of Evie Davis.

I climb down from the chair carefully, making sure I stay quiet as I descend. I am fighting the instinct that tells me I need to show this to someone, to have them confirm it, to run down the list of possibilities until we land on the thing that makes the most sense. I want someone to say: Yes, this does mean that things are just as twisted as they've felt from the beginning. But as I turn to walk back into Evie's room, I can't help but look at everything differently, to imagine what it would mean if there were even more cameras. I look at the bed where I had just been sleeping, where she slept. I spin around and assess every surface that faces the bed, her most private space. My stomach turns, imagining someone else doing the same thing I'm doing now, standing in this room and trying to figure out where she would be the most vulnerable. How to use the knowledge against her.

I look everywhere. Beneath her vanity. In the deepest parts of her closet. On the undersides of lampshades. In her drawers. It's not until I stand on a bench at the foot of her bed, trying to get a different vantage point, that I see something on the ceiling fan that looks ever so slightly off. Unlike in the bathroom, there's no light that's immediately visible. Instead, there's just a small white circle that seems to stand out from the rest of the fan. It's on the central hub of the fan, the same color as it, too, but it doesn't sit flush. If the fan was on or I wasn't actively looking for something, I'd never notice it. It's roughly the size of two quarters, maybe smaller, and when stand on a bench to get closer, I can tell that the material is different from the rest of the fan.

"What the fuck," I whisper.

As soon as the words leave my mouth, I see it: a tiny flash of lime-green light on the fan. It's barely the size of the tip of a ballpoint pen, but it's there. "What the fuck," I say, louder this time, and watch it flash again. Goosebumps rise on the back of my arms as I take a photo of it and upload it to a reverse Google image search.

A million instant responses confirm it's a voice-activated recording device. Less than sixty dollars on Amazon. And it's roughly ten feet from where my little sister sleeps every night. Slept.

I step down from the bench and away from the fan, staring at it as I consider my next move. I want to rip off the device and destroy it, but I know I can't. The police will need to take fingerprints. Maybe whatever is recorded on this thing and the one in the vent is key to finding my sister. But is it possible that they searched the whole room and didn't find this?

Is it possible that if they did, it wouldn't matter to them?

For a moment I sit with what either scenario would mean: they had never taken my sister's disappearance seriously. I trusted the detectives because I had no one else to trust. Not my mom. Not Gavin. Not even myself, after learning how much Evie kept from me. So I trusted the people who did this professionally, and I let myself believe that they would take my sister's disappearance more seriously than the rest of the world did. How could I have been so naive? I think of Buxton flirting with my mom, the way both detectives had seemed so eager to be done with my sister. The case.

I need to make a plan, a checklist of next steps. I take a deep breath.

I'll sleep. And in the morning I'll get some water, then some coffee, and call Buxton and Williams. I'll explain the creepy doll, the devices I found, leaving out the way I was searching my sister's room from top to bottom in the middle of the night. I'll force them to believe me when I say my sister is not okay.

I check my phone, which is nearly dead. It's almost five a.m. My heart is racing. I remind myself of the list again, to calm down: *Get a few hours of sleep. Call the detectives. Make them believe you.* I repeat it again as I do a final scan of the room, and then once more as I open the door to the dark hallway and walk down to the guest room, moving as silently as possible. I try to turn on my phone's flashlight and the battery promptly gives out, powering my phone down.

I open the guest room door and run my hand over the wall, trying to find the light switch, but when I finally do, it doesn't work. I try a few more times before remembering what my mom had told me the last time I was here—that that switch doesn't work, and to use the lamp beside the bed instead. "You'll need it with those blackout curtains," she had said. "You can't see a damn thing with those. Makes for the best sleep." She was right.

I can barely see my hand in front of my face now, let alone a clear path to the lamp. I squint in the darkness with a hand stretched out in front of me, attempting to make my way to where the nightstand is by memory, running my hand over the top of the bedside table to make out the lamp, and then find the switch. As I feel across the smooth ridges of the lamp-shade and then underneath to the switch, my fingers hit something soft and warm. Something that moves.

Knowing what another human hand feels like in yours is human nature, even in the dark. The shock of it makes me pull back my hand instantly. There's someone else in the room with me, who has been sitting there silently as I stumbled through the room and grasped for the light switch.

I jump back, gasping as the light clicks on, and there, sitting on the edge of the bed like she's been there for hours, is my mother.

You know that thing when a celebrity complains about being famous, and suddenly everyone hates them? They say it's hard to have photos taken of them when they're leaving the gym or taking their kids to school. It's hard to go to the grocery store when there are magazines with their faces on them lining the aisles, headlines about who they're dating and who they're cheating on. And maybe you think, for a second: Sure, that sounds miserable. Candid photos on your worst days. Zero privacy for your family. Baseless (or true) rumors destroying your relationships. But then you remember: It's not just any gym they're going to. They're seeing the world's best trainer for three-hour-long sessions, sessions that are the monetary equivalent of buying a pack of gum for them and a month's rent for you. They're not taking their kids home from just any school, but the best of the best. Their school lunches are made from things like kumquats cut into tiny, cute shapes and pea protein snacks that taste like Doritos.

And my God, they're not actually *going* to the fucking grocery store. They're not standing in the aisle like a normie and debating whether or not to get that Kinder Bueno because it's been a hard day and, you know, they deserve it. No, they're getting groceries delivered by people who are also probably doing them the favor of organizing their CBD-infused, ethically sourced iced teas by color or shape or carbon footprint. And their fridges? Their fridges—all their kitchen appliances, really—are sexier than you on your very best day. They are more sensual, more organized and inviting than you as a human being can ever hope to be. They are so nice to look at and to use that they would never forget the healthy dinner they (or their private chef) had planned and cash in on that $5 coupon for Papa Johns. They've never even heard of Papa.

Still, can we all really assume that they don't work hard, too? Even the most bitter of us can probably admit that using your personal image and interests and face and body and platform and everything to sell items, or build interest, must be draining. Or confusing. Both. At least actors get the unique gift of making money by being anyone *other* than themselves.

olivia muenter

But what about when what they're working so hard at (or not working so hard at, depending who you ask) isn't packaging their own lives, but their kids' lives? What, exactly, happens then? I know how it goes, too. You see an ad from an influencer that features her kid in diapers, shilling a bottle, a onesie, a medicine, and you wonder how that kid will feel about that choice one day. If they will ask where that money went, exactly, or if the money matters as much as the fact that they could have never agreed to the photo, or the ad. We turn up our noses at things like this and say that if it was us, we'd do things differently. But would we? Do we? Aren't most of us sharing photos that our children might grow up to hate? Aren't we putting them out into the world anyway? Do any of us know where the line is as we conduct this giant social experiment in real time?

Last week in Colorado, an eighteen-year-old sued their parents for personal damages after the parents had spent years sharing personal and "sometimes embarrassing" photos of the kid on various social media channels. In other words: The kids that have grown up on our phones are grown. And they are not happy. But does intent make a difference? Does money? If someone like Erin Davis had never made a cent from sharing her daughter Evie's every move on the internet, would it still feel as rotten? Would it look so different from how your parents and their friends shared things on social media a decade ago, when there was virtually no discussion about what it meant that a child could never, really, consent to having their photo shared publicly?

I still sometimes share the memes, the viral videos of toddlers doing ridiculous things. It's harmless, right? Cute. Funny. But if Erin and Evie Davis have taught us anything, it's that sometimes a viral video of a cute kid isn't only that. It can grow to be something else entirely. Does that mean Erin should have never posted the video that made them internet famous in the first place? I can't say I know the answer to that.

I've been thinking a lot about these questions lately, about how, exactly, influencers who turn their children into content—and money—should be held accountable. How the privacy and potential assets of these children should be protected. I don't claim to have all the answers, but we can't leave it up to the kids, right? We can't wait for everyone to turn eighteen and sue their parents.

After all, by that point some of them will have been brainwashed into starting influencer careers of their own, continuing the cycle of monetizing their lives without understanding the stakes.

As always, here's what else is trending right now in the world of content creators:

- August Lawley continues her journey to make "thin body pos influencer" a thing, this time advertising a popular weight loss program that's "not a diet" by touting it as "a holistic lifestyle change to boost confidence." Follow along so you, too, can learn how to pay money to feel bad about yourself.
- I have it on good authority that lifestyle influencer and GirlBoss™ extraordinaire Eden Thompson has been posing as an anonymous Redditor on a popular internet snark thread. But it gets better: not only is she snarking on influencer "friends" and defending herself in the comments, she is also posing as a POC, for reasons that are unclear. Talk about a series of bad choices. Nothing on the internet stays secret for long, Eden.
- Ashlyn Price is back at it with giveaways, this time shilling out $500 in cold hard cash to one lucky winner. All you have to do to enter is to like every single photo she's posted in the last month. And she's doing this Every. Single. Week. Ah, sweet, sweet bribery. It never goes out of style.

That's it for this week, friends. See you next week for more tea that will make you realize that everything you see on your phone is fake.

SABI

CHAPTER 24

"You're up early," my mother says matter-of-factly. Her tone is casual, as if the fact that she's in this room, waiting for me in total darkness, is totally normal. She's bright, alert, relaxed—as though she's been up for hours, not even a little bit hungover or tired.

"Why are you in my bedroom?" I ask, backing away, closer to the door. I expect her to get up, but instead she leans back against the cane headboard, crossing her legs in front of her. She smooths the blankets over her lap, and it's only then that I realize she's under the covers.

She laughs. "Your bedroom, huh?"

My cheeks flush in embarrassment at the idea that I'd feel ownership over a space here, in this home that was clearly not made for me at all.

"This room. The guest room. Whatever," I deflect. "Why are you waiting for me?"

"Why were you rummaging through your sister's room?" she replies. "Sleeping in her bed?"

"I fell asleep," I say, and it comes out quietly.

How long has she been awake? Listening?

She smiles, then tilts her head like a dog who's heard a word they recognize. "But not for long, right?"

What did she hear? What does she know?

"I was just washing my face," I mumble.

"Right," she says, the smiling stretching wider.

We stare at each other then. She doesn't blink.

Finally, she sighs and gets off the bed, walking straight toward me. I back up a step but as I do I realize I'm in the corner of the room, with no space to sidestep to the door and out to the hallway. There's nowhere to go. But it's not like I'm scared of her. Right?

She's narcissistic and manipulative, but she's not dangerous, not physically.

Right?

She's inches from me now, and my palms are flat against the wall behind me, clawing for more space, for room to breathe. Finally, she stops and stares at me, lifting her hand. I flinch, but she strokes the side of my face.

She shakes her head, like I'm a stubborn child who's being difficult. I expect her to say something but instead she moves past me, walking down the hall to the spare room—the former workout room, the one I haven't been in in years.

"Come on, then," she says, gesturing that I follow her. "If you insist on knowing everything."

I walk a few steps down the hallway, cautious, as she pulls a key out of her robe and puts it in the lock.

Since when does this room have a lock? Or stay locked?

When she opens the door, it feels like relief. Because for once in my life, in this home, I feel validated. I have spent so long believing that all of it—my sister's career, this family, my place in it—is so much more fucked-up than the world realizes, than even I could understand. And now, looking at this room, I finally know I was right. I was always right.

The room looks almost normal at first glance: a part-time home office collecting things waiting to be sold at a yard sale or moved elsewhere or thrown away. There's a desk, a few framed photos on the wall, grade-school art projects from Evie, her ten-year-old handwriting scribbled in the bottom right corner. But as my mom clicks on a desk lamp, more of the room is illuminated—forgotten childhood toys piled in corners on top of dated furniture. And there are boxes. So many boxes. Stacks of them. I take a step inside the room and look quickly behind me, just a glance, all too aware that my mom is watching me now, hands on her hips. This wall is all boxes, floor to ceiling. All of them labeled.

olivia muenter

I face my mom again, and she's sitting in the desk chair now, her legs crossed. I take a step toward one box and move closer to the tiny label, reading what it says.

Evie. May 2012.

My eyes travel toward the stack next to it.

Evie. February 2013.

Evie. March 2013.

I spin toward a different tower of boxes.

Evie. October 2017.

Evie. December 2018.

"What is all of this?" I manage, unsettled by the sheer amount of stuff, the organization. The locked door.

"It's nearly two decades of doing my job," she says coolly.

I study her face, and there's a strange sense of calm in her expression. Like something about entering this room made her feel that much more at home, that much more relaxed.

"It was a little pathetic, baby," she adds. "Watching you crawl around the floor like that. Stand on chairs. Dig through drawers. I figured this was just easier."

"You were watching me . . ."

She sighs. "I mean, I would have preferred to be sleeping, but once I saw what you were doing . . . well, we're both awake now, aren't we?"

"You were watching *her* . . ."

The texts Ashlyn showed me flash through my mind, the words my sister had written. *I think someone's following me. Listening to me.* What if the whole time it was Mom?

"I was managing her," my mother corrects me. "Protecting her."

Is that what she thinks this is? All of this? Cataloging my sister's life like it's a collector's item?

"By invading her most personal, private spaces . . ." I say. "The bathroom? How is that necessary for what you were doing?"

She waves off my disgust. "Please, Hazel. This is just like when people your age get outraged over photos of naked babies splashing in a tub. Not everything is as dark and twisted and perverse as people your age like to think. I'm her mother."

Yes, I think. That's just it.

You're her *mother*.

Rage is building in my core, dampened only by a low-grade nausea. "Filming your daughter in her bathroom is not practical. It's fucking . . . horrible. It's sick. And . . . illegal. It must be."

"It's my home," she says. "My security system. That footage was auto-deleted every week. On a secure server in the meantime. And if she hadn't started getting paranoid last year and taking calls in there, then this wouldn't even be an issue."

Paranoid. Another bell rings in my head.

"I wonder why she could have possibly been paranoid, Mom," I say, my chest aching at how scared my sister must have felt, and from knowing how much worse it would have been if she knew the truth.

"Why would you do this to her . . ." I say, staring at all the boxes. "I don't get it."

She stands up, grabbing one of the older-looking boxes from a shelf. The date says 2011. The peak of the mommy-and-me content that took over our lives then. Evie would have been seven.

"You, of all people, should get it," she starts, placing the box's lid on the bed and carefully removing a thin layer of tissue paper that covers the top of its contents, like whatever is underneath is fragile, precious. Sacred. "You, so determined to shape her life one way or another . . ."

Before I can protest, she's taking items out of the box—thick piles of papers stuffed into manilla folders. Dozens of DVDs in plastic cases. All of it meticulously labeled with dates and other descriptive information. I see names of brands, but also milestones. There's one DVD that just says: EVIE, LAST BABY TOOTH.

"What is this?" I ask. "Her entire life? Boxed up and categorized like she's . . ."

I trail off, stunned by the sheer amount of information that must be contained in this room if every box is like this, stuffed with data.

"Like she's famous?" My mom snorts. "Like she's worth something? Like she's worth protecting? Imagine that."

"That's what all of this is? That's what the cameras are? Security?" I ask. "You can't be serious."

"At first they were about security, yes. Keeping her safe. Watching out for her when I knew she wouldn't do it for herself. You know as well as I do she was never as scared of the internet as she should have been."

I blink at her, willing her to go on, knowing that this can't be the whole story.

"When she was younger, it was easy. The filming. The content. All of it. But as she got older, she naturally pushed me out more . . . even if I was her manager, I couldn't be with her all the time. She didn't always tell me when she was sad or angry or feeling creative. What she was reading or watching. Who she was talking to. The cameras made it easier to . . . to push her in the right direction. To guide her. To understand. Find angles for brand deals. Narratives for friendships, relationships. I mean, it's not like I saw her crying in front of the mirror and said, 'Hey, hun, I know you hate your body today, want to go post about it right now?' But if a brand deal came along the next week that was about body positivity, about loving the skin you're in or some bullshit, then . . . well, I knew the connection. I knew how to spin it in a way that made sense for Ev. I was already inside her head."

I picture my sister standing in her room, examining her body for changes. Marking her success or failure by the size of her waist, a thigh. I remember those moments, my own versions of them. The idea that anyone but me would be privy to them makes me ill. That it was my mother who saw them makes me want to break something.

"I saw the big picture when she couldn't," she adds. "And honestly, Hazel, you're old enough to know that you can't see any of it when you're a kid, a teenager—not even the tiniest sliver of it, really."

This is exactly like my mom, to weave some piece of truth into a darker, more destructive narrative. It's what makes her effective, why all the campaigns work. Why brands want to work with her, and Evie. It's how she can market anything, anyone. She can find the tiny, jagged piece of universal truth amidst even the ugliest thing.

I'm silent now, taking it all in in waves.

"How else do you think I was going to make us money, baby?" she whispers. "This was my job. *She* was my job."

"What *money*?" I hiss. "Last I heard, most of it was gone. Used up. This isn't proof of some partnership, some beautiful working relationship . . . it's an obsession. You wanted total control of her."

My mom chuckles. "Last you heard . . . you mean last year? When you were so quick to take my help, my money?"

I flash to that day and tell myself the same lie that I have repeated for the last twelve months: That she caught me on a weak day, a weak moment. That I should have been better, but I wasn't.

"Is it really so hard to believe that maybe the reason your sister was so good at all of this isn't because of *her*, but because of me? That it was always, really, because of me? Ever consider that that's the reason she was so eager to stay, Hazel? That *that's* why she didn't want to leave home, go to college? Deep down, she knew, too. She needed me. For the deals. For all of it."

I let the unspoken thing hang between us, the past tense of it all. The way my sister isn't here to clarify, to push back.

My hands are on my hips now, and I'm scanning the room, desperately looking for something. That's when I spot six boxes with no labels. I pull one out from the top of the stack.

"Hazel, stop this. You're making a mess, and for no reason. Stop."

She tries to pull the box away from me, but I'm already opening it. It contains stacks and stacks of paper. I pull one sheet out and it's a photocopy of something, lined paper. Evie's handwriting.

In the left-hand corner, there's a date from earlier this year. Underneath, there's a handwritten note—an entry. Evie's handwriting. The date, the note . . .

"Is this her *journal*?" I whisper, horrified.

"Well, no, obviously not, Hazel. This"—my mom taps on the paper with her pointer finger—"is just a copy. She has . . . or had, I don't know . . . the original. It's hers, after all."

This shouldn't horrify me more than the cameras, maybe. But it does. It feels more like a violation than anything else, confirmation that there was nowhere my sister could bring her own thoughts without the judgment or weight of anyone else. Even this, something as simple and pure as this, had been taken from her. Used. Monetized.

"Why the fuck do you have this?"

olivia muenter

My mother stares back at me like I've just asked the world's stupidest question, like shouldn't it be obvious to me? Shouldn't it make sense?

"How else do you expect her to be able to have her memoir properly ghostwritten one day, Hazel?" she says. "Honestly, you can be so dense sometimes. It's not like I cared about her love life or something. About how depressed she was about her lack of abs. About her secret tattoo. Whatever. I could care less. This is for *posterity*."

She shakes the paper in the air like it's nothing, just business.

"This is for *you*," I snap. "For the money it would make you. And the control. That's what this whole room is. All of it. And it's disgusting."

"I told you it would only be a couple years," she says. "A book deal would have paid for your college loans and then some." She shakes her head. "If everything didn't go to utter shit, we would all be happy."

For a second, I wonder if that's true.

"I would never have taken that money from you," I say. "From a book. Not a chance."

She laughs. "Oh? No? Just, what, the money from other stuff? Partnerships? Affiliate links? That money is better? Come on, Hazel."

I stand up from the box of papers now, make my way toward the door. But my mom continues talking.

"Acting so high and mighty about money is pretty funny coming from someone who can barely afford their rent. Even funnier coming from someone who was so quick to take my help a year ago. To take the money you seem to think is your sister's alone. But, you know, whatever you need to tell yourself, baby. What *I'm* telling you is that yes, I was thinking about money. I always am. It's my job to be thinking about money. To be thinking about long-term wealth and stability. A career with staying power," she explains. "Your sister lived minute-to-minute. It was the fact that I zoomed out and saw the wider, longer game plan that meant she could become what she is."

I'm about to walk out when my eye catches on a crumpled piece of fabric stuffed in a Ziploc bag, just visible at the bottom of one of the open boxes sitting near the door. I reach for it and my mom lunges, grabbing my hand, her nails digging into my arm.

"Leave that," she says. "It's disgusting."

I find it hard to imagine that anything could be more disgusting than what I've seen in the last few minutes.

"I kept the gifts," she explains. "The things people would send her. The . . . intimate things."

I look at the fabric again and now I see it, the tiniest band of elastic that I recognize immediately as underwear.

"I don't know why now, really. Or maybe I do, given . . . everything. I think at the time I just needed to remind myself that she needed me . . . that she needed protecting. Someone who saw everything, who monitored it all."

And then I remember.

"What about the doll?"

I am pacing the room now, wracking my brain for the year, the date. It was 2015, right? The summer, maybe? Or was it a particularly hot fall . . .

"What are you talking about, Hazel?" my mom asks.

"Evianna. That doll she thought was so funny," I say. "The one that the person tried to make look like her. With the face. The painted-on face."

I'm crouching down, moving from box to box, my eyes dancing over the labels, looking for the right one. I choose one at random and rummage through it, tearing out DVDs, framed photos, loose sheets of paper and tossing them aside.

"You're going to mess up my system . . ." my mom groans, picking up the pages from behind me.

"You don't know where it is? Really?" I ask. "It was in her closet a few years ago. I swear it was."

"Oh, *that* thing?" she says, recognition coloring her expression now. "God, that was horrible looking. I hated it. She insisted on keeping it for the longest time. I sold it last year."

My skin prickles. "You sold it?"

"Easy money," she says. "And I—well, *we*, after our little deal—needed it. Someone paid $175 for it. Can you believe that?"

"Do you know who?"

"I guess I could look up the transaction . . ." she says, spinning in the office chair toward the laptop. "On eBay."

She clicks around for a minute, types a few things in.

"Here it is . . ." she says, clicking her tongue as she scrolls down.

"Charlie. Charlie Buchanan."

Adrenaline rushes to my brain, lighting me up.

"Is there an address?"

"Sure is," she says. "It's 12023 Palma Ceia Court. Los Angeles, California."

And then I'm out the door and running down the stairs before I even hear her call after me. Before I can spend one more second in that terrible room.

CHAPTER 25

It's almost seven a.m. now as I start the six-hour drive to Los Angeles. I'm jittery, wired from the last twenty-four hours. The kind of exhausted that lets you make different decisions than you normally would, where your brain isn't fully working through problems or calculating risk the way it should.

There was a split second, right before merging onto the highway, when I thought I should pause. Stop. Call the worthless detectives instead, or bring in Ashlyn or Gavin for help. Consider that I could be walking into something truly terrible, the kind of thing I would never recover from, or maybe never come home from, either. Go home to my apartment and wait for someone to tell me that this was somehow nothing, too.

Then I gripped the wheel harder, pressed on the gas. If I was the only person in the world who thought my sister needed help, then I was the only person who could do this. I was going to find out what happened to her, no matter what the cost.

I force myself to think about Evie: her laugh, the way she smells like jasmine. I'm going to find her, I tell myself. I'm going to find her, I'm going to find her, I'm going to find her. I try to blink away the image of my mom in that room, sitting amid all my sister's things. But it won't budge. It feels grotesque and sticking, burned in.

I used to try to make happy memories stick when I was a kid. The time my parents and I had a picnic somewhere in Zion National Park, when we ate peanut butter sandwiches and sat together in silence, all taking in the splendor of the landscape around us. Even then, at six or seven, I had the sense that you don't get to choose which memories stay and which don't, or maybe even which people stay and which don't, either. But I tried anyway. I'd concentrate so hard on the details of the space around me, the sensations, that I'd practically feel my brain absorbing the colors. "Remember this, remember this, remember this," I'd say inside my head. Now, the exact makeup of the scenery is a blur to me. I couldn't tell you what we talked about, or where we went next. I can't remember whether it was cold or hot outside. But I can remember willing the memory of the three of us into myself, begging it to stay.

I already know that the memories of last night with my mom, the morning, will always be there. I know that there might be a time when I forget specific things she said or did in the moment, the play-by-play. But there will never be a time when I can't close my eyes and see her sitting there, wrapped in her bathrobe, surrounded by the carefully curated pieces of my sister's life. I know I'll always see her face, the way it had looked so different in that room than at other times in my life. There was nothing about the room that looked like the home she had spent so much money creating, year over year. Nothing was beautiful, or neat. New. But I had stared at her expression and tried to place it as the sun streamed in from across the hallway, and it had occurred to me that it was maybe the first time that I had seen her look serene. Like she was perfectly content to stay right there, to remain there for as long as she could. And I guess it did make sense, maybe. At least all that stuff was predictable. At least it wouldn't leave.

The GPS announces that my destination is approaching, and I feel the fear settle deeper into my thoughts. I'm scared because of the obvious— that this Charlie person might be dangerous, that he's obsessed with a teenage girl he knows from the internet. That he could be a kidnapper. A rapist. Worse.

But I'm also scared because part of me wants Evie to be there. What I really want is for her to tell me she's been gone because she couldn't leave. She couldn't call. That someone forced her to post that message on Instagram. That of course she would have reached out to me if she could have. That she missed me too.

I shift the car into park, turn off the ignition.

I'm scared because I know that for all of that to be true, she can't be okay. And I still want to open the door and see her here, anyway.

I'm parked on the street maybe six houses down from Charlie's house, building up the energy to knock on the door. I dig my nails into the steering wheel as I coach myself through how this will go.

Should I have 911 already on the line? My phone hidden in my pocket?

Should I act naive? Like I know nothing?

Should I do anything at all just to get inside, to try to spot evidence of my sister?

I consider it all.

It's a crowded suburb, the homes so close together that you could reach out the window of one and touch the neighbor's fence. The neighborhood itself is a mix—some houses have yards overgrown with weeds, paint peeling off stucco, mailboxes that have been mangled in hit-and-runs but never fixed. Others are bright, newly renovated. Cheery.

I study the house numbers, count down to figure out which one is the one I'm looking for. My stomach drops when I see it. The windows on the side closest to my car are boarded up. A chain-link fence wraps around the property, empty plastic Coke bottles stuck into some sections. I squint, trying to see past the trash in the backyard, and I can just make out what looks like a small shed, cardboard covering its only window. It can't be big enough for more than one person to fit inside.

Oh, God.

The appearance of the house should be the thing that makes me rethink this whole plan, but it has the opposite effect. Adrenaline courses through me. I unclick my seatbelt and get out of the car, closing the door as quietly as I can.

I walk over to the house and take a deep breath as I wiggle through the already-open gate. I'm on the front porch, about to knock when I see it. The house number, just above the front door. 12021. This isn't the house.

I move backward quickly, going out the way I came, walking the few feet to the right house. To what I'm really looking for. And then, I'm even more confused.

It's more a cottage than a house. A bungalow, really. It's painted a faded, friendly shade of yellow with tall, proud-looking palm trees out front. The tiny porch has just enough room for two deep, slightly fraying wicker chairs, each of which is filled with overstuffed blue gingham pillows that match the front door. A reclaimed wood side table sits in between. Every bit of it is inviting. I look back toward the other house, the one I had gone to first. It was what I had expected, I guess. This . . . this is not something I was prepared for. And though everything about it looks cozy, unassuming, it's that thought that makes my chest flutter with worry.

Before I can second-guess myself, I bound up the stairs and knock on the door, hard. If someone is home, they'll hear it. The front door is a cornflower blue, a few shades lighter than it used to be by the looks of it, but it still happily pops against the warm gold of the house. Now that I'm closer, I can see the wind chime from the corner of the porch that lazily sways in the breeze as I wait for someone to open the door. I listen for a sound, a voice, but all I hear is the faint, somewhat distant hum of jazz coming from the back of the house. The backyard, maybe. I peek around the porch and see two small raised garden beds and a thick vine of wisteria winding up a trellis. It's the kind of place I can imagine myself living in one day. I stand up straighter, reminding myself not to get too comfortable. Not to let some nice-looking old man and his adorable garden make me forget what I'm here. Who he really is.

The lock startles me as it clicks, and when the door opens I find that I'm not standing across from a creepy old man, but a woman.

"Hi there," she says, her smile wide and bright, her face lined with deep creases. One thick, gray braid resting on each shoulder, and she's wearing a short-sleeve, oversized linen dress in a shade of blue that matches the door she's holding open for me. I pause for one second, readjusting, and she looks on smiling, a tiny gap between her front teeth.

I clear my throat. "Uh, hi," I say. "I'm . . . I'm looking for a Charlie?"

"You've found her, dear," she says.

This is Charlie? Charlie from the comments. Charlie who bought the doll.

I realize now, of course, that Charlie *could* be a woman. But . . . does that really make sense? Does that track with everything I know about predators, about danger? It occurs to me that maybe I have been very,

very stupid. That maybe all of these clues have been a series of strange coincidences, that I'm just as paranoid as I've felt and for absolutely no purpose. But I want to make sure anyway.

"*You're* Charlie?" I ask.

She smiles like she's heard that before, but the repetition of the question doesn't bother her one bit.

"Well, yes, I think so." She laughs. "I certainly hope so, anyway. Technically, it's Charlotte. But no one's called me that in years except for my orthopedic surgeon, who—let me tell you—wasn't my favorite person in the world."

I notice right away that she's not peppering me with questions, too. That she doesn't seem in any kind of hurry to get me off the front porch, and as much as I think it's plausible that she's simply this friendly and patient with everyone, there's another part of me that sees something in her gaze like she's trying to place me. Like she might recognize me.

"Are you . . . are you a former student?" she asks.

So she's a teacher, then. A professor, maybe?

"I pride myself on never forgetting a face, even if I have taught so many lovely people over the years, but I guess it's possible that I've forgotten . . . I'm not getting any younger, of course, so maybe my memory is—"

"No, no," I cut her off, feeling bad that I'm making her play a guessing game instead of coming right out with it. Should I really be afraid of this woman? Should I really be this cagey? "I . . . I thought you might know Evie."

Her brown eyes light up then, like she's finally got it. Like she sees it. "You're Hazel."

I nod.

"Of course you are, dear," she says. "I hadn't seen a photo of you in so long . . . couldn't find any on your Instagram. But of course you're Hazel. Of course you are. Come in, come in."

Charlie gestures inside toward a love seat that looks like it could fit three people, if it weren't mostly covered in books, blankets, and a quilt that looks like a thousand floral dish towels sewn together. "You're so much like her, you know," she says, sitting across from me on a small couch. "It's something in how you stand . . . how you talk."

I'm flattered by the comparison for only a split second before it makes me nervous, cautious. An alarm bell goes off inside me, saying *Careful, careful.*

"Oh. Well," I say, shifting awkwardly in my seat, trying to avoid toppling the stack of books next to me. "Thank you."

She nods and smiles, saying nothing for a second, studying me, then pushes herself up from the chair.

"I'll get us some tea and something to nibble on," she says.

My eyes travel across the walls, each of them painted shades of bright, vibrant earth tones. Deep, moody hues of blue. Warm, lush greens, like grass in sunlight. One wall the perfect shade of terra-cotta. All the colors poke through the hundreds of frames and art and knickknacks that cover the walls. There are black-and-white photos of Charlie and other people laughing, wineglasses in their hands, heads tipped back with joy. The laughter is the same in all the photos, but the backgrounds are different. There are beaches and cobblestone streets and forests creating the backdrops behind them, all of it seeming so dull compared to the joy on their faces.

The photos are interspersed with colorful, abstract pieces of artwork and photography, as well as framed painting and drawings that were clearly made by children. There are dozens of these, dotted with messy writing that says things like LACEY 6-A and THEO 6-D in the corners. They remind me of art class in school, of the feeling of taking an hour a week just to make things. Of joy. And then I catch myself. Is collecting the artwork of children who aren't your own sweet, or obsessive? I search the wall for Evie's name but don't find it.

There are mirrors, too. All of them reflect the vibrance of the room, their borders lined with tiny pieces of sea glass, or intricate gold molding. There's something on every part of the wall, lining every shelf. It's like being cocooned in the tapestry of someone's life, wrapped in the warmth of all their best days. I pinch the side of my leg, reminding myself why I'm here, and that I shouldn't be comfortable at all.

Charlie is back now, setting down a tray with tea and some cookies in between us. She stirs some milk and sugar into her own cup and then leans back on the couch, tucking her feet under her while she leans one elbow on the armrest.

"You know," she starts, "when I didn't hear back from you on Instagram, I thought maybe Evie was wrong. That I should have been more direct. Explicit about who I was. Where I was."

My spine straightens and cracks at the mention of my sister's name. I look to the stairs quickly, like maybe she'll bound down them at any minute. I listen for a banging, a muffled scream.

"But she insisted," Charlie goes on. "She said I needed to be vague enough that only someone who really knew her would even pay attention. Just in case your mother had access to your accounts, too. Your direct messages."

My head is spinning.

She laughs. "She said you hated that doll. That if you didn't respond to everything else, to send a photo of it. She said that would really get your attention."

Evie had told her to send the doll picture?

"I . . . I don't understand," I say. "Evie told you to message me? When?"

"Before," she says quietly. "Before everything. At first it was just supposed to be for an emergency. A way to get in touch with you should something go wrong and she . . . couldn't."

My jaw tightens.

"What do you mean, couldn't?"

Charlie is visibly upset now, not angry, necessarily, but distressed.

"You have to know that Evie was like a child to me," she says. "All of my students were special, but she was . . . different. How I felt about her was different."

She's speaking about Evie in the past tense. I'm afraid now, charting the distance from my seat to the door. Trying to remember whether she locked it or not.

"Well, as I'm sure you've gathered, I was Evie's teacher. Sort of. A school guidance counselor. I was an elementary school art teacher in Phoenix for many years, but when I got my master's in psychology, I moved to a middle school and started working with students there," she says, her eyes drifting toward some of the art on the walls. "That's where I met Evie. So she would have been twelve when I met her. Sixth grade."

She crosses her legs, straightening the fabric of her dress as she does.

"Those years are some of the most painful in anyone's life," Charlie goes on. "They're horrific years, really. Brutal. Unrelentingly difficult. It's why I became a teacher. At first I thought little kids needed the most support, the most safe spaces during those vulnerable years. But after a while I realized that the tween years are the hardest. The most tender. I wanted to be there for them in a way that was pure. By choice. So many kids feel like a burden to everyone around them, but it was my choice to help them. To love them. So I got another degree to be a school psychologist."

I don't know whether to be comforted by or suspicious of what she's saying. Is it appropriate to talk about your students that way? To say you loved them?

"I wanted to be the person who would sit with them and say, 'This is exactly as miserable as you think it is, honey,' instead of dismissing what they were going through as unimportant. Parents are amazing. They do things I could never do. But they don't want to feel that level of misery in their own child. They don't want to carry it, to fully acknowledge it. I knew I could be that person for them—that I could try, at least."

She tucks a shock of silver hair behind her ear that's escaped from one of the braids. It's the first time I notice all her rings. Turquoise, amethyst, diamond. All of them stacked on one another, every finger dotted with something beautiful and unique, an extension of the walls around us.

"Evie was having a tough time that year. Kids didn't like how famous she was—how many free things she had. How beautiful she was. They sensed the money, I think. The fact that she was already operating like she was an adult with a job and a career. It's that age where all you want is to be older, or at least seem older. And Evie seemed older. None of them understood why that was a bad thing, of course."

I wrack my brain for memories of this. I was twenty-two then, my first years in New York. Distracted, yes. But I should have known. Guilt wraps its way around my throat and squeezes.

"Girls at that age are . . . unflinching. Violent. I don't blame them, really. It's an age that's all change, when you're not sure whether you should want attention or be afraid of it or both. It's complicated. But, sweet Jesus, they can be mean as wasps."

I don't like where this is going.

"Evie had been talking to some boy in the class, apparently. Flirting. I think she had written him a poem or something—a love letter, maybe. Something sweet and innocent. I don't know how, but somehow it got intercepted by this group of girls. And, well . . . you can guess what happened. They threatened to post it online. The poor girl was terrified. She thought the internet would tear her apart."

My heart is breaking for my sister. Oh, Evie.

"I don't know what it was about my office or me that made her want to chat, but she came to me once after school and told me all of it. She was so mortified, poor thing. I told her creativity was never anything to be ashamed of. That she should be proud that she put her feelings down on paper. I tried to reframe the whole thing for her, to encourage her to write it all down—every ugly thought, too. And she really took to it. Every day that she wrote, she said she felt happier. So we spent an hour after school journaling most days," she says, smiling. "And within a month or so, things really seemed to be improving. She was happier. Her grades were better. The bullies had quieted, or at least she seemed better at ignoring them. She made some new friends. She was happy. I expected her to stop coming by eventually, but she kept visiting me until the end of middle school. Even later, when my wife and I moved here for her job, Evie and I kept in touch."

She drifts off then in a way that says there's more to discuss there, but she's not sure where to start.

"She never said anything," I admit. "About you. The writing."

Why wouldn't she have told me that? Not once?

"Don't let that bother you too much, dear," she says kindly. "I got the sense that our time together was always something separate for her. Like it was almost sacred. She never pulled out her phone while she was there. Never talked about that part of her life with me, not beyond that first meeting. She told me once that my office was the only place she'd ever been where she wasn't viewed through the eyes of someone else first."

She looks at me in a way that's a bit pleading, like she needs me to understand that Evie's secrecy didn't have anything to do with me. I'm not sure if I believe that. But I'm starting to trust Charlie, at least.

"She needed something quiet and untethered from everything else," she says.

I'm nodding, taking in the story, trying to access the gratitude that I know I should feel for this person. This woman who seems so kind, so warm. The clatter of a teacup hitting the plate jolts me out of my thoughts. Charlie is fidgeting with her tea like she's nervous. Then she takes a deep breath.

"She's the whole reason I thought it would be a good idea at first," she starts. "She was the inspiration for it all. Why I even took the interview. My wife said, 'This doesn't really seem like your usual thing . . . are you sure you aren't too old for all of that?' I mean, she supported me, she knew that there is endless therapy to be done with people who spend so much time online. But she wasn't wrong. I just thought . . . I don't know, I thought what they were doing would bring people—kids, really—like her some . . . meaning. Some peace."

I don't know what she's talking about now, and uncertainty crawls up my back like an ant.

"Who is *they*, Charlie?"

"ReBrand."

The influencer agency? The one Gavin told me about?

"You worked for ReBrand? The management company?" I ask, confused. "I'm not following."

"That's how Evie found out about them. It was me. I recruited her," Charlie replies, shaking her head. "I should have known when they mentioned Evie in our interview that it was all wrong. Off. Instead, I chalked it up to coincidence. I told myself that they mentioned Evie because she's the textbook example of a child who grew up on the internet. The one everyone recognizes, even an old woman like me. I was proud of myself that I knew her. Really knew her. And I was only so eager to tell them that Evie and I were close. That I had helped her. That I had a unique perspective on all things influencing. I'm ashamed of myself now."

So it was Charlie who told Evie about ReBrand, then. And. . . Evie told Gavin. I think back to our conversation yesterday, when he told me that Evie had chosen the topic for the docuseries.

"So . . . what happened?" I ask, steadying my voice.

Charlie is near tears now, twisting the rings around so many times that one of her fingers has started to swell, angry and red. The calm, cozy person I met an hour ago is dissolving into someone else in front of me.

"For a year, it was fine. I had virtual sessions with most of the clients, until they'd inevitably drop off. Disappear, really. But that's not unusual in my line of work, either. Especially not with young people. I believed ReBrand when they said that the creators were choosing to move on."

All I can hear in my head is one word: *Disappear. Disappear. Disappear.*

"Is it true?" I ask. "That they're using people's trauma to make money? That they force people to donate to them? Is that what happened? Did they want a cut of Evie's money, too? To exploit her? Gavin said they turned her away . . ."

She looks confused for a moment then, like she's not following what I'm saying, and it makes me uneasy.

"It was the opposite," she says. "They went after Gavin for the same reason they went after me. To eventually get to Evie."

I narrow my eyes, trying to make sense of what she's saying.

"There were tiers," she explains. "Levels of influencers. Internally."

"What? Based on follower counts or something?"

"No. It was based on what they thought a person could handle. And what they thought they really needed," she says, a tinge of sadness in her voice. "When it came to Gavin, it was clear that he and Evie were in different places. Different levels. That their ReBrand experience would never be the same. He was in the group that funds ReBrand . . ."

She trails off, and I know this is the place in the conversation where I need to ask the question, but I'm too nervous. Adrenaline is surging through me, shooting down my leg.

"That funds them . . ." I manage.

Charlie looks up now, making eye contact with me, like she's finally ready to come clean. "That funds what they really want."

CHAPTER 26

"They call it their hundred-year-goal," Charlie says, calmer now, but still visibly uncomfortable. "Because that's how long they estimate it will take."

"What will take?"

"For us all to . . . unplug, get off of social media. Learn to live without it," she says.

I pause for a second, and then laugh. "Is this a joke?"

Charlie rolls her eyes, not at me but like she can't believe it herself. "No."

"So let me just make sure I understand this: They want to make money off of influencers . . . but also to . . . what? Wean the world of their addiction to the internet? Explain to me how, exactly, that makes sense?"

She sighs, pulling her braids over one shoulder. "I know more now than I did when I took the job. When I interviewed for the role, they spoke in terms that made sense to me—boundaries, addiction, attachment. The mental burden of growing up and stumbling through your teens and twenties online. I thought it was noble what they were doing . . . a way to make existing online feel better for people like Evie. It wasn't until much later, long after I had signed all the papers that make a conversation like this illegal, that I realized that every client they had, no matter what tier they were, fell into a category of . . . examples. They wanted Gavin not only because they thought he might influence Evie, but because they *thought* he'd say yes immediately. That he'd be lighting quick to monetize his dad's illness. The sadness of it all."

"You knew?" I ask.

"Yes," she says. "And I'm not proud of that. When they told me, I was disturbed, but my contract meant I couldn't say anything. My mother is elderly, you see. Ninety-nine next month. I'm her only child. Her only source of care and income. She was battling health issues at the time . . . I just, I couldn't risk losing the job. The money. I was all my mother had. I'm not proud that I stayed for as long as I did, but there it is."

"And the work . . . I don't care whether they truly believed in it or not, the work itself was important. Giving these young people safe, private spaces to work through the dynamics of sharing their lives online . . . it was vital. I still believe that, even if it turned out that the company never did . . . at least, not when it didn't serve them. "

"So it *was* what Gavin thought, then?" I say. "They wanted to make money off of the trauma. They knew people would engage with it."

"Yes, partially," she says. "They made money from all of it, of course. At the beginning they told me that they needed it for research, for planning. The only way they were going to get people off their phones for good was to market the idea accordingly. That wasn't cheap. But it wasn't just about getting every cent they could from Gavin, or his followers, but about making a point."

I shake my head, struggling to understand.

"Gavin is the best example of how they work, really. They thought they'd recruit Gavin, he'd sell out in no time, and he'd be one more person in the world that would prove their point: The internet is ruining us. Rewiring our neural pathways and dopamine receptors. Dulling and cheapening the greatest parts of life—joy, connection, meaning. All things I had tried to tell Evie, too. That all that money and fame comes at a price. Re-Brand wanted people to really see that, in real time. To feel it. They had whole teams of people who mined and planted embarrassing stories about Tier Threes like Gavin, in Reddit forums and YouTube and Instagram comments. Mistakes they had made. Rumors with a kernel of truth. Reminders of how shallow they were. How warped they were from spending so much time behind a screen."

My mind flashes to the newsletters Ashlyn sent to me, and I tuck this piece of information away for later.

"So they make money off of these people, anyway?" I push. "These 'lost causes'? They set them up to share their trauma, fundraise for it, monetize it to build their brands, and then ReBrand keeps the money?"

Charlie sighs. "ReBrand's philosophy was that they were beating social media at its own game. They were using consumer data and algorithms to get people to spend money, just like any other brand. Anyone on social media is just a click away from the BUY button at all times; those followers would probably be spending money that day anyway. Why not channel that impulse for good, rather than toward a new mineral sunscreen or a matching loungewear set or a course about how to retire off passive income? *Eventual* good, anyway."

For a moment, I can see how this philosophy would take hold, convincing a person that the influencer economy could and should be dismantled from the inside out. Wasn't this same thing I had struggled with a million times, weighing the way social media had changed my family, my sister, my life? Considering if there was ever a way to truly undo any of it? Maybe ReBrand was asking the same question.

And then I remember that they're capitalizing on the most pessimistic view of people, that they're tricking followers out of their own agency, and I'm mad for Gavin. Terrified for my sister. For whatever it means to be in some tier that's above that.

"How is that ethical? Even a little bit?"

"It's not," she says. "It's why I quit last year. The second I had enough money saved to take care of my mother, I was done."

"But?"

"But Evie kept taking their calls. I had only told her about ReBrand maybe six months before that. She seemed interested, but not so much so that I thought she wouldn't believe me when I told her I'd been wrong about it. But even when I warned her, when I told her that Top Tier is a whole different animal, that they would try to keep her involved in the company any way they could . . . I didn't know specifics about that part of things even then, even when I quit. But I knew enough to know it wasn't good. When I was there, there wasn't a single Top Tier that didn't lose everything—their platform, their voice, their career . . ."

"It was either that or . . ." She takes a deep breath. "Or they just disappeared."

I want to feel relieved that I'm being pointed in a specific direction finally, that someone is on my side now, believing that Evie isn't safe. But how can I trust her now? How can I trust this?

"And you didn't go to the detectives any of this?"

"I made a point not to trust the police a long time ago," she says. I don't blame her. "And I couldn't very well trust your mother, could I?"

She raises an eyebrow, like she's testing me, trying to see if I'm on the same page as my mother.

"No," I say. "You couldn't."

"And, truthfully, I was confused at first," she said. "A month before she disappeared, Evie told me that she and Gavin were going to expose ReBrand, to dig deep into what exactly they were doing to people. I was relieved. That Gavin was going to go there. *Him*, though. Not her. But when she disappeared, I thought . . . I don't know, maybe she took his place. Then there were his absurd videos. I messaged you, anyway. And when you didn't reply, I worried that maybe you and Erin were more similar than I had realized. That Evie shouldn't have trusted you, either."

"You think my mom didn't want to find her?"

"Not that," she says, carefully. "I just knew that with your mom . . . the business was always going to come first. If she knew about ReBrand and how the media would foam at the mouth over a story like that . . . well, I'm sure it wouldn't take long before I was sued and Evie wasn't even the priority anymore."

I think of Gavin, how he had been so cautious about how the internet would respond if he kept searching for Evie. How I had wondered why that mattered. Shouldn't all of these people feel exactly like me? I would do anything to find Evie, would lose anything. Risk anything.

Charlie is staring at her hands now, smoothing and resmoothing the same section of her dress.

"She wouldn't know a message from someone who truly knew her daughter if she saw it, anyway."

There's a hum of bitterness in her voice, just barely breaking through the surface. But I hear it. She's not the first person who thinks they could have done a better job with Evie than my mom has. The fact that maybe she's the first person who's tried unsettles me. There are boundaries, aren't there? Between teacher and student. Therapist and client.

"So that's why you sent the photo of the doll," I say, trying to keep my voice steady.

She nods.

"I do really hate that thing."

"I do, too, frankly," she says. "But I thought if I didn't buy it, there was no telling whose hands it would end up in. I can imagine the man—forgive the presumption, but it's always a man, isn't it?—who sent it to her seeing it for sale and spinning into a wild rage. Feeling slighted. And honestly, I also looked at it as some . . . I don't know, some way for her to take ownership of the horrible things that have happened to her. When I showed it to her, she laughed. Told me that you hated it more than almost anything. That if I ever needed to get your attention, just send you a photo."

I have more questions than I can get out: Was Charlie just . . . searching for Evie memorabilia on the internet? Did she have Google Alerts set up? Was she in bidding wars with other fans? My eyes drift toward the door again, the lock.

But there's another thing: why would Evie need her to get my attention?

"I thought she was joking," Charlie adds. "But it's a very Evie thing, isn't it? I think sometimes she made things much more complicated and obscure than they had to be just to see if someone was truly paying attention. If they really cared enough to figure out whatever secret code she had created—to see *her*, not her as a brand, or the character she played when she was growing up."

I think of Evie drawing on walls. The elaborate lies she had occasionally spun. But none of this answers the biggest question I have.

"So where is she, then, Charlie?"

Charlie gets up, shuffling to a bookshelf and pulling out a paperback novel. She flips through the pages and stops when she gets to the center, handing me a tiny sheet of paper with an address written down in neat cursive.

"This is all I have." She shrugs. "It's my best guess, anyway. Somewhere in Joshua Tree, where they have the company retreat every year. I never made it there, but I was looped into an old email chain at one point and . . . well, maybe it will help."

I glance at the paper, the letters smooth and sloping. Even Charlie's handwriting feels comforting, I think, before reminding myself of the facts. The chain of events. The doll. The way she is the person who started all of this, who could have fixed things so much sooner.

"Why not go yourself?" I snap. "Why message me? Why wait?"

A flash of shame moves across her face. "I had seen them go after other employees for breaking their contracts, their NDAs . . ." she says. "I thought we'd lose the house. Everything. If my mother got sick again, and I was battling impossible lawsuits at the same time, I would be in over my head so quickly. I would drown."

I want to feel something for her now. I know what it feels like to live on the edge of something, to feel that if one thing goes wrong, your whole life will come crumbling down. But all I can feel is that she's another person who let my sister down.

"So that's why you messaged me, then," I say. "Because I had less to lose."

"No," she says, firmly. "I messaged you because she loved you more than anyone. And I figured that went both ways."

It's the first time in weeks someone has confirmed what I've always felt, and it feels like relief. I study the piece of paper in my hand, the address. What if this is a trap, though? A way to get me out the door. I could think of a handful of other reasons why Charlie would have the doll, none of them good. My eyes drift up the stairs and Charlie follows my gaze.

"I know you don't trust me," she says. "I wouldn't either. I wouldn't trust anyone if I had been through what you have, dear."

"It's fine," I say. "I'm fine."

Am I?

"Would it make you feel better if you heard it in her own words?" she says. "All of it?"

I stop breathing for a second, imagining Evie making some grand entrance. I know that can't be what Charlie means, but I want it so badly. I want to tell my sister that I'm sorry I missed so much, all of this. Instead

olivia muenter

I stare at Charlie with skepticism.

"Come, dear," she says, making her way toward the stairs, gesturing for me to follow.

I know there's danger in this, but my curiosity wins the battle against my fear, and I follow her. We walk through a hallway lined with more photos and art and then into a bedroom, everything neatly in its place. A guest room, maybe. An old cast-iron bed sits in the corner, pushed against the wall like a day bed, a thick, pillowy comforter spread on top of it, covered with linen blankets and throw pillows. Charlie is going straight for something else in the room, though. A large wooden chest, clearly an antique. It looks like it belongs in a shipwreck, not in a house in the middle of the suburbs of Los Angeles. Before I can say anything, she's on her knees, opening it with a lock.

Inside are journals. Hundreds of them. My sister's journals.

I think of yesterday at my mom's. Her boxes full of photocopies. I always knew Evie could write—I had seen it in emails, texts, the rare long caption. It was part of why Ashlyn's theory about the newsletters didn't surprise me, once I really let myself think about it. So how could I have been so dumb to not realize my sister would want to write somewhere else? Somewhere just for her. All these words.

"Here they are," she says. "You know, I don't know for certain that they'll explain everything . . . or if you even have time for everything, but I imagine they might make you understand her a little bit more. Or understand why she kept all of these with me instead of . . . anywhere else."

I know what she means is "Instead of at home," or "Instead of with your mom," but what I really hear is: Instead of with you.

"It started in school, of course," she goes on. "During our counseling sessions—she asked me to keep them safe, even after she went on to high school and I moved away. It took her years to tell me it was because she didn't trust your mother not to read them."

I lean down and pick up the journal closest to me. The cover is leather, sage green. I begin to open it and then hesitate—am I any different than my mom? Is invading Evie's privacy wrong, even now? Even if it's so I can find her?

Charlie seems to feel my pause.

"You know, I recommended journaling to a lot of kids I worked with over the years, and I never opened a single one. Not once. I couldn't bring myself to do it, even when I knew it would help me do my job better. To understand what was happening in these kids' lives, their hearts. But when Evie was reported missing, I did read this most recent one, and I think you should too. Before you go find her."

She puts her hand on my shoulder then as she stands, and at first I think it's just to steady herself as she gets up from the floor, but it feels comforting, warm. Like she's steadying me, too. I know there's some part of me that craves exactly this: A person to call me *dear*. To gently lead me to a room where I feel safe. To pour me a cup of tea, slice a piece of banana bread, slather it in butter. To tell me about the birds in their garden. To make me feel like I'm in precisely the right place. To remind me that I don't have to perform or pretend here, either. Evie needed it more, I remind myself. She needed this person and place more.

"I'm sure you're anxious to get on the road," Charlie says from the doorway. "But take all the time you need."

I've spent so many hours of the past weeks wanting to crack open my sister's brain, to spill it all out and see what I missed. And now . . . here it is.

I tell myself I'll look at only one of the journals. The most recent one. I look at the first page and see the date.

December 12, 2022.

Six months to the day before she disappeared.

I run my hand over Evie's familiar handwriting, comforted seeing her loopy letters, the way they all connect in a way that only half resembles cursive. The first sentence is bigger than the rest of the text, taking up two or three lines instead of just one. It's underlined in bright red pen.

I was right.

CHAPTER 27

I only spend an hour reading the journal before I tuck it under my arm and jog down the stairs, straight to my car. I plug the address into the GPS and then I'm on my way, music blaring, calming my nerves and steadying me, despite the exhaustion I know I should feel. I've slept less in the last three days than I usually do in a single night. And yet I'm wired. Determined. I couldn't sleep now if I wanted to, not before I get to Evie. It's the only thing that assures me I won't fall asleep at the wheel. The music helps, too, and I turn the volume up.

It's a playlist that Evie made, one she sent to me that felt personal, but that I now realize is public. It has more than 45,000 subscribers on Spotify. Still, I have to admit that it's good. The kind of thing we both loved, indie folk music that mostly sounds like a compilation of sounds used in TikTok videos. I imagine the low, moody tunes being dubbed over videos of people saying goodbye to their elderly dogs or visiting their lonely grandparents in nursing homes, the kind of videos that always seem to pop up on my phone at one a.m. when I'm feeling my most vulnerable.

"There's a kind of relief in sad songs," Evie said to me once when we were listening to a particularly gut-wrenching cover of Patty Griffin's "Rain," one of our favorites. "No one needs an explanation. Everyone knows why you're crying, what you're feeling. How you got there. You don't need to give a play-by-play."

She was maybe fifteen at the time, and I had nodded at what she said, agreeing with her, feeling the truth of it. It was only later that I wondered if she was really saying was something like: *No one would understand if I told them the things I'm really sad about. No one would understand.* I comforted myself with the thought that everyone feels that way at fifteen. Right?

Still, the music doesn't quite fit this place, as I get closer and closer to Joshua Tree National Park. Not on a day like today, with a sky so blue that it looks like something you can dip into or scoop out. It's a perfect day, really. Not too hot. Zero clouds. A cool breeze, and a bright, piercing sunlight. I could understand choosing this particular place to convince people that the world outside their phone is better.

My GPS interrupts my thoughts by loudly announcing that I'm supposed to take a right and continue on for one hundred more miles. I look over the steering wheel and am comforted by the familiar absence of green. It looks so much like the long, terra-cotta-colored stretches of desert that Evie and I had driven through together before, talking about nothing the whole way. I wonder if Evie turned down this road a few weeks ago, if she looked out over the landscape and had the same thought I'm having now, that it looks like another planet here. The moon. Mars. A place to disappear into anonymity, to blend into the quiet.

olivia muenter

Episode 125: "The Cult-ish Influencer Society That No One Is Talking About" | *Darker: A True Crime Podcast*

September 25, 2022

Kira James: Finally, we are giving the people what they want . . .

August Cho: A CULT EPISODE!

Kira: You've got it. This week we're talking about a cult—well, actually, no. Alleged cult. Rumored cult. Cult-ish . . . cult. Whatever. The fact of the matter is that they've never confirmed or denied any of this, so we're just sourcing rumors, theories, and information from the deep dark corners of the internet so you can get all the important information as you drive to work or fold laundry or, you know, whatever it is you do when you're listening to us.

August: It's a weird job, but someone's gotta do it.

Kira: And we're happy to, right? Right. So today, we are talking about ReBrand . . . part possible multi-level marketing scheme, part supposed off-grid community, lots of culty behavior . . . all-around mystery.

August: Can you believe that I hadn't even heard of this until you briefed me on what you were doing for this week's episode?

Kira: Actually, yes, I can totally believe that, because not that many people are talking about ReBrand at all—not the bigger company behind the MLM stuff, anyway. You can find rumors about it online if you dig, or if you know who to ask, but apparently they are very, very good about making real stories about them disappear, which is why I haven't previewed this episode anywhere yet. I wasn't risking getting an episode this juicy killed before we'd even put it out in the world. Plus, more importantly, maybe this could help someone out there steer clear of these people. In other words, they're not shutting us up anytime soon.

August: One thing about cults—they hate when people call them a cult.

Kira: Every time.

such a bad influence

August: So. Kira. Tell us how this non-cult cult works, exactly.

Kira: Okay, yes. Let's get into it. But before I dive in, I want you all to know that I have been looking into this for months. I had to find anonymous sources and scour the weirdest places online for these interviews. And, of course, I will not be revealing anyone's identity who doesn't want to be exposed, but just know that I really, truly fell down a rabbit hole here. Once I started researching . . . I couldn't stop.

August: It's true, folks, she really went off the rails for a bit there. It was equal parts impressive and terrifying. Full Sherlock Holmes mode.

Kira: I agree. I got to some really weird places, personally. I wasn't sleeping. I started speaking in the Keith Morrison voice all the time. But I digress. Let's talk about what we know for sure right now . . . as in, what is recorded fact somewhere.

August: Let's do it.

Kira: So, ReBrand, LLC, is a company registered in California. It is listed as an influencer and marketing agency. Pretty standard stuff. Their website is very bare-bones. Just a completely stark white background with the RB logo and a place to submit your email address to learn more. You can email them and everything, ask to be considered to join the team. But their standards are both high and mysterious.

August: Ah, so that one time I convinced two of my followers to watch three consecutive seasons of Sister Wives would . . . not make me an appealing client?

Kira: I am sorry to report that no, I don't think it would.

August: So, wait. Who's making these decisions? Who's running the whole thing?

Kira: That's one of the many mysterious aspects of ReBrand. Even the creators I interviewed—we'll get to them in a minute—were hesitant to name names when it

olivia muenter

came to the founder. Their identity is a well-kept secret.

August: Creepy.

Kira: Very. But anyway, those creators? Each of them had more than 150,000 followers—and basically the same story about applying to ReBrand, more or less.

August: Tell me, tell me, tell me!

Kira: They were told that they would have to offer an up-front commitment. Basically, collateral. If the creators didn't make X amount of money or get Y amount of deals in a certain period of time, then they'd forfeit the up-front cash. It's rumored that they promised this cash would go toward charities, good causes, but it's impossible to trace it all, of course.

August: Wow, that's . . . kind of fucked-up?

Kira: It is. But based on what I've learned, ReBrand is very good at making it seem like you need them and not the other way around . . . at least for that level of influencer.

August: Now, Kira, what do you mean by level?

Kira: Well, according to their very mysterious Tier System . . .

August: Oh, my God. I swear we need some kind of party foghorn sound that goes off anytime we do an episode on a cult and there's a hierarchy involved. It's like when you're at a club and it's someone's turn to do birthday shots every twelve minutes.

Kira: Wait. You club?

August: What can I say? I was a different person once.

Kira: Wow. You heard it here first. But, okay. Back to the ReBrand Tier System. So,

such a bad influence

bottom tier is minor influencers. But minor to them is like . . . a quarter of a million followers. You pay a flat fee to start working with ReBrand. They take that money.

August: Hmm . . . methinks a pyramid scheme is about to emerge . . .

Kira: You're not totally wrong. So there are two ways to sort of prove yourself to ReBrand after that. One, you get enough partnerships to hit a certain threshold. We're talking very big money. Almost impossible standards, but from what the creators I talked to said, they make it seem like with them, you'll hit those standards easily. No problem. And if you don't, well, there's another way to earn your keep: recruitment.

August: God, what I would give to read a SABI newsletter about this thing . . .

Kira: I know, right?

August: But, okay. Back to the fucked-up-ness of it all. Let me guess: They can't recruit just anyone? Because of that whole exclusivity thing . . .

Kira: Exactly. It has to be people in the levels above them . . . each group is more and more popular, more and more famous. One source told me that she was childhood friends with a mega-influencer. We're talking followers in the millions. Apparently, the source's contract was coming to an end and their manager brought it up to them—suggested that they recruit this old friend. That it would mean this person wouldn't lose their up-front financial commitment. Thousands of dollars. When the source wasn't sure what to do, the manager suggested blackmail. Gave them a whole booklet of things to use against this creator, their old friend.

August: Oh, God. Is that legal?

Kira: Maybe. Because the thing is the contracts. People seem to get so enamored by the exclusivity, the mysterious nature of everything, that they sign without even knowing what they're getting into. They sign away any ability to push back. There are NDAs included in it all, of course.

olivia muenter

August: Okay, so . . . what about the higher levels? What's in it for them, exactly? Are they actually earning money?

Kira: That's where things get really weird. Really, really weird. You'd think that when it comes to those ultra-VIP clients, they'd just want money, right? More clout . . . more deals, whatever. But according to one source who managed to get out—escape, if you will—from their contract with ReBrand, it's so much more complicated than that.

August: Sorry, did you say escape?

Kira: I did. The thing is that if the buy-in for the lowest-tier influencers was cold hard cash, then the buy-in for the Top Tier targets—that's what they call them by the way, targets—is something much bigger.

August: Oh, God. What could they possibly want from them other than money?

Kira: Well, according to this source . . . everything. Your whole identity.

CHAPTER 28

I am in the suburbs.

I expect the address to lead me to some sprawling, mysterious open field. Or a cabin in the middle of nowhere. Or an ultramodern, high-tech, heavily guarded compound surrounded by nothing but cacti and dirt. Instead, I'm in the middle of a fucking cul-de-sac.

The neighborhood is your typical early-2000s-style suburb, cookie-cutter houses topped with terra-cotta roofs practically touching each other. It's exactly the type of place that would make a certain group of people feel inherently safe and another feel suffocated and unsettled. I turn another corner and expect to see more of the same, but instead it simply stops. The houses transition from fully built, seemingly lived-in single-family homes to bare-bones framing to empty lots to desert. I roll down the window and it's completely silent, nothing to hear but the steady hum of my car.

I drive for a few more minutes, my car crawling toward the darker section of the neighborhood, the part where the streetlights start to gradually fade and then disappear entirely. There must be people here. I had passed houses with lights on at the entrance to the neighborhood. But now I feel like the only person on earth, totally alone except for the steady silence that floats into the car with the breeze and curls around my neck, my ears.

The GPS announces that I've arrived and I slow to a stop. There's nothing outside my window aside from piles of construction trash. Scraps of

olivia muenter

lumber. There's nothing livable here, at least not that I can see. I know I should get out of the car, look around. Drive back toward the entrance, maybe. But I feel frozen. I remind myself that there's nothing scary about a place like this. I remind myself that part of what I'm feeling is adrenaline, the fact that it's getting dark, that I've barely slept in the last couple of days. That I'm still processing everything I've learned about my sister, my family over the last month. I've seen a million places just like this back home. They were everywhere after the housing bubble burst.

"It's just a neighborhood," I whisper to myself. But I don't believe it.

I try to count how many houses are here—maybe twenty, twenty-five.

I finally put the car in park, force myself to get out and look around. I close the door gently, quietly. Every step I take sounds loud, like every single person here could hear it, if there's anyone here at all. But there has to be, right? This address exists for a reason.

I spin around, hands on my hips, deciding which direction to go in first. It's then that I spot something in the distance, just beyond the half-framed houses and the empty lots, in a space of flat, clear land. The ground there looks rocky, like it's dotted with objects, all of them the same exact size and shape. I walk toward them, curious, and I'm almost to the edge of the paved road when I realize what they are: Dozens of tiny identical markers. Like gravestones. It looks like a makeshift graveyard without any grass.

But it can't be, right? This is a neighborhood full of normal houses— and what will be normal houses one day, when some developer buys this land and turns it into a chic, off-grid Airbnb paradise. The land surrounding the neighborhood is gorgeous, vast and completely unique, flat and studded with occasional spikes of green, everything contrasted by the endless background of blue sky (now painted with streaks of orange and purple). The last house I had passed while driving to the neighborhood was thirty minutes south of here, maybe. Miles and miles away.

As I move closer, it's clear: those things are markers, and each of them is engraved with tiny letters on the back. Initials. I walk through ten or so rows, searching for some explanation. It's not until I make it to the end that I turn around and see a marker that looks new, shinier than the rest, less coated with dust and dirt, with three letters I recognize. EED.

Evelyn Elliot Davis.

Oh, God. No.

My stomach lurches and goosebumps cover my arms. I look back toward my car, wishing I had brought something to defend myself with. Pepper spray. A knife from Charlie's kitchen. Anything. I tuck my car keys into the crook of my hand, my only weapon.

Suddenly, I feel the urge to look up. To scan my surroundings and make sure I'm alone. There's no one in sight, still, but something is different. One of the closest houses, just down the street from where I stand, has its lights on now. In the glow, I can make out the unmistakable, unmoving outline of a person that is staring directly at me.

My gut is screaming that I need to get in the car. Now. I can't leave the area, not when I'm so close to finding out what happened to Evie. But I need armor. Distance.

I jog to the car and throw myself into the front seat, click my seatbelt, and head out the way I came as quickly as I can. I'm driving so fast that I almost can't stop for the person standing in the middle of the road. Not on the sidewalk, or on the front porch trying to wave me down. But directly in the middle of the road, barefoot, a smile creeping across their face.

"What the *fuck*," I say as I slam on the brakes.

What the fuck, what the fuck, what the fuck

They're walking toward my passenger door now, features shielded by the darkness—and though I'm tempted to peel out then and there, something makes me wait. I take a deep breath and look to my left. Part of me harbors a wild hope, for just a moment, that I'll see my sister standing there. But the figure crouches down at the window so they're at eye level with me, and it's someone else. Someone who looks familiar to me, but I can't place.

"Hazel, hello," I hear the figure say through the window. "We've been expecting you."

I blink at her through the glass, then turn away, moving to shift my car back into drive. All of this feels wrong.

"Not so fast," she says, raising her voice. "Don't want to damage the car more. And trust me, you'd have to walk for miles before you get enough service to call AAA. And out here? In the middle of the night? That's no good, is it?"

olivia muenter

I look at her, confused, and she's pointing behind the car. I look in the driver's side mirror and I can see small, raised strips on the road behind me. They look sharp. As if answering my question, I watch a light on my dash turn on right then: low tire pressure warning.

Shit.

I glance back at the figure, who is still smiling at me through the window, as if she's waiting for me to connect the dots. To understand.

I crack the window, just an inch.

"Where is Evie Davis?" I ask.

"She's inside," she says. "Waiting for you."

CHAPTER 29

I'm sitting on the floor when I see my sister for the first time in almost two months. The woman who stopped me in the street led me to a house a few yards away. My sister's house? She ushered me in the front door and motioned to a spot on the ground, a cushion.

"Sit, please," she says. "I'll tell Evie you're here."

My mind is racing with questions. What is this place? Am I in Evie's house? Is Evie actually coming out, or is this a trap?

But when my sister walks through the living room door, every question melts away and full-body relief takes their place. She's here, and real, and alive. She's safe.

"Haze," she says quietly, wrapping me into a hug when I stand, like there are no other questions hanging between us. Like she owes no other explanation. "You're here."

"I'm here," I say back. I'm still overwhelmed with relief but the questions are coming back.

"My furniture is on the way," she says, answering the one that was maybe last on my list.

She throws me another cushion from a pile in the corner of the room, and I take it as an invitation to sit again. Everything is beige. Even the light coming from the few fixtures in the room feels intentionally dulled. "The first month we give up pretty much everything just to be present."

I take a deep breath, conscious that the woman I had met earlier is still here somewhere. As if on cue, her voice cuts through from an adjoining

olivia muenter

room.

"It helps you figure out what you really do need, and what you don't," the woman says, coming in to sit cross-legged against a wall, sipping something from a ceramic mug. She's wearing an oatmeal-colored linen jumpsuit, her loose waves of thick blonde hair blending into the fabric around her shoulders. "And that's the whole point of what we do, really. But Evie will tell you all about that."

I glance from the woman to my sister, noting the changes in Evie's face. The hair extensions I had become used to are gone. The makeup is nonexistent. There are two single remaining eyelash extensions hanging on for dear life. Her clothes are old and mismatched, items I've never seen her wear before. It's her, of course. Freckles. Eyes the color of green grapes. Auburn hair. But something else has been pulled away from her. I can't tell if it's left her lighter, or dimmer.

"Right," I say to the woman, digging my fingers into my cushion. I look around the room, trying to make sense of the space, this place. "So what would be the point of giving me two flat tires on my car, exactly?"

"That wasn't how I wanted to meet. I'm Natalie, by the way," she says lightly. "And the tires . . . that was an accident. With as many VIPs as have here, there's no such thing as being too careful."

"So your goal is to make sure your biggest stalkers can't . . . leave?" I say, trying to calculate the logic in what she's saying. Trying to find it.

Evie shoots me a look that feels like a warning, but Natalie seems unfazed.

"Our goal is to give law enforcement easier access to people who wish to do our clients harm," Natalie says smoothly. "In fact, we have a very good relationship with law enforcement."

"Right," I say, and at first, I think the comment is odd, but then something starts to click. Maybe Natalie was the detectives' source, the one who told them Evie was just fine.

"The institution has its issues, of course, but they understand privacy," she says. "And ultimately, that's always what we're asking for. When things don't just die down, sometimes we need their assistance to protect the privacy of someone like Evie."

"So that's what the Instagram post was about," I say, staring at Evie, who just blinks back at me while Natalie responds.

"Well, yes," she says coolly. "It was to keep Evie safe. That's all we care about here. That's why our security measures are what they are."

She lifts her mug toward the front door, toward my useless car down the street.

"But you don't wish to do your sister harm, I'm sure," Natalie says, her gaze intense and unblinking. "You'd never do that, would you?"

The question feels exaggerated, like she's implying that I'm somehow dangerous to my sister.

Again, I look to Evie, but she's staring at her hands.

"No," I say, firmly, finally turning to meet Natalie's gaze. "Never."

"Great," Natalie says cheerfully. "We're on the same page then."

I glance at my phone and notice there's a blank space where there are usually bars and symbols. I have no service.

"No service out here," Natalie explains, pushing herself off the ground and walking toward the adjoining kitchen. "No internet either, of course, for our clients. A total dead zone. Though, you know, I've always wondered why we call it that, as it's the disconnection that makes you feel more *alive* than ever. That's why I started this."

"ReBrand, you mean?" I say. I can't keep the disgust out of my voice. "The so-called influencer agency . . ."

She smiles again, kindly, like she's slightly amused by my question. "The mission," she clarifies. "Evie can tell you all about that, though. I'm sure it would mean more coming from her. We're not for everyone, after all. Not yet, anyway."

I look around, studying the bland home, exactly zero trace of what I had imagined ReBrand would look like: clean lines, modern conference rooms, shiny glass surfaces. "So this is . . . what? Company headquarters?"

Evie tucks her knees toward her chest, nodding.

"It's like . . ." Evie starts. "A giant factory-reset button. For your life. Your brain. An opportunity to relearn how to be in the world."

"A rebirth, if you will," Natalie chimes in. "I believe that once you do truly start over, from scratch, there's no way you go back to the rot and hollowness of a disconnected, digital world. You want something more.

olivia muenter

But you can't get there if you don't kill everything that came before."

She stops herself with a laugh. "Metaphorically speaking, obviously."

I think of the markers outside. Evie's initials.

"The graveyard . . ."

"Yeah," Evie says, a little like she's embarrassed. "It's . . . symbolic."

"Like I said, a metaphor," Natalie adds, but my eyes are fixed directly on Evie.

"Don't you think that's a little . . . absurd? Cheesy?" I ask. "Both?"

"What I think is absurd," Natalie says with a withering look, "is a child growing up with millions of people watching her every move. A mother monetizing her daughter's biggest successes and failures."

"And you don't do that?" I push, emboldened by the urge to help my sister. To protect her. "With Tier Threes? With Gavin? That isn't what you're doing with all of them, too? Exploiting the people you think are too stupid and meaningless to be helped?"

I want her to be surprised by what I know, how ReBrand manipulates and take advantage of people. But she doesn't even flinch.

"Tier Threes are a lost cause," she says with a wave of her hand, like she's brushing off my implication. "They're never coming back. They're not like Evie—craving a different way to be. They'll never get past how they exist now. So the best we can hope for is that they show everyone else how not to be. The worst ways to exist in this world. The clearest examples of how a life lived online sucks the soul out of you, changes the way you make choices."

I shoot a look at Evie, whose face is blank. This is her boyfriend Natalie's talking about. Why doesn't she seem more offended?

"Look," Natalie says lightly, placing her mug in the sink. "You don't have to get any of this, Hazel. That's the whole point. The only thing that matters is that your sister gets it. That she's choosing to be here. It's like any good form of therapy—designed to challenge you, to make you better and happier than before."

I think of Charlie and wonder how many other therapists ReBrand has on staff.

"The only thing that really matters is if it works for the client. If it serves them," she says, heading toward the front door. "I think you'll find that this serves Evie right now. Even if it's not comfortable or convenient for you."

This feels like a dig, a reminder that I forced myself into this world without being invited. That I showed up here unannounced.

"I'll see you two in the morning," Natalie says. "We will handle your car, Hazel—the damage. You'll be good as gold by tomorrow afternoon."

The word *we* lingers after she shuts the door, and for a moment Evie and I sit in silence, the hum of the air conditioning filling the room.

"So," I finally say. "All of this . . . mess. All of this anxiety and *fear* was just so . . . what? So you could just stay here with Cult Leader Barbie?"

Evie sighs, though it comes out a little like a laugh.

"I needed some space, Hazel," she says. "A chance to regroup, to reset. Like I said."

She sounds so sure of herself that it catches me off guard.

"And this is how you do it?" I push, following her into the kitchen. "I was terrified. I thought you were being held in a basement somewhere. Dead in a ditch. I haven't been sleeping. I was at Mom's for a week. A nightmare. And just so you could . . . what? Take a break? Just so you could do a little social media detox?"

"Look, I know how it seems on the surface. I know ReBrand's methods seem extreme. I know that because at first I felt just like you do—I didn't get it, didn't see it. Thought it was fucked-up. But then it clicked. Half measures don't work when it comes to resetting everything, not when you grew up like I did. Not when you're as broken as I was."

I cringe hearing my sister talk about herself this way.

"You weren't broken," I say, the last word coming out like a whisper. "I didn't think that."

"No?" She laughs. "I thought you, of all people, would get this. Would see it. The way you despised the world Mom and I were in. The way you looked down on it. I couldn't tell you about this place because of the NDAs. But I thought that when I had healed enough, when it was time to reach back out again . . . that when you saw me here, you'd understand. Forgive me."

I feel a pang of regret for a moment, ashamed to have disappointed her. And then I remember.

"The resources you wasted, Evie . . . the police, the time spent searching for you . . ." I argue. "The aftermath, what Mom did . . ."

"Oh, so now we feel bad for cops?" She snorts. "And *Mom*? That's new."

"I just mean—you caused chaos. Everyone was so worried about you. And then even after the Instagram post, I knew something was off . . ."

Her voice softens now. "I'm fine, Haze," she says. "This was a hard boundary, and I needed to draw it. I thought that would be clear."

I consider a different angle.

"What about Gavin, then?" I say. "You just left him in the dark, too? To spiral? To freak out? Even after he was so excited about the docuseries thing . . . even with everything with his dad? You just . . . left him?"

She's laughing for real now, and it chills me. "So you guys hung out, I guess. You finally got the full Gavin Ramirez charm offensive. Figures."

I'm thrown by her knowing this, embarrassed at the memory of being attracted to him. That afternoon in the kitchen.

"He'll be fine," she says. "I'm sure of that."

"But are *you* fine?" I push, putting a pin in the Gavin conversation. "Are you really fine with all of this? This place? The rules? The isolation? Being here for . . . for how long?"

"As long as it takes. And I'm getting there," she says. "That's the whole point of doing this program. It takes time. If it was easy to reframe how I think about connection, the internet, my selfhood, maybe I'd have figured it out years ago."

Years ago?

"You're eighteen, Ev," I say. "You don't need to have it all figured out."

"No?" she asks. "Is that why you were always pushing for me to leave home, go to college, get a real job?"

A burst of shame spikes my bloodstream, warming me.

"I . . . I just wanted you to have options," I say. "Beyond what Mom wanted."

She smiles. "Same. That's why I'm here. Hazel, it's not about you . . ." she says. "I've just never been truly on my own, cut off from everyone else's opinions. All the pressure. ReBrand gave me the opportunity to do that."

"So . . . is this . . . I mean, how long does this last?" I ask, afraid of the answer.

"It's for now," she says. "For a while."

I lean against the countertop and nod, telling myself I'll push back on this later. That maybe now it's best to just take a beat.

She finishes drying the mug that Natalie left in the sink and puts it away in a cabinet before turning to me. "You know, none of it means I don't miss you," she says. "That I haven't missed you. What I need and what I want are two very different things right now."

Are they? Did Natalie tell her that?

"I missed you too, Ev," I say instead, and I can feel the adrenaline of a day that started in Arizona and ended in a compound in California finally wearing off. It's past ten p.m. now. The relief of being near my sister is mixed up with sadness and fear now, too. It's a different kind of fear; after all, she's right here in front of me. Physically safe, a reality that wasn't guaranteed this morning.

This fear is for tomorrow, when I feel sure that I'm going to have to leave her here. To do the one thing that she really wants, even if I think it's wrong. Even if I think there's a better way. Even if I think it's going to hurt her in the end.

She stretches out her arms and walks toward me like she's read my mind, pulling me in for a hug. I close my eyes, and everything about her is familiar again. Her smell, the way her hand wraps around me and rests on my shoulder. We stay there for a minute, quiet, and I don't think she's going to say anything, but just before I pull away, she whispers.

"I thought you'd be proud of me, Haze."

I swallow, tears finally pricking my eyes.

"Always," I lie.

olivia muenter

CHAPTER 30

Evie's bedroom is arguably more boring than the front room. It's a box with beige walls, a beige carpet, and a small air mattress resting in the center.

"You can sleep on the mattress," Evie says, and I can tell she's a bit embarrassed by the room, the plainness of it, maybe. The way I know it looks nothing like her. "I'll take the floor."

"No way," I say. "Floor is fine for me."

"Suit yourself," she says, but she's smiling. She heads to another room and comes back with an armful of blankets and pillows, so many that there are throw pillows falling out of her arms when she enters the room.

"Sleepover it is," she says, tossing it all on the floor, pulling the comforter off the air mattress so we can lie there together, just like we did for so many years when she was little. It's the second time I feel like I'm going to cry, but I hold it together.

"A whole house, all to ourselves," I say. "Just for a sleepover. Our younger selves would be dying right now."

"My younger self would expect far more unicorn-themed items in the room," Evie says. "But yes, we would be thrilled."

I laugh. "Oh, so unicorns aren't coming with your new furniture?"

"Who knows," Evie says, and it gives me pause.

Didn't she say that she picked out her furniture? I wonder if that was something she said because Natalie was there, to make things seem more comfortable than they really were. But if this is the last evening I have with my sister for a long time, then I'm not going to spend it arguing about this place.

We burrow into the blankets and turn off the lights, and now it's easy to imagine we're kids again, that we're back in my mom's house, and there are so many years stretching before us when we can change and fix whatever we want.

"So you knew," I say, breaking the silence. "About the cameras."

I feel her eyes on me, searching for something.

"I met Charlie," I explain. "Found her. Or she found me, I guess, depending on how you look at it."

"Ah," she says, stretching the word out. "Of course."

"And she showed me the journals," I admit, then remember the moment at my mom's. The photocopies of Evie's diaries. I clarify: "The ones you wrote when you were with her."

She doesn't respond, and I wonder if she feels like this is a violation, too. Like even this little bit of privacy was something I wasn't willing to give her.

"I only read one before I came here. Just part of it, really," I said. "An entry about how you found the cameras. How you realized what Mom was doing."

There's a pause again, like she's waiting for me to go on. "Right," she finally says, though something in her tone sounds confused, like she's piecing something together.

"That's why you're here, right? That's what all of this is about?"

She's staring up now, studying the ceiling fan. I wonder if she's thinking of the voice recorder, too. "The cameras were part of it, yes."

"Part of it?"

"I felt like I was drowning, Hazel," she says. "Like I couldn't breathe. Like I had to change all the time, and at the same time, I couldn't. Like people would hate me either way. I couldn't think of a single choice I had ever made where I didn't account for everything else first—the internet, the followers, the money. Mom's feelings. Your feelings, too." She says the last part quietly, and my heart drops. "I couldn't think of one moment when I was able to trust myself to make a decision that was separate from it all. Not when I was fifteen or ten or five, or even before then, maybe.

Before Dad."

I hear what she's saying, of course. I understand it. But does all of that really mean that we had to end up here? Like this?

"You could trust me," I offer.

A long pause hangs between us before she goes on, seemingly ignoring what I had said.

"When everything is material or content or something that can be packaged in a better way . . . by you, or the people around you . . ." she says. "It just becomes this thing, this monster that makes you believe that if you really are good enough or smart enough or savvy enough, then you can optimize it. You can optimize anything. You can optimize yourself. And when that happens, nothing is real anymore."

"I know it's hard, Ev," I say. "I tried my best to make it easier for you, even when I was away. It's part of why I came home. I just . . . I couldn't. Nothing I did was enough. Your world, you and Mom . . . it was all so much bigger than me."

"You know," she says, and I can already tell she's about to do the same thing again—talk around what I said. Not ignore it, necessarily, but not engage with it, either. What isn't she telling me? "In a way, I don't even think that any of these problems are unique to me. I think it's maybe how everyone feels, living in the world we do, always connected online but disconnected from ourselves. It's part of what I like about ReBrand. They're honest about the thing that the rest of us have spent so long lying to ourselves about."

She's using that specific brand of therapy-speak that sounds like Natalie, and it makes me uneasy. My sister was always more grounded than this.

"We all like to believe that these online versions of ourselves don't rob us of something, but that can never really be true. Right? It just can't. If one version is the optimized version of us, then what's the unedited version? The kind that doesn't end up in photos or videos? How can any of us walk around and feel okay as is when that's how things are? We've all been set up for failure. Eventually what happened to me will happen to everyone . . . the real version gets sanded down into nothing."

"You are so far from nothing, Ev," I push. "Whatever else you are, you're never that."

"I don't . . . I don't need that, Hazel," she snaps. "The pep talk. I can do that for myself now. That's what all of this is giving me—the chance to see myself. The good, the bad, the ugly. To just sit with it. To be okay with it."

I'd imagined what it would feel like to see Evie again a hundred times over the past two weeks. I'd wondered what questions I would ask. But this reality is like an alternate universe. I feel desperate to comfort my sister, to convince her to change her mind. And she just keeps pushing me away.

"We need to sleep," she says eventually, turning to face me in the darkness. "But let's go on a hike tomorrow, okay? Before you leave."

You. Not we.

"Okay," I say. "That sounds good."

"Night, Hazel," she says sweetly.

I blink into the darkness of the room for a few minutes, noting the steady change in Evie's breaths, the way she settles into sleep. It comforts me, the rhythm of it, how it's so similar to how it was when she was little. I want to wake her and tell her all about it, to point to something and say that some things are unchangeable. Instead, I let myself feel like she's seven again and I'm seventeen. That she's dozed off and I've promised to stay awake next to her, to keep away the monsters as she sleeps.

CHAPTER 31

I wake up to the sound of a kettle boiling in the kitchen, and Evie is gone. For a moment, I have to remind myself where I am, to play the events of the last two days in reverse and remember how I got here. The apartment is soaked in light now, the exact opposite of how everything had felt last night. The beige had made everything look slightly dirty last night, shadowed. Today, it all looks bright and warm. I pad out of the bedroom to the kitchen and Evie is pouring hot water into a French press.

"Morning," she chirps, not looking up from what she's doing. "Half-and-half is in the fridge."

I've never seen my sister make coffee. Never seen her in her own space at all. I didn't even know she knew how I take my coffee. It's a strange thing to feel proud of, this little moment of simplicity. Of independence. But I feel it make the tiniest chip in the resentment I felt last night—the anger that she could have orchestrated this elaborate stunt despite how it affected everyone. How it affected me.

There are two insulated mugs sitting next to the French press, already filled.

"Think you'll be ready in fifteen?" she says. "I want to make sure we have time to get a couple miles in before Natalie comes by with your car."

The car. That's right. Instinctively, my eyes search the counter for my keys. Hadn't I left them there?

"She picked it up this morning," Evie says. "I thought you wouldn't care. She's handling the repairs, like she said last night. It should be fixed by the afternoon. I'm sorry about that, by the way . . . your tires."

She had said that, right? I rub my eyes, trying to wake myself up. The mention of Natalie and last night makes me feel disoriented again. Maybe I didn't sleep as well as I had thought. Maybe it's the crack of dawn.

I check the time on my phone. It's not that early—almost eight, but my eyes are stuck on the top right corner, the SOS symbol. Then I remember. No cell service. No internet. No car. I suddenly feel sweaty, trapped. Fresh air sounds good.

"Yeah," I say, trying to seem unruffled, casual. "Fifteen is fine."

"Natalie brought by some clothes for you this morning," she says, thrusting a freshly poured cup of coffee my way. "For the hike. She figured you wouldn't have brought anything."

"Oh," I say, trying to figure out how early, exactly, Natalie had been by. Why she had known we would go on a hike. "That's . . . thoughtful."

"Yeah," she says. "She thinks of everything."

Apparently.

I grab the leggings and T-shirt on the counter and head toward the bathroom, changing quickly. I stare in the mirror afterward, and realize I look nothing like myself. I wonder if it's the clothes or just this place. The exhaustion. I lean closer to the mirror, smoothing my hair back into a clip. I run my tongue over my teeth and they feel gritty. I open a drawer, searching for some toothpaste to squirt on my finger. The first drawer is mostly empty, but in the second I find a single tube of toothpaste next to some sunscreen. Nothing else. I "brush" my teeth, spit in the sink, and am about to throw the toothpaste in the drawer when I see it—a mark on the side of the drawer. A tiny stick figure, a strange smile, drawn in Sharpie. Evie.

"Ready to go?" she yells from the kitchen.

"Yeah, just brushing my teeth," I say, testing something. "Borrowed your toothpaste—hope that's okay."

Silence. I wonder if she heard me at first. But then she responds.

"More than okay," she says, the three words standing on their own for a bit before she goes on. "You're much more fun to hang out with sans coffee breath."

"Ha," I say, walking back into the kitchen where she sits in full hiking gear, ready to go. It feels good, to be laughing. Teasing each other. It makes me feel hopeful that maybe we can work our way through everything that's happened, that maybe we'll emerge from our hike and she'll get in the car with me, and all of this will be something we laugh about next month, next year.

She smiles, her green eyes flashing my way. "Ready?"

I shrug and start walking toward the door. "As I'll ever be."

· • • ● • • ·

There's a trail behind the neighborhood, not far from the fake graveyard.

"When I got here these scared the shit out of me," I say, studying the markers as we walk toward the trailhead, noticing how much less ominous they look in full daylight. "I mean, come on, Ev. You have to admit this is kind of ridiculous. You'd think, with all the money ReBrand has, that they'd have some other plan for a metaphor . . . something a little more chic and a little less Spirit Halloween."

She's walking a few paces ahead of me, not stopping to look down, or back at me.

"I get it," she says. "That it seems ridiculous. It did to me to, at first. When Charlie told me about it, my first instinct was pretty much exactly what yours was. It seemed utterly absurd and also fucked-up. The kind of thing you hear about on a podcast and think, *how on earth did that ever appeal to anyone . . .*"

"Hence why you brought the idea to Gavin . . ." I offer. "As the docuseries subject."

"Yes," she says, pulling on the straps of her backpack.

"So what changed, then?" I say.

She looks back toward the houses, most of which are getting smaller in the distance.

"Everything," she says. "Last year changed everything."

My mind flies to last year, the conversation I had had with Mom. The deal we had made. Did Evie know about that? Had she somehow found out?

"Right," I say, directing the conversation elsewhere. "The cameras. Mom."

She's still walking ahead of me, her pace faster than I can keep up with, making it impossible for me to see her face. "Sure," she says. "And the newsletter."

My mind races to my conversation with Ashlyn, the way their friendship had fallen apart.

I try to sound sympathetic. "I heard about what happened. With Ashlyn. What she accused you of. The way things fell apart between you . . . how she ignored you later. It's horrible, Ev."

She stops in her tracks then, looking back at me, like this surprises her. "You did?"

"Yeah, she was at the search party that Gavin organized . . ." I say.

Evie faces forward again, continuing at the same pace as before. She exhales, a *psh* sound floating into the desert air. "I bet she was."

She sounds amused more than bitter or angry. But it confuses me.

"What do you mean?"

"Her and Gavin."

I stop walking then, calculating what she's saying in my head, but she's still going. I jog to keep up with her.

"Wait, what do you mean, her and Gavin?" I push. "Ashlyn and Gavin are a thing?"

"Sure are," she says. "Have been for a while."

I want to ask so many things, like what that means about Ashlyn's former fiancé. How it happened. If this was part of their fight. I try to do the math in my head. "He cheated on you? Last year?"

"Not exactly," she says. "We were never . . . exclusive, he and I. It was just easier for everyone to think that."

Now my head is really spinning.

"Hold on," I say. "Stop, Evie. Stop."

She pauses then, glancing back at me casually. None of this seems painful for her. It's old news.

"We were always better as friends," she explains. "The internet seemed to love us together way more than *we* loved us together, if that makes sense. And honestly, being in a couple was better than the stupid TikTok speculation of who we were seeing, flirting with, talking to . . . a long-term relationship makes you likable and also a little bit boring. Or safe, I guess.

So we just kept it going—publicly, anyway. And we stayed friends."

I think of the photos I had seen of them, the ways Evie had draped her-self over Gavin at the beach last summer, his hand flat against her bare stomach. I had heard them FaceTime each other, had seen the way they talk. How is it possible that there wasn't more there? All that chemis-try . . .

"Friends," I repeat. "Just friends . . ."

"Well, I mean, you've seen him," she admits. "I'm only human. We hooked up. A lot. It was fun. Easy. Exactly what we needed. Don't get me wrong, we talked about making things more serious a few times. But in the end, we always came to the same conclusion. We understood each other. And we liked things the way they were. It's what made the idea of working together actually appeal to me. We weren't partners in *that* way, so we could be partners in this other way."

"And then . . ."

"And then he met Ashlyn," she says. "And suddenly he did want some-thing serious. With her."

"When was this?" I ask, though I already know.

She turns around and starts walking again, facing forward, her tone neutral. "The same time that she accused me of writing the stupid news-letter."

I swallow, thinking of the excerpts of the SABI emails Ashlyn had sent me, the sentences that sounded so much like Evie's voice, her sense of humor.

"So it wasn't you, then?"

She shakes her head, and because I can't see her face, I don't know whether it means *no*, or *I can't believe you're really asking me that*.

"Of course it wasn't you," I say. "Maybe it was Mom. Those cameras . . . everything she heard."

She doesn't reply, walking ahead, her hands set on her hips.

"Or maybe it was ReBrand. Maybe it was one of the ways they were planting stories about influencers. That would make sense, wouldn't it?"

"Yeah, Hazel," she says. "That would make sense."

I pick up my pace, and I'm beside her now, but her expression is un-readable.

"So that's why Ashlyn didn't reply . . . when you thought someone was watching you . . ." I say. "Because she . . . wanted Gavin?"

"She was pissed Gavin was still working with me on the docuseries idea. That we wouldn't talk to her about it because we were trying to make sure something didn't leak before we were able to pitch the idea. She thought we were still hooking up. So when I decided to take it all into my own hands, to come here anyway, and then to stay and really do the work . . . well, I thought I was doing everyone a favor. They could have each other."

I'm putting together the pieces now, remembering my conversations with Ashlyn, Gavin, Charlie.

"So you did come here to expose what ReBrand is doing . . . how they're taking advantage of creators?" I say.

Evie reaches for a water bottle on the side of her backpack and takes a swig, wipes her mouth, but doesn't slow her pace. "I didn't understand anything about what they were doing, Hazel. I had it all wrong."

"And Charlie did too?"

She stops walking for a minute, guilt flashing across her face.

"Yes," she says, but I can't fully tell if she believes it. "She did, in the end. But she was the one who *told* me about ReBrand, who thought that they could help me, change my life . . . and she was right, even if she questioned things eventually."

I don't reply, waiting for her to continue.

"I love her, you know," she says. "Charlie. She's like a grandmother to me. Or a mother. She made me feel completely at ease in a time when I felt like I couldn't trust anyone. She gave me the space to write . . . to find comfort in that. But when she started working at ReBrand, I felt . . . I felt like she was doing what everyone else has ever done with me. Maybe she wasn't trying to monetize me, but she was trying to fix me. I resented it, even if by the time I realized she was right, she was the one second-guessing it all . . . the process. Just because the program wasn't a fit for her doesn't mean it isn't for me."

The program. I wonder if she hears herself. How it sounds.

"I know that some of it seems extreme on the outside . . ." she continues. "Or unorthodox."

"How about hypocritical, Ev?" I say. "They're making money from all of you . . . the lower-tier people, even the Tier Threes like Gavin who don't end up committing to anything . . . they're digging up this personal information about them, taking advantage of all of them just so they can . . . what? Spin some ridiculous story about how the internet is actually the enemy? But in the meantime they're making millions of dollars from it? From you? Come on."

"I know how it looks," she says. "But it's exactly why ReBrand will work, eventually. Maybe not in my lifetime, but one day. When all the stories about the Tier Threes, or people like me who give it *all* up, trickle through everyone's phone and apps month after month, year after year, then people will start to realize that none of it serves them."

"And until then, ReBrand will just rake in the cash, right?"

"How else do you think they could afford this?"

She gestures toward the neighborhood, which is now small in the distance.

"So *that's* the plan? Convince everyone in the world to join their weird, off-grid suburb?" I say. "Make sure no one can just show up without getting their tires popped?"

"It's a *retreat*. A detox center," she says. "And it works, Haze. It does. I'm happy."

I flash through every emotion I've experienced in the last two weeks. The fear. The paranoia. The many ways I've imagined my sister could have been hurt, maimed, killed. And meanwhile she was here. Happy. Hiking through the desert, alive and strong.

"I don't understand how any of that is worth making people worry like we worried," I say. I picture the TikTok Live, the figure approaching the car. "The video made people think you were *abducted*. Hurt, or worse."

"That . . ." she starts, and finally drops her hand, shifting her body so she's facing another direction, away from the sun and me. "Was a mistake. Natalie thought it would . . . I don't know, make people pay more attention. That if we had as many eyes on the story as possible, it would make everything that came after even more impactful."

She's walking again, and I'm trudging behind her. We must have walked a mile already, and I'm feeling sluggish, thirsty enough to drink a gallon of water. I can feel the first prickly sting of a sunburn crawling up my neck.

"Impactful *how*?" I ask.

"I'm not the first person to do this, you know," she says. "Not the first person to do the program here."

"Not the first *Top Tier*, you mean," I say, rolling my eyes, but Evie doesn't seem to catch my sarcasm.

"Do you know Dani Tan? The super-famous beauty blogger who disappeared a couple years ago?" she asks. "She was the first Top Tier and now she's . . . well, you met her already, I guess."

I put the pieces together. "Natalie? That's her?"

I conjure up an image of the Dani Tan I had seen online before and can't reconcile it with the person I met last night.

"The blonde hair helps. And the lack of makeup," Evie offers. "People see her around and guess, but no one ever really puts it together. But there have been others, too. When there are enough of us here, who have left all of that money on the table and a lifestyle rooted in comparison and disconnection, and we've found something better . . . well . . ."

"You'll influence everyone else to do the same?"

"Something like that."

She pauses, studying the endless stretch of desert in front of us. It's undeniably gorgeous here. The dusty grays and scraggly Joshua trees look wavy in the heat, a bone-dry watercolor. It's suddenly obvious to me that everything around us is exactly where it should be, and we're the ones intruding.

"We should head back," Evie says eventually, as if she feels it too.

She turns and we're facing each other now.

"I don't get this, Evie," I say. "I'm trying. But I don't."

She smiles, just a little, the corners of her eyes wrinkling slightly. "I know."

"I just want you to be . . ."

"Normal?" she asks, and it comes out with a little laugh.

"Happy," I correct.

She grabs my hand then, squeezing it. "I'm getting there, Haze. I promise I am. And for the first time, it feels sustainable."

"Because you're away from Mom?"

"Because I'm away from all of it. I don't think I knew how to access happiness that wasn't tied to the thoughts of a million strangers' opinions before this. A million and two, because your and Mom's opinions mattered more to me than anything. It's like I had all of these tiny strings tied to me, pulling in different directions. When it was good, when everyone was happy with me, I went up and up and up. No one could touch me. And when it was bad, I was down for days. Weeks. Stuck. Does any of that sound like happiness to you?"

I imagine my sister with a pair of scissors, cutting the strings away from her body only for new ones to appear in their place. "No," I say.

"I'm sorry for how this has been for you, Haze," she says. "I am. I knew it would hurt you, maybe, or scare you, but you know me. I can't . . . I can't gauge it. Can't picture the scale of things. Or measure consequences. Not like other people. For a while I thought it was because I was just . . . broken. Fucked-up. Drawing on walls because I was, like, malfunctioning. Getting teachers fired because I was evil. Now that I've been away from it all for a while, I'm realizing I just always believed there could be an upside in reach. Always a way to spin my choices. I mean, think about Dad. Losing him was the worst thing that ever happened to us, and it created this life that Mom had always dreamed of. It gave us vacations and cars and college funds."

I freeze at the mention of college. Money.

"It didn't make any of it less sad," she goes on. "But it made it easier. To distract ourselves with a million other things."

I nod, taking in everything she's saying.

"I was selfish. I've been selfish," she says, her eyes focused on mine, unblinking. "And I'm sorry."

Relief floods my bloodstream, and I realize instantly this is what I've been waiting for. Not just to know that she was okay, but to know that we were. The two of us.

"I forgive you," I say. "Of course, I forgive you."

She beams, dropping my hand as she walks back toward the neighborhood. "Ditto."

What did she say?

"Ditto?" I ask.

"Yeah, ditto," she says, her tone light. "I forgive you. For the money stuff."

My stomach twists. "The money stuff . . ."

I watch the back of her shoulders as they shrug.

"Hazel, it's fine. The money stuff with Mom. The student loans. You knowing how much of my money she had taken . . ."

It feels like the temperature has risen fifteen degrees is as many seconds. I'm on fire, panicking.

"I . . ."

"It's okay," she says, looking back at me over her shoulder. "I get it. It was easier to make a deal with Mom than to just ask me for it. You were embarrassed. Stuck. I saw how guilty you felt afterward, how awkward you were around me. How you avoided me. Screened my calls. I was hurt, but it didn't take me that long to figure it out. How you had seen my bank account . . . the way Mom had mentioned you'd hung around that night after I left. When I asked her about it outright and she told me that you had asked for money, some of my money . . . I had the common sense to know that wasn't the whole story, of course. That she held something over your head in return."

"She did," I try. "But . . ."

"But I acted like I didn't want to go to college anyway, right? That I wanted to keep working with her?"

All this time I'd been trying to understand my sister, and she was the one who had my number all along. I wonder what else she hasn't mentioned, what else she could be saving for the right moment.

"Yes," I say. "I thought . . . I thought if you never knew, then it wouldn't make a difference. How you felt about me, about the money, the industry . . . none of it would change. But it was wrong of me, Evie. It was your money. I never even got any of it, in the end, just so you know. But still . . . I've felt horrible. It was just like her, what I did. To assume it didn't matter. That you wouldn't notice."

"It's okay, Hazel," she says. "It is. There are far worse ways to hurt someone than with money, right?"

The question doesn't feel rhetorical, but I don't know what to say. What she expects me to say.

"You mean Mom, right?" I ask.

She doesn't reply right away.

"Yeah," she answers finally. "Mom."

· · · · ● · · ·

We walk in silence the rest of the way to the house, and when we arrive, my car is in the driveway, complete with four new tires.

"Ta-da," Evie says, gesturing toward the vehicle. "Good as new."

I'm relieved it's there. That I have a way to leave. But I don't want to leave my sister, either.

"You can go whenever you want, you know," Evie says as I follow her through the front door of the house. "We're not going to keep you here. Despite what you might be thinking."

But you're here, I think.

"I mean, someone thought the tire strip was a good idea . . ."

She laughs, nodding. "It was a bit much," she says. "I do admit."

I'm so happy to be joking with my sister, free from guilt and fear and questions, that I almost don't ask the next question that pops into my mind. But then I do.

"So what about you, then?" I say. "Your car is in Palm Springs . . . or it was, anyway."

"There are community cars here," she says, turning the key in the front door. "Mostly for emergencies. Leaving the car there was just . . . easier. Less of a chance of being followed here by some crazed fan who knew my license plate number. Or Mom. Or Charlie."

"Or me," I say.

"Well," she says. "Yes."

She hands me a glass of water and nods toward my keys, back on the counter where I left them yesterday.

"If you want to stay for a few more days, Haze . . ." she starts, but I hold up a hand.

"No," I say. "I understand. This is your choice. If you're safe and happy, then okay. I can let you do this."

Her smile stretches out slowly, pushing all her freckles together, and I can see everything in her face then. Her at five, my dad, the ways I could have been better for her. The ways I should do better now.

"Thank you," she says.

"I should head out, I guess," I say. "Back to Vegas. Real life."

Evie is back in the kitchen now, loading our water bottles into the dishwasher.

"How's the job hunt going, by the way?" she says.

I pause while taking off the boots Natalie lent me. How does she know I lost my job?

"Oh, it's . . . going," I lie.

"Mom told me," she says. "When she mentioned the student loan stuff . . . I didn't want to embarrass you. You seemed so determined to make me think that everything was okay."

"Yes," I say, busying myself with the other shoe, grateful she can't see my face from where she's standing. "I'll figure it out, Evie. Don't worry about me."

"If there's anything we've established here," she says, her voice moving closer, "it's that the whole 'don't worry about me, I'm fine' thing doesn't really work for us."

I chuckle, trying to keep things light, easy. "True."

She's standing above me now, in what would be the dining room, and I push myself off the ground to meet her. "I'm going to change, and then I'll be out of here."

"In the bathroom?" she asks. It's an odd question.

"Yes . . ." I say, unsure. "If that's okay."

"Perfect!" she says.

I quickly change into my clothes, splashing my face with water to remove the sweat and dust from the hike. I want to shower, but it feels like overstaying my welcome. I keep waiting for Evie to say, "No, actually, stay. Let's keep talking. Let's go through it all. Let's watch *Lost*. Let's do nothing. Let's pretend like everything is how it was before." But I know it's not coming. I can feel the space for me here shrinking by the minute.

I study my sunburn in the mirror and cringe, imagining how the drive home will worsen it, the setting California sun beaming through the windows. I remember the sunscreen in the drawer and open it, my eyes searching for the tiny stick figure again. The "Evie was here" mark. Something about it comforts me, reminds me that she's still the same person she's always been, and I am, too.

But there's also a piece of paper folded neatly into a square, taped next to the drawing. I crouch down. HAZEL is written on the front in Evie's handwriting.

I grab it and begin to open it, but then there are voices from the kitchen. Not just my sister's.

"Is she . . . staying?" I hear Natalie ask from the other room.

She's back, I guess.

"Just leaving," I answer, stuffing the note in my back pocket and opening the door. "Thank you for the tires."

"Our pleasure," Natalie chirps.

"I'll walk you out," Evie says quietly.

As we make our way to my car, I open my mouth to ask about the note, but nothing comes out. I can't shake the feeling that there must be a reason she didn't just hand it to me. Is she afraid to talk about this with Natalie so close? Is it a coded message? Is there something else she needs to tell me that she can't bring herself to say out loud?

"I used your sunscreen in your bathroom drawer," I say instead. "Hope you don't mind."

She nods, like she understands. "Great. I was hoping you would."

It feels strange, to be so cryptic after so many hours of honesty, but I choose to trust her. That's what this is all about, right? Trusting my sister to make the decisions she wants to make, regardless of how I may feel about them.

"Look, Hazel, you won't . . . tell Mom about this, right? About where I am?" she asks.

"Never," I say. "I can't think of anything I'd want to say to her again . . . ever, really."

"You and me both."

We laugh for a minute, and then it fades, like there's more we should say but we're not sure where to start.

I open the car door. "I should go."

She nods, and there's my push.

I'm about to climb into the driver's seat when she stops me. "Hey, Haze?" she asks.

I look at her, waiting.

"You remember when you asked me once if I ever wanted to just throw my phone into the ocean . . . or off a cliff . . . into a volcano? Something like that?" she asks. "A long time ago."

My mind sorts through memories, remembering the text. The game with Sasha. How Evie had seemed so uninterested in the idea. "Yeah. I do."

"I said I couldn't imagine it, I think. That it would feel like a different world. But now I'm realizing that I think what I really meant was . . . it would feel like throwing myself off a cliff, into the ocean. Swan-diving into a volcano. I couldn't imagine existing without it. It felt too pathetic to admit. It is pathetic, right?"

I remember the game I would play with Sasha, the way neither of us would follow through with what we were saying we needed, either. That we'd open the apps back up, scroll until our minds were mush. "It's not pathetic."

"I guess this is me seeing if I survive it," she says. "If I even exist without it. If I matter."

"Of course you matter," I say instantly, but I know what she means. I've wondered the same thing before, if the perception of me is what is keeping me afloat more than anything else. If anything beyond that even matters, really.

"And so do you," she says. "Fancy job or not. Fancy apartment or not. Money or not. Boyfriend or not. Whatever. None of that ever mattered to me as much as you thought it did. I would have looked up to you no matter what you did, Hazel. You could have told me anything. You still can."

My heart aches at what she's saying, the kindness of it.

There's a beat where I know I should reply, say something, but I'm frozen. Afraid of the way my voice might crack if I start talking.

Finally, she smiles at me, though it's a little sad now. "You know there was this kid in middle school who used to tease me relentlessly about YouTube and Instagram . . . the followers, all of it. And then when he learned Dad had died, it was this whole other thing. 'Too bad your dad missed out on all the free shit you get sent every day,' blah, blah, blah . . ."

"That's horrible," I say, but she waves my comment away.

"It bothered me at first, until I realized that it didn't matter. He might have a dad. Two parents. But I had something even better. I had you. And you were cool and funny and beautiful. And you got it. You got *me*."

I want to cry now, but it feels too dangerous, like if I let go even a little, I will fall apart. Why is she making it even harder to drive away now?

"It's what made all of this . . . the last year . . . so much harder," she adds. "Because I love you so much. Always have."

"Same," I say. "So much."

Natalie appears in the doorway now, walking out toward the car. "Almost time for meditation hour, Evie," she says. "You ready to go?"

I picture the two of them in some beige room, sitting in silence for hours. I raise my eyebrows at Evie.

"Okay, yes, it is a *little* crunchy here," she says, smiling. "Whatever."

I put my hands up in defense as I climb into the driver's seat. "I said nothing."

"We'll talk soon, okay, Haze?" she says, backing away from the car. "I'll reach out when the timing is right. When I'm good. Promise."

I nod, and I hope she knows that what I'm trying to say is: *I hate this. I love you. I'll leave if you want me to, anyway. For you.*

I roll up the window and back out of the driveway, exiting the neighborhood the way I came. I drive for forty-five minutes before I arrive at a gas station, pulling into a parking spot to read the note. I wanted to be still when I read it, not looking over my shoulder. I open it slowly, taking a deep breath as I do.

It's typed, which surprises me. Is there a computer there I didn't see? Did she bring this to Joshua Tree?

   1. Go back to Charlie's. Read the journals. Start from the beginning.

   2. Have you ever heard of ghostwriting?

   3. What do you think of this for the first chapter?

And then I keep reading.

For as long as I can remember, there have been a million mes in the world. The me that my mother wants, which splinters into a thousand other versions, too—versions of me that she can mix and match, depending on which iteration will get the most likes, the most cash, the most engagement. There's the me that men seem to want, someone who is just enough of everything: Just old enough. Just sexy enough. Just confident enough. Just natural enough. There's the me that my sister wants, someone who is a little more like her, who shares the same insecurities, the same struggles, the same pain. That's the only version I ever really pine after, the only one I wish would stick. If anyone deserves it, it's her. But the thing about knowing all these versions of me exist, and pulling them in and out of rotation since I was a child, is that eventually, they made it hard to even think. To form a single thought that was mine. To make a single choice. I couldn't do anything without wondering who I was doing it for: My parents, the internet, my sister, my boyfriend? The likes, the clout, the money, the fame, the approval? I felt paralyzed. Overwhelmed. Convinced that any choice I made would be something I was doing for someone else—anyone except me. So at some point, I decided that there would be only two of me. That if I was ever going to survive social media, my mother—any of it—there could only be two.

There would be the version of me at home, the one who writes every day in a diary that I know my mom will read. The version who will give her what she wants in heaping spoonfuls. The one who survives. And then there would be the real me, the one who writes here. The one who doesn't hold back, who tracks every violation, every manipulation.

It was the only way I could separate that world from my own. To know that there was a difference. To be able to recognize and point to my real thoughts. My real feelings. My real self. So I've recorded every horrible thing in these journals for years and stored them somewhere I knew they would be safe.

For a long time, I didn't know what I would do with them, if anything. They existed mainly to keep me balanced. Sane. To remind myself of the truth. And then I learned about the cameras. The ways my mom had been watching me more closely than I ever realized for most of my life—at least since I was nine, based on the boxes I found. She knew exactly

olivia muenter

how to optimize my pain because she could see it every day, even when I hid it from her. I realized it wasn't a coincidence when I started purging after most of my meals and suddenly a campaign benefiting the National Eating Disorders Association landed in my inbox. I realized that my mom knew how to pitch my pain. It wasn't a coincidence when I would come home with a bag of candy or chips or fast food and my mom was at my door first thing the next morning, talking about what amazing things Noom is doing now, how they're looking to enter a younger market, too. And it certainly wasn't a coincidence when, directly after a major fight with a boyfriend or friend, my mom was there with a camera, cataloging the day—the ups and downs of growing up, as she said. They were my ups and downs, sure, but they were everyone else's, too. That's what made people care. My mom would look at my face and see I'd been crying and know other people would wonder, too. That curiosity was a type of currency.

I could have told her at any point that I knew, I guess. I could have thrown away the cameras. Disabled the recording devices. I could have demanded she burn the diary photocopies. I could have threatened to go public the moment I realized the extent of how she was controlling me. The content my audience would consume about a child who never could have chosen this career, who grew into a young woman who made the most of what she had.

In the end, though, I wanted to provide them the opportunity that they never gave to me, not even once: I wanted to let them be themselves. And that's exactly what they did. And every night I went to sleep knowing that, at the very least, I was protecting myself. I was keeping a record of it all, too. And, someday, everyone would know that that version, and that version only, was the truth.

TWO YEARS LATER

Evie Davis is back!

That's what the chyron on the bottom of the television screen reads, the one that sits just above the well-lit mirror in front of me. It's the teaser text that viewers at home will see before this interview—the first one I've given since returning to the public eye with a bang, a book deal. A million secrets to tell or sell, depending on who you ask. It's not a particularly creative set of four words, but it works, I guess. It makes people ask: Where did she go? And why did she leave? And why should I care? The questions that sell books.

A stranger fluffs my hair as I check the giant digital clock on the wall, just to the left of the mirror in front of me. Hair and makeup now, and in an hour, it'll be time to go live. To tell everyone why they should care that I left, that I'm back, that they can read about all of it. I text Hazel: "Almost here?"

I don't blame everyone for thinking the book was a money grab at first, a way to double down on an already successful career, a cushy bank account. It made it that much more satisfying when everyone learned that the money was actually gone, that my mother had whittled it away over the years, bringing her bank accounts and mine down to almost nothing. People felt *bad* then—that they had assumed I was in control of it all. As if any child, any teenager, can ever really be in control of anything. I had assumed the money was safe, that *I* was safe, because that's what you do when you're growing up, living in your parent's house. You trust them. At least I had my sister, right?

My phone lights up. A text from Hazel: "Car's about to pull up! Kind of freaking out!!!" I smile. "I'm excited, too," I write. I snap a photo of my hair in rollers and send it to her with a text.

"Does this or does this not make me look like George Washington?"

An instant reply: "It definitely does, but to be honest you're pulling it off and I hate you for it."

I've missed this. Talking with my sister. Joking. It was six months after she showed up at ReBrand that I got my phone back, my first-ever flip phone, which I was shocked to find do still exist. All new contacts. No social media. Simple. By then, Hazel had gone back to Charlie's and found the rest of my journals—the real ones, the ones that I had poured every dark thought into, every way my mom had failed me, every detail of manipulation, and started outlining chapters. Six months after that, she had a first draft.

It was a perfect plan, really. She put everything she learned in journalism school into the structure of the draft, polishing the flow of the chapters, the narrative, thoughtfully interviewing me over the phone to fill in the gaps. There were parts of the book when I wanted more details from Hazel, more about her perspective, her choices. More vulnerability and honesty. "You're sure there's not anything else you want to include?" I'd push, but she'd say no, that this wasn't about her. Obviously.

It wasn't until we got to the chapters about ReBrand that I realized I couldn't stay in Joshua Tree any longer—that I didn't need them to hold my hand anymore. I had known for a long time that what Natalie was trying to build wasn't as pure as she claimed, that maybe it never was, but I didn't care. It had given me everything I needed. I would have never been able to find the balance I know now if I hadn't started from scratch. Of course, there was also the fact that the docuseries was still rolling around in my brain. I had taken the ultimate step that Gavin and I discussed: I was in it. They trusted me. I knew the ins and outs of how the program worked, how the money flowed. Maybe the docuseries wouldn't work anymore. But a whole chapter of the book dedicated to the ways they had failed me, too . . . well, that had potential. Plus, I had my suspicions about the finances at ReBrand. The spending versus the income. The way houses were always half finished, construction projects halted. The advance for the book had been significant, enough money for Hazel and me to be set for a decade if we lived modestly. Simply. And once Natalie (Dani now, again) left, too, exposing even more about them than Hazel and I did—well, that was the end of that.

"I'm here, I'm here," Hazel says as she rushes into the room, sweat coating her brow. She settles into the chair next to me, a makeup artist already plastering her face with foundation. "So. This is happening, huh?"

"It is," I say. "You ready?"

"Absolutely not." She laughs. "Still completely open to you excluding me from this whole thing."

I insisted that Hazel join for the interview, that I would explain to the interviewer how amazing she was at her job. How I couldn't have written the book without her. All true, of course, even if it wasn't the whole truth.

"No way," I say. "We did the book together, and we're doing this, too."

She nods, and she can't help herself; she's beaming. Her eyes travel to the screen, where the book is being shown in another preview, the cover plastered with the now-infamous photo of the cactus with a balloon attached to it. I do love that cover. I watch her eyes travel over the text, the authors' names: mine in giant, stacked type, and hers in smaller text just below. That had been agreed upon in the book contract, too, that her name would be on the cover in addition to mine. I had to fight the publishers on that, and I had to fight Hazel when it came to the profits. It was important that she made more than me—sixty-five percent compared to my thirty-five, to be exact, even though she pushed for fifty-fifty, for a while anyway.

An intern pops their head into the makeup room after a few minutes. "Hazel, Evie—almost ready to head to the studio?"

Hazel turns white instantly, but I take the lead. This is like riding a bike.

"Ready to go!" I announce, hopping out of the chair and grabbing Hazel's hand.

We follow the intern to the studio, which is all bright lights and clean, smooth surfaces. Producers buzz around the room while makeup artists touch-up anchors.

"Five minutes, and then you'll go there," the intern says to us, pointing toward a couch up ahead. "Any questions?"

"Where are the nearest exits?" Hazel quips, and the producer shoots me a brief panicked look.

"We're fine, thank you," I cut in.

I squeeze Hazel's hand, reminding her that everything will be fine. Why wouldn't it be?

A producer waves us over a few minutes later and we settle into the couch easily, though Hazel keeps talking through her teeth.

"Oh, yeah, okay. I remember exactly why I hated this as a kid," she mumbles. "It's all coming back to me."

"You'll be great," I assure her, adjusting my posture, my skirt. I ask the makeup artist for a mirror, quickly check my teeth for the remains of my breakfast, dab an oil-blotting sheet on my T-zone. Mom taught me well.

The anchor sits and smiles at us politely, though I know we're just two of a dozen people she'll talk to today. No need for small talk before we do this.

They count us in, a light goes on, and just like that, we're live.

I smile during our intro, though not too big. I laugh, though not too loud.

The anchor gives the perfunctory pitch of the book to the camera, and as expected, she turns to pepper me with questions first.

"Evie, I think that most of us were quite shocked by the contents of this book, the ways your mother . . . well, violated your privacy, to put it lightly. Can you tell us what it's been like to share all of that?"

I tone done my smile a degree or two. "Yes, well," I start. "It wasn't easy, of course. To go through all of that, to relive it all in detail, even with my sister's support."

The anchor turns toward Hazel, who is shifting awkwardly on the couch, crossing and uncrossing her legs even though I told her not to. But then her eyes are on me again.

"And how are things with your mom now?" the anchor asks. "I know many people are calling for her to be arrested and charged with something . . . child pornography, even, given the cameras that you outline in the book. That was incredibly hard for me to read, I have to admit."

I've practiced this answer before, of course. Disappointed, but not angry. Sad, but not angry. Seeking justice, but not angry. Never angry.

"I don't speak to my mother now," I say. "But I do forgive her. And I'll always love her, in spite of everything. I do think, though, that there need to be consequences for the ways that people take advantage of the children of influencers. There are protections in place for child actors, after all, who are often managed by their parents in much of the same ways. So why shouldn't the same apply to people who grew up like I did?"

"I totally agree," the anchor says. "Absolutely."

I think of how I had seen the anchor's face on my screen yesterday, interviewing a twelve-year-old who had gone viral for starting a dog-walking business, how she looked at the girl at the end of the interview and said, "So, do you have a boyfriend?" and then caught herself and added, "Or a girlfriend?" as if that was the problem with her first question.

"I also know," the anchor continues, "that it was important to you to have your older sister, Hazel—your ghostwriter—here today. Is that right?"

"Absolutely," I say. "I wouldn't be here without Hazel. And the book definitely wouldn't be here."

Hazel laughs nervously.

"Tell us a little about that," the anchor says. "What made you think that Hazel would be a good fit for this project?"

"Well, she is an incredible reporter. A great journalist. She was the person who really pushed me to do things outside of my comfort zone, outside of Instagram," I say. "And then there was the fact that I had already seen how creative she could be when it came to writing about the world of influencing, and influencers."

I feel Hazel flinch next to me, just slightly, but I keep my eyes on the anchor.

"I'm sure Hazel would be embarrassed that I'm getting into this here, but she deserves the credit, really. Hazel actually started an extremely popular, very lucrative newsletter all about influencers a few years ago. I think it had—what was it, Hazel? Like, 20,000 paid subscribers at its height?" I turn to Hazel for her response and she's the color of a paper napkin. "I mean, people loved it. It was hilarious. And so much about this stuff, when it isn't dark, is kind of funny, you know? You have to laugh at it all sometimes."

The anchor is sensing something is off now, her eyes darting between Hazel and me.

"Oh," she says. "That's . . . well that's very cool."

"It really was," I add. "She even wrote about me, choices I had made. My friends, my boyfriend at the time. She saw it all. And anytime I told her about something going on in the industry, a faux pas someone had made—and, God, there are so many, you know?—she found a really creative, intelligent way to write about it. Anyway, I just thought she would be perfect for this."

"Right," the anchor says, gazing between us, and then her eyes shoot toward her notes. "That's why you wanted Hazel to earn most of the money for this book, right? You said that was important to you."

"Well, I mean, of course," I say, adding a slight hint of confusion to my face as if to say: *Why wouldn't I want that, lady?* "I didn't know how all that stuff worked then, but once Hazel explained it, it made perfect sense."

A sound comes out of Hazel's mouth like she's about to talk, to protest, but the second I turn to her, her mouth snaps shut. Like she doesn't dare say anything.

"That's really generous of you, Evie," the anchor says. "Especially after everything you went through with your mom . . . the money . . ."

I fix my eyes downward, looking embarrassed, uncertain, sheepish. This part is important.

"Oh, it's nothing," I say. "It's what's right. She's my sister, after all. Family."

The anchor's eyes narrow. "But so was your mother, right?"

"Of course." I nod, confident, measured, like of course I don't miss the similarities here. Of course I thought through them. "But Hazel and I . . . we've been through so much together. We understand each other. We trust each other."

I don't have a smartphone anymore, but I can practically hear updates from Reddit pinging in my head: *Wait, is Hazel Davis . . . SABI? Holy shit. And now she's making even more money off of her sister's story . . . this is sooo fucked-up.*

I never could stop people from theorizing. From talking. People can't help themselves, you know?

"Hazel knows what I mean." I turn to her, my smile wide and generous. Expectant. "Right?"

She looks terrified, truly frozen in fear, and then something in her snaps. A reminder to act normal. Human. "One hundred percent."

"That's . . . that's really special," the anchor says, a little cautiously.

"Besides," I add, "if there's one thing you should know about Hazel— the thing she's always reminded me herself—it's that she's nothing like my mother."

Hazel swallows so loudly then that I wonder if the mic picks it up. Couldn't hurt.

And then there's that sound again, the imaginary pinging.

Hazel Davis is a monster. Jesus.

Ping, ping.

Are you honestly telling me that Hazel Davis monetized her sister's secrets?

Ping, ping.

And we thought Erin was bad . . .

Ping, ping.

God, poor Evie. Poor, poor Evie.

ACKNOWLEDGMENTS

It probably shouldn't surprise me that writing acknowledgments for a book feels a lot like writing the book itself. Despite years of reading other people's novels and daydreaming about doing exactly this one day myself, I'm still sitting here with the same annoying voice in my head that often pops up while writing. It's shrill and panicked and is usually screaming something like, "It's happening! It's happening! Don't mess it up!" I'm confident that without any of the people I'm about to mention, that voice would never, ever shut up, and this book that I'm so proud of wouldn't exist.

Thank you to my agent, Dana Murphy. The first time we met, I went home and wrote in my journal that I met an agent who really seemed to get me and my writing, and it made everything that felt too big and out of reach to me before suddenly seem possible. (I didn't mention the oyster incident, don't worry.) I'm so grateful for your wisdom, support, and guidance, always.

Thank you to my editor, Alex Arnold, without whom this book would simply not have been possible. From the first time we discussed SABI, I knew that I had met someone who appreciated the same things I did (and went down the same internet rabbit holes, too). Through every phone call, text, revision, and email, I've been astounded by just how lucky I have been to work with someone so full of talent, empathy, and creativity. There is truly no depth to my gratitude. You have made me a better writer in every way, and I am so honored to call you a friend.

Thank you to Jhanteigh Kupihea and the entire Quirk Books team, especially Jessica Yang, Jane Morley, Elissa Flanigan, Ivy Noelle Weir, and Nicole De Jackmo. I am so grateful to each of you for your consistent support, collaboration, and excitement. I'm so proud to have worked with such a talented group of people who all understand the particular magic which is Philly.

Thank you to Becca Freeman, my podcast cohost extraordinaire and fellow published author (!). I couldn't have done this without your constant support and encouragement. Joining *Bad on Paper* as your cohost has changed my life for the better in so many ways, and I can't ever thank you enough for sending that email back in January 2021 (and waiting two weeks for me to reply—sorry about that, again). Tiny tongs forever (or as long as listeners will allow us to hold on to that inside joke).

Speaking of *Bad on Paper* listeners . . . where do I even begin? The community of supportive, positive, witty, wildly interesting people that I have been able to connect with because of *Bad on Paper* has blown me away. Thank you a million times for welcoming me into your little podcast family, and for the support you have shown this book and my writing.

While, yes, it does feel incredibly meta to be thanking my Instagram followers in these acknowledgments, it wouldn't be right for me not to mention the people who have supported, engaged with, and followed my work (on Instagram and beyond) for years now. One of the things that makes social media so hard to quit is also one of the best parts about it: it helps you find your people. To anyone who's ever shared something I've written or cheered me on from afar (or simply tuned in to Tipsy Candles), know that you've helped make my dream of writing a book possible and helped me feel less alone so many times. Nothing could mean more to me. Thank you, thank you, thank you.

Thank you to Ayana, Haley, and Gabrielle aka The Rat Cult, who together encompass what is (in my mind) the single most prolific group chat of all time. Throughout writing this book, you have been there for my greatest wins, my most painful lows, and everything (*truly* everything) in between. Each of you makes me feel seen and safe and laugh hysterically on a daily basis. I couldn't ask for more.

Thank you to my therapist, Emily, who gave me the space for me to get

olivia muenter

to know myself, and then to like myself, too. Our work together made me the writer and person I am.

Thank you to Kirsten and Kate, for being like sisters to me.

Thank you to my brother Grant for being the funniest person I know, and for sending me the most bizarre memes I've ever seen on a daily basis. I love you.

Thank you to my parents. To my mom, for encouraging me to love reading and writing, and for always supporting my independence even when it may have been hard to let me go. To my dad, for showing me how to have a sense of humor about almost anything, and for your lifelong, steadfast commitment to singing "You are my shining star!" at me even during the moments when I was not, in fact, such a shining star. I love you both and am so thankful for your support.

Finally, thank you to my husband, Jake. If there's any single person who makes that loud, panicked voice in my head shut up every time, it's you. It's always you.

Such a Bad Influence Playlist

A soundtrack to influence your reading experience

"All-American Bitch" by Olivia Rodrigo

"Have to Be Around You" by Brooke Bentham

"Surface Tension" by Genevieve Stokes

"I Love You, But I Need Another Year" by Liza Anne

"Quantum Physics" by Ruby Waters

"Yeti" by Paris Paloma featuring Old Sea Brigade

"At Least I'm Pretty" by Harriette

"Anything but Me" by Muna

"It's Called: Freefall" by Paris Paloma

"I Did Something Bad" by Taylor Swift

"Unlovable" by Delacey

"Pedestrian at Best" by Courtney Barnett

"Nothing New" by Taylor Swift featuring
Phoebe Bridgers (Taylor's Version)

"Boys" by Indigo De Souza

"As Good a Reason" by Paris Paloma

"Hold On" by Brooke Annibale

"My Tears Ricochet" by Taylor Swift

"Hard Times" by Ethel Cain

"Narcissus" by Paris Paloma

Scan to listen